A.J. Pengelly is the pseudonym for renowned author and inspirational speaker Anne Jones. Her books in the fields of self-development and spirituality have been translated in over 17 languages. She lives in the New Forest National Park in England with her husband Tony and two Labradors.

Her latest book, *Master of the Keys*, is an entirely new genre designed to bring symbolic thought and self-empowerment into the periphery of the mainstream. Her aim is to help others tap into their inner resources so that they too can discover their true potential.

To Dearst Kim
who heard the
dreams a
Master of the Keys
clearly too!
XXX
Amee

A.J. PENGELLY

Master of the Keys

Vanguard Press

A CIP catalogue record for this title is
available from the British Library.

ISBN: 978 1784650 58 2

Vanguard Press is an imprint of
Pegasus Elliot Mackenzie Publishers Ltd.

www.pegasuspublishers.com

First Published in 2015

Vanguard Press
Sheraton House Castle Park
Cambridge England

Printed & Bound in Great Britain

I dedicate this book to Tony who has been there for me, my rock and loving support throughout my journey – thank you sweetheart.

Acknowledgements

Huge thanks to Doggy, my ever patient editor. To Debbie and Tony who have been splendid mentors, critics and healers of the fragile confidence of a writer. To Colin for saving me embarrassment with diligent proof reading. Thanks too to all my long suffering friends and family who have been involved finding holes in the plot, inconsistencies and outright mistakes!

Thanks to Penny and Tanya for endorsing my original plot by putting muddy paws all over it – with love of course, and to Harry and Super who continued their roles of silent supporters.

Many thanks to Dave Welch of Ramora UK, EOD, Portsmouth. His experience from his own navy days plus his expertise in mine and bomb disposal was invaluable.

Thanks to Paul and Tom the Wizard for technical support, expertise and website design. Thanks too to Judy Piatkus who has supported me through many of my previous books and gave me support and ideas for this publication too. Big hugs too to Debbie and Brenda who are supporting me constantly and lifting me when I stumble. Thank you girls.

1

The two-seater sports car sped through the dark lanes. The little girl bounced on her mother's lap with excitement. "We're going to see fireworks, fireworks, fireworks. Will there be a real guy, is it a man dressed up, he won't get burnt will he, Daddy? Will there be rockets? Oh, Daddy, I can't wait."

Her mother, Annabelle, looked out of the car window. "It's a full moon tonight, just perfect for the party, look."

The little girl leant forward and touched the windscreen. She peered up at the sky, her attention diverted. "I can see the stars, and, oh yes, I can see the big moon."

Jonnie turned to Annabelle and smiled. "This was a great idea; I just hope the Blakes have built up a good fire. It'll be cold, the temperature's dropped, must be below freezing now."

"Just watch the road, darling, there'll be icy patches on these back roads."

"How long, Daddy, how long?" She touched her father's arm.

"We're nearly there. Just a few more minutes. Why don't you count the stars?"

Annabelle put her arms around her daughter and smiled. "Thank goodness the roads are clear. It's a small miracle after all that snow. I've never known so much so early in the year."

The little girl peered out into the night sky once more. "Daddy, what's a miracle? Is it anything to do with the stars?"

"A miracle is... well now, what is a miracle? I would say a miracle is something so wonderful that you can hardly believe it can actually happen." He smiled. "Just like you coming into Mummy and Daddy's lives."

She smiled. "I think going to the fireworks is a miracle."

"Oh, Daddy, Daddy, look, look another angel. Just like yesterday." She grabbed out to her father's arm, missed and caught the steering wheel instead. She pulled in her excitement. The car skewed on the ice, went into a screaming skid, slammed into a tree and they were thrown onto the windscreen.

The night was filled with the screeching, searing sound of metal breaking, glass shattering, the popping of the hot engine and the dying echo of their last screams.

2

In a cool dusty cavern deep inside the earth a slim beam of sunlight found its way through a minute crack. It illuminated the old casket that lay in its hiding place; the small chest that held the secrets of ancient powers, lost symbols and forgotten magic. The sun moved on, the light faded and the chamber returned to darkness.

3

Charlie glared down at the river. She sat at a window table in the Oxo Building Restaurant. The winter sun shone on the Thames and a pleasure steamer slowly made its way down the river; decks filled with groups of laughing women holding champagne glasses and obviously having fun. Down there they were having a lot of fun.

Opposite sat her boyfriend Andy Jamieson, thirty-five years old, ex navy, specialist in mine and bomb disposal now working in his uncle's hotel business. He was considered good looking by most women. They all noticed his eyes; dark brown, deep pools, quite difficult to read, soulful, a gentle touch in his strong chiselled looks. He wore his dark wavy hair cropped short and he looked good in his smart buttoned down shirts with cool double cuffs. In this moment she wasn't impressed by anything about him.

Her fingers tightened around the slim stem of her wine glass, dangerously so. The pain in her solar plexus was so real she felt an urge to crush the glass into tiny pieces. She didn't normally indulge in self pity but she felt a welling of tears that were about to spill out of control.

She looked up at Andy and glared.

"I don't know how you can do this to me," she said. "You know how much I wanted, no not wanted, *needed* this holiday. I've been working fourteen hour days for months now."

She wrapped her long legs around each other, tightening them in an effort to take back control. Her patent black shoes squeaked as she

14

gripped them together; she clenched herself, desperate not to show the hurt. She tossed her head in a pointless act of defiance. Some of her curls sprung loose making her look less formal and more vulnerable. "At this moment I hate you, Andy Jamieson."

He pushed his chair back a little, distancing himself from her hurt. "Sorry, babe. It just came up. It's an important merger, joint venture with the Maharaja Hotel chain. It means a lot to the company. I have to go to Mumbai; glitches in the contract to sort out."

He fingered his napkin nervously, avoiding her glare and took a sip of red wine.

She continued to stare, fists tight, fighting the tears.

"Anyway... " he said, "you're the one who cancelled every plan we've made in the last six months. You're so besotted with your work and," he dropped his voice, "quite honestly, I think they run rings around you. Howard makes you jump through hoops and you don't seem to be able to say "no" to anyone there and the clients have you totally at their beck and call. Personally, I think you're a fool to yourself."

"Bloody hell, Andy, so I love my work, so the Agency is my life. What else? In the four years we've been together this is the first major commitment you've made and you've grabbed the first excuse to walk away again. You've been on any number of trips, even in the last few months, and never once have you included me in on any of them. If you don't want us to be together, for God's sake just tell me so now." She turned away and stared out of the window. Her voice a little softer now, her lip quivered, "You know how much this trip meant to me."

"Let's just delay it; Egypt will still be there next month."

"I don't want to *delay it*. I want a holiday now, right now." She hit her hand on the table, glasses jangled. She stood up decisively, "Forget it. I'll see what Jacqui's doing."

She shrugged into her silver grey trench coat, grabbed her bag and stalked out of the restaurant. She caught a glance of her glaring face in the lift mirror. Her cheeks were flaming and her wayward mop now totally out of control. She had really tried hard to be the cool woman about town, to show some steel and resolve but as ever, when she tried to be strong with Andy, she felt like a child having a tantrum.

* * *

Upstairs, Andy called for the bill, sighed, picked up his phone and selected a number. "Yeah, yeah I told her. This is going to cost you. She is not happy, not happy at all. I feel an absolute arse. Anyway I'm free now, where shall we meet?"

4

Immediately she stepped onto the pavement her heel became wedged into the pavement. She bent down and yanked at it. It snapped.

Hell. So much for the stylish power woman. Charlie stared at her broken shoe. Tears started again. *Oh no, Charlie Masters, get a grip.* She took off her shoes and carried them. She felt conspicuous and slightly silly, but she also felt free. At least she could walk now.

Stupid shoes.

She started to walk along the South Bank then stopped. What was she doing? She went to the curb and raised her hand to hail a cab. After just a minute one pulled in. "Waterstones in the Strand, please."

* * *

Andy gulped down the last of his wine and paid the bill. He gave Charlie a few minutes head start then made his way out of the building. In the entrance he paused and watched as she jumped into the cab.

Why was she carrying her shoes?

He waited till the cab had disappeared from sight and then stepped up to the curb. The black limousine pulled up. He peered through the darkened windows, checked, looked around once more then got into the back.

5

In the cab Charlie made a call. "Hi, Jac, how's you?"

"Great, darling, just great, I'm in Lymington, enjoying a cocktail or two at Stanwell's."

"What, already? It's only two-thirty."

"James was in a good mood; we got the Wentworth's order so he gave us the afternoon off, so hey ho what to do but come and celebrate. How's you?"

"Dreadful, how do you fancy a trip to Egypt next week?"

Jacqui screamed down the phone. "You kidding? I'd love to, but weren't you going with Andy?"

Charlie brought her up to date with her latest upset with Andy. "I really let off steam; do you think I'm being unreasonable getting mad at him?"

"Of course not. You are the easiest going person I know. Far too soft. I love Andy, but he's been a bit distant lately. Like he's preoccupied. Do you think there's a problem with the business?"

"Not that I know. He's supposed to be linking up with a whole chain of hotels in India so there can't be any money worries. I feel he hides behind a perspex wall at times. Even Dave at the yacht club mentioned it last week. He acts like he's got something on his mind. Just hope it's not another woman." She turned down her lip and stared out at the traffic in the Strand. She shrugged her shoulders. "Anyway, let's go and have fun. I'm off to grab a guide book then I'll pop down to stay the night with Nan. It was her idea for us to go to Egypt. She was there in her hippy days; I'll get the low down from her."

"OK, Charlie, sweetness, you find out about the old buildings we need to visit and I'll put my mind to what the hell does a girl wear for a Nile Cruise. I guess it's linen, linen and more linen. I hate the stuff. I always look like I've slept in it. I'll pop into town tomorrow and see what I can find. Maybe a khaki mini would do the job. Do you think there will be any free men on this trip? I could do with a new man; one of those dark dusky Arabs would be perfect." Jacqui took a sip. "By the way can I pay you off over a couple of months, I'm a bit skint; the bloody lawyer's bill just came in."

"No, sweetie pie, it's my treat. Call it therapy; you need it after all you've been through."

Jacqui had just been through a bad time taking her abusive father to court. So many tears, so much blame, so much guilt and the ripples had affected the entire family.

Jacqui protested. "No way. You can't do that."

"Yes I can. Nan gave me a hefty Christmas present and I'd love to share it having fun with my best friend. We need this Jac, we need this – anyway, I'm at the bookstore now, speak later."

* * *

Jacqui pivoted on her bar stool. She pulled at her short black skirt that had ridden up showing long slim legs clad in black tights and black patent boots. It was impossible for Jacqui to look anything but hot; her appeal for most men was obvious, too obvious for her own good. With a swig she finished her champagne and indicated for another from the barman.

"You look pleased with yourself, Jac," he said.

"I'm delighted with myself, John, delighted. I am off to Egypt with a dear friend and am putting this last year's nightmare behind me. Life feels good again."

She swung round the bar stool again, leant over the bar and gave John a big smacking kiss.

"Hey, careful, I'm spilling your bubbles." He laughed.

* * *

Charlie climbed the stairs to the first floor of the bookstore making for the travel department. She felt a bit self conscious of her bare feet. In the centre of the store a group sat listening to a lecturer standing in front of a screen. She began manoeuvring past them when an aerial photograph of Egypt flashed up on the screen. She took another look at the old academic. Beside him was a table piled high with a display of books. The book title sent a tremor through her. 'Ancient Egypt Secrets Revealed'.

"As you know there is a constant search for temples and graves in the desert and recently we've had a major breakthrough. We've been able to see beneath the surface of the desert with new infrared technology. The camera picks up any change in the desert surface, showing slight outlines of buildings below. So far we have discovered quite a number of lost pyramids, tombs and temples. This is a very exciting time for us and we know there are many more great lost treasures to be found."

Charlie raised her hand. "So do you think you might find more treasure like Tutankhamun's tomb?"

He turned towards her and smiled. "I believe there is so much more to discover," he paused, "and so, so much more to learn from the Ancient Egyptians – I am convinced time will bring knowledge from that wise and ancient culture for the benefit of us all. And as you will read in my latest book, 'Recovering the Hidden Treasures of Ancient Egypt', the Ptolemaic Dynasty and the Greeks brought dissent…"

Charlie felt a shiver run down her spine and the hairs on her arm stand to attention. She turned to the shelves and looked for a travel guide, selected one and ran to the pay desk. As she stood waiting she noticed the lecturer's book by the till. She picked it up then shook her head. *Hey no, I don't need woo hoo about lost treasure, I need nice hotels and cocktail bars.*

She paid the clerk. "Is it really cold in here? I feel frozen." The cashier looked at her in surprise. "Heavens no, it's like a hot house."

Charlie shrugged and left the store, still shivering.

* * *

Three blocks away a large dark suited man picked up his phone and selected the name stored as 'D', just 'D'. Unconsciously his lip curled into a sneer as he waited for a response. *Fascist, capitalist bastard.*

His sneer turned into a mean line of a smile as the cold upper-class voice cut through. "Yes, what is it?"

"All in place, your lordship, all set."

"Good." The line went dead.

Jared looked down at the phone. His thick Bermondsey accent at odds with his dark Middle Eastern looks. "Yeah, you w****r, don't worry, it'll cost yer, and some."

6

The taxi from the station dropped her at her nan, Miranda's cottage on a quiet lane in the New Forest. She opened the door and let herself in.

"Hi, Nan," she called out as she stepped directly into the living room and threw her shoes and her bag into the corner. As she shut the door the draft brought a waft of a familiar fragrance – Miranda's favourite lotus incense. She glanced around at Miranda's collection of memories brought back from her many travels hugger mugger with unsuitably large furniture.

"Charlie, darling, bless you, how lovely to see you. Have you eaten?" Miranda appeared from her bedroom and clasped Charlie close in an all-enveloping hug. She was dressed in her favourite caftan, old and faded turquoise silk decorated with appliquéd exotic flowers and butterflies. Her long grey hair was swept up into a purple turban, a small strand of hair escaped and curled down her back. Although, now in her seventies she still had great presence and filled the room. She stepped back to view her granddaughter and cast a gentle but discerning eye over her; tall and slim, intelligent blue eyes and strong face.

"You're stressed," she said. "Your aura is all over the place. You're angry with someone."

She looked over at the discarded heels. "What happened to them? Did you throw them at someone? God, Charlie, you should stick to pumps, whatever made you wear those things? You are quite tall enough. Anyway, come tell me all about it. I've some spaghetti left over and I'll knock up a salad."

Although large she moved gracefully and she swept Charlie into the kitchen and pushed her into an old carver at the end of the battered oak table, rescued from the servant's hall of her own parents' manor house. She pushed an ashtray towards Charlie and pulled a bottle of opened Chablis from the fridge and in one seamless movement placed a glass before her and filled it. She turned and took a glass for herself.

Charlie, let out a huge sigh. "Nan, you're a star. But you are also an old witch. Yes, I have been angry. Andy can't make our Egyptian holiday." She pushed the ashtray away. "I'm determined to keep off them – I've managed a whole week. I feel sick. He says it's a work project he can't get out of. I don't know if it's true or not in any case I feel so, so side-lined; shut out."

"Don't be melodramatic, sweet child. You know you've been pretty elusive yourself these last few months."

"Yes, but that was because of the McKinty account. That was a must do. I need to prove myself to Howard. It's all done and dusted now and I so desperately wanted this trip. I just wonder if Andy loves me at all. I'm not sure if we really have a relationship. Maybe I'm kidding myself that he cares about me."

"Well, this is something you'll have to sort out for yourself. Bless you; I know how much you wanted this holiday. Can't you go with someone else?"

"That's just what I am doing, Nan. I've asked Jac and she's jumped at it."

Charlie sighed, and took a large sip of her wine. As she put the glass down firmly on the table she looked up at her grandmother. She took deep breath. "I'm seriously considering whether to end it with

Andy. He's such a miserable sod at times. The other night he had the most awful nightmare; he was screaming and thrashing about in his sleep for ages. I asked him about it when he woke and he just shrugged me off and went and poured a large whisky. We've been going out now for four years yet I actually don't feel I know him at all."

"Well, I'm sure he'll tell you what's troubling him in the fullness of time. God, Charlie, he's a gorgeous man; I think the current term is 'hot'. I've always been partial to men with dark brown eyes; he looks vulnerable to me even though he's physically a toughie. And he definitely has prospects in his uncle's firm, the shares have rocketed in the last few months. I thought his money was part of his attraction?" Miranda raised an eyebrow.

"Yeah, well, it helps." Charlie laughed. "Still, I'm doing OK myself now." She stared into her glass and touched her neck and ran her fingers over the ribbed scar that ran from the neckline of her top to her left ear. She shook her head, dismissing negative thoughts. "I guess it'll work out, I suppose everyone has their issues, their hidden stuff, baggage, that sort of thing."

"Of course they do, my darling. It's what makes us interesting."

Charlie looked up at her and smiled. "Well, I must say I'm very excited about this trip to Egypt, Nan."

"Well, you're going at a good time for the weather. It's warm in the day but not too hot and it's cool at night. It's their high season for visitors though."

"Yes, but with all the trouble they've had apparently the tourist numbers are really down."

Charlie drank the last of her wine and leant over to take the bottle. She poured herself another glass and topped up her grandmother's.

"There was an archaeologist, an Egyptologist, in Waterstone's talking about lost and hidden pyramids and treasures. I must admit it really spooked me when he spoke, like a touch of déjà vu." Charlie shivered.

"Are you cold, sweetie? It should be warm enough in here." Miranda swept her hand around her cosy home.

"No, it's OK, Nan, I'm fine." She tossed her hair again and smiled as Miranda handed her a bowl of spaghetti and jug of homemade tomato sauce. She added a tossed salad in an old Wedgewood bowl and a block of cheese with a grater and refilled Charlie's glass and her own.

"Hey, this looks good. I haven't eaten all day. I left before our order came at lunchtime and this wine is going down a little too well."

While Charlie ate, Miranda pulled up an old barrel back chair and sat holding her glass in her hands. She stared down into the wine as if reading a crystal ball. She frowned as though disturbed by what she saw. "I know you don't believe in spooky, but, my cherub, I will just say that this is going to be a very important trip for you. Be prepared for the best and the worst. I sense you'll find it life changing. In fact I have something I need to give you."

She put down her glass and took off purposefully to her bedroom where Charlie could hear her rummaging in one of her drawers. Charlie shrugged and focused on eating.

"Here it is." She returned carrying a small purple cloth drawstring bag. She pulled the cords and she slipped the contents into Charlie's hand.

She looked up at her grandmother. "Nan, your hands are shaking what's up?"

"Nothing, nothing, I'm fine."

Charlie looked down at the object in her hand. "Oh, my God, what is it?"

7

In a side street in Cairo an old match seller carried his tray filled with cheap novelties and souvenirs into the dark shop. The only light a single naked bulb. He nodded to the young man behind the counter. "Marhaban, Malik," he muttered.

The young man stared back at him, his eyes glinting in the dim lamp light, "Marhaban bīka," his voice thick with suppressed emotion. "I've had a call. She's coming. In ten days, In sha' Allāh."

The old man's shoulders dropped and he sighed. "Thanks be to Allah. At last." Now he had to get things prepared, in place. He pulled his beard. *Let Allah be merciful, let this go well.*

The youth beamed at him, his anticipation tangible.

The match seller nodded again. He touched the scarabs in his tray as though for confirmation, of a blessing. A frission of an old fear made his ancient hands shake a little. *Sure it will go well, it must go well. In sha' Allah, In sha'Allah, if God wills it so.*

8

"This was given to me by someone very special and as my travelling days are over I feel it's time to pass it to you." Miranda opened her hand fully to show Charlie a silver pendant, in the shape of a disc the size of a fifty pence coin. It was embossed with the form of a beetle.

"This is a scarab, a lucky charm in Egypt. It will keep you safe, it will protect you from danger. Promise me you will humour this old lady and wear it while you are away."

Charlie took the talisman and turning it over noticed a symbol engraved on the other side. She felt a shimmer run through her. "Yes I'll wear it, just for you, Nan, you old carpet flyer."

They laughed and Nan touched her hand. "Thanks, my sweetness. Are you OK, you seemed to shiver then?"

"No, no, I'm fine. I just keep getting the chills today, probably overtired. I need a good night's sleep that's all."

"Now tell me exactly what you will be doing on this trip. Do you start in Cairo? It's a filthy place. You won't want to hang about there for long. Terrible traffic."

Charlie passed Miranda their itinerary and while her grandmother listed out the sights that would be of most interest she scribbled notes on the side of the brochure and sipped her way through another glass of wine.

"And finally watch out for the street sellers. Egyptian hawkers are some of the most persistent salesmen in the world," she laughed.

"They start as young as eight and nine. The men will call you Habibi, which means 'dear one' and will tell you that you are beautiful and then try to fleece you. But treat it as a game and don't let them upset you. Now pet, you look really tired. To bed with you." She shooed Charlie up the narrow stairs that led from the sitting room up to two upstairs rooms and a small bathroom.

Charlie stopped halfway up the stairs. "Do you think it's safe to go to Egypt at this time, after all the unrest and political changes they've had there, Nan? Hilda in the office said there may be further problems and it could be dangerous."

"Oh, you'll be OK, darling. I'll send you psychic protection and you have your lucky talisman now. Anyway it'll be far less crowded than normal. It's usually teeming in January. At least you will have space and you won't have to queue everywhere."

"Good, that's what I thought you'd say," Charlie laughed. "It was about half the normal price." She continued up the stairs.

Miranda watched her and touched her heart. The smile left her face and she stared after her. The old lady couldn't help thinking. *Stay safe, please God, you will stay safe, my precious one. Please, God, keep her safe.*

9

Charlie looked around her old bedroom. Nothing had changed. This cottage had been her home and at times her refuge since she was three. On the table by her bed just the one photograph. A faded picture of her mother Annabelle and father Jonnie, sitting on the bonnet of a red Triumph TR7, the love of Jonnie's life and the car that had killed them and left her scarred. Scarred inside and out. Once again she felt the sharp stab of guilt, still unresolved; the cause of some of her darkest moments; a faint, unclear shadow of a memory that she had played a part in their death.

She sighed and turned and walked to the window and drew the curtains with their old roses faded to the palest pink. There under the window her oak bookcase. She ran her fingers over her book collection, childish things and the odd uni book. She opened a drawer and pulled out a pair of pyjamas and threw them and the guidebook onto the double bed still covered with the pink candlewick throw of her childhood.

She took a shower then climbed into bed with the guidebook. She felt the heightened emotions of the day subside as she delved into the mysteries and wonders of Egypt. What adventures had this ancient land in store for her? Instinctively she clasped the pendant that now hung round her neck. She shivered again.

10

The sun shines relentlessly. Despite the panoply carried by the slaves, the elderly priest can feel his right arm burning from the scorching metal as his golden armbands become searing hot. But he is focussed; physical discomfort will not distract him from his purpose, a divine and sacred purpose, a purpose prescribed by the gods themselves.

He steps forward, faces the huge sphinx and begins his magical chant:

O poh ker ray men

O poh ker ray men

Ban di poh key

Ban di poh key

Bah lah so ray

Bah lah so ray

The great stone paw gradually shifts, grinding and crunching across the desert floor revealing the dark entrance. The tall priest steps from under the panoply carefully carrying a golden casket. He looks down into the darkness and calls out a command; a young man steps forward holding a flaming torch up high. The boy hesitates at the edge of the dark pit, then starts down the steps with the priest following on his heels. A rush of escaping, stale air hits their faces as they descend. After a few steps the priest grabs the torch and takes the lead down the uneven spiral staircase. The flame from the torch flickers on the rough walls creating distorted shadows.

He steps off the steps into a cavern. The torchlight lights up a lofty underground chamber filled with baskets, leather trunks, huge earthenware pots and brass caskets. The light flickers on the walls of the chamber illuminating the forms and characters that had been painted by many priests and their helpers over the centuries. The young man looks around wide eyed at the walls and the golden hieroglyphics.

"What are they?" he asks pointing to the walls.

"Incantations, spells and prayers to the gods. The wisdom of ages. Ancient knowledge of the Wise Ones," the priest's voice is hushed with reverence.

He moves through the chamber hands the torch to the boy and places the casket on the stone floor. He opens it to check that the precious contents are still safe. In the casket lies a scroll, tightly rolled and bound with red silk ties. He unrolls it carefully and studies its familiar shapes one last time.

"These symbols, my boy, are the keys of world power."

He rolls up the papyrus, re-ties the scarlet ribbons and with a great flourish he kneels down, picks up the casket and places it at the feet of the statue of Amun that towers above them.

"O Amun, I, High Priest Hornedjitef, familiarly known as Khamet, on this 66th day of the 22nd year of the reign of our leader Ptolemy the Third, do bring The Sacred Scroll of Symbols for safe keeping. I vow these shall stay hidden from the eyes of mankind until the beginning of The New Dawn, the Great Spiritual Era when individuals will take ownership of the powers for themselves."

His deep resonant tones continue, "The sages have prescribed a moment in time when these symbols will be revealed and gifted to the common man for they are the keys to their personal power and man will be set free from the dominance of the mighty few."

The priest slowly stands up, his old joints cracking with the stiffness of age. His face softens. He looks down at the young man at his side.

"These ancient symbols were rescued from the dying glory that was Atlantis and brought here by the Temple priests. When they come forth they will awaken the sleeping and dormant force that lies within every individual, the hidden inner power to take them beyond the limits of their expectations, to manifest and create whatever they choose, to heal and be healed, to reach the unimaginable heights of human endeavour. The symbols are the key to personal power and I, Khamet, the High Priest of Lower Egypt, am the guardian of their secrets."

He pauses and listens. "Quick now, Hapu," he calls the boy, "Aapep is close by, we must make haste and seal the chamber."

He takes one final look around then bows before the statue of his spiritual master one last time.

He climbs the stone steps followed by the boy. His breath is laboured and rasping as he hurries to seal the chamber with its precious sacred texts. He must perform the closing ceremony before his enemies arrive.

Khamet steps out into the sunlight and stands at the top of the stairwell. He raises his arms and slowly draws the closing symbol. His deep resonant tones delivering the ancient spell to seal the entrance.

"Ya wan say kah
Ya wan say kah
Ya wan say kah
Bren y mar kar
Bren y mar kar"

He raises his arms again and sweeping his hands down with total authority he commands: "All is hidden; all is sealed, now, right now."

He raises his hands one more time. "I, Hornedjitef, Priest of Aman, High Priest of Karnak and all of Egypt, do solemnly vow, from my heart *and soul, that I will divulge this sacred seal to nobody, in this or any other lifetime, so be it."*

A flock of ibis fly overhead, circle three times in perfect unison then fly away and a soft wind blows across the desert in acknowledgement.

The paw slowly slides back into place.

"My work is done. The spell is set and can be released by me alone. Osiris, Isis, Sekhmet – my Masters, I have done my duty, I can now leave – the boat of death awaits me."

He bows deeply before the Sphinx. "Quickly, we must return to Thebes, I will not die in this godforsaken city."

A rhythmic and purposeful drum beat stirs the air, bringing a sense of primeval force and urgency.

Charlie woke with a start, she was sweating and shaking. The sound of drums still resonated in her head, touching her with fear and a danger from times long past. The words of the spell repeatedly looped through her mind like a song that becomes a fixation. With a sense of urgency she picked up the guidebook and scribbled them down.

She looked down and saw a red welt circling her arm.

11

The next morning in the kitchen Charlie prepared herself some toast. Miranda sat at the table sipping orange juice and watched her. "What's that mark on your arm, sweetie?"

"Oh, it's nothing. I must have lain a bit heavily on it. Do you want some toast, Nan?"

"No thanks. Did you sleep OK?"

"Mostly, though I did have a weird dream. Can't remember much about it now but I think there was a priest and he was doing something with a gold box which seemed to have some sort of secret scroll. The Sphinx was in the dream too."

"Well, my dear one, dreams are either portents of things to come or memories of things past. Tell me more about it."

"Well, whatever, I can't recall the details." Charlie shrugged. "It spooked me a bit at the time but it was the middle of the night and things always seem more disturbing in the dark. I was reading the guidebook before I went to sleep so that's probably the reason Egypt came up."

"But, darling, it could have a message for you."

"Nan, will you please leave it alone." She glared down at her grandmother, daring her to say another word.

Miranda shook her head. "All right, all right, you don't have to be quite so niggly."

"Sorry, Nan. Anyway I'm off, I have to catch the early train. I've a number of meetings today and I need to clear my desk. Can I stay with you for the rest of this week? I don't want to see Andy."

"Course you can, sweetheart. Bye."

Charlie gave Miranda a big hug then rushed out with toast in hand. "I'll jog to the station I could do with the exercise."

Miranda stood at the door as her whirlwind granddaughter disappeared round the bend. She smiled, sighed and shut the door. She had never felt like a nan and had tried for ever to get Charlie to drop the 'nan' for 'Miranda' with no avail. She made her way to the little altar in her bedroom downstairs and lit a candle.

Moving slowly Miranda walked back to the sitting room and picked up her telephone book, selected a number and waited patiently while the international call connected. "It's started, be alert, bye."

A slight breeze blew through the cottage swirling the curtains and spinning dust balls across the floor.

12

Jared Mustof picked up his phone and made a call to one of his men. A watcher. "She knows. She's booked a flight to Cairo travelling with a Jacqui Millar. Check her out. Works for Michelle Wilmot Agency, Bournemouth. Lives at Kings Hide, Middle Common Road, Pennington, near Lymington, Hampshire. Five foot five, green eyes, long dark brown hair. From the reports and shots we have so far she's hot to trot so keep cool, no messing. Peters has a full file on Charlie Masters, I've sent an encrypted download; should be with you by now. She looks fit too. Remember keep it in your trousers, don't get distracted."

Jared paused and listened and stared out of the window at the Thames, dull and grey in the winter light. He picked up his phone. "They're staying in Cairo at The Mena House Hotel. Watch and wait for instructions."

In a training camp in Libya near the border with Egypt a man called Binwani replied. "Gamda, good, that's great, salām." He closed his phone and smiled. "Action at last."

13

The scene from the taxi was chaotic, cars with blaring hooters, motorbikes cutting up through the traffic. Loud, dusty, and vibrant. The taxi driver screamed insults at any driver that came into range, with fingers pointing abuse into their most private parts. Charlie and Jacqui laughed and clung on to each other as the car swerved from side to side to duck into the moving lanes of the crush of Cairo traffic. Forty-five minutes later they arrived at their hotel, situated just a quarter of a mile from the Pyramids in the village of Giza that had become an outer suburb of sprawling Cairo. The taxi dropped them at the entrance and porters wheeled away their luggage.

They stepped out into the heat of the late afternoon. Charlie stretched and followed Jacqui as they entered the lush gardens that surrounded the hotel. "I am so looking forward to this holiday. I can't wait to chill out and be spoilt in luxury, champagne at a flick of a finger for a week, how wonderful," she said.

"Me too," said Jacqui.

* * *

It was a cool night by Egyptian standards. They were sat in the grounds of the hotel sipping cocktails. Charlie was on her third Tom Collins; Jacqui was working her way through a bottle of Pinot Grigio. The exotic shrubs and plants of the garden created dark and shadowy shapes. The lights on the hotel patio lit their table and cast long light fingers across the lawn.

Jacqui complained at the price of the wine. "It's six times more than I pay in Tesco."

"Anyway it's brilliant to be away, I feel more relaxed already." Charlie kicked off her shoes and stretched back in her chair.

Her mobile phone beeped. Charlie picked up the phone.

"It's from Nan," she said. "Let me read it to you, bless her, she writes a text just like a letter. 'Hi, girls, hope all is well. Just to remind you that you should visit the Holy of Holies in the Temple when you get to Luxor. It's the inner sanctum where only priests were allowed in the old days. Tutankhamun's tomb in The Valley of the Kings is a must do. Also you should visit Abu Simbel. Have a great time love Miranda. Ps. look out for tall dark strangers!'"

Charlie looked up and shook her head. "God, I feel a bit faint, the word Tutankhamun is making me feel even more peculiar, look at the hairs on my arms standing up."

She put the phone down on the table and leant her head on her arms. "Oh, I feel so weird." She looked up at Jacqui and her eyes rolled back into her head. Her head dropped back onto her arms and she started to mumble.

Jacqui quickly moved to her side, stroking her hair, "Hey, honey bun, don't go off on me now."

Charlie whispered to some unseen being. "Yes, yes, I'm coming."

The voice calling her faded and she felt caught in a swirl of light mist. A powerful light pulled her forwards. She felt herself morphing into the body of a young boy.

Young Khamet is lying in bed. His head throbs with pain; he puts his hand to his forehead to check that the bandage is still in place. Good.

The bandage is a sign that he will get the best sweetmeats and the tenderest cuts of meats for the next few days. Better still, he won't have to attend the temple preparation lessons which have filled his days this last month or two. He turns to look at his mother sitting beside the bed. She is dressed in purple robes and around her neck the Sacred Seal of the Temple, a golden pendant encrusted in brilliant cut amethyst and carnelian gemstones. It dazzles him. She is fearsome, aloof and generally above his childish world but today she has taken time out to sit beside him. He feels a little in awe of her, the head priestess of the temple and revered by all. Today her voice is gentle.

"My boy, you must take time to recover from this injury. In future you will have to take more care. Camel jumping is not for you. It is too risky at this time. You will have plenty of time in the future to test your mettle and show your bravery when you join the initiates at the Temple School."

"Your family lineage is impeccable. Your grandfathers were the Great Khalida and the architect Ami Ka Ra. You are destined to become the High Priest of all Egypt Upper and Lower. It is also written that you will return to this world one day in the future at the time of the New Dawn, when men and women will become initiated with their own power, at the birth of the Great Spiritual Era on Earth."

"There are rumblings and dissent in the land and these will grow in your lifetime. Our Hellenic rulers do not have the power of the old Pharaohs. Peace and stability in our land is being challenged now as never before. You need to become familiar with the magical powers of the symbols. At your initiation you will be given access to all of the sacred knowledge but now I will share with you a symbol that unlocks the key of manifestation; the ability to create or attract whatever you need. Use it wisely, if you hold any negative or egotistical thought, it will bring forth negative energies and it will destroy your peace of mind and eventually destroy you."

She picks up a tray on which lies a papyrus scroll, a scribing tool and a small jar of paint, puts it on the bed and then demonstrates to her son how to draw the sacred symbol.

She turns the tray around.

"Now you practise drawing this – you need to draw it three times only, then the key unlocks your inner power to manifest, to create, to attract whatever is in your mind – to turn thought to matter. Do it now, my son."

"Is it like a magical wish? Can I request anything?" *The boy is excited now as he considered the possibilities.*

His mother frowns. "Use caution and responsibility and remember your lineage. Do nothing to disgrace us or bring shame to the family or your position."

He tentatively picks up the brush and dips it into the ink. Carefully, his tongue in cheek to aid concentration he draws the symbol three times, then looks at his mother for approval.

"Good that is correct," *she smiles a rare smile and pats his bandaged head.*

There is a knock on the bedroom door.

"Enter," *she calls in the imperious voice that was more familiar than the gentle tone she was using today.*

A man servant enters carrying a golden tray to the bedside. "Your sherbet, young master." *He passed the boy a vessel of his favourite lemon sherbet drink.*

The boy nervously looks up to his mother.

She laughs. "Not the noblest use of the symbol but it proves you have learnt it well."

"I also requested that I would fully recover from this head injury, Mother and would perform my responsibilities well."

"Good. It is of the utmost importance that you do."

The boy slurps his drink quickly before she can change her mind and the pain in his head begins to ease. As it fades entirely he can hear the sound of distant drums. The soft chill wind of his destiny swirls around him.

He slips away into sleep muttering quietly, "I will, Mother, I will, at any cost."

A chill wind blew through the garden and Jacqui shivered. She strained to hear Charlie's words against the ever constant sound of Cairo traffic. "Charlie, can you hear me? Are you all right?"

Charlie's voice came clearer now. "I vow I will."

"Are you OK?"

Charlie lifted her head and opened her eyes. "Mmmm, I just dropped off. I think I must be overtired."

Jac took her arm and they took a gentle stroll through the gardens then let themselves into their room through the patio doors.

* * *

"Got them in my sights, this'll be a breeze, they haven't got a clue." He shut the phone, smiled and stepped back into the shadows.

14

Andy threw his gym kit into the hall cupboard. He stepped into the kitchen of his apartment in St Katherine Dock and took a beer from the fridge on his way to the living room. He picked up his phone from the table by the window and tried to call Charlie. After a few moments he was put through to voicemail. He slammed the phone shut and cursed. Immediately the phone rang. He smiled.

"Hey, oppo, how're you doing?" A male voice boomed in his ear.

"Oh, it's you Guthers, you old bastard."

"Sorry to disappoint – sorry I'm not Beyonce. Thought I'd get in touch – must be at least three months. Can't talk on the phone but how's about getting together for a pint and you can fill me on in on your progress. Heard your bird's been a bit upset by things."

"Yeah, well, she not too happy with me for sure. When are you free?"

"Tomorrow any good for you?"

Andy paused for a second. "That'll do fine. Say eight at the All Bar One, at Butler's Wharf, over the bridge. It's good and noisy there."

Andy shut his phone and stood staring out of his floor to ceiling window. Staring at but not seeing one of the iconic views of London. Cruisers, yachts and dinghies moored below his window, the Dickens Inn overflowing with tourists and the lights of the Tower of London in the distance. He refocused, shrugged his shoulders and went to run a shower.

The next night Andy and Tim Guthrie spent a couple of hours drinking beer and reminiscing on their days in the Navy as divers and mine disposal operatives. Then they moved on to double Chivas and the darker days with the SBS.

"Glad you're back in the fold?" Guthrie peered hard into his old friend's face.

"Of course. Finished the training. Got an op coming up in Libya. Can't wait to go live again. Thanks for dragging me out of the cold."

Guthrie continued to read his face then slammed down his empty glass. Broke into a grin. "One more for the road." He staggered to the bar for refills.

Andy let go the breath he'd held onto so tightly, shook his head and dropped his shoulders and waited for the next round to appear.

Two hours later the two men helped each other up the stairs of the bridge. Stopping from time to time to rebalance, laugh, curse and slowly make their way back to Andy's apartment.

A figure stepped out of the shadows and made a call. "They're on their way back. Have you done?"

"Yeah, all done, you'll be able to pick up any calls on the landline and we put one in the bedroom and a tracker on the car."

"Good." The man shut the phone and walked off into the night.

15

On board the cruise ship, The Golden Pyramid, the girls joined the queue to register for the cabins. The boat felt opulent and exotic; decorated in a colourful Moroccan theme; mirrors on every wall reflecting light and colour from Kasbah style brass lamps and vibrant wall hangings. The dark wood deck was covered in oriental rugs. The fragrance of burning Frankincense and Jasmine completed the atmosphere of a mystical East.

The reception hummed with the chatter of thirty odd tourists. Charlie and Jacqui were talent spotting. Male crew members, smart in white, confident and perky, smoothed through the crowd preparing the cruise boat for sailing.

"Got him, saw him first, he's mine," Jacqui nudged Charlie and nodded towards a dark Egyptian hovering around the reception attempting to speed up the ponderous paperwork.

"He must be the tour guide, great, he'll do for me."

Jacqui's eyes sparked as she threw him one of her, 'here I am, just what you have been waiting for' looks. He looked back at her. She smiled. He smiled.

"The poor man hasn't got a chance," murmured Charlie.

She caught sight of a solitary man standing a few feet back in the queue; out of place in a two piece business suit, he looked Indian or Lebanese. She found herself attracted and cast a surreptitious glance his way.

"No," she said more to herself than Jacqui. She shook her head emphatically. "Definitely, no, Charlie, my girl. No, I'm going to be good. I'm going to immerse myself in the sights – this is one of the richest places on earth for temples, tombs and ancient monuments. Nan has given me a list of places that we must see. Mind you, that guy does look rather special."

"Which one?" Jacqui pulled herself away from her own prey.

"The one back there who looks like a modern day Maharaja."

"My, your fantasies are flying already, Charlie, I can see the story unfolding: Indian Prince, Rajput castles, blonde maiden held in love nest, there's no stopping you."

She pretended to pout. "Well, Andy has really upset me so why shouldn't I enjoy a bit of an adventure?" The girls laughed.

Charlie tossed her hair and threw a glance back to check him again. Their eyes made contact. He smiled. Without a thought she smiled back then blushed. She quickly turned back as the queue moved forward.

Jacqui was watching and laughed. "Good to know you haven't lost the gift, Chas."

* * *

Eventually, the purser passed them a key and led the way dragging their cases up two flights of stairs covered in deep red carpet to their cabin. The oriental theme of luxury and opulence continued: deep red and black bedcovers and wall hangings, gold lamps and embossed wallpaper.

"God, this room is beautiful but so small, where will I put all my gear?" Jacqui threw her case onto the nearest bed.

"It's a cabin not a room. There'll be lots of hidden drawers and things. I like boats. You have to be orderly and tidy in a boat. Goodness knows how you're going to manage, my sweet." Charlie started unpacking and stowing her light linen pants and tops in the small wardrobe.

Jacqui was fixing her lipstick in the bathroom. "I'm going to unpack later. Let's find the bar, that sexy tour guide is giving his introductory talk, I need to check him out."

* * *

The girls joined the rest of their group for the overview of the week's events and the cruise schedule along the Nile. Charlie was excited to hear so many exotic destinations: Temples of Karnac, Valley of the Kings, Crocodile temple at Kom Ombo and so on, many names that she had heard from Nan over the years. Jacqui was more interested in the tour guide, Mohammad, and spent the entire talk grinning at him.

After dinner Charlie and Jacqui found the bar, and took their drinks out onto the open deck. Fellow passengers occupied the luxury deck sofas or stood leaning over the guard rails watching the activity on the riverside walkways. Their boat was one of many moored at the start of the Nile experience. Tourists strolled on the riverside path and negotiated the street merchants persistently pushing statues of ancient gods, Egyptian cotton shirts and gelabeyas, postcards and cheap souvenirs. The night was warm and balmy and the air was filled with the high pitched sound of cicadas.

"This weather is sublime. It's so good to feel warm. I am ready for anything Egypt has to offer me," Charlie said.

She stretched out her arms to the stars overhead and gazed out into the gloom to the far side of the Nile. There they would find the road to the Valley of the Kings with its ancient tombs. They moved to a table where they could watch the world go by and relax.

* * *

The girls chinked their glasses. "To us and our Egyptian Adventure," said Charlie.

"Let it include fun and sexy men," replied Jacqui.

"Did you see your Indian Maharaja? He was sitting in the corner of the bar when we were having dinner and he was definitely looking you over, Charlie."

They started to giggle, the exotic atmosphere making them giddy and girly.

"Oh, no, Jac, he's here!" Charlie blushed.

He sauntered over to their table. "Good evening, ladies, I hope you are enjoying the night air? May I join you?"

Jacqui gave him her welcome smile. "Of course."

"Would you like to share a glass?" He held up an opened bottle of Louis Roederer Cristal and a glass.

"Yes, of course, thank you." Jacquie was quick to respond.

He waved his hand towards the nearest waiter. "Waiter, bring two more glasses, please."

Charlie was tongue-tied. *My God, Cristal! This man is cool.* He looked smart but more relaxed now he'd changed into navy linen pants, blue short sleeved open neck shirt and Gucci loafers. He had the good looks of a Bollywood star: straight nose, full lips and black hair neatly trimmed. He reminded her of the Pakistani cricket heartthrob her friends had sighed over at college, what was his name, something Khan, she smiled to herself. This was a great start to the holiday.

He sat next to her but directed his conversation at Jacqui. "Sorry for barging in like this. Let me introduce myself, my name is Garneesh, Garneesh Vellupillai."

He grinned at Charlie and she smiled back. "I'm Charlie and this is Jacqui. Thanks for the champagne, you're welcome anytime," she laughed. They raised their glasses, chinked and shared smiles.

"Here's to a great holiday, ladies. What brings you onto this cruise," he asked.

Jacqui answered, "Just for some sun; it's freezing back home and Charlie's interested in the ruins. And how come you're here on your own, it's rare to find a tasty man like you alone."

Charlie flinched.

He laughed. "Well, it was a last minute plan. I'm a consultant plastic surgeon. I come from Kuala Lumpur in Malaysia; I work there and in London at The Cromwell Hospital. I was visiting Cairo to speak at a conference and also teach a new technique I've developed for breast augmentation. But they've had a noro-viral outbreak at the clinic so, lucky for me, I have a free week before the conference starts. I've never seen the ruins, as you call them, of Ancient Egypt so I'm taking a well needed rest with some culture thrown in."

He refilled their glasses and smiled again at Charlie.

Garneesh's Blackberry chirped an incoming call. "Sorry, ladies, this may take some time. Finish the bottle and I'll see you around."

He left the deck and the girls started to laugh. "Hey, he's hot and wealthy, how bad is that, Charlie. I think he fancies you."

"Well, I must say, he's a great distraction – he does have the wow factor." Charlie twirled her hair as she sipped her drink and thought through the possibilities.

Her thoughts were interrupted as Mohammad arrived. "Hi, may I join you?"

Jacqui smoothed her skirt, flicked her hair. "Of course," and she pulled up a chair close to hers.

Charlie moved away as Jacqui started her flirting routine and took her drink over to the boat rail. She leant back looking at the stars, thinking about Andy and their last conversation, *damn him*. She checked her phone. Her heart thumped. A missed call. She was about to call him back when she stopped. *Hell no. I am not going running after him again. Let him stew.* She remembered Miranda's words of wisdom. "Hold some of yourself back, Charlie, you will frighten him off if you act too keen. Don't smother him."

OK, Nan, I won't smother him. Anyway, you have to catch someone before you can smother them. No chance of that with Mr Andrew Elusive Jamieson. I'll have some fun in the sun instead! She kicked back her leg and sipped her drink as she peered over the rail.

As she watched couples enjoying the night air strolling arm in arm along the riverside she recalled Miranda's enthusiasm for the sites and their powerful energies.

"The veil between spirit and man has been thin at two places, in two times. One was Avalon, in England at the time of King Arthur and the other was in Egypt, when the pharaohs ruled the country. The men and women of Egypt were very connected to their gods and had mystical experiences. They believed fervently in life after death and the nobility spared no expense filling their tombs with their prized possessions. Anything, just about anything can happen there."

She continued to lean over the rail as she pondered on Miranda's words. Suddenly she realised that she was being watched. Her arm hair stirred. A man was leaning against the paper kiosk opposite their boat staring straight at her. She could see smoke curling up from his cigarette. His face was in shadow, no real form, just a shadowy figure.

16

Andy threw his field pack out of the back of the Chinook and jumped down onto the sandy floor of the Libyan Desert. The drivers of the two Land Rovers stowed in the helicopter belly revved up and they too carefully disembarked down the ramps. Within minutes two field vehicles, eight men, weapons and supplies for mission Y0ZX were unloaded. As the last pack hit the ground the four man crew waved a cheery goodbye, the idling rotors picked up speed and it was up, off and away leaving the eight man cell of the black ops task force to load up the Land Rovers, set their GPS systems and move off. The whole unloading operation had taken five minutes.

In the back of the first vehicle Andy gritted his teeth, clenched his fist, determined not to show his absolute delight to be back in live operations again. He cast his eye over his pack. This was planned as a short sharp attack on a training ground in the Libyan Desert so his assault pack was light by his standards. In training he had carried a one hundred pound pack in temperatures over thirty-five degrees.

His grenades, rocket launcher and other serious weapons were propped on the seat beside him. Next to him sat his oppo, Wayne Gardener. The two of them made up the Improved Explosive Device Disposal (IEDD) team on this operation. He was the senior so it was his choice of ordnance disposal equipment that lodged behind them – everything they would need to find a clear path through the mines planted around their target.

The troop leader, Jimmy Percher, leant over the seat in front. "Now, guys, remember this has to be swift. No one knows we are here including our own armed forces. We take out the training camp and get the hell out of there pronto."

Andy looked up. "Is it an Al Qaeda set up then, Jimmy?"

"Yeah. The bastards are seeking to get a stronghold here. They used the confusion of the civil war to infiltrate and this is just one of two training camps our counter terrorism intelligence boys have identified. Another cell is working on the second one. I don't even know where it is or who's involved. You know the score. Absolute secrecy."

Wayne leant forward. "How are we going to do this without the Libyan authorities sussing us out, guv?"

"Take a look outside." Jimmy pointed to the miles of empty Sahara desert in all directions. "There are only six million Libyans and ninety-nine percent live in the cities. The whole country is about seven times the size of the UK with a tenth of the population. Since they got oil rich they've given up their camels and tents and live in blocks of flats like you and me, mate. We would be very unlucky to catch sight of one of the few Berber tribesmen still roaming the desert. And this ain't the usual terrain preferred by dog walkers." He laughed. "However, if we are sighted then the rule is leave no one left to tell." He glared at them defiantly daring for a reaction. "Jo will give us the full run down when we reach A Zone."

He turned back to look at his maps and give directions to the driver. Andy looked at Wayne and grimaced. "Stroppy bugger. Makes it sound just a bit too easy for my liking," Wayne muttered. "Never known an op to go a hundred percent to plan. The w*****s in HQ never get the full picture."

Wayne glared out of the dust covered window. "Wouldn't want to be left out there alone for long. Looks like hell."

Andy nodded. "Yeah, the dark side of the moon."

17

Charlie stared hard at the man in the shadows. He seemed completely motionless apart from his cigarette; a touch of red light in the gloom.

How long has he been watching me? Who is he?

She turned to tell Jacqui, but she was completely immersed in Mohammad.

She looked back at the smoking watcher, but he had gone. Again the shiver chased down her back.

* * *

"Hi, Charlie, how about another champagne?" Garneesh was back.

"Great idea."

Mohammad and Jacqui untangled themselves. "Not for me thanks." Mohammad called the waiter for a Coke and the three of them started a second bottle of Cristal. They relaxed as Mohammad entertained them with anecdotes from previous tours and Garneesh told indiscrete stories of celebrity cosmetic surgery. Charlie watched Jacqui with Mohammad. *They look good together.* He wore a white cotton shirt that showed off his dark skin and good looks. He laughed and twinkled at Jacqui and she flashed her eyes at him.

I wonder how long she'll hold out. Maybe all of ten minutes. Charlie laughed to herself. *God she's hopeless.*

She and Garneesh wandered over to the side rail and she looked over to see if the dark stranger was still there. No sign of him.

They people-watched for a while. Vendors were hassling the stream of passers-by, but there was one in particular that caught Charlie's attention, an old man standing with a tray tied around his neck selling matches, postcards and lucky charms. Despite his age he stood upright and strong and quietly sold from his tray, without the constant blitz of sales patter of the other hawkers.

Charlie pointed him out to Garneesh. "Look how upright he stands, do you think he was a soldier? He looks so impressive even though he's dressed in rags. Maybe he's a war invalid. How sad that all he can do is sell matches, oh that's so sad." She put her hand to her chest and her eyes filled with tears.

"Bless you, how sweet you are, all those people are just walking by and not even noticing him."

He turned and looked at her closely. He took out his handkerchief and wiped her eyes. She stepped back a little confused and turned away to look down at the shore again and noticed a familiar dark figure, cigarette in hand, walk up to the match seller.

God, that's the watcher.

The two men started an intense conversation which quickly developed into a full scale argument. Their voices loud now, attracting attention from the passers-by.

"Bouse tizi, khalet," the match man swore, dismissing the watcher with the back of his hand.

The man yelled back a torrid stream of Arabic, snatched something from the tray, and then punched him in the face sending him flying onto the dusty path.

"Oh my God, stop him, Garneesh." Charlie was distraught.

As they started to move to the gangway a young man came running up, helped the old man to his feet and holding his hand the two of them walked off together.

"He doesn't look too badly hurt does he?" whispered Charlie, tears streaming down her face now. "Oh how awful, that man was a bully, did you see him punch the old man in the face, that's dreadful… "

Garneesh took the opportunity to put his arms around her. She snuggled into them.

"I think you may have a misconception of the man's background; his walk is too agile for a fellow that has been severely wounded."

"Yes, but… "

Jacqui and Mohammad came over to see what the fuss was about and Garneesh told them about the fight.

Mohammad shrugged. "Happens all the time, probably arguing over a sales pitch."

"Honey bun, we're off for a walk, will you be OK?" Jacqui untwined herself from Mohammad and hugged Charlie, whispering, "Don't wait up for me, I have a key to the room, see you when I see you."

"Cabin, it's a cabin," Charlie laughed after her as they sauntered off arm in arm. They smooched off down the gangplank onto the riverside path.

"Take care and watch out for dark strangers," Garneesh laughed as they waved goodbye.

"I don't feel like sleep yet, my mind is racing all over the place now, I'd love a coffee," said Charlie.

They spent the next hour chatting about their lives. He shared memories of his humble childhood on the rubber plantation in Malaysia, where his Tamil family had lived and worked for three generations before he escaped through a scholarship to The School of Medicine in London.

She told him of her life. The sense of feeling different from the other children with her unconventional and eccentric home life – the bullying of the children at the local school and at boarding school where she went from the age of ten. Her grandmother's need to travel had meant that the blissful times in the New Forest were interspersed with hateful times at boarding school. She admitted that she often had nightmares and woke up screaming with flashbacks of the night her parents died.

"Didn't you have any counselling or therapy for the trauma?" Garneesh asked taking her hand.

"A little but I rejected it. I just wanted to forget it and move on. I don't want to dwell on it. Most of the time it's OK. I sometimes think I had… " She stopped and her face fell and her dark eyes became clouded. "Sorry, but I would rather not talk about it." She gave Garneesh an embarrassed smile.

"Of course, of course. But it sounds like it has left a difficult legacy for you to cope with."

"It's OK, there are those who go through worse and my grandmother has been a gem, a lodestone. I got into trouble in uni and made a disastrous marriage to a man damaged and struggling with his own issues." Her eyes went dark as she recalled the drugs and alcohol that they used in an attempt to numb their pain.

"Bad choices," she muttered. "I tried to rescue him and he ended up hating me for it. He dominated me and I just went under. Eventually, when the abuse went just too far, thank God, I managed to get myself away and ran back to Nan."

Garneesh squeezed her hand.

She sighed. "They were bad times but after rehab and TLC from Nan I got over it then went to uni and I got a reasonable degree in graphic design and with a connection of Nan's got my current job with J J Blacks Advertising Agency. I love my work but I've felt for some time that there's more; even as I've become successful I still feel unfulfilled, it's strange."

She started to yawn. "I'm sorry, Garneesh. I must be boring you and I also feel exhausted now."

"Don't be ridiculous, you are far from boring." He took her hand and looked deep into her eyes. "You are the most interesting woman I've met for years. Most of my clients are shallow and lightweight, too much money and too much time. But you have a depth about you that you probably don't even realise yourself. Anyway, it's time for bed. I will walk you to your cabin."

He took her to her cabin door where he kissed her lightly on the cheek. "Goodnight, Charlie, my dear. Sleep well."

"Night, Garneesh."

She closed the door and smiled – a great start to the holiday. She slipped into her bed and curled up waiting for sleep. As she drifted off she dreamt of a tall man wrapping brown arms around her holding her close and safe. As she looked over his shoulder she saw a dark figure watching her. She shuddered. She pulled the covers up over her head and after tossing and turning for a few moments fell into a deep sleep.

18

The next morning she stepped out of the shower and grabbed a towel. Her phone announced a text message. "Hi, Charlie, don't forget to visit King Tut's tomb. Love, Miranda x."

She looked over to the other bed and the heap under the bedclothes began stirring.

"Hey, are you awake? It's the visit to Valley of the Kings today and Miranda says we should go to King Tutankhamun's tomb.

There was a mumble from under the covers.

"Come on, Jac, breakfast is at six-thirty, seems it gets really hot there by mid-day so we have to make an early start."

Jacqui threw back the bedclothes and pulled back the curtains on the porthole, letting the early morning sun stream in.

"Dare I ask how you got on last night?" Charlie said.

Jacqui laughed. "Last night was good, thank you very much; he's hot."

Charlie stood in front of the mirror struggling with her hair. She frowned. "Are you OK about being the pick of the week. He probably pulls at least one woman on every cruise? And don't forget he's Muslim, he won't be looking for a long term relationship."

Jacqui shouted over the sound of the shower. "Oh, cool it Chas, I'm not looking for a husband, but anyway, he spent four years in London. He's more Western than most of the local guys."

"As long as you know what you're doing; strikes me you two seem to have shot out of the starting gate pretty quick."

Jacqui laughed. "It's my magnetic personality. He does seem quite keen I must say. He says all the right things and he's great in bed. And hey I'm living in the moment."

Charlie smiled. "You're impossible." She was still struggling with her hair and tried holding it back from her eyes with a clip. "God, it's a frizz bomb, I need a scarf or bandana then I can tie it back. I think it'll be hot today and I forgot to pack any scrunchies." She touched her neck where the old scar was still visible.

A faint voice from the shower called out. "How about you? Did you score?"

Charlie ignored her and dressed quickly. As she was leaving the cabin she stopped and went to her case. She took out the pendant that Nan had given her, looked at the engraving and slipped it around her neck.

"See you at breakfast."

* * *

Charlie scanned the breakfast crowd for Garneesh. No sign.

She found a quiet table but was immediately joined by a tall, fit looking, sunburnt man with longish blond hair. He wore fatigues covered in pockets, with a video and digital camera slung around his neck. "Howdy y'all. OK if I join you, ma'am?" He gave her a huge smile and she nodded. He sat opposite her. She jumped up to join the buffet queue but he held out his hand.

"I'm Sam, Sam Burnett, from Austin, Texas, USA. I'm divorced, blessed with two kids, boy and a girl, fourteen and sixteen, and I'm fulfilling a lifetime dream to visit the antiquities of Ancient Egypt. And your name, ma'am?"

Reluctantly she shook his hand. "I'm Charlie Masters and this is my friend, Jacqui Millar," she indicated Jacqui coming towards their table and made her escape to the buffet table.

Sam Burnett from Austin Texas took over the conversation at breakfast and after a full interrogation their entire life stories were laid out on the table with the feta cheese and tomatoes.

As soon as she'd finished eating, Charlie excused herself. "Sorry to leave you, Sam, but we've got half an hour before we set off so I'm going to see if I can find a bandana for my hair, see you."

"Yes, I've got to pick up my bag and our water from the cabin." Jacqui also jumped up to escape.

As they hustled out of the dining room, Jacqui pulled a face. "My God that man's a pain; I hope he doesn't try to tag along with us all the time."

Charlie laughed. "He looks like a sad old surfer but he's probably a bit lonely travelling on his own. Anyway, I must dash, see you in a bit."

She ran up the stairs to the reception. She paused at the top of the gangplank taking in the quayside scene in the fresh morning light. As she looked up at the blue sky a white ibis flew past. She ran down the gangplank to the path and spotted the old match-man. He had taken a pitch just fifty yards along the riverside path. She skipped towards him. As she came closer she could see him more clearly than the night before. His skin was very dark, his beard grey and dishevelled, his garments flowing and he wore a turban typically worn by older Egyptians. She noticed that one eye had the milky hue of blindness and she wondered if the young boy she'd seen last night was his guide.

"Sabaah el Kheer," she said tentatively.

"Sabaah el nuur," he replied and smiled a welcome.

"Do you speak English?" she asked hopefully.

"I do, Madam, I have worked with tourists from your country for many years."

"I saw you being attacked last night, are you OK?

"You are very kind, Madam. I am very well, do not worry about me," he smiled again showing teeth brown with tobacco stain and decay. "How can I help you?"

"Do you have a bandana, a scarf, for my hair?" She took out the clip and let her hair fall to her shoulders.

"I do. They are very beautiful, Madam, like you," he smiled again.

He showed her a bundle that hung from his tray. She picked one with a black background covered in a small beige pattern. Her eye fell on a crystal crucifix. "Are you Christian?"

"Me, I am Coptic Christian," he replied.

"I'll take that crucifix too, please."

He pulled a piece of newspaper from his pocket and wrapped up the trinket and bandana for her.

"How much?" she asked.

"Ninety pound," his face filled with crinkles and wrinkles, his eyes twinkling as he broke into a full smile."Ha, Egyptian pound, of course, Madam."

She handed over a hundred note thinking, *I love this man,* "Please, keep the change."

Her eyes fell on a box of small silver beetles in his tray. "What are they?" she asked, her heart thumping.

"Scarabs, Madam. They are for protection and luck."

"My nan gave me one – look here." She pulled out the pendant from her shirt and showed it him. "I think she may have got it from here many years ago."

"Madam," he looked at the pendant and stared at her intensely. She interrupted. "Call me Charlie."

He smiled. "Madam Charlie," he took her hands. Her smooth manicured hands in stark contrast to his rough, brown and weather-beaten. "Everything you thought you wanted in life is about to change. You will start to discover true happiness, my dear."

He looked up and peered deep into her eyes. Looking down again he frowned. "But you must take care. I see danger. Please, you trust no man."

He opened her left hand, pushed something into it and closed it again. He smiled now. "My name is Joseph. Joseph Sayyid." He looked at her intently. "This will make your dreams come true. Remember, my dear, that you get what you ask for and what you visualise, good or bad. Use this and one day you will create your own magic."

He smiled and his face lightened. "You will find yourself on this journey through my country, my dear lady. As you visit each temple, tomb, sacred site, hidden in the stones of the ancient relics there are important messages for you and your purpose here on earth."

His eyes glistened with the intensity of his words. She felt mesmerised by the fervour in his voice.

"So, start by visiting King Tutenkamun's tomb. It is very important that you look at the West Wall. Your first message waits for you there."

Charlie felt herself welling up once again. "Oh, thank you, thank you, Joseph."

"Ma'as salaama, Rohi," he touched the centre of his chest and bowed his head to her. "God bless you."

"Goodbye, Joseph, bless you too and thank you so much."

"Charlieyyyyy," Jacqui's call cut through to her and dragged her back to reality. She looked up and saw her waving from the deck of the boat.

"Coming," she called.

She looked back at Joseph once more. He waved his old gnarled hand towards the boat. "Go, Madam Charlie, go now."

She ran back to the boat and joined the tour group as Mohammad led them to the coach.

"OK, Charlie?" Jacqui grinned at Charlie as they hugged.

"Jesus, Jac, you look like you've got the cream."

"Well you look like you're flying pretty high yourself."

"Yes and no, tell you later."

Charlie got on the bus. Jacqui slipped into a seat by Mohammad and Charlie walked further back, looked around to see if Garneesh was on board but he was nowhere to be seen so she found a free window seat. She looked down at Joseph's gift.

Oh my God.

Her hand shook as she looked down at a silver ring embossed with a strange symbol. She clasped it tight then tried it on – it fitted her index finger. It made her feel good, comforting. She looked out of the window; the sky was still a brilliant blue, such a stark contrast to the white sands of the desert dunes. Small farms and communities lined the road as they left the East Bank to cross the bridge to the West Bank and the Valley of the Kings, the burial ground of the ancient kings and queens of Ancient Thebes.

What will be waiting there for me? She thought back on his words. *He seemed so believable. Maybe there is something in this idea of signs and portents.*

Her daydream shattered as Sam moved back up the bus and stood by her adjoining seat. "Hey, Charlie, I hope you don't mind but I get sick at the front of a bus. This here would suit me so much better. Do you mind if I join you?"

"No sure, of course not." She took her bag off the seat but avoided eye contact and turned her face to the window, closed her eyes and muttered, "But sorry, Sam, I'm catching up on some sleep."

She felt guilty shutting him out but her head was full of the old man's words. *How weird that he knew about me. He sounded a bit like Nan, with her tea leaf readings – maybe he's a bit of a nutter.* Her head whirled.

Sam's voice burst through her musing. "Charlie, are you OK? You look mighty pale to me."

She gave in, opened her eyes and sat up. "Yes, thank you, I'm fine, just a bit tired."

He peered at her chest. She flinched.

"Hey, I like your scarab; do you know that one was always put on the heart of the deceased before being entombed. Meant to be some kind of protection, where did you find it?"

"It was a gift."

"Sure, that's great."

He pointed out of the window. "Now, do you see here, these old houses, they are still built the same way as when our Dear Lord visited Egypt, all those years ago. Isn't that just remarkable?"

She sighed as she accepted the end of her peace.

The bus continued through the desert, passing villages with houses carved out of the soft rock that dominated the landscape. Charlie become absorbed with the scenes of everyday life and she felt she was stepping back into the past. Sam kept up a travelogue pointing out the country lifestyle that had changed little since the time of Jesus; donkeys carrying huge loads of everything from bricks to hay, families existing on simple farming methods using bullocks and manual labour; houses made from mud and straw. She felt slightly uncomfortable looking into their lives uninvited, like a voyeur, a peeping tom.

Eventually they reached the site of the ancient burial grounds known as the Valley of the Kings. Hundreds of other tourists milled around their tour guides, surrounded by dusty young boys selling postcards, guidebooks and grimy souvenirs. Mohammad was giving his usual spiel in the background when suddenly she sat upright.

"If anyone wants to visit Tutankhamun's tomb you have to pay a big extra fee. Our government is worried all the visitors in this small tomb will spoil it. We have good story from this. You like to hear? Good I tell. Two Englishmen, Lord Carnarvon and Howard Carter were digging here and found the tomb of a young pharaoh in 1922. This was a big story that filled the world's newspapers. Why? All the other sixty-two tombs were robbed by grave robbers before excavation but here all the treasure was still in place. On April 5th Lord Carnarvon died in his hotel in Cairo, the lights all go out same time. Also they say his dog in England cry and die at same time. Other members of the team also die. So the newspapers say there is a curse on the grave." His voice hushed. "Death will visit all those who enter the grave, whoooow."

The bus load of tourists joined in, "Whoooooow."

Charlie shuddered at the story of the curse but put up her hand for the extra entrance ticket.

19

Jacqui, Charlie and Sam stood together looking down onto the sarcophagus that still held the body of King Tutankhamen, an ancient pharaoh who died mysteriously in his youth. Charlie clutched Jacqui's hand as she looked around the three walls that enclosed this part of the grave complex. All were covered with paintings, symbols, simple graphics of ancient myth and spiritual belief. The book of the Dead.

"He said it was on the West Wall. Which is west? Oh my God, how will I know which is west," she panicked.

Sam put his hand in one of his prolific pockets. "God darn it, what do you know, I just happen to have a compass right here."

He lined up to magnetic north on his pocket compass and pointed to her left. "That's the one, sure thing, that's the West Wall."

They all looked. "There's the scarab, look, there's the scarab just like the one on my pendant," Charlie's voice squeaked with excitement. "What are those figures in the boat doing?"

"They would be the baboons healing the soul on its journey to the afterlife." Sam gently touched her arm.

Will I be doing something like that? Surely not.

She turned to Jacqui. "Hey, they are monkeys. Maybe the message is I am being made a monkey of!" Her laugh a little brittle, touched with hysteria. She blushed.

She felt so hot and so stupid. "Is it me or is it boiling hot in here?" she turned to Jacqui. "I feel so strange, sort of hot and cold together, shivery but also hot."

"Hey, hun, sit down here," Sam said. He placed his backpack on the ground and she sat on it, resting back on the dirt wall. Sam and Jacqui looked at each other over her head.

"Sweetheart, this is what happened in the garden in Cairo. Do you feel OK?" Jacqui asked her.

"Just woozy, leave me for a moment will you? Please don't be worried, I'm just… " Charlie closed her eyes and Sam and Jacqui stepped away.

She felt she was falling into a tunnel, the atmosphere misty and dull. Suddenly the mist cleared and a scene appeared before her.

The young Khamet, an initiate priest, is looking up and meeting the intense gaze of an elderly priest, dressed in golden robes whose voice, deep and penetrating, booms out.

"Your initiation is nearly over, my boy. You have the sacred symbols in your consciousness now where they will stay till they are needed. Your final tests are to use the healing symbol and then there is just the test of courage with the crocodiles. I have no doubt that you will succeed. So, Khamet, designated to be High Priest Hornedjitef, you will succeed for you are a healer and the guardian of the sacred symbols – the keys to empowerment."

"Remember well my words. These powers are sought by many for evil purpose. Your life will often be in danger. The drums will be your warning. Take care when you hear the drums for danger lurks nearby at that time."

"Now follow me."

They enter a darkened chamber and kneel before an elderly man who, slumped in a gilded chair, struggles for breath.

The priest closes his eyes and lifts his hand. Bracelets of gold embedded with precious gems jangle as his arms move through the air. He traces a simple shape above the seated man, who sits quite still apart from his laboured breathing. Twice more his hands slowly draw the mystical form. He holds his hands before the man and a strong force flows from them into the man as he struggles to breathe.

A few moments pass and the old man's breathing starts to calm and colour comes back to his face.

He opens his eyes. "Khamet, I, Ptolomec, thank you from my heart. Your destiny is sealed. I honour you and your forbears. Thou hast brought life back to this enfeebled old body."

Khamet bows low before his king and touches his feet in reverence. "My lord, your health is affected by the negative forces of the dark priests.I will prepare a ritual of protection for you. You must keep me informed; whenever you feel your energy leaving you call for me. I will always be here for you, my lord, while there is breath in my body I am your faithful servant and the servant of all Egypt. It is my destiny."

The scene fades.

Charlie opened her eyes, stretched her arms and legs and looked up to Sam and Jacqui, standing wide eyed above her.

"Oh my God," she whispered. She jumped up. She looked down at her hands. "My hands are tingling." *What is going on with me?* She looked up frightened and confused by the sensations that she was experiencing. She felt embarrassed by the stares of Sam and Jacqui and blushed again.

Jacqui laughed. "Hey, girl, what's up?"

Charlie shook her head to clear the confusing thoughts. "It's OK, Jac, it was just a dream. Yes, it was just a dream. There was this boy and he was using a healing symbol and my hands are still tingling. Oh my God!"

Jacqui whispered close to her ear, "Maybe your nan was right. You are a reincarnation of that priest."

"Don't be ridiculous." Charlie blushed again and pushed back at her hair. "It was just a dream. I AM NOT A PRIEST AND NOT A HEALER." Her whisper became a little shrill and startled Sam who raised his eyebrows.

"Hey, gals, what's going on along here? Did you say you are a priest?" He smiled but looked confused.

Jacqui looked at him. "Oh, Sam it's too complicated to tell you now."

"Did you see the symbol?" whispered Jacqui.

Charlie stopped short. "Well, no, not actually. Oh, no."

They'd drawn a small crowd by now. Charlie grabbed Jacqui by the arm and drew her away.

Mohammad walked up, smiled at the girls. "Happy?" he asked.

"Beyond happy," Jacqui laughed and hugged Charlie. "Don't look so serious, sweetie, it's all good."

Jacqui did a twirl and cried, "I love Egypt!"

"Now you make me happy, too," grinned Mohammad. "But we must move on, more wonders for you to see yet."

Charlie decided to give a miss to the rest of the tombs. She felt a little unsettled so she moved further up the valley away from the tourist throng, where she found a rock in the shade. She sent a text to Miranda to share her latest dream, vision or whatever it was. She looked up and the sky was still the most brilliant blue. A kite circled overhead. She closed her eyes.

Her phone brought her back to earth with a text from Nan. "I'm not at all surprised. Be prepared, darling. I know you are cynical but keep your mind open. Keep everything secret for now."

She started to feel the heat of the valley affecting her. She reached into her backpack for her water bottle and pulled out the bandana that she had bought from Joseph. She recalled his words. *Maybe I can create a little magic. That would be a turnaround from designing ads. It would certainly surprise a few of my workmates! I could use a bit of magic on Howard – but I think it would probably be black magic.*

She laughed as her thoughts went off into the realms of the ridiculous. She pulled her hair back and tied it with the scarf. She felt her hands tingling again. She looked down at them and started to rub them together. She could do with a touch of Andy's down to earth approach. *Maybe one text.* She pursed her lips as she thought about the pros and cons of contacting Andy. *No, he'll be gadding about in five star hotels, this will seem completely batty to him.* She decided not to contact him.

"Charlie," a familiar voice called her, "Charlie!"

She looked up to see Garneesh walking towards her. "I thought I'd missed you," he called. "I was delayed with calls from Malaysia this morning and missed the coach; I came by taxi, what a ride. How's it been, seen anything interesting?"

"Yes it's certainly been interesting. Quite extraordinary in fact. I'm still trying to make sense of it. I had another funny turn where I had a sort of dreamlike experience. I thought I saw myself in Ancient Egypt. Anyway, despite my nan's conviction it's a past life I am extremely sceptical. Quite honestly I don't believe in reincarnation. I suppose you do – Indians are into that aren't they?"

"Well Hindus believe in a cycle of life, that's true. I can't say I've ever thought too much about it, but reincarnation and karma are inherently part of our culture."

"Well, I don't believe in it but it was very vivid. It's left me a little confused and spacey."

Garneesh held out his hand to help her up. "Can I suggest you wait till we meet tonight then you can tell me all about it when there is no one else around. We have to join the group now as they are moving onto the Valley of the Artisans. They might think you a little odd if you start talking about past lives and visions."

She stood up and brushed off her white linen trousers that were beginning to look less than fresh. "Yes, you're right. To be honest I find it unbelievable myself, I think we have enough to cope with this lifetime without worrying about any previous ones! I'll leave that to the New Age lot. But I am interested in the concept of destiny; maybe you can share your take on that tonight."

They linked arms and sauntered down the valley to join the rest of their group.

The kite continued to draw its own swirling patterns in the intense blue sky. The sun beat down ever stronger on the tourists, the tombs, the ancient rocks.

The man stepped out from the shadows, checked his watch and opened his phone and made a call. "She's waking up."

20

Andy put the last of his kit into his tent. He looked around at their camp at Wadi Qorm, a small gully where they could rest up out of sight. They planned to hit at dawn. The target a terrorist's training camp; the source of many attacks on innocent victims around the world, including the hostage disaster at BP's Algerian gas facility. He looked around at the red desert sand, red and strewn with small rocks, barren apart from the occasional tuft of hardy grass.

God forsaken place.

Jimmy had brought them up to speed with the plans for the attack. Everything in black ops was always on total shut down until the very last minute before the actual moment of action. Secrecy and stealth were their greatest assets alongside the talents, skills and incredible expertise of the handpicked troops that made up the various cells.

Overall he was glad Guthrie had enticed him back in. He had missed active service after he left the Special Forces; it physically hurt at times. He loved it and hated it equally. The adrenaline; the thrill of combat; using his skills and expertise; the camaraderie versus his own personal sense of shame.

He decided to take a walk; he was stiff after the long flight and drive from the drop zone to the wadi. At the end of the small valley were a group of large rocks and here he found Wayne his attack buddy on sentry duty. He was leaning on the rock, night glasses round his neck.

There's one cynical bastard

But whatever, he could be his saviour. They used the buddy system in the mainstream Special Force operations and it worked – well most of the time. The idea was to have your back protected at all times – have someone to watch out for you.

He called up to him. "Hi, mate, anything going on out there?"

"Just a f**king load of nothing, pal, a load of nothing." Wayne's grim face peered down to him through the fading light. They could expect a short twilight then total darkness till the moon arrived.

He walked back to his tent to get some sleep.

Unaware to Andy, on the far side of the wadi, Jimmy Percher was on the field radio, his voice just above a whisper. "All instructions passed on. Yeah, yeah, I know your thoughts about Jamieson. So far he seems OK. I know, I know, I'll try and keep an eye on him. Just wish I hadn't been landed with an op with baggage. I've buddied him with Gardener, he's a tough bastard. Any sign and he'll sort it. Yeah, I know but it'll be a hard tight pitch tomorrow, can't take any passengers. Yeah, I know – no one better with mines," he mimicked.

He was annoyed. "He's checked the image scan and there are hundreds of the bastards around the camp but he reckons he can find a way through. Just hope he keeps his nerve… Sure… Wish we could have done a direct drop into the camp… Yeah, yeah I know, OK. Time out, got to go."

Unaware of the call, Andy slipped into his tent. He looked down at his hands, they shook. *Excitement or fear?*

21

It was dark by the time Charlie and Jacqui's tour arrived back at the boat. They were tired, hot and dishevelled. They came face to face with a large poster placed in the centre of the reception area.

Fancy dress – Galabeya Party.

Live music and Whirling Dervish dancers.

"Now that sounds fun, Mohammad was telling me about these parties, they have them on all the boats. They sell outfits in the ship's shop on the deck above our cabin. Let's go and choose something special, this could be a great crack." Jacqui bounded up the stairs with Charlie behind her.

Two pairs of eyes watched them.

* * *

On the quayside children stopped playing and paused to wave as the boat slowly pulled away to start its journey along the Nile. First stop Edfu.

The girls were dressed for the party. Jacqui wore a deep blue full length sequined galabeya, with matching scarf covering her hair. Her eyes were lined with kohl and blue eye shadow, her full lips painted with vivid red lipstick. She looked absolutely stunning.

Charlie had chosen a simpler crimson outfit, embroidered with gold thread that perfectly showed off her blonde hair. She felt more than a little self-conscious as she followed her friend down to the bar for a pre-dinner drink. Appreciative comments from the barmen and the arrival of other members of their group also dressed for the occasion soon made her feel less conspicuous and she began to relax into the spirit of the evening.

Garneesh arrived as the second round of drinks and canapés were served. "Hey you look scrummy," said Charlie admiring his imposing black and gold outfit.

He kissed both girls on the cheek. "Not nearly as scrummy as you two, can I join you?"

The girls nodded.

"Permit me to buy you a drink, this wine looks a bit ordinary, would you prefer champagne?"

"You say all the right things, Garneesh, I would always prefer champagne if it's on offer," Jacqui pushed her wine glass to one side.

"Well, yes please, that sounds great," Charlie moved her bag from the seat beside her.

"How are you feeling now? Have you recovered from your time warp adventures?"

"Yes, thanks, I feel just fine."

Garneesh called the waiter over and ordered champagne for the girls and a campari and soda for himself.

Once they were served he looked around, most of the group had wandered onto the deck outside.

"So, Charlie, tell me more about your experience this morning. What exactly was happening in that past life of yours?" Garneesh leaned back in his chair and sipped his drink.

Before Charlie could reply the ship's bell rang for dinner, so they picked up their drinks and moved towards the dining room.

Jacqui whispered into Charlie's ear as they walk downstairs. "I don't think you should tell even Garneesh what you told me. Remember what Miranda said about keeping it secret. Anyway, he'll probably think you're losing the plot, don't forget he's a medical doctor and I doubt if he believes in healing. As it is, Sam was asking me what it was all about – he could be Christian fundamentalist or something. I really think you should keep it quiet for now."

"Funny, that's what Garneesh said – he said I should keep it quiet." Charlie looked at her friend. "Well, as I don't even believe it myself it suits me fine to keep it to myself."

Garneesh walked up close behind them. "What're you girls whispering about, hey? Can you share your secrets?" He laughed.

They moved to join the table allocated to their group and sat with Sam and a couple from Canada. Sam had the tour schedule in his hand.

"Geez, tomorrow should be a stunner, two great temples, Edfu and Kom Ombo."

Maryanne from Quebec joined in. "Sure, I'm keen to see the Kom Ombo Temple, it's famous for its crocodiles."

Sam read from the guide. "Yeah, it says so here. The Temple known as Kom Ombo is actually two temples consisting of a Temple to Sobek, the crocodile-headed God of the Nile and fertility and the second the Temple of Haroeris, the hawk headed god of the underworld. In ancient times, the Nile was full of crocodiles and sacred crocodiles basked in the sun on the river bank nearby."

Maryanne added, "I heard somewhere that they used it for initiation rites for an Ancient Mystery School. Apparently to prove their courage initiates had to swim through water-filled tunnels not knowing when they would come face to face with a crocodile."

"Sounds exciting though, maybe we can bag one for dinner," laughed Sam.

"Nice one, you can count me out of that excursion," laughed Jacqui. "And I'll give your dinner a miss too, thanks, Sam!"

Charlie felt a shivers run through her spine. *Initiation, the fear test. Oh my God.*

22

Once the tables were cleared from dinner they made their way back to the large bar furnished with velvet banquettes and sofas in rich reds, blues and greens, gilt armchairs and screens and tablets intricately carved with Moorish designs. Everyone had made an effort to dress up and their colourful costumes added to the exotic atmosphere. There was a constant flow of wine and soon the room came alive with the throb of high octane eighties pop. Mohammad was off duty and he and Jacquie danced with Garneesh and Charlie. After a few more glasses of wine Charlie could feel herself getting rather wild and out of control. Behind her she could hear Jacquie's laughter became louder by the minute as she too threw herself into the party atmosphere.

She was swept away with the heat and the powerful rhythms – her dancing became more and more abandoned. Garneesh was laughing as he spun her around, catching her and throwing her from arm to arm in a parody of a sixties jive. She felt slightly queasy and was rather relieved when the disco music stopped and the Whirling Dervish dancers were announced.

Three male dancers came onto the small dance floor dressed in full floor length white skirts and tall brown hats. The atmosphere became charged as the musicians started up zither, drums and pipes creating a hypnotic sound. The men began spinning with arms outstretched, their long skirts swirling around them creating a blur of spinning white. Faster and faster they twirled, the music growing louder and louder. Faster and faster whirled the dancers and the effect was powerful and evocative. Spin, spin, whirl, whirl, faster, faster. The volume continued to rise with the dancers spinning into a vortex of white. As the pipes wailed their figures blurred into spirals. Faster, faster.

The hypnotic swirling, spinning figures mesmerised Charlie. Her attention began to drift and she struggled to keep the dancers in focus. The sound of the pipes and zither faded and the music changed to the hypnotic rhythm of drums. The whirling, swirling figures in front of her became diffused and blurred.

She became dizzy and disorientated. The sound of the dervish music was overtaken by the sound of distant drums. She drifted off.

Gradually her vision clears and she sees the young Khamet, priest initiate, lying in bed – a strange bed with simple covers in a dark spare room, a cell. The moon's soft beams shine through the small window high in the room. They pick out the ceremonial robes hanging on the wall waiting for the initiation rituals due in three days time. He has one last hurdle to overcome; swimming with crocodiles. Then his great moment will arrive and all the hard work of the last eight years will culminate as he reaches his majority. He will then be accepted into the Temple Service. His life purpose can then begin.

He lets go his reverie and becomes alert, what was that noise? He holds his breath to hear more clearly; stealthy footsteps in the corridor outside his cell, heavy breathing from someone behind the old wooden door, the cautious lifting of the latch.

The door begins to move, little by little opening to let danger and menace enter his sanctuary. He shivers and tenses. He has no weapons; he has no recourse, just his strength and wits.

He calls out, "Who is that, who enters my domain?"

Suddenly, the door flies back and a body hurls itself onto his bed. Hard, cold hands grip his throat. He looks up into the gloating and evil face of his arch rival and enemy Aapep; the one boy in the class that hates him, who lusts after his position as senior, as the leader of the class, the favourite of the masters.

"I have come to kill you, Khamet, O favoured one, Hornedjitef, I shall take your karma and position. When you die, it is I who will become High Priest Designate in your place."

The drums play out their harsh rhythm. Aapep squeezes his throat tighter and tighter. Khamet starts to choke and feels himself slipping out of consciousness. He draws his sacred symbols in the air behind Aapep's head then with a huge effort brings his hands together in front of the boy and throws him off. The symbol's powers with his anger and indignation have given him strength and Aapep falls to the floor.

"Get out of here; you are an imposter in the Temple. You are an evil conniving beast."

Khamet reaches up and grabs his sacred ritual dagger from the wall and advances towards Aapep. He puts the dagger to his throat and the point pierces his skin, a tiny drop of red blood oozes onto Aapep's white robe, a scarlet teardrop.

"Get up and get out, right now. Get out of here, get out now and never threaten me again."

He holds the dagger before him with both hands to prevent the trembling in his arms.

Aapep sneers but backs out of the room, the sharp knife glints in the candlelight and he can see steel in Khamet's eyes; he senses that he will not hold back from using it.

Khamet stays back, controlling his anger. Now out of reach of the dagger Aapep's bravado returns.

"Watch out, Khamet, you will never lose me as your enemy. I shall succeed, if not tonight, tomorrow and if not tomorrow, some day nigh. It is I that shall have the glory not you."

He laughs and slams the door – the wall hangings rattle and the room settles back into peace.

Khamet puts the dagger back in its place and lays back on the bed, emotional and shaking.

Gradually she morphs back into life. As she transits between lives a voice booms in her head.

"You are in danger, beware those that would steal the symbols and their powers." The drum beats became louder and more menacing. *"Beware, Aapep, your mortal enemy, has crossed over from the past. He is near. Take care, take great care."*

The drum beats began to fade and the dancers came back into focus once again. She shook her head and looked around her. Had anyone noticed her slipping away? The dancers held everyone in rapt attention; no one appeared to have noticed her own experience.

Her heart was beating fast and furious in her chest. She reached out to take her glass and her hands shook. She held the glass tight and leant forward breathing deeply in an effort to regain control.

The dancers had now finished and were replaced by a single man dressed in a full skirted robe of multicoloured fabric. As he began to whirl he became a swirl of colour. Just to see him made her feel giddy again; she closed her eyes. After a few moments she felt able to talk and turned to Garneesh and Jacqui.

"Guys, I feel a little nauseous, all that whirling and swirling has made me giddy. I think I'll just go and lie down for a while. You carry on. I'm sure I'll come good in no time and I'll come back and join you."

Jac looked at her hard. "You OK? You look deathly white and what are those red marks on your neck?" She leant towards her.

Charlie touched her neck. It felt sore. She trembled. "No, Jac, stay." She pushed her back down. "Thanks, but don't worry, I'm fine."

But Jacqui was a little high and not to be deterred. "You know they look like fingerprints to me. What's been going on?"

Garneesh leaned over her and peered at her throat. "They certainly do look like fingerprints. Good heavens, this is really most intriguing."

Charlie looked at Jacqui and whispered to her, "Oh, Jac, I'm frightened. I just had another dream, trance or whatever it is. I really felt I was a boy and someone was trying to strangle me. What have I got myself into?"

Jacqui pulled her into her arms, hugged her and smoothed her hair. "Relax, Charlie, sweetheart, it was just a dream. You're in the twenty-first century; you are safe and there's nobody trying to kill you."

Garneesh shook his head, he looked worried. "But, Charlie, I must say, it feels as though the past is coming back to haunt you. But why would someone want to kill you? Do you have some deep, dark secret?" He laughed as he pulled Charlie back to her feet. "I am wearing my doctor's hat now. I think you should take a rest in your cabin. Come I will take you there, you look so very pale."

"OK, I do feel sleepy, Jac, don't worry about me, you go on and enjoy your evening. If I feel better later I'll come back up. Go find Mohammad and enjoy yourself."

"You sure, Charlie?"

"Yes, I'll be fine. Garneesh will help me. See you later."

He put his arms around her and half carried and half led her down the stairwell and along to her cabin. He took her key and opened the door. The porthole was open and a night breeze from the river blew the curtains. Charlie felt sick. "Oh, the curtains, why are they fluttering like that?"

Garneesh stared at her. "It's just the night air, nothing to worry about."

He pulled back the bedcover. "Would you like me to stay here with you?"

"No, no I'm OK. I just need a little rest, bless you."

"Try to sleep; I'll catch up with you later."

He helped her onto her bed. He kissed her gently on her head and quietly left the cabin. "Lock the door after me, just to be on the safe side."

She watched him leave and lay there for a while. Thank God for meeting a kind man, just when she needed him. He was tasty too. She suppressed the sensations of desire that were starting to creep over her. She sighed, got up and locked the door. She picked up her bag and hunted through it, pulling out the contents. She tipped it upside down and there it was – the talisman, the pendant that Nan had given her. With shaking fingers she slipped it around her neck. Immediately she felt calmer. She picked up her phone and began a text to Miranda.

"Is it possible to be physically affected by a dream?" She told her about the imprints on her neck.

Almost instantly her text reply came back. "If what you call a dream is actually a past life recall then yes, you most certainly can be affected. You can hold imprints of past life trauma in your etheric body, your energy body. Because we are holistic and mind, spirit and body are all connected, when you are facing the same situation or danger in your current life the energy memories can come back in your physical body. Sweet child, I have a sense that you could be in danger, take care. So glad you have a knight in shining armour looking after you."

23

Charlie woke with a sudden start. She could feel the vibration of the engines as the boat throbbed its way towards Edfu. Her senses were on full alert and her heart was beating wildly. She looked around to see what could have woken her up so suddenly. She listened intently, what was it that had disturbed her? Was it from a dream? But why the sudden jolt? Was it the engine noise? Hardly likely as that was a constant background noise. She looked around the cabin but all seemed in order. Her heart continued to race as some inner sense warned her of danger.

She looked across at the door. In the dim light of the cabin she could just see the door knob and her body tensed. Was it her imagination or was it moving. She peered through the gloom.

Yes, oh, my God it moved.

She stared hard at the door knob. Again it moved just ever so slightly. Her heart beat even faster now.

Oh, God. Angels protect me. Oh, no, it's my dream coming true.

She sat bolt upright and pushed herself back against the cabin wall. The handle moved once more. Now she could hear heavy breathing on the far side of the door.

I locked it, I know I locked it. Or did I?

Her mind filled with doubt.

She looked around to see where she had left the key. The handle turned again. She tensed and got ready to spring up. She searched through the gloom looking for a weapon. Her chest heaved with the fear, her heart thumped, her whole body tensed. Now the door itself started to shake, someone was leaning on the door, testing to see if it could be pushed open.

Nothing happened for a moment. She started to relax.

Maybe they will go now. Maybe they will give up.

But the door rattled again a little louder. More effort, more force. The door frame started to creak.

Oh, my God, he's going to break in.

The door handle rattled loudly; no subtlety now. This was an outright attempt to get into her room. She continued to look for a weapon but there was no handy dagger on the wall! She grabbed the bedside lamp and pulled out the plug and started to move closer to the door. Again the door handle rattled. Any minute the wood would splinter.

She stood by the door with the lamp in her hand. She would catch him as he came in, catch him unawares; surprise him with her own attack. Fear slithered through her body, her hands trembled and she was sweating, beads of water dripped down her back. She felt cold inside and her stomach churned. She braced herself ready to strike.

Another sound.

Someone else is coming!

In the distance, far down the corridor she heard approaching footsteps.

Then relief. Blessed relief. She heard the knocking on cabin doors. The purser preparing beds for the night. The door stopped creaking. The intruder went quiet then she heard his soft thudding footsteps as he ran off down the carpeted corridor.

Thank you, angels, thank you, thank you, purser.

She shuddered as her fear subsided and she put down the lamp. She took gulps of air and started to breathe again. She found the key on the side table and with shaking hands she cautiously opened the door. The purser, Ahmed, appeared from the cabin two doors away.

"Oh, Ahmed, Ahmed, thank God you have come. Did you see someone at my door?" she gasped.

"Yes, a man, dark clothes, he ran off. Your friend? Are you alright, Ma'am?"

"Yes, yes. No, I don't know who it was. Oh, I am so scared. Could you please... " her voice broke. "Oh, please can you tell the captain? Someone was trying to get into my cabin." Her voice shook. She leant on the wall for support.

"So sorry, so sorry, Ma'am. I tell Captain. You OK? Sit down, sit down." He put out his hand to steady her.

"Sure, yes, I mean, well, not really, but I'll go out and get some air on the deck. Don't worry, I'll be fine. Thanks, Ahmed. Really don't worry."

She turned away, the intensity of Ahmed's gaze and concern embarrassing her. Too much attention. She went back into her cabin. She was still dressed in the galabeya. She felt in no mood now for fancy dress. She pulled it off quickly and dragged on a pair of jeans and a sweatshirt. She looked into the mirror and checked her throat. It was now back to normal but she could see the fear in her eyes.

Stupid woman. Get a grip.

She gritted her teeth and tried to smile but she only managed a grimace, so she turned away from the mirror, picked up her bag and quickly left the cabin.

Ahmed was just next door; she could hear him on the phone speaking excitedly in Arabic. She slipped away and ran up the gangway. She hurtled up the steps two at a time, desperate to get away from the gloomy corridors below decks. When she stepped out into the open deck she was relieved to see it brightly lit by a full moon. All seemed peaceful and normal up there. A few passengers were leaning on the rails peering into the darkness as the boat throbbed its way up to Edfu. She looked back and realised they were one of a dozen boats sailing in convoy up the Nile; an impressive procession. She looked around for Jacqui but the deck was quiet and her friend nowhere.

Probably sloped off with Mohammad.

She found a secluded spot away from the other passengers and leant over the rail. She wished she still smoked.

She felt calmer now and her breathing began to return to normal but her heart still raced and she could feel the anxiety still in her muscles. She stretched to release the tension. She took deep breaths and focused on the scene before her, willing herself to release her anxiety and tension.

The moonlight lit up the banks and she could see past and present merge. The banks were lined with small family farms with a couple of cows tied to a stake outside simple mud homes. Piles of alfalfa and hay. Donkeys rested in the gloom of the night light with their loads of sticks and rice beside them. In the dusk children played in the dust, shouting and waving at the cruise boats. Overhead the clear dark sky filled with flickering stars. How easy to drift from the past to the present and back again.

Her heart still thudded from the very real fear she had experienced in her cabin.

Her phone beeped and she looked down at the latest text from Miranda. Dear Nan, always her blessing, always there for her. "Dearest Charlie, everything you have ever been is with you. Everything you have ever experienced is locked into your cellular memory. That is your spiritual development and your spirit is the core of who you are.

You were born to this and you have the strength to cope with the challenges you will meet. But with this knowledge comes danger. Do be careful, my darling. I love you, Miranda."

Charlie shivered, this was not what she wanted to hear. She wanted Nan to tell her that it was all a fanciful dream, a result of visiting a land of ancient myths. Her warning re-enforced the sense of a sinister presence that seemed to be lurking around her, not just in the past but right now in the present moment.

She thought about Andy away negotiating deals in five star hotels. *Lucky thing.*

Despite her anger at him she yearned for his presence, his strong energy, his down to earth approach. He would dismiss her fears in an instant. Tell her to pull herself together and get a grip. Get a hold on reality. She sighed and reached for her phone. She tried calling him. "This phone is turned off, please call later."

She stared out into the shadows as the boat continued on its journey into the dark night. The menace was palpable.

24

Andy crawled into his sleeping bag. He felt the tremors leaving him as exhaustion numbed his senses. He fell into a fitfull sleep but his past refused to rest and the memories reared up from the recesses of his mind and filled his dreams.

The smell of cordite fills the air, the residue of shots just recently fired. Fateful and fatal shots. He looks down and sees his buddy lying in a pool of blood as his life force seeps away in the mud. What does he feel? Nothing, nothing at all. The guilt, the rage, the despair will hit later. He turns back to the family huddling in the corner of the hut, the fear on their faces lit by the flames of the burning shacks. The night is filled with the screams of the victims, the smoke from burning roof reeds, the smell of seared human flesh. He gestures to the man to take his family away. They rise quickly and step over the fallen bodies of the two rebels that Andy has shot. Saving them he has forfeited the life of his buddy. Later, he will think of this, later. He runs over and picks up their third child in his arms and leads them out of the burning village. They stumble into the jungle taking a well worn path, used by the women to the nearby washing pool. "Vite, vite, allez, allez" he calls back to the mother and father who have the two other children in their arms. Gradually the sound of the carnage behind them dies and they reach comparative peace as they run deeper and deeper into the safety of the jungle.

In the papers the next day a small paragraph mentions another massacre in Western Africa, another village destroyed by militants. No mention of the British armed forces sent under cover to track the insurgents, monitor the situation. No mention of a young man killed while his buddy broke the rules of his mission. No mention of the guilt that this act of mercy would eat away within him for years to come. His legacy of war.

Andy tossed back and forth, back and forth as he relived that night once again. His body soaked in sweat. He swore. He tossed and turned. He ground and gnashed his teeth with anger at himself, the memory and the futility.

A soft call came from the nearby tent. "You all right, mate?"

"Yeah, yeah, I'm fine, no worries."

He felt the tension in his arms and realised his fists were still clenched. He released them. *What the hell am I doing here? Where will this end?* He looked at the illuminated face of his watch. Three hours to go. Three hours before the possibility of more carnage, more death, more guilt.

25

The boat continued to chug its way along the Nile. Charlie pulled her thoughts away from the fear of the unknown and shadows that lurked all around.

"Hi, beautiful lady. How are you feeling now?" She looked up as Garneesh appeared before her.

"Oh, Garneesh, I'm so glad you're here. I've just had a really ghastly experience."

"What, another one? Come, sit down and tell me about it." He put his arm around her and guided her to one of the deck sofas.

"This one was awful and very real. Someone was trying to get into my cabin. I saw the door knob move and… " She felt tears start to flow. "Oh, I'm sorry, Garneesh, I'm not normally the crying type but I feel a bit… "

"A bit discombobulated, maybe?" He laughed. "I should think so, you've had some strange experiences and this one is serious. I shall go and find the captain immediately." Garneesh stood up.

"No, no, it's OK, the purser has done that."

"But we can't have you girls troubled by this. You should feel safe on the boat. Maybe he was an opportunist petty thief. Everyone needs to be made aware."

"Please, Garneesh, please don't worry about it. But you could get me a drink," she smiled at him.

"Of course, of course, how terribly remiss of me. Do you want to stay here? Let me find a waiter."

He walked briskly to the steps leading down to the saloon bar.

She watched him as he disappeared down the steps. Again she felt gratitude for his kindness. So good looking too! She felt a surge of desire, followed by a twinge of guilt as Andy's face slipped into her mind.

No, I will not be tempted. I will not.

She refocused and picked up her phone to text Miranda her latest developments, changed her mind and started to text Andy. Then again had second thoughts and selected his number. The phone rang for a few moments and Andy's recorded voice told her, "I am unable to answer your call, please contact my office where you can leave a message."

26

"I just don't trust him. He's not stable. He had the night terrors just last night. It's my bloody life that'll be at risk. You have to pull him." Wayne looked fierce as he whispered into Troop Leader, Jimmy Percher's ear.

Jimmy stepped back and pushed Wayne away from him. He swore. "Get off, don't crowd me, mate. I know your concerns. Don't think we're not aware of it. But the guy had an impeccable record till that incident."

"Bloody incident," Wayne interrupted. "His buddy getting slaughtered due to his negligence is more than an incident."

"There were mitigating circumstances."

"All I know is that Pete Jones died, whatever the circumstance and Jamieson was responsible." Wayne poked his finger into his leader's chest. "He didn't cover Pete's back and because of that he got clobbered." He poked him again.

"Stop that. Just stop that. Calm down." He pushed Wayne's hand away and bent down to continue packing his gear. "I'll be keeping a close eye on him too. You'll just have to be ultra vigilant. Sorry, mate, there is nothing we can do now. We hit the camp in half an hour. No time for change of plan. Jamieson is the best ordnance operative we have. That camp will be ringed by mines."

Wayne glared at the kit at their feet, but said nothing.

"Now get a move on. Get a move on." Jimmy turned his back and started loading the jeep.

Wayne moved off. He kicked a rock in his path. Once out of Percher's hearing he muttered, "Well, I'll be taking bloody good care of myself one way or another, mate, that's for sure. Make no mistake on that score."

27

Horses' hooves clattered over cobbles. The atmosphere was full of impatience; everyone in a rush to grab an opportunity to make a few pounds. Arabic profanities coloured the constant thrust and parry of battered taxis, dust covered private cars and horse drawn carriages hurtling tourists to and from the cruise boats and the Temple of Horus. Charlie and Garneesh looked out from their carriage at this street scene of modern Edfu; the Egyptian mix of sacred and profane, ancient and modern.

Charlie had been reluctant to use the traditional horse drawn carriage. "Are you sure they treat the horses well?" she asked Garneesh.

"I believe there is an English charity here that ensures they do so. I don't think any of them look too bad."

But Charlie insisted they spend time searching for the healthiest looking horse. They eventually found a horse without sores. To calm her anxieties Garneesh insisted there would be no tip if the driver used his whip.

After a short dash along the cobbled streets avoiding cars and other carriages they arrived in front of the temple gates without mishap. The place teemed with foreign tourists arriving in coaches, carriages, taxis and on foot. Garneesh guided her protectively through the throng.

"We won't bother to go with the rest of the herd," he announced. "I'll buy tickets for us and then we are free to wander unfettered." He laughed. "I'm not very good at these package tour situations."

He bought their tickets. Charlie watched with admiration as he skipped the queues of jostling tour guides and back packers that teemed around the ticket office.

"You have the knack of cutting through the red tape. You seem to attract respect and attention, is it because you are a doctor?"

He laughed, "Not sure about that, doctors aren't held in awe any more. To these guys I could be anyone."

Once inside the compound walls they walked around the well preserved temple. Huge sandstone pylons created an impressive frontage, towering above them looking splendid against the blue sky. Charlie asked a passerby to take photos of them standing by the huge statue of the god Horus as a bird.

Garneesh laid his arm around her shoulders as they wandered away from the statue. "Horus is the god you need just now as he is the god of protection. His is a good story. Isis's husband Osiris was murdered and dismembered. She collected all his body parts to put him together again. She found them all except his penis which had been thrown in the Nile and eaten by a catfish then, using magic, she recreated him and gave him a golden penis, lucky fellow! She then became pregnant with Horus. Years later when Horus ruled Lower Egypt he was attacked by his uncle, Set. In the battle one of his eyes was gouged out by Set and the eye became a symbol of Horus – hence the Eye of Horus symbol that you see everywhere as a talisman to ward off evil."

Charlie gasped. "Oh my God. Did you say an eye?"

"Yes, look there it is on this wall here." Garneesh pointed to a stylised eye embossed into the surface of the outside temple wall. Charlie stared at the symbol of the eye.

Where had she seen that symbol before? It looked so familiar.

"How do you know all this?" she asked.

"Simple, I read it in a guidebook on the boat. The stories of Ancient Egypt are fascinating."

"I bought a guidebook but after my first dream I've tried not to read it before bed. Can we go inside?" she asked.

"Yes, of course." At that moment his phone trilled a cascade of bells. "Sorry, Charlie. I must take this one."

"OK, I'll go on in. Catch up with me when you can."

She wandered into the vast temple and made her way towards the Holy of Holies, the innermost sanctum, the sacred domain of the Temple High Priest. She felt a little daunted by the high pillars that lined the inner corridors; the energy of the great temple seemed to overwhelm her. She felt small and vulnerable. She decided to say a prayer to Horus for protection when she reached the inner temple. But, she was disappointed for it was jammed with a large group of new agers omming and chanting. So she wandered off along one of the many side corridors which led to minor chambers. Temple guardians dressed in long grubby white tunics, stood at strategic points throughout.

One of them stepped up to her and touched her arm. "Madam, would you like to see special place. Please to follow me. I show special and very sacred ancient place. Not for public."

She looked him up and down. He was quite young and his big eyes almost implored her to follow him. She had heard that guides often offered to show you closed rooms and crypts. He looked dirty but harmless.

She dug out her purse from her bag. This was going to cost her but she felt compelled to follow him, her pulse was racing and she felt a familiar whoosh.

"Well, OK, then," she said.

He lifted a rope with a No Entry sign and led her further away from the crowds.

God, how much should I tip him? She tried to remember the exchange rate.

They left the bustle and noise of the main temple. The only sounds her footsteps and his shuffling sandals. It was dim here with just the odd light high on the grey granite walls. It felt cool, even cold, after the heat of the city. The temperature dropped even lower as they walked further into the heart of the building. Suddenly the man grabbed her arm and pulled her through a narrow opening.

"Madam, Madam, come." His hoarse voice was insistent. His tight grip hurt her arm and his forcefulness made her suddenly very scared.

"No, no, let me go," she shouted. He held tight onto her blouse. "Let me go!" She was really frightened now.

They tussled and he got his arm around her throat. "Please, please come," he shouted into her ear.

He dragged her into a side chamber. She tried to kick him but he was too close and held her tight. She could smell his breath through the cloth that covered his head and mouth.

"Oh, Angels, help me."

Her phone was ringing in her bag, but she couldn't reach it. She struggled and tried shouting but he held her closer and forced a hand tightly over her mouth.

"Shhhhhhh," he whispered fiercely in her ear. "Shhhhhhhhhhhh, quiet."

Charlie tried to bite his hand but he just pressed her closer to his chest. She wriggled and pulled at her arm to jab him with her elbow but the man was strong, she could feel hard muscles under his galabeya.

Suddenly the chamber echoed with the sound of a strong and forceful voice. "Hey, what's going on here? Let her go. Take your hands off her."

The man immediately released her and thrust her away then ran off disappearing down the nearby passageway. She staggered against the wall, her legs buckling and knees trembling. Garneesh came running up. "Are you OK? Oh, I am so sorry that I was not with you. Who was that man?"

"I don't know. I thought he was one of the temple guards. It's my fault I should never have followed him. Thank God you found me."

Charlie was shaking and she rubbed her arms as they left the small room. Garneesh put his arms around her and gently led her out into the light.

"So much for Horus protecting me. But I guess he sent you, didn't he? I was saved whichever way you look at it. Thanks so much, Garneesh, I was just a bit naïve I think. It sounded such a good idea to see something that is closed to the public. I was stupid."

Garneesh shrugged. "Well, I must say, I quite like the idea of being the champion for a beautiful damsel in distress, a modern day Sir Lancelot to your Queen Guinevere."

Her hands went to her face where the man's hands had tried to gag her. She recalled her most recent dream. *A coincidence, surely a coincidence?*

2 8

The phone rang. Jared stretched over the desk and lifted it to his brown, podgy face, the diamonds on his watch sparkled in the office down-lighters.

He listened and frowned. "Yes. I have no idea. No, I did not authorise it… No, nothing from this end. Find out."

He put the phone down gently. The desk was empty apart from two phones and a silver embossed paper knife. He picked up the mobile and hit a speed dial. In his other hand he twirled the knife. "Get over here now. We need to talk strategy. There may be another party getting involved."

He closed the phone, walked to the window and looked out. The central London square looked a chilly and uninviting place on this dull day. A few pigeons grovelled around for specks by the walkways. A watery sun shone but a sun without warmth. The man glared out at the scene then nodded to himself. A decision had been made. He looked down; he still had the knife in his hand.

29

"This will steady your nerves, sweetie." Jacqui walked up to their table in the bar and plonked down a large vodka and tonic. Charlie noticed the sphinx at the end of the plastic swizzle stick. She stared at it for a few moments then realised that Jacqui was watching her. She shook her hair out and ran her fingers through it and picked up her drink.

"Thanks, this will go down well, I need fortification. I seem to be going from spooky scary to real time scary. I shall be a nervous wreck by the time we get to Luxor."

Charlie had brought Jacqui up to date with her stories of the night-time intruder and the Edfu attacker.

"I still think he was after your body. These guys just stand around all day watching the hot young women tourists in shorts and T-shirts, they must get frustrated. After all they are Muslims and not allowed women."

"Well, that's not strictly true, Jac, they are allowed to marry. They just aren't supposed to be with a woman who is not their wife. I know that's a novel idea to you."

Jacqui laughed. "Certainly is, anyway, you know what I mean, women are protected here and not so available. So what do you think he wanted then, if not your fit young bod?"

"I don't know, but I have had a sense of being watched a lot since we started this cruise. Nan keeps warning me that I may be in danger. If it wasn't for Garneesh I don't know what would have happened to me in the temple. I felt so vulnerable. Actually I started to feel really angry too. God, it really makes me mad when men use their strength on women. I could feel myself full of rage and I might even have been able to fight him off except he'd pinned down my arms; his grip was so strong. His breath smelt as well. Urgh it was revolting."

"Garneesh is turning out to be a knight in shining Versace. At the right place at the right time." Jacqui looked at Charlie sideways. "Have you slept with him yet?"

"Oh, Jac. Leave it. No I haven't nor do I intend to. I tried to call Andy last night but I couldn't get through. I don't know why. He's in India but there's perfectly good network coverage in the cities. Don't you think that's a bit strange? Mind you it's typical of him. Elusive and unobtainable. Anyway, although I feel a bit guilty about enjoying myself with Mr G it's not enough to stop me!" She laughed. "He is gentle and charming but strong too. He definitely knows how to make me feel good." She laughed again and blushed.

"You'd better stick to him like glue – at least I won't have to worry about you if you have a protector. Mind you, he looks too well turned out to be much use as a bodyguard. I would have thought he'd be too frightened of getting his trousers dirty. What are his muscles like?"

Charlie ignored her and sipped her drink. The boat was on the move again, heading towards Kom Ombo and crocodile territory.

Mohammad came into the bar and walked towards their table. "Ladies, can I join you?"

"Sure, of course," Charlie smiled and Jacqui jumped up and gave him a kiss.

"I see you're not keeping *your* relationship a secret then," whispered Charlie to Jacqui as Mohammad ordered himself a fruit juice.

"No, but he's not married and he's a free agent."

"The passengers won't mind, they're all western but I think you should be a bit circumspect when you're in town."

Jacqui glared at her. "Don't preach," she hissed.

Charlie retreated. "OK, go your own way, just warning you that's all. It's not like you to be so touchy."

Mohammad had heard her. "It's fine, Charlie. The younger generation are more open and this isn't an extremist country you know. There are a few fanatics but generally we are fairly liberal in Egypt."

Jacqui laughed and ruffled Mohammad's hair. "Bring it on – I like liberal."

Mohammad's eyes softened as he looked down at Jacqui then turned to Charlie. "I'm actually quite proud to be seen with your friend. She is quite a woman. She has the character of a peacock and the heart of a lion."

Jacqui laughed and blushed. Charlie looked at them and felt a stirring in her chest. *My, God, he really has fallen for her. Who'd have thought it.*

"I guess that's a compliment." Jacqui laughed again.

Mohammad smiled and turned to Charlie. "The captain wants to offer his apologies for the incident last night. He's reported it to the police. We are all so very sorry for the upset for you."

"Thank you, Mohammad, it's kind of you. So now, tell us about the crocodiles."

Jacqui leant forward. "Yes, Mohammad. What's in store for us next? Marian mentioned them last night at dinner, something to do with initiation rituals."

Sam and Garneesh sauntered into the bar chatting. They came up to the girls. "Can we join you?" Garneesh gave Charlie a kiss on her cheek. Sam pulled up a couple of chairs. "What's this about initiations?" asked Garneesh.

"Hell, yes, Mohammad, is it true they used to swim with crocs? Sounds like an extreme sport. Just my kinda thing," Sam enthused.

Mohammad laughed. "Well, yes, there is some truth in that story. The temple at Kom Ombo is known as the crocodile temple because it was the temple for worship of Horus and the Crocodile God, Sobek. You'll see the image of the crocodile carved on the temple walls. In ancient days there were many crocodiles in this stretch of the Nile. Any threat to life was worshipped and there was – what you say – reverence because of the fear. There is a story, not proven to us Egyptologists I might add, that the young men who wanted to be priests belonged to Societies. You call them Mystery Schools. They were educated in mathematics and astronomy and also tested for their courage and resolve. Our Ancient Egyptians believed crocodiles represented birth and death; there could not be death without life or life without death. The purpose of the initiation was to open new knowledge and wisdom. So the school at this temple made the boys swim underwater through tunnels next to a big tank where crocodiles lived. Very nasty surprise for some of them, hey!"

The men laughed with him and the girls looked at each other.

Garneesh smiled. "I heard that this test was for them to trust their intuition rather than fear. So if they were fully connected to their higher consciousness – the whole point of their training – then they would be able to negotiate the dangers of the tank and avoid the crocodiles. Quite a seriously severe way to see if you were connected, it would certainly keep you focused wouldn't it?"

"It certainly would, most definitely not my idea of fun," said Jacqui, pulling a face of distaste.

"Nor mine," said Charlie, shivering. "There must be other ways to test your gut instinct. Personally I'd even take a chance of making the odd wrong call than face those crocodiles." Everyone laughed but Charlie couldn't get rid of her shivers.

30

Early the next day, Charlie found herself at the site of Mohammad's story, Kom Ombo. The water looked cold, dark green and very, very deep. Charlie and Garneesh stared into the depths of the water tank. The water eddied and swirled and she felt herself being sucked down into the murk, spiralling down and down.

Her heart began beating faster. She could hear the rhythmic beat of drums and she tried to hold back sensing danger but the swirling motion sucked her in.

"Remove your sandals. Leave them here." The priest indicates a large wicker basket.

"Khamet and Aapep, you are the first to go."

The boys look at one another. Both doing their best to appear fearless. Aapep whispers under his breath. "So, feeble one, are you ready to die?" His taunting voice just a little less strong than usual.

Khamet ignores him. He concentrates on his sacred breathing techniques. He knows that if he holds fear in his solar plexus he will not be able to take enough air in to make the underwater journey. He will need a reserve in case he has to fight a crocodile. Has he done enough to please Sobek? Will he be spared? He will find out soon. He turns his back on Aapep and quickly draws the Symbol of Protection as his mother has taught him. Immediately he feels stronger.

"At the count of eight you jump. I will meet you at the other end."

The boys use the count to bring air deep into their lungs. At eight they jump.

The searing cold shoots through Khamet's body. He uses the pain to project himself forward. His legs work hard with strong purposeful strokes, following the dim sides of the tunnel.

He senses rather than sees Aapep his rival swimming behind him. This is not a race. He must hold his nerve. He must keep calm.

The underground waterway consists of three stretches that follow the outside of a large square cistern where the crocodiles are kept. They are not fed for two days before the initiates' challenge and there are a number of unknown entry points from the cistern to the tunnel. He swims the first leg with steady strong strokes. He turns the first corner. No sign of danger so far.

He is nearly at the end of the second leg when he senses Aapep alongside him. He feels a sting in his leg and looks round. In the dim light he sees the grim face and cruel eyes staring myopically at him with hate. He kicks forward and in a flash he is ahead of him again.

"Oh, Master Sobek, he has cut me," his heart pounds. "I am now nothing but bait for your sacred crocodiles."

He senses the danger approaching. He feels violent water movement and hears the ominous swishing of a large tail nearby. He is now in pitch dark water. A thrill courses through him and his heart misses a beat.

"Faster, faster," his brain tells his thrashing legs and arms.

His arm is touched by a cold scaly body.

"Oh, no, Sobek, oh, Master, spare me. I am your student, your disciple. Oh, Master, spare me." A swirl of light fills his head and he sees a symbol emblazoned on his inner sight. He immediately feels a surge of strength and hope flows through his body.

He thrusts deep with his legs and propels himself even faster through the murk. He feels the water turbulent and swirling behind him. Maybe Aapep is in trouble. Should he stop?

"CONTINUE, GO FORWARD. YOU ARE MY SERVANT. I AM TELLING YOU DO NOT STOP. THE SYMBOL IS YOUR PROTECTION. YOU ARE MY CHOSEN ONE."

The powerful force of Sobek's words resounds through his head. One more hard drive forward and he rounds the final bend. He can see a dim light ahead and above. All the fibres of his muscles scream for mercy. His lungs are at the point of bursting. Ahead the exit wall. Will he make it? No breath left. He feels faint. One last thrust. He throws himself up the iron staples set in the end wall.

The Priest pulls him out of the water. "Well done, Khamet. You are a faithful servant. Sobek has saved you." His assistant runs towards him holding the greatest accolade - a medallion representing the highest level of spiritual achievement; The Golden Scarab inscribed with the sacred face of Sobek, the crocodile.

"Stand."

The High Priest takes the medallion and places it around Khamet's neck.

"Hornedjitef, known as Khamet, I hereby initiate you into the Eighth Level of Sobek. You are acknowledged and activated to the Highest Degree. You are now a Master of the School of Sobek. You are Blessed and Honoured, my brother. You are now a priest to serve the Gods, the Rulers and the Citizens of Egypt. You are designated to the Temple of Amun, at Karnak.

The ceremony over the other boys crowd round to congratulate him, but The High Priest sees the cut on his thigh.

"Aapep?"

"Yes, Master." The priest looks grim.

The boys are crowded around the tunnel exit waiting for Aapep to appear. They watch the water and pray to Sobek to spare their brother.

"He's here," one cries.

With a huge crash Aapep hurls himself out of the water and throws himself onto the ground at their feet, blood oozing from his thigh where he has been bitten.

The Priest looks down at him. "You survived so I acknowledge you. You too have been saved by our Master Sobek. You have passed to the next level of your evolvement. You are spared by the god but you are reviled by man."

He turns on his heel and walks away leaving his assistant to present the medallion.

Aapep glares at Khamet. "You may have survived this time but one day I will kill you. It is I that will take the place of that feeble old man. I shall be High Priest one day. Always remember I am your mortal enemy now and forever into eternity."

Khamet stares Aapep directly in the eye without a flicker. "I have passed my test of fear with honour. I neither fear you nor ever will in this or any future lives. Save your histrionics for those who follow in your evil footsteps."

Charlie shook her head and opened her eyes. She was slumped on the ground. She looked around; she was lying beside the sacrificial table of the Holy of Holies, a broken slab of black granite, the pillars of the temple open to the sky. She felt woozy and confused as she tried to bring herself back to reality.

Garneesh was staring at her. "I carried you into here out of the sun. What happened? Where have you been? You seemed to go into a trance as soon as we approached the waterway."

Charlie shook her head in an attempt to dislodge the vision. It felt too real she could still feel the strength and adrenaline that had coursed through her body as Khamet had confronted Aapep.

What is wrong with me? I actually thought that I was that boy. Oh my God I am losing my mind.

She recalled the blind fury and hatred on Aapep's face and felt it would haunt her forever. Questions hurtled through her mind.

Why did he hate her so much? What had she done to him?

She realised that she was beginning to feel connected with this Khamet in a surreal way. Ancient and modern were becoming seamless in her consciousness.

Maybe the symbols are real after all. She shook her head again.

Nonsense, nonsense, gobbeldiegook, New Age nonsense.

Her body began to shake as though the close call to death and the hatred of Aapep in her vision began to affect her physically.

"Charlie, Charlie, what's wrong. Answer me. What did you see?" Garneesh's voice probed through her thoughts.

"Sorry?" She looked up at him dazed, unsure of where she was for a moment. "Oh sorry, Garneesh." She shook her head. "I'm sorry. I don't want to talk about it just now. It was very scary. It was more like a nightmare than a dream. I'll try to tell you all about it tonight."

They walked back to the boat hand in hand. For Charlie the warmth had seeped from the day and clouds of foreboding swept the sky.

She looked up and indeed storm clouds were approaching. "I think there is going to be a storm."

The waters of the Nile looked dark and menacing as they climbed the steps of the boat.

31

After dinner Charlie and Garneesh were sharing a nightcap in the saloon bar. Jacqui and Mohammad had disappeared and much to her relief the others had decided to stay in the dining room where the tables had been pushed back for a belly dancing lesson.

The boat continued its journey towards Aswan and the storm that had shaken and rocked them throughout dinner had quietened to an odd rumble and distant flash.

Charlie had been staring out at the night sky with its rolling thunderclouds and once again her mind dragged her back and once again she was mulling over her latest past life experience. She recalled a day when she was about twelve when she and some friends had picnicked by the river in Brockenhurst near Nan's home.

After lunch they start a series of dares. Who can swim longest underwater, who can pick up the most stones from the river bottom? As the afternoon progresses the rain clouds are starting to build; the sky becomes dark and foreboding. It is her turn to pick up stones. She is the last of the ten and the others are getting bored. Some of them have already decided to run home before the rain. Again and again she dives through the swirling dark waters to find pebbles. When she eventually came up she finds just five of her friends remained on the bank. She still has to complete the time trial. "Let's leave it," one of them suggests. "John's done the longest; let's say he won"

"No, no," cried Charlie. *"I want my turn. It's not fair. I haven't been yet."*

"OK, but get on with it. There's a storm coming."

She dives into the black river and slices through the icy water. She has to beat John. She searches the bottom and finds an old tree root to grasp as an anchor. Slowly she counts the seconds away, then the minutes. She forces herself to go through the barriers of fear and pain in her chest as the pressure built. She refuses to give in to the urge to go up for air and recover. Her determination chants through her mind.

"Stay down and win, go up and lose."

She feels herself becoming faint and the words morph to, "Stay down and die, go up and live."

She forgets to count and her mind becomes confused with the words repeating, "down and die, up and live". As her thoughts weaken, so her grip on the root grows stronger. Will of survival and will to win battle in the dark water.

"Charlie, Charlie, wake up, wake up."

She feels a cold hard slap on her face and her chest explodes as trapped water surges out of her mouth. She comes back to consciousness to see her last remaining friend, Jacquie Miller, peering into her face.

"Oh, Charlie, you fool. Why didn't you come up? "

"Sorry, Jac, did I win?"

"So what did you see in Kom Ombo, Charlie?" Garneesh's voice cut through her thoughts. "Charlie, Charlie!"

She suddenly realised that someone close by was calling her name. "Sorry, what did you say?"

Garneesh smiled. "You were far away, somewhere where I couldn't reach you."

"Sorry," she repeated. She shook her head to clear her thoughts.

"Charlie, what is it? Another trance?" Garneesh's voice penetrated her memories.

"Oh, no, Garneesh, so sorry." She told him about her childhood experience. "I don't know why it all mattered so much."

"I have heard that we are here to learn from our experiences, learn our lessons, and if we don't then we have to repeat them till we do learn either in this lifetime or the next," Garneesh said.

"Yeah, well I nearly drowned from being competitive. I don't know why I am so determined and stubborn, why did I risk my life in the river? Maybe my lesson is not to put myself at risk just to prove a point. I think I should learn when to back down. Well, it's something for me to think about." Charlie nodded her head and ran her hands through her hair. She laughed.

"I would say you are a woman who is driven and determined once you have a goal or cause. From what you say you throw everything into your work. I can't imagine you would give up easily whatever you take on."

She blushed. "Oh I don't know about that. I guess I get a bit intense at times and act like a dog with a bone. But that day at the river I would say I was just plain stupid – maybe that's my life lesson, not to be stupid!"

Garneesh laughed. "Anyway, you were going to tell me about your recall at the crocodile tank – you can tell me while we have another drink. Champagne? Then I think you should focus on the present."

"Great advice. I guess the past is always going to hold bad memories – it's a bit like beating yourself up twice over when you go back over bad experiences. Like picking a scab and re-opening a wound. I feel like having some fun now, I came on holiday to have a good time."

The wailing chords of Egyptian belly dancing music flared and died as the door from the dining room opened and closed. Garneesh bought drinks from the bar.

"So what *did* you see in the waters of the temple?" Garneesh enquired as he sipped his malt whiskey.

"Lots of weed." She laughed. "OK." She told him of her latest dream. "Most frightening of all was the intense hatred and the venom in Aapep's eyes. I saw the same look in the other dreams. He's definitely evil." She shivered, something dark stepping on her grave.

Garneesh put his hand on hers. For once she didn't sense the comfort and protection that he normally brought her. Her sense of danger magnified her sense of anxiety – no gentle hand could shift that. It was too deep, too vivid.

"Maybe the attacker was the same man who tried to get into my cabin and the watcher from the bank. Hell. Do you think I am in danger, Garneesh?"

"Maybe, maybe, Charlie. But you have survived all the attacks so far. Maybe you have a magic charm that protects you?"

They could hear the wail of lute, castanets and drums as the door opened again.

"Hi, guys," the cheery voice of Jacqui broke the moment. "You must come and join in, it's such great fun. I think I've mastered it. I've discovered you don't need a big belly to do this, just flexible hips and to think of sex."

Jacqui gyrated around their table. "Come, Garneesh, I insist you partner me." She dragged him by the arm and pulled him into the dining room.

"Do you mind, Charlie?" Garneesh asked.

"Not at all."

She followed them. As she entered the bar she reeled from the impact of the noise and laughter of the party. As she stood in the doorway she began to open to the hypnotic sound of the music. She felt herself flow to the magnetism and rhythms of the dance. The rhythms touched something deep inside her and before she could stop herself she too had stepped onto the dance floor, gyrating and twisting; dancing with sheer exuberance; swept along with the evocative sound of the music. Sam stepped up and flexing his muscles, danced with her, matching her steps and copying her every move in an earthy masculine way. She closed her eyes and let all sense of danger and menace drift off into the night.

"This is great. Let's party."

From the far side of the boat the watcher answered a call. "No, she's just dancing. Great dancer. No nothing else." The line went dead and the man continued to appreciate Charlie's gyrations and smiled.

3 2

Garneesh and Charlie were on the prow of the boat as it moved slowly towards Aswan. He had suggested they cool down with a nightcap on the top deck and enjoy the evening air.

Charlie leant back in the sofa gazing into the night sky. "It's so beautiful out here at night. Look at the stars – we see them in the New Forest but in London they get lost in all the city lights."

"Yes, light pollution. Same as Kuala Lumpur."

"Now, tell me more about you, it's your turn to bare your soul."

"Are you sure you want to hear? I don't want to spoil this wonderful atmosphere."

"Of course, I do. Go on, tell me all. You've only given me the basic outline of your life. I want to see the inner layers. I want to know what makes you tick." She snuggled down further onto the sofa.

Garneesh sighed. "OK. Where to begin? Because I was smart and picked up my school work easily I was taunted by the village boys." He went on to describe some of the humiliating experiences of his childhood. "I learnt to keep my feelings to myself but it also gave me the impetus to work hard and climb out of the poverty in which my family lived."

He went on to describe life as a student in London where he arrived on a scholarship, out of his depth, socially unsure and naive. "After being mocked for my accent and lack of 'good manners' by some of the privileged students and their friends I had many lonely sleepless nights. Then I decided to re-invent myself. I copied their accents and learnt to put on a show. So actually I'm a sham, I'm not what I seem." He turned and looked at Charlie. "The urbane and sophisticated man you see here now is an act." He grimaced.

Charlie touched his face. Her eyes were filled with tears. "Oh, but Garneesh, we are all putting on an act of some sort. We are all acting out a part. Everyone is wearing some form of coping coat, a mask to hide their fears or sense of inadequacy. Nobody knows how I sweat at night as I recall the night of the car crash. Nobody knows how the memory and guilt paralyze me. My nan says that the reason I act like a doormat to the men in my life – not sure I should be telling you this one – is that I feel weak inside and want to please. No, we all put on an act so don't worry about yours. Hey, yours is a good one, it suits you. I like it." She smiled up at him.

She felt a warmth and understanding for this vulnerable man lying beside her. She turned towards him and looked into his eyes, her heart missed a beat; he was truly gorgeous. He wrapped his arms around her and pulled her close. She felt his breath on her cheek. He kissed her gently on the side of her mouth.

She turned towards him and offered him her full lips. He gently parted her lips with his tongue and kissed her deep and with passion. She felt her body responding. Her pulse started to race. He looked deep into her eyes and ran his hand over her shoulders and down over her breast.

"You have the perfect body, Charlie. Perfect."

She relaxed against him. She could feel his heat.

He licked her lips and kissed her again. His hands travelled slowly over her body.

Oh, yes, oh yes.

As though reading her mind he gently whispered, "Would you like to join me in my cabin?"

"Yes please," she whispered. "Yes please."

33

The troop arrived in the two Land Rovers at six-fifteen a.m. It was still dark.

"We leave the vehicles here. Unload and we continue on foot. Silence now. The camp is over that rise. It should take us thirty minutes to reach the perimeter. Jamieson, you will then have thirty minutes max to check the path through. We have to hit the camp by dawn, seven fifteen a.m."

Jimmy turned to Wayne. "Gardener, you cover his back. The rest of you have your instructions. Right, any last questions?"

They carried their weapons and essential equipment. Andy had more than most as he had his IEDD kit so Wayne helped him.

After half an hour the troop slid and crawled over a small hill. Most of them were wearing night glasses but the predawn light highlighted their target. They looked down on an old settlement; the remains of a fort surrounded by a small village around a water hole. This had been a vital watering stop for the camel trains of the date traders. Now produce was shipped around in trucks on the country's new tarmac roads that linked major towns and settlements. The tumbledown mud homes were now the hiding place and shelter for the terrorists that used the village and fort as a training site. Most of the buildings had lost their roofs and were a collection of crumbling walls. Accomodation was supplemented by ten tents erected around the site.

Wayne looked at the camp and turned to Percher. "How many are there down there?"

"We estimated twenty but seeing the tents it could be more." Jimmy looked worried. This was a much larger camp than their intelligence had indicated.

"Those tents look like new arrivals," whispered Andy.

"Yeah, I think you're right, mate," said Percher. "Well, we're here now and there's a job to be done." He gestured for them to wriggle up closer. "You all know what to do. Jamieson will be checking and identifying a path through what we must assume is a mine field around the site. Our thermal imaging reconnaissance shows it as highly probable. He will indicate a clear path so make sure you follow his markers."

They nodded and slipped off in the dim light to take their positions. Andy moved away more slowly carrying his gear and Wayne followed just a few yards behind with their rifles and pistols. Other members of the troop had the grenade launchers and heavier weapons needed to destroy the camp.

As a senior Bomb Disposal Officer, Andy had a certain amount of independence in black ops. When he was recruited for Covert Operations he was given the opportunity to choose his own equipment. He picked the latest Mantis lightweight disrupter, a non magnetic prodder, a Needle Plus – as well as the usual kit and a can of his favourite fluorescent green marker paint! His role was to find a safe path through the mine field. Only in extreme circumstances would he have to actually neutralise a bomb.

He started to crawl cautiously down the hill side. He had studied the images fed back to them by the reconnaissance team so had some idea where the mines were placed. He used a prodder to check the path.

Bomb disposal is nerve-wracking work but safe enough given all safety measures are taken and set procedures are followed exactly. But in an active operation like this, when time is of the essence and where they could be detected at any minute, he was bound to take short cuts. Short cuts were a recipe for disaster in ordnance disposal. He knew this and despite his familiarity with his role, his expertise and his years of experience he still felt a nervous thrill run through his body as he started to move down the hill.

He spray marked the way as he checked every inch of the path he had indentified from his image map. Minutes ticked by and he continued to crawl forward, checking as he went. He knew that if new tents could be erected since their intelligence was gathered then new mines could easily have been planted. His hand shook a little and he moved forward. Wayne crawled after him.

Back up the hill, Jimmy Percher and the rest of the troop started to slowly follow him down the hill towards the camp. Their lives were in his hands.

34

Charlie stood looking out of the porthole. The sun was coming up and the dark sky gradually turned a soft morning blue. She stretched and sighed and looked over to the bed. The top of Garneesh's black hair on the pillow was just discernable in the dim light of the cabin. *What a beautiful night.*

She hugged herself.

She gathered her clothes and dressed quickly. She felt a shimmer of guilt as a swift image of Andy flicked in and out of her mind. Where is he now? She felt the need to return to her own cabin before the boat woke up. She slipped out and ran down the corridor carrying her shoes.

35

He had five minutes to go and they were close to the tangle of barbed wire that circled the camp. The light was a little brighter and it made Andy's job easier but it also exposed them. They could see two guards at the entrance to the camp. But this was a cut and run operation. These men would pack up and move on given any chance of exposure so there was no sophisticated surveillance equipment; no guard towers; probably no electricity apart from a portable generator or two. The men and women in this camp would be taught how to create handmade munitions, how to wrap a bomb around oneself and how to blow oneself up. They didn't need much equipment, they didn't need sophisticated armaments; they needed faith and the call of a cause or blind hatred.

He froze. His prodder had located an object buried right in front of him. This one was not on the plan. He looked around to warn Wayne that he would have to stop and check it out and work around it. He gasped. Wayne had moved off to the left of the actual path that Andy had marked. He couldn't see why, maybe he'd lost focus, maybe he'd seen something. But he could see that just by Wayne's right hand was a telltale indentation in the sand. There was something very, very close to where he lay. He now had two potential mines to work around.

He whispered back to his buddy. "Stay absolutely still, mate. Do not move a hair."

Wayne stared at him petrified. "I can hear something coming from it."

"Right, OK." Andy braced himself. He had no time to check the land he had to cross. He started to wriggle backwards but to get to the mine he had to cross uncharted territory, an area of sand that he hadn't made safe. He could detonate a mine with his weight at any moment.

He inched his way back pulling his pack. Slowly, slowly but with careful attention to the sand, like a tracker it told him what he needed to know. He relied on his experience and intuition to guide him. He had no time to use his monitoring equipment. He had to rely purely on his luck and divine intervention to keep him safe.

After a few moments that seemed like hours he reached Wayne. His buddy was trembling. A pool of sweat had turned the sand under his face black.

"It's OK, mate. We'll be fine. You can breathe but don't move," Andy said. He too could hear the slight pulsing sound of a live detonator sensor. He pulled open his pack and grabbed the disrupter equipment used to neutralise mines in operational situations. No help from Cyclops or other remotely operated vehicles here. Once he was in place he signalled Wayne to move to the side – the side where he had checked the path, the safe route.

The defusing operation took him three minutes. Three minutes of concentration and use of all his personal expertise and the technology of his kit. Thank God he had insisted on the very latest equipment. When he finally cleared and disabled the detonator in the mine he realised that he had been holding his breath. He looked up and saw seven faces staring at him; as he put up his thumb there was a collective outbreath.

A hoarse voice whispered, "Thanks, mate. I owe you one."

Andy turned to Wayne. "It's no worries, mate, all in a day's work. You'd do the same for me."

Thank you, God. And thank you the inventor of this little baby.

He put his equipment away and continued to crawl forward marking the route leading them around the mine he'd detected ten yards from the wire.

* * *

Just five minutes after their ETA the troop gathered safely by the fence. The wire cutters came out, they crawled through and taking their weapons forward they quietly entered the camp. Working in pairs they took up their positions. They set up their weapons all the time carefully keeping out of view of the guards.

Once they were all ready Jimmy gave out one blood curdling shout and they attacked the camp with their rocket launchers and grenades.

36

"Pretty lady, look at us."

The Felucca boat boys flexed their muscles and posed for Jacqui. She snapped their photo and applauded, encouraging their ego.

The girls were on a sailing boat, a traditional Felucca, on the way to the island of Philae, the Island of Isis.

"Please, Madam, you put on the jacket," the boy passed both of them bright yellow life jackets.

"Naff, darling, do we have to?" Jacqui screwed up her nose at the dusty jacket.

"I believe it's something to do with our UK insurance companies – our travel insurance, health and safety and all that. They won't pay out if we don't wear these ghastly things," Charlie said.

"How embarrassing, our nanny state smothers us even out here! You can spot the Brits, they're the wimps in bright yellow plastic!" Jacqui picked up her jacket with disdain. Reluctantly the girls put them on then sat back to enjoy the ride.

The storm of the night before was spent and sunshine filled the skies.

Garneesh had dashed off to manage a business emergency and had gone into Aswan to find an internet café. Before he left he hired them a boat and crew to visit the island of Philae. The island sat in the middle of the Nile which was wide at this point due to the dam built to control the annual flood. Charlie was interested in the Temple to Isis, the most famous of the female Egyptian deities. According to Mohammad, this temple had been transported block by block to the island to take it above the new water line created by the dam work. Jacqui was interested in improving her tan and scanning the boat boys.

Charlie lay back on the cushions and looked up at the large brown sail flapping overhead. She felt relaxed and dreamy.

Jacqui touched her arm. "Have you heard from Andy?"

"No, not a word and his office phone just has a recorded message saying he's away. His secretary is a dragon and won't give me any contact numbers. Anyway to be honest I'm enjoying the attentions of Garneesh. He's hot and he makes me feel good, sort of cherished, if you know what I mean."

"Yes, it's an old fashioned word but I feel like that with Mohammad."

"Jac, have you fallen for Mohammad?"

Ducks flew overhead in formation, calling out directions to each other. The gentle lapping of the water on the bows was reassuring and relaxing. The boys murmured secrets and giggled quietly at the end of the boat.

For a few moments Jacqui focused on her question. Finally she replied, "I may have, but I don't want to spoil what we have by bringing in the love word. It seems that for the first time I can recall I am in a totally mutual relationship. We have fun and we have great sex. He treats me as though I am precious and that actually means more to me than I could ever imagine. He makes me feel great and that is a first. But love, well I don't know about that. I'm not completely sure I know what that is. Seems we use the word a lot but I'm not sure it means very much. The only love I've ever come across has ties, conditions. You know what I mean." She lay back on the cushions and stared at the sky."No, I'm not sure that I know about real love apart from with you and Josie."

Josie was Jacqui's younger sister. They had been through a lot together. Jacqui had tried to protect her but had failed and even now she felt she needed to make it up to her sister.

Charlie turned and saw a tear seeping from her friend's eye. She felt a lump in her throat. "Your father's got a lot to answer for, my sweetheart; a lot to answer for." She sat up and went to put her hand to Jacqui.

The boys called a warning,."Head down, Madam, we here."

The boom swacked across and the boat lurched as the boys brought it alongside a wooden quay. They looked up to see stone steps leading to the temples of Horus and Isis set among trees on the top of the island.

"What time we come back, Madam?"

Charlie looked at her watch. "Let's take an hour and a half here, OK, Jac?"

She nodded. "Great idea, let's go." She shook off her melancholy and ran up the steps two at a time.

Charlie turned to the boys before she joined her. "At one o'clock sharp, here at this place." She held up one finger.

"One o'clock," the boys chanted back to her. "Bye, bye." Their faces full of smiles they deftly pushed off and sailed into the river.

* * *

They explored the Temple of Isis. Then Jacqui had wandered off to find a place to relax outside and Charlie had braved the inner sanctuary of the temple, the Holy of Holies, without incident. She knelt on the cold slabs and prayed to Isis for protection from the dangers that seemed to be constantly with her these days. She asked for clarity about her dreams. "Am I really Khamet reincarnated? Do I really have to find those symbols?" So many questions.

She left the temple and shrugged off the mystical and the unknown and found Jacqui sitting in the shade of a cluster of trees looking out over the river.

"We've three quarters of an hour before the boat is due; I feel sleepy let's take a rest." Charlie flopped down under a tree. The ground was covered in dead leaves and dried berries. She didn't care. She smoothed out her long white linen skirt, put her back pack down as a pillow and lay down in the shade of the trees. The light breeze rustled the leaves gently and the river water lapped on the shoreline beneath them.

Jacqui lay down beside her. The women held hands. "Thanks so much for bringing me to Egypt, Charlie, my dear. I feel happy here."

Charlie laughed. "Apart from feeling that my life's threatened, I'm enjoying it too."

"Oh, don't let a drop of mortal danger spoil a good holiday, Chas."

They giggled together.

"Anyway, I wouldn't have missed my time with Mr G. He's an amazing lover. In fact he's almost too good to be true, so gorgeous. Bollywood comes to Egypt." She had a smug smile.

Warm soft breezes blew gently. The midday sun filtered through the leaves overhead. They drifted off into quiet contemplation. Gentle sounds lulled them to sleep; the lapping of small waves of the river drifted up from the shoreline. Brown sparrow-like birds quarrelling nearby joining the lazy chatter of tourists meandering through the groves.

Charlie floated into a dream. She could feel the gentle tug as she was pulled back in time again.

The priest lit the candles and sconces in the Holy of Holies of his temple. The pungent fragrance of incense purifying the sacred space. Helping him with this work is a younger priest.

"Thank you, Hapu, you are a faithful servant and I value you."

Khamet puts his arm around his helper's shoulder, intense love flows between them.

"Today we perform a ritual prayer to Renentutet for a successful harvest, Hapu, go and fetch the holy water."

Hapu brings forward two large urns and places them at his master's feet. He takes a ladle, fills it with purified, sacred water and pours it over the old man's hands. Then he takes a small jug filled with aromatic sandalwood for the purification anointing ceremony. He pours a small amount into Khamet's hands and watches as his master completes the ritual essential before any ceremony of worship; drawing signs and symbols on their foreheads and sweeping his hands over their heads.

Hapu then removes the vessels and the two men move towards a wall of the temple chamber where an entire section of the wall paintings are dedicated to the goddess. Her familiar python image with double plumed headdress shines in the candlelight.

The two men bow before her. Khamet pulls a papyrus scroll from his robes and reads the ancient text honouring the Goddess Renentutet.

"Oh, Great Renentutet, Goddess of Plenty of this wondrous land we request you bring the rains, bring the waters of the Nile to fertilise the seed, use your magic to bring us plenty, oh Mistress. We make our oath that after this harvest we will honour you with a great offering of our finest produce."

He and Hapu clasp hands after the ceremony. Their work finished they step outside and look down on the Nile. The Temple had been built on high ground above the danger of flooding. Together, still hand in hand, they descend the steep steps down to the water's edge. Suddenly,

Khamet pauses and raises his hand. They stop and listen. He can just hear the warning rhythmic thud of drums.

"Careful now, Hapu, danger is near."

He looks around cautiously but all seems at peace. A small felucca bobs gently by the river's edge waiting to transport them down river.

The boatman steps ashore and walks towards them. Suddenly without warning he throws a sack over Khamet's head. A second boatman rushes up and grabs Hapu, pinning his arms behind him.

Khamet tries to fight off his attacker but the younger man's superior strength is too much for him and he is thrown roughly into the bottom of the boat. As he falls he hits his head on the seat. On the bank Hapu puts up a strong resistance as he fights off the second boatman; kicking and gouging he manages to push him from the bank into the swirling water of the river. He turns to the boat and hurls himself onto the back of Khamet's attacker who is now forcing the old priest down into the boat's well.

Charlie started to feel unfocused, she lost the clarity of her vision as she came to the surface of her dream; she felt a searing pain in her head. With a soft moan she sank back into her dream again.

After a few minutes of intense hand to hand fighting the strength of Hapu is enough to overcome Khamet's attacker and he manages to throw him also into the Nile. He kneels down by Khamet who has blood seeping from a gash on his head.

"Oh, Master, you are harmed. What can I do?"

Khamet slowly and carefully pulls himself up on his elbow and draws a symbol into the dust on the floor of the boat.

"My son, you must use this sacred symbol of healing."

Hapu kneels beside him and copies the sacred form over his master's head. Immediately, he feels the energies of healing flowing through his hands. He places them on his master and in no time he starts to revive. As his strength returns Khamet pulls himself up and embraces Hapu.

"Bless you, my son, bless you. Into the distance of eternity I shall never forget your love, our destinies will intertwine forever."

A leaf fell onto Charlie's face. She blinked and opened her eyes. Gradually she came back into the present. She looked over at Jacqui who was also stirring from her sleep.

"Oh, my God." Jacqui sat up. "I have just had the most amazing dream. I saw myself rescuing you. I had to fight off these awful men who attacked you. They were dressed in old fashioned clothes – like something from Ancient Egypt. There was a boat and river; it must have been the Nile. At the end of the dream I saw this shadowy figure stand in front of me. He told me that I am here to protect you and help you! Isn't that amazing? It feels right though. I do love you, you know." Jac blinked as tears began to form. "Hey, you'd better do as I say now!"

The girls laughed and hugged. "I'll try to keep out of trouble but I can't promise! But this is mega spooky as I had the same dream. Oh, this is very, very odd. In my dream Khamet, the priest, was there again but he had a young assistant and I think it was you. Khamet showed you the healing symbol and you used it on him and as I watched I could feel my own body responding. That's the really weird part. I could actually feel the energy in the here and now." Charlie looked at Jacqui with tears in her eyes.

"Oh, heavens. What is it? How does it work?" Jacqui asked.

"Oh, don't, Jac, you won't believe this but, although I know we were using it, I couldn't see it. I don't remember what it looked like." She beat the ground with her fist. "This is so frustrating. I do know that you had to use it three times and it brings in magical healing energies, but I can't tell you how to draw it! Hell." She jumped up and started pacing around. "I could feel the energies pulsing through me. I guess I must have been that old priest. I clearly saw you as his assistant."

Jacqui sighed. "At last. I was getting to wonder if you would ever accept all this. I have been texting Miranda and we were despairing that you would ever wake up to the truth and believe in yourself."

"Well, I do now, I really do. I have passed the dreams and visions off as my imagination but I can't deny what I felt. I don't know how this could happen – I'll work that out later. But I know I must find these symbols, Jac. I must."

"What about that first dream you had at home, you know, the one where you put them under the Sphinx in that hidden room. Do you think the scroll and the symbols are still hidden there?" Jacqui was excited now. She grabbed Charlie's hand and with huge eyes she stared at her intensely.

"Do you think you could open the Sphinx and find them?"

"My God, Jac, I don't know. Maybe I could. As I recall, there were two chants, one to open and one to close. I wrote them in the back of the guidebook. Though come to think of it, that wasn't a very smart move, especially if there are people out there trying to get hold of them."

She pulled the book out of her pack and turned to the back page. "Here they are. Fortunately they are short." She said the words quietly to herself. "I've got a good memory, I'll memorise them."

She walked around and around beneath the trees, in and out of patches of sunlight, the words resonating in her as she said them over and over.

Jacqui watched her entranced. "God, Charlie, you look just like a priest as you read that book chanting those words, did you wear white today on purpose!" She laughed.

Eventually, after about ten circuits Charlie was word perfect.

"Now I must destroy this." She tore out the back page and shredded it.

"If you really wanted them to be safe you should eat it now," Jac said then scrabbled in the dead leaves close to the tree.

"But better for your digestion if you hide the bits here, they'll break down eventually."

Charlie pushed the tiny fragments under the leaves then placed a rock on top. "Good that's done. I feel better now."

Jacqui looked at her watch. "We're late, it's already one fifteen. Quick, we can talk more about this later."

They gathered up their bags and brushed themselves down.

"Before we go – give me a hug." Charlie pulled Jacqui into her arms. They embraced and laughed. Come on, Hapu, let me buy you a lunch in the town for a change."

"Good idea, getting a little tired of the same old buffet."

They ran down the steps hand in hand and looked for the boat. But it wasn't there.

37

It was early morning in Brockenhurst. Miranda stood by the back door of her cottage wrapped in a blanket. She watched as Tabitha took her first stroll out for the day. The bare trees waved dark branches in the gale that blew in from the coast; a seasonal south westerly bringing rain. She looked up and clouds sped across the early morning sky.

She thought of her granddaughter and she wrapped her blanket around her more tightly. She felt a shimmer of fear for her. Her instincts were on high alert and she feared for her safety.

Tabitha swished her tail and stalked back inside. Miranda took one last look around her garden and stiffened.

Is that a figure lurking behind the oak at the bottom of the garden?

She stared hard for a few moments. No movement other than the branches dancing in the wind.

Stupid, fanciful, old woman.

She stepped back into the cottage and locked the door behind her, just in case.

38

The girls stood by the water's edge. The murky water lapped at the bottom of the steps. They looked out over the river to Aswan on the far shore. There was no sign of the dhow.

"Hmmm they're really late now; it's twenty past one already."

They stood waiting for a few more minutes.

"What shall we do if they don't come?" Charlie said. "We can't hitch a ride or call a cab?"

"I'll call Mohammad, I'm sure he'll be able to send another boat, but I'm famished, where the hell are they?"

After another ten minutes of waiting Charlie started pacing again. "Where are they? What could have happened? Maybe they've abandoned us here."

Jacqui had planted herself on a rock and was letting the sun top up her tan. "Oh, don't be so melodramatic Charlie. Chill out. This is Egypt. They may have been caught by the tide or another customer. Relax. Anyway, here they are."

"Hey, Madam." The felucca with the two smiling boat boys sailed around the island towards them.

"Sorry we late, Madam."

With relief they climbed into the boat and settled down for the journey back to the cruise ship. The Nile is wide at Aswan due to the High Dam built across the river in the 1960s to control the flood waters and bring a consistent supply of water to the riverside farms. The boat meandered around some of the many small islands to be found in the river opposite Aswan Town. It slipped effortlessly through the water. The sails flapped as a strong breeze blew up and the boat moved faster and faster.

"This is fun," said Jacqui as she trailed her hand in the cool water. Small waves broke over the bows and sprayed the girls. They laughed. Everything seemed fun again.

Charlie looked over at the rocks around the island and realised they were taking a different route – not at all the way they had come. In fact they were moving further away from the bank where their cruise boat was moored. "Where are you taking us," she asked, annoyed that her voice sounded shrill.

Jacqui looked up. "This isn't the way back," she called to the boys. They too had lost their smiles. They looked grim and ignored the women, staring fixedly ahead.

Charlie grabbed Jacqui. "Where are they taking us do you think? Are they kidnapping us? Oh, Jac, the dream. This is the dream!"

39

Jared struggled with his umbrella as he pushed his way through the early morning push and shove on the city streets. He was making his way to his office. He swore under his breath about the English weather. His girlfriend had been bending his ear for a holiday in the sun.

"Not yet," he had told her. "Not till this job is wound up. Won't take long. One chit of a girl and an old woman. Not much of a problem. So, love, get yer bikini ready and I'll take you to the Caribbean in a week's time."

I'll take her for a week of sun, sand and sex then I'll dump her. 'Er bleeding whinging is getting on me nerves.

His phone rang. He answered it. "Mornin'. 'Ow's your lordship?"

He listened to his latest instructions. "If you say so, me Lord. Get onto it straight away." The phone had gone dead before he could say goodbye.

Ignorant bastard. One day…

The wind caught his umbrella and flipped it to one side and a squall of rain caught him full in his face.

Bastard.

He ducked into the shelter of a Starbucks. He went inside and made a discrete call to organise a phone tap on a mobile. Main location of use – Brockenhurst.

40

"Just you take us back to the boat right now," shouted Jacqui pointing at the boys.

Charlie stood up and moved towards the younger one who held the tiller. "Turn it around right now, do you hear me, right now."

"Down, down," the eldest boy shouted, waving his arms menacingly at her. "Sit down."

"No. I will not," Charlie screamed.

Thud, the boom hit her alongside the head as the boat swerved towards a small island.

She fell onto the deck and hit her head hard on the wooden planks of the deck. Her head filled with pain.

"Oh, my God, what have you done?" Jacqui turned to the boys. They stared back terrified.

"We tell her, we tell her, dangerous to stand," the youngest one shouted.

In her anger Jacqui went to hit him. As she raised her hand a voice called across from the island. "This way. This way." Garneesh stood on the shore. He was waving his arms, directing them to land.

The boat drifted in and one of the boys jumped off to tie up the boat.

"Charlie, my dear, what's happened to your head?"

"The boom hit me. I fell and cracked the side of my head on the deck. It was my own stupid fault," she said.

She looked over to where Garneesh stood. Beside him he had laid out rugs. In the centre of the rugs a tablecloth was covered with food, a feast.

"It's a picnic," he laughed. "I thought I'd surprise you, ladies."

"Oh, Garneesh," Jacqui laughed. "We thought we were being kidnapped. We are two very stupid paranoid women. How ridiculous of us. Thank you sooooo much."

She and Garneesh helped Charlie out of the boat. Charlie fell onto a rug and laughed. "Oh how ridiculous. I really thought we were living out the past life dream especially when that boom hit me on the head. Oh, Garneesh, we actually thought… " She peeled into hysterical laughter.

Jacqui hurled herself down next to her. "What we need, Garneesh, darling, is a large drink."

"And a Paracetamol for my head," said Charlie, "although, the pain's going already."

"Not sure of the medication but I have a good supply of champagne." He opened a cool box. "A glass of Cristal to revive Madam," he laughed and draped a white napkin over his arm, filling two glasses and bowing.

Jacqui and Charlie hugged, their spirits restored and they turned to the mezza of humus, falafel, pastry triangles of spinach and cheese, tahini, broccoli and pitta bread.

"Wow my favourite food. Bless you, Garneesh."

41

Charlie sauntered onto the deck of the cruise boat. She felt restless. The sun had gone and she could hear the night sounds of the busy town of Aswan. The constant thrum of traffic, the honking of car horns, the sound of a thousand stereos, TVs and even street musicians filled the air. She leant against the guard rail and looked up at the early evening sky streaked with greys and pinks. It was a beautiful night to end a great day.

She pondered on her relationship with Garneesh.

A holiday romance, pure and simple. She knew that. *Her thoughts turned to Andy. What was he doing now?* She felt a tweak of guilt as she thought of him, wondering where he was, whether he was still in India and if the deal had been sorted. She touched her chest as she thought of him. She frowned.

"No good chasing someone who just doesn't want to know." Her nan's words came back to her, "and never throw your precious pearls to those that don't appreciate them, my darling, there are plenty out there who will."

His reluctance to commit and his reluctance to let her in close was finally closing the door of her own heart. She had to be realistic; he just wasn't made for settling down. She wiped away a tear. *Never look back.* She would look forward now. What was it Nan was always saying? "Live in the moment." *Good idea.*

She thought of the experiences of the last few days. Her old beliefs had been well and truly challenged. The past life recalls had unsettled her and she felt her normal pragmatic and firm attachment to life slipping. Now she was sensing that there could perhaps be more to life than she had previously believed and this shift and change in her understanding was making her feel vulnerable. She leant on the side of the boat which, thankfully, was the last boat in the row so she could see across the river to the far side where there was little development. The soft sandy banks and dunes had a mystical charm and the moonlight illuminated reeds and a number of moored small boats. A flight of white ibis flew past. The swirling and constantly moving water of the Nile lapped against the side of the boat and in the background the distant roar of Aswan traffic. In the context of this country where the ancient and the modern were side by side effortlessly she was again touched by the sense of her own past and present melding into one time frame. Khamet and Charlie seemed to be merging into one person.

Miranda's words came back to her. "We are what we have experienced. Nothing leaves us untouched whether in this or a past life." She was fully aware of that truth now.

A footfall behind her startled her out of her reverie and she spun round to see Mohammad coming towards her. "What a beautiful night. Charlie, can I talk to you, can I share something with you?"

"Of course, Mohammad," she said and gestured towards a table and chairs nearby.

They sat down and Mohammad sighed. "You know that Jacqui and I have been spending a lot of time together, of course you know that. Believe it or not, and you may find this hard to take in, she is my ideal woman. She is fun, she is lively, she is caring and well, I cannot believe it has happened as, well, I have to admit, I have had a number of girlfriends but, you see," he looked up at her, his eyes sparkling with tears, "I think I have fallen in love with her." He smiled sheepishly.

"I gathered that. You're a great looking man and you certainly aren't short of opportunities." Charlie smiled back and reached over and touched his hand. "I think you make a fine couple, although I wouldn't have thought that Jacqui would have been your sort of woman."

"Thank you." He smiled. "You know that I lived several years in UK?" Charlie nodded. "Well, that sort of opened my mind to things that are, well, either forbidden or frowned upon in this country. Our women are repressed and they are by nature less outgoing than western women. I had a girlfriend in London, she came from Essex and Jacqui reminds me of her. Really crazy! I love Jacqui's ability to laugh, be honest and share her thoughts and so on, but at the same time I feel she's a woman of depth too and I sense a great sadness within her and that makes me want to protect her and take care of her."

He paused. "However, I have a small problem with Jacqui. I've shared my feelings. When we make love she is intense and full on but I also sense a real resistance from her. It seems as though she is scared of something. I could understand her being scared of commitment, after all we have only just met and we are from different cultures, different countries, so I could easily understand her reluctance to make promises. But it's not that, it's as though she is deliberately holding her emotions back. Whenever I say anything loving she either jokes it off or changes the subject."

He looked hard into Charlie's eyes. "Charlie, does Jacqui believe in love?"

"Hey, that's a big question, Mohammad." Charlie paused for a few moments as she considered how to answer. "How much of her past has she shared with you? Did she tell you about her father for instance?"

"Yes. She told me that he abused her and that she has recently taken him to court."

"Well, that has left her very confused about the difference between love, sex and loving sex. She appears very light and frothy, some of that's an act, some of it's her character. She is a fun loving girl and she is a very caring woman too but, she is a troubled soul underneath. She has her gremlins – as do we all, but hers are deep and painful. She has learnt that it's easier not to trust, not to open her heart, not to get involved. It may take some time to break down this resistance. She will have to feel safe to change her beliefs. I think you are going to have to be patient, Mohammad, my dear. But, I am so happy you two have come together. You are just what she needs. So far on this holiday she has only eyes for you and she isn't roaming already. So you're actually doing really well. Just give it time. But just don't push it too hard or you might frighten her away."

"I did wonder if it's the culture barrier. Many women fear that Muslim men will shut them away and turn them into domestic slaves. We don't come with a very good press!"

"No, Mohammad, I don't think that will be a problem with Jac. She wouldn't be scared to speak out if there was anything that troubled her like that. It's a matter of trust; trusting you and trusting her own feelings. And that will take time. After all you've only just met, it's very early days."

"Thanks so much, Charlie, this is all new to me – this is the first time I've felt it here for a woman." He touched his chest.

They stood up and Charlie gave him a hug. "Persevere, Mohammad; she is pure gold and has been a brilliant friend to me."

"Good."

A clatter of heels on the stairwell and Jacqui appeared. "Hey, guys, so here you are. What a beautiful night. Are you off duty now, Mohammad?"

"Yes, sure, I'm all yours," he replied. She sashayed over to them and took Mohammad's arm. "Let's visit the night market before dinner. Do you want to come, Chas?"

"No thanks, I'm enjoying the peace and quiet here for a moment and I'm meeting up with Garneesh just now. You go off and find bargains."

"Did I hear my name mentioned here?" Garneesh appeared grinning broadly. "I fancy a glass of champers before dinner, any takers?"

"We're off to the bazaar, but thanks anyway, another time. And thanks again for the lunch what a great surprise that turned out to be." She and Mohammad said their farewells and strolled off.

42

Charlie and Garneesh sat finishing their dinner in the dining room.

"Garneesh, I feel a bit odd." Charlie held her hand to her forehead. "Everything feels a bit strange, I feel faint and my head is swimming."

"Maybe you're having another vision?" Garneesh peered into her eyes. "Your pupils are dilated."

"I don't think so, it feels different than before. I feel very tired. I think I'll go back to my cabin." She pushed away her half eaten tiramisu.

"I'll help you." He pulled her up and half carried her from the dining room. Her legs were weak and she leant heavily on him. As they entered the cabin she collapsed completely onto her bed. "Zank you," she slurred. "Zank you."

He slapped her hand. "Charlie, Charlie can you hear me?" He lifted her eyelids but she didn't respond. Her breathing was light but regular. She was unconscious. Garneesh smiled, the Rohypnol had done its job well.

He locked the door and dimmed the lights. From his pocket he took a silver toothpick holder. He pricked her arm with the toothpick but there was no response.

He pulled out a small burner and incense sticks and lit them. The room filled with the pungent fragrance of frangipani.

"You are asleep and going deeper and deeper. You are breathing slower and slower. You are going deeper and deeper. You are safe to tell me all your secrets."

He pulled her into a sitting position, she flopped and her head rolled, he propped her up again. He placed a notepad by her hand and put a pen in her hand. "You can draw me the symbols, Charlie, it's OK, you are OK."

No response.

"Charlie, your life is in danger, you need to share those symbols with me"

Still no response.

"Speak now. If you don't know the symbols then tell me the opening spell for the Sphinx, tell me right now."

She said nothing. Her breathing was even and strong now.

Garneesh looked grim. He drew his own dark symbols in the air and muttered incantations learnt at his grandmother's knee. He took out of his bag another small burner, a piece of charcoal and set it alight. After the yellow smoke had died down and the charcoal was glowing he took out a packet of herbs and sprinkled them onto the hot coal. A pungent aroma filled the room. He put his arm around Charlie and lifted her head and he held the burner with its powerful concoction; a truth serum from the East that had never failed him. "Speak. Tell me the breaking spell, what is the seal. Draw me the symbols."

A small sigh from Charlie was her only response.

How could she resist him? What extraordinary power had she that allowed her to withstand his magic? Was she subconsciously sabotaging his efforts?

His phone buzzed. He answered quietly. "No I haven't, no she is under the influence still... Yes, still drugged... No, there is absolutely nothing more I can do now... She told me that she hadn't got the symbols yet... No, I'm not entirely convinced, but she has a very powerful protection and maybe she made a vow that holds it all locked inside her... Yes I hear you... No, she will remember nothing. Yes, I will do that tomorrow... I can't do that on the boat, too many connections to me... Yes, tomorrow, I promise. Yes, of course, no trace." He shut the phone and swore.

Charlie I need your secrets.

He picked up his incense and opened the porthole window. He undressed her and placed her in her bed. Softly, he left the cabin and disappeared into the night.

43

Jared slammed down the phone, missed the socket and swore as he reseated it. "Idiot, bloody idiot."

He picked up his mobile and called a number. His podgy fingers gripped the phone in frustration. "That bloody idiot has failed, Lord D. The subtle approach isn't working – he's not the bleeding lady's man, the great seducer, he thought he was. Don Juan's out and Mr Nasty's in or else he's kaput." He listened to the clipped Eton tones on the other end of the phone and curled his lip.

"Yeah, yeah I know he's your boy. I know, I know, but I think he's gone soft. Anyway, he's promised to sort it in the next two days."

"How precious is the dear doctor to you?" He picked up a toothpick from a carton on his desk and started to pick his front teeth.

"Good. I'll see how it goes. On the other 'and I haven't put all my eggs in one basket. I've got other things going on out there."

"Not on the mobile. I'll pass by your place later and fill you in."

"Yeah, no probs. We're onto it. She'll be sorted one way or the other; no don't you worry about that."

He closed his phone and put it into his jacket pocket, flicked the toothpick into the bin by his desk, licked his lips and straightened his tie.

Shaking his head he picked up the phone again. "Your lordship, so sorry, forgot to tell you. We've sorted out the old lady too."

44

It was early, really early. Charlie stirred. She put her hand out to touch Garneesh.

Oh, he's left already.

She threw off the bedclothes and went into the bathroom. Her head felt heavy.

I must cut down on my drinking. It's getting out of hand.

She sniffed. She smelt a slight whiff of a perfume – a tropical flower, what was it? She frowned and shrugged. She slowly entered the shower and let the hot water revive her.

As she dressed she mused on the fragrance in the room and her heavy head.

What on earth was I doing last night? What happened to Garneesh, he must have started off very early?

Her head began to clear after the shower. The cool early morning breeze flowing through the open porthole helped as well. She dressed and on her way to the upper deck stopped off at the kitchen which was just beginning to come to life. She took a coffee up onto the upper deck now bathed with pre dawn light.

Her phone pinged – a text from Nan.

"Hi, Charlie. Hope you are all right. Don't forget to keep complete secrecy. My guides tell me you are in danger from someone close to you. I see a dark stranger, who has already attacked you. Take great care. Enjoy Abu Simbel. Giza a good idea. Love Nan Miranda."

Dark stranger? Must be that man at Edfu!

"Hiya, Charlie." Sam's deep throated voice woke her from her reverie.

"Hi, Sam."

"How are you doin'? Say, won't you tell me what's been going on. I know something strange and mysterious is happening for you. Have you anything to share with little ol' Uncle Sam."

Charlie's nostrils flared. *God that man is so annoying. Why did he want to know?*

"No, there's nothing to share, Sam. I'll let you know when there is."

"Shame, I could do with some spice. The journey has been quite dull so far. Are you guys going to Abu Simbel? Is Garneesh coming?"

"I think so, he was planning to. Jac and I are definitely going."

"Hi, Darling," Jacqui's lively voice cut through her thoughts as she bounded into the room. She looked cool, really cool in white linen blouse and pants. Charlie noticed that she no longer wore skimpy tops. "These early starts will kill me."

"Hi, Jac. Glad you made it. The coach'll be here at six thirty a.m. Let's grab a quick breakfast."

Charlie hurried after her slipping away from Sam. "That man gives me the creeps," she said.

"Me too. I think we should watch out for him."

"Yes, Miranda says someone on the boat is a danger to me. By the way did you notice a sweet smell, a type of perfume in the cabin?"

"Can't say I did, sweetie, but I did notice it was cold, you left the window open."

"Porthole," corrected Charlie. "Yeah, I noticed it was open this morning, don't remember opening it last night but I must have been blasted, I woke up with a hangover. I don't remember much about last night at all. Last thing I recall was sitting down to dinner, after that it's a total blank. I'm definitely going to have to cut down. I think I'm drinking too much champagne."

"Not possible. That's like saying you can have too much of a good thing." She laughed. "Anyway, let's get going, I'm looking forward to Abu Simbel, I've heard it's a really romantic place and I feel like that just now." Jacqui dashed ahead into the dining room.

"Just a moment, I want to call Nan. I have a real urge to speak to her." With a sense of great extravagance she called Miranda. The phone rang and rang. No answer.

45

It was way past midnight by the time Jared left. It took him an hour to get to the Sussex village of Dunsworth and Lord Dennington's country house.

The butler showed him into the drawing room where the Lord was waiting. He was a slight man, trim and lean, more from limitless energy than from visits to a gym. Dressed for the city in an immaculate navy suit he looked what he was, a powerful and confident business baron.

He looked impassively at Jared and nodded. No niceties, no welcome drinks. He moved to the fireplace and taking the poker thrust it deep into the burning logs. "We have to stop this wretched girl. I've spent years destroying the credibility of the Masons and their secret powers – there is no way I will allow a simple girl to bring out more. She's even a greater threat – she would share it with any Tom, Dick or Harry. She's daft enough to let the unwashed proletariat get their mitts on powers that would upset the entire world order."

He stood up, squaring his shoulders and glared at Jared. "She must be stopped, do you hear? Stopped."

He threw the poker into the hearth, filling the room with the cold clatter of steel.

Silence.

Dennington sat down. The only sound in the room the thrumming of his fingers on the arms of the chair.

Jared stood silently for several moments then cleared his throat. "I understand, my Lord. After you called I contacted an associate of mine, Binwani. He will hire men and I have given him the task the doctor started but is failing to deliver."

"Good, good. Is he to be trusted?" asked Dennington.

"He has always proved to be and his men are ruthless. They will do the job, never fear." He grinned.

"He had better be good. I hold you accountable." He glared, his dark almost black eyes, bore into Jared. He stood up. "Right, Jared Mustof, come with me to the office, we need to talk money." He walked briskly to the door and led the way out of the room. "Remember, nothing must lead back to me. Cover your tracks. Keep your messages to me short and change phones from time to time. I will give you a new number to use for me from now on."

Jared followed him, careful not to step on the priceless rugs that covered the flagstones in the hallway.

"Yes, of course, me lord, of course," he muttered trying to keep up as the slight figure disappeared down the corridor to the back of the house.

Anything your lordship wishes, posh bastard.

46

The girls sat at the front of the coach so that Jacqui could talk to Mohammad. He was taking them as far as the airport where they would pick up the small plane that would fly them to the Abu Simbel site.

Charlie's phone buzzed an incoming text. She looked at it and frowned. "See you tonight as arranged. Thanks for sharing the secret. It's worth a lot to have such insider information. So glad you have agreed to this. Remember very important to keep this quiet. I will bring the money tonight. S."

What the hell is that all about? She stared at the text. A shimmer of fear disturbed her solar plexus. *Money? Secret? What on earth is this?*

Then she noticed a red heart stuck to the corner of the phone.

"Oh, Jac, I've picked up your phone by mistake."

Jacqui laughed and looked in her bag and brought out Charlie's iPhone. "Same, same!" They swapped over.

"What's that mail about?" Charlie asked.

Jacqui stiffened. "Oh, nothing, nothing at all." She immediately turned around and started talking to Sam who was sitting behind them. "What do you know about Abu Simbel, Sam dear?" she simpered.

Charlie felt cold. This was so unlike Jac. Miranda's words were ringing in her head. Maybe Jac was the danger.

Suddenly, the coach door opened and Garneesh leapt up the steps. He took a seat behind her next to Sam. He had lost his usual calm and contained manner; he was flustered, even his hair was messed up and he didn't appear to have shaved.

"I didn't think I was going to make it on time. Sorry, Charlie, I had to dash away. One of my patients had a complication and I needed to find a landline and email. How are you today?"

The bus started with a jerk and they all fell forward. With a roar and a belch of diesel it started off towards the airport.

"I'm great. A bit of a thick head that's all. Too much Cristal last night I think." She laughed.

He leant forward and kissed her ear. "How about skipping this trip? It's such a long way for a day. Let's take off down the Nile on a Felucca," he whispered.

"It means Jacqui will be on her own. Mohammad's not going; he's visiting his grandmother."

"Oh, I'm sure she will be just fine. She's not slow to make friends is she?"

"Well that is true. OK, then."

"We'll slip off at the airport."

Charlie turned to Jacqui and told her what Garneesh had proposed. She shrugged her shoulders. "No probs. Just watch out for the crocodiles."

At the airport they left the coach and jumped into a cab. Charlie fell back onto the mock fur seats and relaxed. Soft Egyptian pop music filled the cab.

She turned to Garneesh and told him about the strange message on Jacqui's phone. "Mmmm, well that sort of confirms something that I should have said to you. I'm not sure she is totally honest with you."

"Why do you say that?" Charlie said sharply.

"Well, it's just something I overheard her saying to Sam the other day. But, listen, sweetie, it might be just my imagination, I'm sure she's a loyal friend to you."

"Well, she is, but even so. I feel I have to be careful of everyone. What was it, what did she say?" Charlie pressed him.

"Well, they were whispering so I couldn't get it all. But he was pushing her hard for something. He was using words like, most important that she gets it, that he would pay her well for it. But I didn't hear what it was he wanted from her. He was very pushy though and she seemed reluctant but in the end he mentioned something like five thousand US dollars, I couldn't hear too clearly, anyway I think that swayed it. She seemed as though she was going to go for it then someone came by and they were interrupted. He said he would mail her."

Charlie blanched and covered her face with her hands. "Oh, no, not Jac. Not Jac." Her thoughts went straight back to the pile of stones – the hiding place they had set up on the Island of Isis. "Hell."

"Why don't you confront her tonight and find out what's going on. You can't do anything right now. Forget it and relax, we're going to have a great day. Let it go now."

"OK, but it's so upsetting, Jac of all people." She reluctantly sat back and tried to relax, staring without seeing at the traffic and bustle of Aswan.

The taxi took them back through the town to the quay. "I feel as though I'm playing truant, this is exciting." Charlie skipped along the quayside as they made their way to the Feluccas to hire. Garneesh was surrounded by a throng of boat boys trying to get his custom.

Further down the quay, a man in local dress, grubby white galabeya and thick brown sandals, leant against a hoarding advertising

Sony computers. He watched Garneesh haggling for the boat hire then pulled out his phone.

"They are getting a boat." He listened. "Sure, I follow by car." He put the phone in his pocket and slowly walked to his car parked by the quayside, inside his companion turned to him. He nodded. "Ready?"

"Yeah, ready." The older man looked grim. "I will drop you off in town – you know what you have to do."

47

The felucca sailed upstream with the river flow; there was a good breeze and they were making steady progress. Garneesh glanced at his watch.

Charlie lay on the cushions, in her white linen trousers and shirt and large straw hat she looked burnished and healthy.

She is so beautiful. Any other time, he thought pursing his lips, *Any other time.* He pulled out his phone and took a photo.

"Are we planning to be somewhere at a certain time?" Charlie put her hand to her eyes to stop the sun glare as he stood over her.

"No agenda, just thought it must be time for a drink," he smiled and pulled forward his backpack and took out a bottle of red wine and two plastic glasses.

"Where are we going?" Charlie leant over the side of the boat and looked into the depths of the Nile as they swirled past her.

"Nowhere in particular but I thought we would sail up the river some way, find a spot to stop then we can get a cab back."

Charlie shivered. "Strange, the sun is shining but I feel cold." She pulled out a cardigan from her bag.

"You may still be reacting to the last few days; it's been quite a journey for you so far. You are also probably hungry; it's past lunch time already. This morning in town I found this little shop run by a momma, just like the ones back home in the kampong and I bought us some food." Garneesh pulled out pitta bread, hummus, olives, goat's cheese and tomatoes wrapped in grease paper and brown bags.

Charlie took the bags and started to lay out the food on the cushions.

Garneesh's phone sounded. "Hello?"

He frowned as a torrent of sound poured from the phone into his ear. He pulled it away at one point and glared into it. Then moved to the end of the boat and whispered. "Enough. Enough. I hear you. Leave it to me."

Charlie looked up. "What was that about? You look so cross."

"God, it's the organisers of the conference. They are trying to get it together again and want me to recall the other speakers. I am the president of my chapter of the Association of Cosmetic Surgeons in UK and I get roped in whenever we have these international conferences. But they are being very pushy and because the conference was disbanded most of the speakers went home. Now they want me to jump through hoops to get them back. Let's forget them. I'll sort it out tomorrow. Eat now."

He crouched down beside her and took a tomato which he sucked, tore a piece of pita in half and dipped it into the hummus. "Sorry there are no knives. My, this is good, just like the picnics of my youth, simple basic and great food."

"I love it too. Food always tastes better this way." Charlie smiled – she felt warmer now and more relaxed.

Half an hour later Garneesh instructed the boys to moor up the boat on the bank side. They slung their packs on their backs and prepared to leave the boat.

48

The elderly Egyptian shouted into the phone. "Hakim, you old blind fool, can you see them?"

"Joseph, calm down. You one-eyed donkey, of course, I have them in my sights. I can see the boat from the road. Don't you worry; I am on target. I will keep you informed."

He closed the phone and wiped a sweating palm on his robe. This reminded him of days gone by, dangerous days, but exciting days. He grinned. Life was beginning to perk up, at last.

He started the car again and crawled along. The boat had slowed and looked as though it was about to moor up.

49

The battle had been fought hard and fast. Bodies lay all around the camp. Blood spattered the walls of the tents and congealed in pools.

The men looked at each other. Wild eyed. Tense. Hyped up by adrenaline; life saving adrenaline. They were still jumpy. One of the 'bodies' had already resurrected and taken a pot shot at Jimmie.

"Jones. You and Bonavita go and check every single body. Then back here. You have five minutes." Jimmy's voice was harsh with the shouting during the attack. Yelling, shouting, screaming, supposedly to frighten and confuse the enemy but also the way to muffle the sound of inner voices.

Percher nodded at Andy. A sign of approval. His spirits lifted. Accepted. Good.

Wayne put his hand on his back. More approval. He squared his shoulders. Accepted and approved. Good enough. He busied himself packing up his kit.

The sound of helicopters in the distance. They could be heard landing half a mile away.

"Quickly now. Get ready, men." Percher gave out one last vocal blast.

There was a large enough space for a landing zone thankfully so no need to retrace their route through the minefield. Their vehicles were being picked up from the desert then they would come and take them away. Take them away from this hell hole.

But Andy didn't feel the heat of hell; he felt the blessing of redemption.

50

"Do you know where we are, Garneesh?" Charlie looked around; they were in a quiet spot of the river. The Al Khatar-Awan road could be seen further away inland. There were a number of tilled fields and some large banks of sugar cane and down a dirt track opposite to their landing place a farm which looked deserted, no sign of the donkeys, chickens and goats that surrounded most of the farms they had passed. No sign of life at all.

They climbed out of the boat onto an old concrete landing stage, crumbling at the river edge and lined by wooden hitching posts eroded away by time and the swirling currents. Garneesh paid off the boat boys and they tacked the boat around and sailed back down the river towards Aswan. As they stood alone on the pier there was no sound but the swishing of the river as it coursed by.

Charlie looked up and down and for once there were no cruise boats to be seen. She shrugged. "This is a strange place to stop, Garneesh."

"Don't worry, follow me." He walked confidently on ahead up the farm track. "Come along, little one. Let's explore."

She followed him as instructed. "It's too hot to go so fast. Slow down, what's the rush?" She was sweating now and her cardigan went back into her bag.

51

Hakim stopped his car when he saw the felucca moor up by the bank and he parked up by the side of the road. He leant over, took binoculars from the glove compartment, got out of the car and quietly pushed the door to. He took up position leaning against a nearby tree where he could watch unobserved. As he focused his binoculars he saw Garneesh and Charlie leave the boat, climb the bank and start to walk along the track towards the farm. "Ibn El-Sarmoota," *(son of a bitch)* he muttered, "he's got her."

His head whirled with options. His choice took him scrabbling down the roadside bank and tracking across the barren land to circle around and catch them before they reached the farm.

He ran doubled up taking what shelter he could from a field of sugar cane from a neighbouring farm. After a while he came below them on the path. He had to be extra cautious; if they turned he could be seen.

He kept to the side of the track taking what cover he could find. As he drew closer he could hear their voices as Garneesh encouraged Charlie to walk faster. She was complaining about the heat. They walked past another stand of cane and he used this as cover to get close. He gathered his strength to make his attack. Now…

He hurled himself at Garneesh and threw him to the ground.

Charlie screamed. "Get off him, get off him." She threw herself onto Hakim's back thumping him with her fists. Hakim flung her off and he and Garneesh continued to roll around on the ground, each one trying to get on top. Charlie could hear her own voice screaming as she searched for a weapon. By the path she saw a large stone and picking it up she waited till Garneesh was underneath and with a huge effort brought it down hard on the back of his attacker's head. He let out a huge sigh, lay still, inert, lifeless.

She immediately dropped down beside him. "Oh, God, have I killed him? Do you think he is dead?" Charlie's voice trembled. "Oh my God, please don't say I killed him."

"He was trying to kill us, my dear, now is not the time for sympathy."

"But I couldn't bear it if I'd killed him. Who do you think he is?"

Garneesh brushed himself down. "Probably the man who has been stalking you. Remember this isn't the first time he has tried to attack you. He got what he deserved."

"Please, Garneesh, you're a doctor, just check his pulse, for my sake check it." Charlie was close to hysterics so he bent over and held the man's wrist for a few moments.

"He's alive. Just unconscious. Come along now."

Garneesh put his arms around her and helped her along the path towards the farmhouse. "You're limping," he said as Charlie rubbed her leg.

"He caught me on the shin before I knocked him out. It hurts but it's OK I can walk. I just feel shaky, that was so unexpected, how awful. Why would he want to attack us?"

In the dusty courtyard at the front and side of the house there were a few piles of straw and concrete posts where animals had once been tethered. A number of rattan sheds that had been animal shelters were now full of holes. The place was neglected and dismal. The sweet whiff of decay wafted from a pile of putrefying vegetation. The walls of the

house, once whitewashed, were now peel
political slogans had faded to a pale memor
reached the door, weather-beaten and ajar. Ga
"Anyone home?" The only reply the sound of the dc
the insects humming around the sugar cane.

Garneesh grabbed her arm. "Let's go inside and ta.   ʌк
around."

"Why? It's revolting. Why would we want to go inside?" Charlie pulled back, screwing up her nose and curling her lip. She turned to go back down the path.

As she walked away he strode towards her, grabbed her arm and pulled her roughly back inside the house, slamming the door behind him. He threw her onto a mattress that lay in the centre of the room.

She screamed in shock and glared up at him. "Stop it, stop it. What are you doing? What do you want? Garneesh what's come over you?"

He ignored her and spoke to two men quietly standing in the corner of the room. They were poorly dressed in long tunics over cotton pants. Garneesh spoke slowly and clearly. "There's a man on the path outside. Tie him up and stop him from speaking."

He bent down and handed them a rope and a roll of masking tape that lay beside the mattress ready and waiting.

"Find his car; it'll be up on the road nearby, hide it in the cowshed. Then stand outside and guard us." With a slight nod of acknowledgement they left the room.

Beside the mattress were plastic bags, another coiled rope, a pair of scissors, a knife and a further roll of masking tape. Apart from these items, the mattress and a pile of tarpaulins on an old wooden chair the room was bare. It smelt damp and musty; clearly abandoned and neglected.

h, my God. Are you kidnapping me, you bastard?" Charlie tried to sit up.

He pushed her back down with his foot.

"You could say that, my dear." He sneered at her. His handsome face distorted into a mask of hatred and disdain.

"I don't believe it, I don't believe it." Charlie was hyperventilating now. "How could I have been so stupid? Oh, God, help me."

"That's unlikely. It's time for us to talk. I've had enough of playing games. It's simple. You have information I need to know so you are now going to give it to me. Either you do it voluntarily and painlessly or I shall force you and it will hurt. Your choice. You are always spouting that we have choices, well here are yours. Tell and be set free or don't tell and suffer."

Again she started to get off the floor. Again he pushed her back down. He put his foot on her stomach and reached for the masking tape. He flicked her over and wound the tape around her wrists. She kicked out. He grabbed her feet and tied them together too. In moments she was trussed, well and truly trussed.

"Christ, the man outside wasn't my enemy – you are. You must be the one that Nan warned me about."

Charlie felt hot tears on her cheeks; tears of anger and frustration, disillusionment and fear. She lay still as the emotion flowed. She was stunned by his deception; she felt helpless, disempowered, useless and stupid, so, so stupid. "My God how could I have been so taken in so easily? You completely fooled me. Oh, my God."

"You have no idea – you have no idea, you silly bitch. You have many enemies. You have no idea. The others want you dead. At least I am prepared to do a deal with you."

170

Anger and frustration kicked in, bringing her to life. "I hate you, I hate you. Who are you, you bastard? I hate you, let me go, I hate you." Charlie thrashed around on the mattress, swinging her bound legs from side to side, up and down.

He sat down beside her. "Well, my dear, calm yourself. You may hate me but guess what, who cares?" He laughed in her face. "What does matter is that you have knowledge, memories and information that I need to know. And I need it now."

She glared at him, her mind whirring, unable to process what was happening. All she could think was what an idiot she had been to be deceived by him.

"I'll get straight to the point, my dear. I know who you are. I know you hold the key to ancient symbols of Atlantis and I want, need and desire those symbols and their power."

Charlie stared up at him with wide eyes.

"There are many who want to destroy you and the symbols. Those who want to hold the power of the world. They will destroy you rather than let the symbols get into the hands of the common herd, the hoi polloi, the Joe soaps in the street." His voice harsh and strident now, his passion rising. "You know I've become quite fond of you over this week. It's a shame you are being difficult – I would much rather not harm you. You were hot in bed too, such a shame." He leered into her face. She stared at his wet lips and flushed hot, flaming with shame.

"Bastard," she yelled. "Bastard, bastard, two timing deceiving bastard. I will never tell you anything. Go on torture me, kill me, I will never give you the secrets."

She could hear the drums beating in the recesses of her mind. She started to connect with that ancient energy. As she lay there, desperate and so very vulnerable, she sensed her past whirling around her. She knew she had the strength and determination of Khamet flowing through her veins.

After all, I am Khamet; I can draw strength from him. I need his courage and wisdom. He's an aspect of me. Khamet and I are connected.

She knew she was in real danger in the present and she must call on those reserves of power and strength from her past and bring them in to her right now.

"Give me the code, NOW," he shouted in her face.

She gritted her teeth and returned his glare. She could feel herself getting stronger. She pulled back her shoulders and tensed her muscles. Power flowed through her voice. "I draw strength from the very fibre of my being, from the deepest recesses of my soul, from the essence of who I am. I will never, never surrender the sacred knowledge to you. Kill me if you will but I will return again and again. The secrets are locked in my own cells, in my own memories. You will never find them."

She heard her voice become stronger, louder and clearer. Its resonance filled the farmhouse, echoing off the dark dank walls. "I've vowed never to surrender the knowledge and I never will. I know who you are. You are Aapep, The Evil One. I will never give you what you want. Go to hell."

The drums were louder now. The past and the present came together, merging into one time, one place.

52

Jacqui finished fumbling all of her possessions back into her backpack and stepped down from the bus. The rest of their group had long gone, rushing to catch a late dinner. As she turned to take the steps down to the boats, two dark figures stepped out of the shadows and followed her.

Her phone signalled an incoming text. "Hope you had a good day. Waiting on the boat for you. Love, Mohammad. xx"

She stopped for moment, head bowed as she sent back her response. "Just arrived back, see you in a moment. Love J."

She hesitated as she heard the padding of sandaled feet on the steps behind her. She was almost thrown over as two men jostled her, one on either side. The smaller one grabbed her elbow, pinching it tightly.

"Hey, get your hands off of me, you bastard." Jacqui swung her bag at the man.

The second man, dressed in a grubby white galabeya and face shrouded in an old red and white headscarf, grabbed her hand. "Come, come."

Jacqui kicked out, aiming for their shins. "Let me go," she screamed. "Take your stinking hands off me."

She fought as though for her life and the men jumped back surprised by her violence.

"Madam, madam, please we are friends." The older man pleaded as Jacqui continued to swing her bag, hitting them on their arms and legs. "Madam, listen to us please. You are in danger. So is your friend, Charlie. Please we are your friends, please listen. Please, come with us."

"Who the hell are you?" She swung her bag one more time for good measure.

"Please. Just listen to us for a few minutes." The older man's soft voice broke through her fear. She stopped. Wary. She was breathing heavily now from the exertion.

"Well, this had better be good." She backed to the side of the steps, still not certain.

"Please, come, sit over here. I will explain." He led her to a wooden bench under the trees. The twilight was turning to night and the pathway was gloomy. The lights of the moored cruise boats illuminated the river creating a separation of worlds; the one light, full of fun and laughter and the other one dark, filled with intrigue, danger and secrecy.

"Let me introduce myself, Madam. My name is Joseph Sayyed and my young friend is Malik Hussein. I have met your friend, Charlie, in Luxor – I am the match seller."

Jacqui turned to look more closely at the two men. The young one slight, with a fresh smooth face; he looked about eighteen. The older one had a lived-in face, scarred and worn by life and the harsh Egyptian sun.

"The match seller. Yes, Charlie did speak about you. She quite took to you and you gave her a ring, didn't you?" Jacqui felt a little more relaxed now.

"Correct. That is so. I have important things to tell you so please relax. We bring you no harm. On the other side of the coin there is much danger about both you and the Miss Charlie. I and some friends are here to keep a watch for you, to protect you. Miss Charlie is not what she seems. I can confirm that she was here as a High Priest known as Khamet in the rule of Ptolemaic Third. In those days all the power and magic were in the hands of just a few high priests. A group of dark priests who used the black magic and dark practices wanted these powers for themselves. They became the Society of Ammonites – The Hidden Ones. This society is still around today and they are evil and ruthless. They want all the power in the world for themselves and nothing will stop them. They threatened and killed Khamet in the past and they are threatening to kill Charlie today for she holds the key to the powers of sacred symbols hidden in ancient times."

Jacqui gasped; her hand flew to her throat. "So it's really true. She's been getting a lot of dreams about this."

"As I said, I and a few others have been given the task of keeping you and your friend safe. We are known as the Guardians and we were on Earth at the time when Khamet lived, but we were unable to protect him fully at that time. This time we must keep him, I mean Miss Charlie, safe."

Jacqui turned and looked deep into his eyes. "You better had. Oh, poor Charlie."

"We will, we will," the old man's eyes misted. "She is precious to us." They clasped hands.

"How do I know you aren't part of this group, anenomes or whatever you call them? How can I trust you?"

"Please, please, Miss Jacqui; you just must believe in us, as there is much worse to tell you. The doctor, Garneesh, is a spy they employed to get close to Charlie, to gain her trust and to discover the seal to the Sphinx and the symbols. Charlie is the only one who knows this. If she is killed before she can recall the symbols then, well, then not only will it be a personal tragedy but one for the world as the powers will be lost for this lifetime."

"Oh ,my God," Jacqui looked at Joseph wide eyed. "Garneesh a spy! Oh, they have been getting really close, I mean really close. She felt tears on her cheeks. Oh, God, Charlie!"

"And I have worse news. Your friend has been kidnapped. The doctor has taken her up river in a felucca and my colleague Hakim went to follow by car. The road follows the river. He went off just before lunch but we have not heard from him for some hours and… "

Jacqui interrupted him as tears poured down her face. "Oh, no. This is terrible. Oh, God, Charlie. What can we do? Can't we go to the police?"

"Our police? The Egyptian police? I think not. Not such a good idea, some of them are donkeys, some are in the pay of the society and quite honestly, I don't know which ones are which, I just don't know who we can trust, it's too risky. I have one friend who is a very senior officer, but firstly I would like to try and find her ourselves."

"I feel I should let Charlie's boyfriend know what is happening." Her voice was shaky and for the first time for a long time she felt out of control of a situation. "I don't know where he is. I think he is in India." She fumbled in her bag searching for her phone. "This is terrible, this is so terrible." She found his number. The phone rang and rang, no answer.

"He also is not what he seems," Joseph said. "We have information that he can be very helpful to us in this situation."

"Really, what do you mean…?" She stopped and lifted her hand as the answerphone clicked in.

"Andy, this is Jac. I've got terrible news. Charlie's been kidnapped."

53

Darkness had placed a shroud over the farm buildings. The wind blew through the few trees surrounding the compound. There was no sound other than the far distant murmur of traffic on the lower Aswan road with the occasional warning hooter of a cruise boat on the river. Another storm was building and the clouds rushed over the half moon, allowing a brief moment of bright light to highlight the shapes of the buildings and the two men standing still and alert guarding the edge of the farm enclosure; paid hands, thugs employed by Garneesh to protect his evil work.

Inside, one dim light hung from the ceiling casting a pool of light on Charlie lying inert on the mattress. Beside her the rope and tape discarded in lieu of new tactics. Garneesh sat on an old tarpaulin beside her; a macabre bedside comforter.

"Charlie, Charlie, my dear. All is well. You can trust me." His voice, soft and coaxing. "Relax and let me share your deepest fears, your far off memories, I can help you. You can fulfil your commitments. Together we can take this sacred knowledge to the world."

Her breathing came heavy and laboured from the drugs he had injected into her an hour before. His new approach so far had produced little response.

He continued. "Come, awaken, my treasure, it's OK to come back now. You are safe now. It is I, Hapu, your friend and supporter. Bless you, all is well."

Charlie stirred and opened her eyes briefly. "Oh, Hapu, thank the Gods you are here. Has Aapep gone now?"

"Yes, yes, he was taken away by the Guardians. We are alone now." Garneesh smiled.

Charlie sighed. "That one is pure evil. He wants the secrets of the symbols for himself. We are in great danger, Hapu. There are many who would destroy the sacred knowledge."

"I know, Master. Maybe it is time for you to share with me the spell and the symbols, so if you are killed I can carry it forth."

There was a long pause.

Garneesh held his breath.

"Let me consider this." Charlie closed her eyes.

54

The car bumped through potholes and the man in the passenger seat was finding it difficult to sit still. "Slow down, I'm trying to dial London, Binwani told us to report to Jared Mustof with any news, slow down."

The driver shook his head. "Can't. I don't want to lose them."

"Got it." The phone rang.

"Put it on speaker, I want to hear what he has to say."

A crackly voice came through the phone. "Hey, Hussein. What's up? Have you traced them yet?"

Hussein, the driver leant towards the phone. "Hi, Boss. No, we missed them, but we are following that guy Sayyid and his sidekick, They f**ked off at a million miles an hour, they must know where he's taken her.

"How come you missed G in the first place?"

"We saw them on the coach going to the airport so thought they'd gone off to Abu Simbel; we were told they were booked on it. They were definitely on the coach. They must have slipped off."

"You f**king idiot. He could be anywhere now. He hasn't reported in for over four hours. He's definitely on his own agenda. He was told to silence her, but I think he's trying to get the info for himself. You have to get him. Silence him and the girl. Make no mistakes this time, else you'll be silenced too. Get it?" The surly voice ended and the line went dead.

"F**king bastard, easy for him in his ivory tower in London, bastard." The driver's lip curled. Someone will pay. Someone will pay. Wait till I get my hands on the double crossing, boob making, f**kwit."

"Boobs, did you say boobs as in titties? Hey is that what he does? Tell me about it."

"Idiot." The car tyres skidded as the driver put his boot to the floor throwing his passenger against the door. "Serves you right," he muttered.

55

Joseph looked in the car mirror again. "I think we're being followed. There are two cars and a motorbike. And behind them a car that I am sure has been following us all the way. My bet is the Society men. They must be backing up Garneesh. Ya Homaar."

Malik was peering out into the night searching for Hakim. "We'll never find him like this. The clouds are hiding the moon; it's too dark out there most of the time."

They sped along the dark road, passing the occasional farm and from time to time a well lit roadside café where trucks and travellers stopped for supper.

"This is useless, he could be anywhere." Malik frowned as he continued to peer by the roadside, hoping to catch sight of Hakim or his car.

"I've got an old friend from army days; he's head of police in Cairo now. He's tracing Hakim's mobile. Even if he's turned it off he can fix it to turn it on and identify his location. He should come through anytime. I guess they'll be somewhere between Daran and Kom Ombo. He was following the boat so would be on the lower Al Khatar Aswan road."

"We can pick that up in about half a kilometre."

As they slowed to search the roadside the two cars and the bike overtook them so there was nothing between them and the following car.

Joseph's phone rang. Malik answered. "Thanks, that's great, thanks, hold on I'll write those down." He scrabbled in the glove compartment and found paper and pen and scribbled down an address. "Thanks again, will tell him."

"They picked up Hakim's mobile. He's near Al Mulaqqatah, half a mile from the river and not far off the Al khatar Aswan road – just as you thought. I've got the co-ordinates. He sends you his regards, says you owe him now, says your daughter will do."

Joseph chuckled. "No chance, he's far too ugly for Sareem, his kids will look like goats. Good. I'm not going on the lower road, I'm going to try and get rid of those bastards before we get close."

He pushed down on the accelerator and took off, pushing the old car to its limits. "This car is a donkey. Where did you get it?"

The following car kept close behind.

Joseph swerved around a huge Coca Cola delivery truck just missing an oncoming wagon of alfalfa. "I'm going for the interchange maybe we can give them the slip there."

They roared on down the road, sliding past trucks, cars, cabs, donkeys leaving a trail of curses and angry hooting. But still the car stuck behind.

They came up behind a slow moving trailer piled high with sugar cane. The lorry and load hung way into the middle of the road, bringing them down to five kilometres an hour. Joseph found another dozen swear words and vented his frustration by beating his hands on the steering wheel. "Those monkeys will block this road for the next five kilometres."

He looked into the rear-view mirror. "I can see those bastards in the car behind. They're laughing at us. He shouted out the window. "Tiizak Hamra, I show you. F**k them. I'll teach those donkeys."

Like a crazy man he drove out into the oncoming traffic and just blasted his way through, narrowly missing a bullock drawing a cart of hay. The driver cracked his whip at them but they got away.

"Let's go." He drove the car around two more bends then turned off the lights and skewed onto a track leading off to the left and drove behind a couple of old cow sheds. A moment or two later the car sped by followed minutes later by the rumbling sugar cane truck.

"Hell, I've not had such fun since the army." Joseph grinned and turned to the younger man.

Hakim stared back at him.

"Yeah, little kid, didn't your daddy tell you about how your uncle Joseph won his Gold Medal of Bravery? In my service days I fought in three wars."

"Three? I don't remember any."

"Well, you're a kid still. I was twenty-three when I first went to war – it was on the border with Libya; shame it was all over in four days. Had another blast in the late sixties when we tried to get back the Sinai Peninsula; that one went on for a couple of years – they called it the War of Attrition, I spent most of my time undercover in Israel for that one – bet you didn't know your uncle spoke Hebrew like a native did you? My medal came from the Ramadan War, they called it Yom Kippur. We attacked them on our feast day, still remember that one – the troops were mad about fighting on our festival, still it caught them unawares to start with. Again I had to get behind the lines."

"Did you win, Uncle?" Malik was hopeful.

"No, boy, we lost – shouldn't have, but those Syrian dogs let us down. Lost the sight in one eye too.

"Anyway, still got my SIG P226, and my damn Helwan, temperamental bastard of a gun, but still it could be useful. Pass me that canvas bag on the back seat. Looks like we might need them today.

Hey, I can feel the old fighting blood coursing again. Malik, my boy. We'll wait here for a few minutes to make sure those goons have lost us, meantime let me show you how to slow a man down." His eyes glittered as he took out his SIG.

56

Charlie was kneeling with her hands on the ground in front of her in a form of abeyance. Three times she bowed. She sat back on her heels.

Her face calm and her voice deep and strong, she announced, "I have consulted with the Wise Ones. I have asked for their permission to break the vow and share the sacred knowledge with you, my dear friend, Hapu. I have asked for their blessings. But they declare that the vow made to the Great One cannot be broken. These Symbols must stay hidden until the Day of the Citizen, The New Dawn. Only then can they be disclosed and then never to one individual but to all the Citizens of the World. They tell me that the day is not yet arrived although it is nigh."

She clasped her hands before her as she completed her connection with her spiritual masters then slowly sunk back onto the mattress. Still under the influence of the drugs she fell into a light sleep.

Garneesh glared at her; grimaced and gritted his teeth and in something similar to a growl, "Bitch, you will pay for this." He kicked out at her in his anger. She screamed from the surge of pain through her ribs.

He then kicked the wall, picked up the tarpaulin and threw it in the corner. "You'll regret this, my darling, you'll regret this."

He turned and picked up the plastic bag that had been lying beside the mattress and pulled out a large torch, a pair of pincers and a cattle prod and laid them by the bed. He reached up to remove the light bulb.

She watched him, eyes full of fear, her heart beating super speed. Her ribs throbbing. Despite the pain she felt herself slipping away as the drugs overtook her again.

57

Jared reached across his large antique desk and picked up the cordless phone, taking no chances with mobiles. He banged in the speed code.

"Hussein, so, have you found them?"

He listened to the garbled reply.

"Soooooo, you lost them. You w****r, you f**king w****r. How the hell am I going to explain that? He'll have me for toast. Keep looking for them, they can't be far. You've got the bastard Garneesh Vellupillai to find, the girl and the old w****r and the boy. Can't be too difficult, Christ you guys are supposed to be professionals. Call me as soon as you have a result, or else…"

He slammed down the phone and glared at it, the panelled wall, the designer room and cursed.

He picked up his mobile and hit a short-cut. After one ring it was answered. "Lord Dennington, I'm so sorry but we have a few 'itches. Seems your friend, Garneesh, has gone walk about. He's taken the girl off somewhere and my boys haven't yet been able to trace them. I've no doubt they will and I've told them to silence the two of them – just checking that is your intention, my lord."

He got the answer he wanted and put down the phone, reached over and turned off his voice recorder. He muttered, "If I go down you're going too, your lordship."

58

Babylon was heaving even though it was early evening. The club was a popular night spot for locals and visitors and tonight it had kicked off early. A local football team had turned up to celebrate a win and a bus load of fans followed. The DJ had cranked up the decibels and the thud of the bass rocked the building.

Andy wiped the sweat from his face. He turned to Wayne. "And this is meant to be R & R," he laughed. "Feels more like mayhem."

"You're surely not complaining, mate. Not often we get a piss up paid for by the brass. This local brew aint at all bad." Wayne was into his third bottle of Luxor Classic.

"Why don't you find yourself a bint and get off for the night. I am. The local talent looks OK to me." He grinned and looked around to take his pick of the girls crowded by the bar. The eight tanned fit guys were getting plenty of attention from the clusters of girls in high heels and strappy tops sipping cola. The men's suppressed excitement and tension acted like a magnet to the local girls. They'd arrived back in town only two hours previously and after a shower and change they were ready for a good time. Time to celebrate.

Jimmy leant forward and in a hoarse whisper said, "Remember you're on a stag do, keep mum. Enjoy yourselves, boys. I'm going to. See you in London. Find your own way home and claim your flight." He swaggered off towards the girls, pulled a couple close and started dancing with them, still holding up his beer.

Andy looked around. He felt uncomfortable. His mind was spinning. A tall blonde started to walk towards him and he immediately thought of Charlie. He felt a stab in his chest. He shook his head at the girl. He turned around and pushed his way out of the crowd. *Bloody hell, I'll join her. Why not? She's just up the road somewhere on the Nile.* As he stepped out of the club into the noise of Cairo's traffic he reached for his phone. A missed call. He listened to the message. *S**t.*

He looked at his watch. Eight o'clock. Time to catch a late plane. He ran across the road to the cheap hotel where the troop had taken rooms. In ten minutes he had booked out, collected his personal kit, hailed a cab and on his way to the airport to catch the 22.15 to Aswan. He called Jacqui, listened to her garbled story and told her he was on his way.

His heartbeat was still in overdrive from the shock and he felt his stomach squeeze with anxiety at the thought of Charlie in danger. *Kidnapped? What the hell. Symbols? Kidnapped by a doctor, how did that happen?* He leant back in the cab and cradled his pack. *Breathe and relax. This is your training. You can save her.*

* * *

At midnight Andy jumped out of the cab and ran down the steps of the quay to the first moored boat. He dashed through the adjoining boats and into the lobby of the Golden Pyramid. Jacqui was waiting for him in the bar.

"Oh my God, Andy." She reached up and put her arms around him.

He put her at arm's length. "What's the latest news?" he asked briskly.

"The two guys who stopped me, the ones I mentioned on the phone are Joseph and Malik. Mohammad says we can trust them. They have a friend, Hakim, and he was following Charlie and Garneesh but they lost track of him. Now we have just heard they have traced Hakim through his mobile phone. We think he must be with Garneesh, the guy who was posing as a doctor, oh my God, Andy, he took us all in. He was such a smoothie, hell…"

Andy interrupted her, "Yeah, fine, none of this really makes sense now but we can analyse all that later. Now we need to focus on getting Charlie. So our best bet is this Hakim fellow. Who is Joseph by the way?"

"Oh he's a great old guy, he's been trying to help Charlie and then there is Malik who is also a good guy, and Hakim, well we thought he was a baddie but it turns out he's a good guy too. Oh, it's all so confusing, no one seems to be who we thought they were."

"Come on, Jac, pull yourself together. We have to get out there and find Charlie now; we can talk all this through afterwards. I've told the cab driver to wait. Have you got everything you need?"

She nodded. She was dressed in jeans and T-shirt and carried a backpack and a black fleece. "Mohammad got me a torch. He can't come but we can be in phone contact with him in case we get into trouble too."

"Great, let's go and in the cab you can tell me who this Mohammad geezer is too."

Andy was dressed ready for action in fatigues and soft army boots. He took off his backpack and held it in his arms as they ran through the deserted lobbies of the adjoining boats and leapt up the steps and hurled themselves into the cab.

"We need to get onto the Al Mulaqqatah Road. Joseph will direct us once we are on our way."

Andy passed the taxi driver a fist of Egyptian pounds and a few US dollars. "This may take some time, mate, there will be more if this works out, right?" The driver grabbed the money and pushed it into a bag by his side.

"Make it speedy." The driver put his foot down hard and the car's wheels screeched into the night as they sped away.

Jacqui put her hand to her chest. "Andy, I hate to say this, but I have a bad feeling that Charlie is in real danger. I can feel a pulsing in my heart which I am sure comes from her. I just sense she is in a terrible place." She wiped away a tear. "The bastard, the bastard, you would never have believed it, Andy." She turned towards him angry now. "You know, none of this would have happened if you'd been with her on this trip. She only went with him because she was mad at you. You would have kept her safe. Bloody men, always have to do their own thing. Why *didn't* you go with her?"

"Sorry, Jac, I just couldn't, I really couldn't. One day I will explain. God, I feel bad enough as it is. Please don't go on."

She looked at his face, and could see the pain. She also noticed how tired he looked. She squeezed his hand. "OK. But we need you now for sure. Thank God you are here, how come you're dressed like that; you look more like a soldier than a tourist."

"Long story, I'll tell you later. But I did get a panic telephone call don't forget; I thought I should be prepared."

"By the way where's your luggage – did you only bring that pack?" she pointed at his navy backpack on the floor between his knees.

"I booked into a hotel in Aswan and left it there."

"Oh," she looked out of the window. "Looks like another storm coming, those trees are almost bent double. That's all we need."

Her phone rang. "Hi, Joseph, yes we're on our way. Where are we meeting you? Good idea."

She passed the phone to the cab driver who spoke for a few minutes to Joseph, nodding his head then passed it back to her.

"OK, yes Andy's here, do you want to speak to him?"

She passed the phone to Andy. "Of course. Yes as a matter of fact I do. Mmmm in my bag. Also night goggles. Good. See you soon, mate. Thanks." He closed the phone and handed it back to Jacqui without comment.

She stared at him. "What did he say?"

"Nothing, just asked me if I was prepared to fight and I said yes, of course."

Jacqui gave him a long look and frowned.

The car continued along the dark streets of Aswan towards the place where Joseph had parked up, the nearest safe place to the location of Hakim's phone.

59

Garneesh kicked Charlie in the ribs a second time, enough to rouse her. She mumbled as she became conscious, unaware of where she was; she looked up confused and disorientated. A torch laid on its side by the bed; the only source of light in the room. As she opened her eyes she saw the cattle prod swinging from the lamp socket. It curved a menacing arc just above her thighs. Her stomach lurched. Evil energy pervaded the room. Her eyes flicked to a dark shape looming above – Garneesh.

"One more chance before I let my friend here," he indicated the swinging cord with its gruesome attachment, "before I let my friend get closer. What is the code to break the seal to open the Sphinx? Your last chance, my pretty one." He smirked – his face pure evil.

She stared at him. "I loathe you, no way will I tell you. You are the devil."

She turned her head away from him, in her head she silently prayed. *Angels, Nan, Andy, anyone who can help me please, come, please rescue me.* She clenched her fists and braced herself for pain. As her hand went to her throat she felt her nan's pendant. She held it hard in her fist. She thought of her nan and a sense of calm and detachment came over her. She felt strong again.

Garneesh picked up the prod and moved it closer to her. She twisted herself away, pushed her hands to the floor and using the torque of her body swung over with all her force and knocked away the torch and caught him with her feet. He was caught off guard and swore as she then rolled in the opposite direction away from him. As he pulled on the cord there was a fizzing and bang and the electricity failed.

"Blast and damnation, you whore. You will pay for this," he swore again. He kicked out at her viciously but only managed to connect to the torch which bounced against the wall and died. The room was now in total darkness. The only sound the first drops of rain falling on the roof and their heavy breathing.

Where are you, Andy? Where are you? Oh, please come, please come.

What an idiot I have been what an idiot.

She shook her head and gritted her teeth.

Silently she got onto all fours and, doubling over, very slowly crept towards the door. As her hands touched the old wood she felt the bar that Garneesh had placed across it. *Oh my god,* she felt a surge of fear blast through her. She was locked in darkness with a servant of darkness.

God, Angels, spirits of light, please help me and I will do anything you wish, I will do anything, get me out of here alive, please, please.

She heard two heavy steps followed by two muted ones as Garneesh crossed the room and stepped onto the mattress towards her.

60

"Don't use it unless you have to. Leave the serious stuff to me. Andy, Charlie's boyfriend is on his way and he and I will go in first." Joseph handed the old gun to Malik.

He had his eyes on the road. He had parked under a tree just up the road from the farm track. The storm was almost upon them and the tree's branches were flailing wildly in the wind. They sat tense and alert as they waited for Andy and Jacqui to arrive.

Malik peered out of the window, the clouds dark and menacing, the moon completely obscured now. It was pitch black outside. A few large drops of rain fell.

An owl screeched as it flew past, Malik jumped. "Uncle, I'm scared."

"That's normal, my boy, that's normal. Before any action I always get a touch of the heebie jeebies. Just remember to keep your back covered at all times. Don't worry, nephew, I've been in worse fixes than this."

Down the road they could see the lights of an approaching car. It slowed as it came closer. "This must be them."

Despite his uncle's reassurances Malik felt his heart pounding in his chest and he clenched his fists.

Once the car got near the lights were dimmed and it drew up behind them quietly. Andy and Jacqui jumped out. Joseph and Malik joined them on the roadside just as the rain started. They introduced themselves and huddled under the tree.

"From the co-ordinates that Ali has given me, Hakim is in that farmhouse down there," Joseph pointed down the track. "You can just see it, there was a dim light showing through the windows awhile ago but it's just gone out and the place is in total darkness. We have to presume he's not on his own and that the farm is guarded. Also you should know that we were being followed. I managed to give them the slip but they could turn up at any time."

Andy took charge. "Jacqui stay here. You can keep guard from here in case those other guys turn up. If they do send me a text or call me on my mobile. I will have it on mute but I'll feel its vibration.

"Joseph, you and I will go down, Malik, follow us halfway down the track. Then you stay there and watch and listen. If we don't come back out in five minutes call the police."

Joseph handed Malik his phone. "Yes call Ali, my friend, he will organise a rescue but only if you really have to. I would rather the police are kept out of this. His number is in my phone. Let's be quick."

Andy put on his night goggles and led the way down the sandy track. Joseph followed close behind him. They dropped over double as they got closer to the compound entrance. Suddenly Andy stopped and put his hand out to halt Joseph. He grabbed Joseph's head and pulled it close to him and whispered in his ear. "There are two guards standing by the entrance. You take the one on the right and I will take the left. Try not to shoot but use this."

He passed Joseph a knife from his pocket and pulled out a second one for himself. Joseph smiled; his favourite weapon, good.

"Now!" whispered Andy.

Joseph threw a pebble ten yards in front of the right hand guard. The man startled and moved forward. Joseph hurled himself from his bent up position and threw himself at the man, knife aiming at his stomach. He caught him unawares and they both fell to the ground. Joseph could feel the knife entering the soft tissue of the man's abdomen. He sighed and flopped forward, limp and breathing lightly. Joseph took tape from his pocket and tore off a strip and plastered it over the man's mouth, turned him over and bound up his wrist. All over in a minute, his old guerrilla training invaluable once again.

Andy had circled behind his man and caught him from behind, his arm looped round and held him in a neck brace. Without hesitation he pulled the knife across the man's throat. One gurgle and he too was silent. Joseph joined Andy and tied up the second man, although there seemed little chance of a recovery; blood was seeping from his neck and there was no sign of life. They pushed the bodies to one side and Andy made off towards the door of the farmhouse.

Joseph stared down at the dead man and looked up at Andy's back as he moved quietly down the track. "Knows his business," he muttered and followed him.

61

In London the phone on Jared's desk rang. He picked it up and waited while the connection was made then put it on speaker and continued to caress the woman in his arms.

"Binwani here. Hussein has tracked Garneesh's phone. They have the coordinates. They are on their way."

"Good, if they get them I will spare you. Aren't these meant to be your top men over there?"

He didn't wait for a reply and replaced the phone and continued with his pleasure.

62

A scream tore through the night. Andy and Joseph glanced at each other then Andy nodded towards the farmhouse door. They both threw themselves forward and onto the farmhouse door. It shuddered but held firm. It was jammed from within. The bar solid and unyielding.

"The window," yelled Andy, all caution now gone.

Another scream seared the night followed by sounds of scuffling; a fight inside the room.

They found the window and Andy took his backpack and threw himself at the window using the bag as a battering ram. The glass splintered and flew in all directions.

"We are armed. Drop your weapon, we're coming in," Andy yelled.

He rolled through the window and across the floor in one single movement. His night goggles showed him the red figure of a man bent over another form on the ground near the door. He crouched and held his knife ready as the man whipped around to face him. They circled each other but Andy had the advantage and could see clearly while the other man was dependent on his knowledge of the room layout.

Outside Joseph was about to follow Andy through the window when he heard the screaming of tyres and a car hurtled down the track towards him. The headlights full beam illuminated the scene; the house and the bodies of the guards on the ground. The car came to a sudden halt in a cloud of dust and two men hurtled out with guns in their hands.

Joseph drew the SIG from his tunic and threw himself to the ground. Instinctively he took aim and shot the leading man in the side. The second man continued coming forward, shooting at Joseph surrounding him with spurts of flying sand and grit. One shot caught his pistol and sent it spinning into the darkness.

Joseph rolled away then bending double ran around the side of the house where he used the wall as protection and looked back to see what was happening behind him. The first man was lying on the ground groaning but the second was making for the window of the farmhouse.

A figure appeared from the darkness and ran across to the car and jumped inside; instantly the lights went out.

Inside the house the sudden arrival of the car and the light from the car headlights had given Garneesh an unexpected advantage and he used it to hurl himself at Andy.

Andy saw the knife in Garneesh's hand as he flew towards him and at the last moment turned and spun around but the force of Garneesh's body caught him. Andy's goggles flew across the room. He continued his spin to the side of his attacker. He lunged and caught Garneesh on the arm. A spurt of warm blood hit his hand. Andy leapt to the other side before he had a chance to retaliate. They circled each other for a few moments then the car lights went out. Andy, aware of fighting outside avoided the window and kept his back to the wall. From the sound of Charlie's groaning he could tell where she lay by the door. Both men were in the dark now and equally matched. Andy held his breath and listened for the breathing of his opponent. Garneesh was labouring and his wound was weakening him. Andy coiled his body, tensed his muscles and ran full tilt at him stabbing him in the chest and throwing him to the ground.

Outside the second man from the car had hesitated once the lights went out. He stood by the window looking in. He could hear Charlie's low moans and Garneesh's heavy breathing and the sound of the rain on the reed covered roof.

He could see nothing at all. He drew back.

Behind him Joseph silently felt his way around the wall of the house. Every muscle in his body tense to the point of pain, his eyes almost closed in his effort to see in the dim light with his one good eye.

Suddenly he focused on a figure moving across his path. With a blood curdling scream he threw himself onto the man knocking him to the ground. His gun flew out of his hand. Joseph, working on instinct found his neck and his fingers tightened around his throat. He hit the man's head on the ground, but the man was stronger and younger and he reared up, throwing Joseph off his back.

Digging deep Joseph found reserves of strength and dragged himself upright against the house wall. The rough sand bricks gave him purchase as he regained his breath. He could just make out the form of the man advancing towards him. The man had pulled a knife and Joseph felt vulnerable without his pistol. He started to back around the wall of the house, but the man was getting closer and closer.

Suddenly a piercing yell filled the night air and the small figure of Malik landed on the back of the advancing man. Joseph threw himself into the fight and caught the man's wrist and the knife dropped to the ground. He hit him under the chin then in the stomach, once, twice, three times, thudding into flesh, each time a gush of air left the man; he doubled over in pain. Malik was still holding on, arms looped around the man's neck. As the man fell he too fell with him. The man didn't move but the boy still held on his back like a limpet.

Joseph stopped his onslaught and pulled Malik to his feet. "Let go now. Well done, lad. Quickly find a rope, there's some in the car."

The boy ran back to the car, trainers sending a spray of dust and stones up behind him. He returned in moments with the rope followed by Jacqui, her hair slicked down on her head, soaked through from the storm.

"Do you want any help? I couldn't stay up there any longer. Let me help you with him." She started to kick the man in the ribs. Joseph put out a restraining hand.

"No need, both are beaten already. Tie them up. I'm going to see if Andy needs help in the house." He picked up the man's knife and moved towards the farmhouse.

The rain was easing now and the storm was moving on. The moon slipped through between the clouds casting a silver glow.

Joseph peered through the window, in the dim light from the moon he could make out Andy sitting on Garneesh. He climbed in and slipped down beside him. He felt his pulse. "That man is going nowhere. He's alive but lost a lot of blood. Your fight's over."

Andy stood up and moved quickly over to Charlie where she lay motionless by the door. "Charlie, darling. Where are you hurting?" He felt her pulse. Very faint. Not good.

"Charlie, Charlie." He slapped her face lightly to bring her round but she was unconscious and far away.

The drums are rolling out their persistent beat. The drums of death. Deep strong beats reverberate around his head. Khamet sighs and looks up from his couch. His eyes are still bright although his joints have succumbed to the stiffness of old age. He spends his time on the couch these days resting his body and working on his papyrus. He shares his duties as High Priest with Hapu and the younger temple acolytes, the spiritual servants of the great God, Amun. He takes a long look around his room, deep in the great Karnak temple. It is filled with his writings and sacred tablets.

Hapu enters with his favourite sherbet drink.

"Put it there, my dear friend. I am about to leave you. It is time. I have done my work and the injuries sustained by the evil Aapep have weakened me. Hold my hand for I am about to take my journey to the other side."

The old man lies back on the couch, sighs again and closes his eyes. He feels his soul lifting up and beyond his body as his spirit soars towards the afterlife. Below he can see his old friend weeping as he calls the temple servants to send a message of his passing to their rulers. The servants carry his body to the embalming chamber where his sarcophagus is ready and waiting for this day. Decorated in gold and the sacred hieroglyphics it will assist him on his journey, as befits Hornedjitef, High Priest, servant of Amun and Egypt.

His awareness shifts. He has a sense of being a woman now, in another time, another life. There is someone, a man, nearby emanating fear and anxiety. She is aware of the pain in her head. She feels disorientated and has a sense of letting go to the vital thread of life. Her life force fades, no energy flows through her body and the pain fades. Her life force is seeping away. She disconnects from her body entirely and feels herself floating up towards a powerful intense light that seems to draw her upwards. A cold wind blows and a voice clear and loud overpowers the anxious pleading voice in the far distance.

"Charlie, you are to return. It is not yet your time. We are not ready for you and you have much to do. You will return now and complete your life's purpose; fulfil your destiny. Go now my dear, all will be well. You have all you need to do what you have to do. Remember the symbols they are the keys to the New Dawn."

The voice repeats. "Return now. Return now. Return now."

Gradually the voice, reassuring and gentle but firm becomes fainter and fainter and she feels herself being pulled through a vortex of spinning energy down, down, down, towards the Earth plane.

"Oh," she opened her eyes. Staring down from the dim light was a kind and concerned face. "Oh, Andy, darling. How lovely to see you." Her voice soft and blurred. She squeezed her eyes shut then opened them wide. "Oh my God. It is you isn't it, Andy? Tell me it's not a dream. How did you get here? Are you here?" She closed her eyes again.

"Charlie, Charlie, are you OK? I thought we'd lost you, thank God you are back."

She opened her eyes. "Thank God you're here. It will all be all right now." She slipped off again for a few seconds.

"Are you OK, Charlie, are you hurt?" Andy's anxious voice penetrated the fog in her mind.

She opened her eyes and stretched. "No, I'm fine. I feel a little woozy, just a bit confused and spacey. Otherwise I'm OK. I just saw myself die as Khamet. Almost felt I was going too. Seems they're not ready for me yet. Sorry you must think I am speaking gibberish. Maybe I am."

She winced and touched her forehead. "I think I hit my head when I fell. Oh, God. That man, where is he? He tried to kill me."

As her short term memory returned she recalled the horror of the last few hours. She became agitated and sat up. But the room spun and she had to lie back down again. Andy caught her in his arms. He checked her over, running professional hands over her, checking her pulse and ensuring that no bones were broken or skin damaged.

"You are physically OK as far as I can see apart from a big bruise on your shin, a bruised rib or two and a bump on your head, so I am taking you out of here now. The man is no longer a threat to you, don't worry, sweetpea. It's OK." He picked her up and carried her out of the farmhouse followed by Joseph.

Jacqui came running up. "Oh, God, is she all right. Oh, my dear sweet Charlie. What did that bastard do to you?"

"No lasting physical harm, thank goodness. He must have drugged her, once that wears off I think she will be OK." Andy almost managed a smile. "Jac, you and I will take her back in the cab. We'll drop you at the boat, Jac, then I'll take her back to Aswan to my hotel. Tomorrow morning we'll meet up at the boat."

"It's almost morning now," said Jacqui looking at the sky which was showing signs of an early dawn.

Joseph went towards the outbuildings. "Malik, come here, boy. We must check for Hakim. I am sure he will be here somewhere; this was where they located his phone. We'll meet you at your boat at ten o'clock. There is much to discuss."

Jacqui led the way back to the taxi, and woke the sleeping driver. Andy lifted Charlie into the back and directed the driver back to Aswan.

63

Andy and Charlie sat opposite each other in the hotel dining room. Charlie wore a long white cotton skirt and a sleeveless turquoise cotton wrap-around blouse, the best she could find in the hotel shop. She felt refreshed and relaxed after a shower and few hours sleep. Her hands still shook a little and she felt fragile and unsteady. But her appetite was back and she and Andy had cleared a large plate of cooked breakfast each.

"That feels better. Didn't get much to eat yesterday – I don't suppose you did either, Charlie."

He wiped his mouth with the napkin and pushed his chair back and crossed his leg over onto his knee and clasped his foot in his hands. "So now let's do some serious catch up."

Charlie gave him a day by day run down of her experiences since she'd arrived in Egypt. "I don't expect you to fully understand a lot of this, Andy, it's so farfetched that even I have had a problem in taking it all in, in fact I have been in total denial until the day before yesterday on the Isis Island. But I can't deny what I've seen and felt; the experiences have been profound to say the least."

She told him about the dreams that were actually past life recalls. She took him through the scary attacks and the menace of hidden watchers.

"Some of the scenes that played out in the dreams or past life recollections, whatever you call them, seem to match what is happening here and now. Like I'm reliving that life all over again."

She told him about the symbols and the promises she had made in the past to make them available to the world.

"Good God, Charlie, this is like a movie."

"I know, I've felt a bit like Angelina Jolie!"

"I wish," said Andy.

Charlie laughed and hit him. "Bastard, you know what I mean."

"But how did you get involved with this Garneesh fellow; how come he could have been such an evil bastard and you not realise it?"

This was just the question she was dreading.

"God alone knows. What a devil he turned out to be. I feel so stupid."

"Jacqui says it's my fault you went with him; seems I'm the culprit here, driving you into the arms of a demon."

"Well, no, it's not your fault. Although, I was really mad at you when I left for this holiday. I felt you'd let me down big time. And, well, this intelligent and handsome man found me attractive and I suppose I was seduced by his attention and champagne. I was feeling fragile and unwanted and he was there and, well, you weren't." She shrugged. "I feel an absolute idiot now, of course. But, if I had felt a bit more supported by you, well maybe I wouldn't have fallen for his charms. Sorry I'm rattling on. I feel very stupid, though." She blushed and found it difficult to look Andy full in the face.

Andy uncrossed his legs and leant forward, rubbing his face.

He sighed. "I can't make up my mind how I feel, mad that you went with him, or pleased that you're OK. The latter is winning you might be pleased to know. By the way it was totally out of the question for me to come on this trip with you. Anyway, the danger seems to be over. Joseph sent me a message that his friend has been to the farm and buried the ones that we killed and he has handed over the others to his friend, Ali, chief of police in Cairo. So that's put an end to that. As for the Garneesh fellow, well he's quite badly injured and is in the hospital; he won't be doing anyone any harm for a while."

"Thank God for that." Charlie sighed. "I'm sorry, Andy, but you did make me mad." She put out her hand to touch his knee. He patted her hand in response.

"Charlie, I owe you some explanations too. It's time for me to come clean. My story is a lot less spooky than yours but just as scary. It will probably explain some of my behaviour and attitudes. Will you promise to hear me out and forgive me for keeping it secret?"

"Well, you'd better tell me first, then I can decide if I forgive you. If this is about missing our holiday, it had better be good." She frowned at him, holding herself tight with her arms crossed in front of her and bent forward expecting the worst.

"Well, you can make up your own mind. I have to tell you that I haven't been entirely truthful about my life, and my past life, not your kind of past life but my life before I met you. You know about my marriage to Mel and you've met my kids. I've not hidden anything there. It's about my working life that I've not been entirely honest."

Charlie shivered.

"I told you I've been in the hotel business since I left the Navy. Well that's not entirely true because I went from the Navy to the SBS."

Charlie interrupted. "God, Andy, why didn't you tell me? What's wrong with that?"

"Well, I'll come to that. Let me go back a bit. As you know I joined the Navy as a warfare officer when I was eighteen. I trained as a diver and worked on minesweepers. I got promoted to lieutenant and then I joined the SBS."

"What's that?" asked Charlie.

"Special Boat Services, similar to SAS – all Special Forces. I loved the work. It gave me an adrenaline rush. I was an ATO – an Ammunition Technical Officer, and I was the best around, de-fusing and neutralising mines and bombs – dangerous and exciting."

Charlie frowned. "Sounds it."

"I loved the life, loved the danger, the adventure, the camaraderie but it destroyed my marriage, I guess, although there were other reasons too, but it's a life that takes you over. Even when I was posted in UK I was on one hour call. Call outs always seemed to clash with one of the kid's birthdays or school events. It's a shame she was a sweet girl, and I'm not sure the kids have really forgiven me." He paused and looked down. After a minute he raised his head and continued. "I became a complete danger junkie. Anyway this went on until five years ago, just after I turned thirty. Then one op went badly wrong and I lost a mate. Suddenly I didn't feel like doing it any more. I spoke to my uncle and he offered me a position in his hotel business."

"Why didn't you tell me all this before?"

"That's a good question. I'm not sure really. Our work with SBS was always very secretive and I sort of got out of the way of talking about what I did. But mostly it's because I didn't leave in a good mind space. I guess I've seen too much behind the scenes to allow me to think of myself as a hero. I don't think it's a job I can brag about or feel proud of. I have what you could call dark secrets that I just can't share, not just with you but anyone. So, anyway, I sort of got into the habit of avoiding the subject."

"So what's this got to do with our cancelled holiday?" Charlie felt a sinking feeling in her stomach and wished she could have a cigarette.

"Well, last year I had a phone call from an old mate from the service and he introduced me to some guy in a mysterious department

– probably an offshoot of MI6. They called me in – all very cloak and dagger stuff, and offered me a job. You could call it part time! I'd be what they call a reservist. They invited me to join a small group of ex SBS and SAS guys to form a covert project group to work in the Middle East – a black ops unit. Anti terrorist work, knocking out training camps, disrupting their communication lines, the odd hit on a leader, that sort of thing." He took a sip of his coffee. "I just couldn't resist – just talking to the guy brought the old adrenaline back on. Anyway, I've signed up on a project by project basis. It's a sort of civilian/forces mix working directly for a government department – although we're on our own, they won't acknowledge us if anything happens, wipe their hands so to speak. Totally, hush. There are a number of cells and no-one knows who's in what. So you mustn't breathe a syllable about this, Charlie, my sweet."

He looked deep into her eyes and clasped her hands in his as though creating a pact.

"Well, I must say you do secret squirrel well. I had no idea. But it sounds so dangerous, Andy. What about whatever it was that pushed you out the last time, won't that feeling come back?" She stared at him, eyes wide, trying to take it all in.

"It may, but I think I've got that covered now. I just get the odd bad dream. But, Charlie, I feel alive again. You just don't know how it feels to be tied down to a desk when all my life I've been out there on the edge. I shall continue to work at the hotel business on a part time basis – it's a good cover. One of the reasons we have to be so secretive is that there is a constant danger from the counter intelligence from the other side – the terrorists are getting more sophisticated and they are aware that we are out to break up their cells and training camps. So if they can identify any one of us they will send out a fatwa and we are as good as dead."

He stood up and stretched. "Anyway, I feel better now you know. By the way, several of my supposed overseas business trips were actually training sessions. One was in Wales, one in Borneo and one just outside of Dubai." He laughed and grabbed her hand again.

"So, sorry, my sweet pea. Sorry to deceive you and so sorry about our holiday. I was more than pissed off when this op clashed with our holiday. In fact, on the day we had that lunch at the Oxo restaurant." He looked sheepish. "You know the one. Well that afternoon I was supposed to be having a briefing about an operation on the Libya Egyptian border, which seemed an ironic coincidence. I had asked them to let me turn up late for the briefing meeting as I knew I had bad news to break to you. Anyway you let me off the hook by stomping out."

"Not sure I like the word stomping – I thought I walked out quite graciously, well, until I broke my heel that is," she laughed. "Great coincidence that you were so near when I needed you. Nan always says there is no such thing as a coincidence. She says that coincidence is the universe acting in harmony with our need. Anyway, it was most fortunate for me that you were in Libya and able to get to me, like a white knight."

"Well, yes, I never saw myself in that light but I guess it turned out to be fortuitous and timely."

"How did the operation go then?"

"Successfully, thanks." He shrugged.

"Was it dangerous?" she asked. He seemed different somehow, as though he was bigger, stronger, more in command.

"Yes, but no more than any of them are," he responded quietly.

"I feel I've got to get to know this different aspect of you, another side that I've not met before," she said.

"Well, hopefully you won't need to see it again."

211

"Yes. But you really looked the part there today. It must be your destiny. Something you were born to do," she laughed tentatively.

"It seems so." He leant towards her and kissed her then took her hands in his. "So what do you want to do next? We're meeting the others at the boat in just over an hour's time but do you want to plan something for the next couple of days before your boat returns to Luxor? I've never been to Egypt as a tourist and I need something to help me unwind. Personally I would love to visit Abu Simbel."

"Well, I must admit I don't feel too bad now, all things considered. My pride is hurting of course." She laughed sheepishly. "I hope I don't get nightmares or there could be two of us screaming our way through the small hours! I don't know what the neighbours will make of that."

"Probably that we're having rough fun! But listen, if you feel you need to rest I'll understand. You've been through a really awful time, you must have been terrified." He continued to hold her hands.

"Well, I was, but I did feel that I had help, it's strange and not easy to explain but I felt almost as though I wasn't all there some of the time, and I also felt that I'd been given extra strength."

Andy leant back. "Well you were drugged, that might explain some of it."

"Mmmm, well I'll have to talk to Nan about it; it's a bit too way out for you to understand, but I felt a lot of spiritual presence. Anyway, I feel fine at the moment. And, I feel I owe you big time for rescuing me. So, OK, let's do Abu Simbel. Maybe Jacqui would like to go again if she's with Mohammad, I think he's off duty today and tomorrow. He's a brilliant guide."

"Great, do you want any more coffee?"

"No thanks. By the way, there's something I want to check out with you."

"Fire away."

"You know Jacqui well. Do you think she would ever deceive me?"

"Never in a million years. She's been your friend for ever hasn't she? She may be dippy and she may be a sex addict but as for being faithful to you I would have thought one hundred percent. Why do you ask?"

Charlie told him about the mysterious text and her fear that she had shared the hiding place of the Sphinx code.

"Well, I can't imagine she would give it away, but you were taking a chance just burying it like that, especially as you now know you have been followed. You may well have been seen."

"Oh, God, you're right. Oh, Andy, what shall I do?"

"To put your mind at rest why don't we go over to the island and fetch it. I'll call Jac and tell her we'll be late."

"Yes, yes let's do that, otherwise I won't have a minute's peace. What was I thinking of?"

They quickly picked up their bags.

"OK, then we'll get a trip to Abu Simbel arranged. I have to meet this Mohammad chap yet, just saw him briefly when I arrived. Fancy Jac falling for an Egyptian."

He sang a chorus of 'Walk Like an Egyptian' by The Bangles as they left the hotel hand in hand. Charlie felt a little more relaxed with him beside her. Life felt good again.

Just one more hurdle – find that paper.

64

It didn't take long to hire a small motor boat with a boatman and in minutes they reached the island. Charlie ran up the steps to the tree where she and Jacqui had rested.

"Oh God no! It's gone." The sandy soil was churned up and there was no sign of even the smallest shred of paper.

"That's it! Either she's taken it or someone saw us. I can't believe it; it really must have been her." Charlie turned to Andy with tears in her eyes. "She's my dearest friend. How could she?"

Andy shrugged. "It certainly doesn't look too good. If the crowd that the Garneesh bloke worked for had taken it they wouldn't have needed to kidnap you. Anyway no good crying." He passed her his handkerchief.

Charlie wiped her face as she clambered down the steps to the boat, completely deflated. "If it wasn't Jacqui then who?" she muttered as they got on the boat. The implications started to come home as she realised that the symbols could be in the hands of anyone, anyone with evil intentions.

65

"You know I'm amazed that Charlie didn't give in to that evil f**ker. I saw torture instruments in that room and he's much stronger than her. He's a master of the dark arts, a black magician, apart from everything else."

Joseph sipped his coffee and shook his head. He and Hakim were sitting in the bar of the cruise boat waiting for the others, sharing a pot of Egyptian coffee served in dainty decorated glasses.

"And you, how come he managed to overpower you? You, the regimental boxing champion. 1988 wasn't it? Heaven fall upon you! I would never have believed it; he must have used some spell on you."

Hakim grimaced. "Well, I don't know – it all happened so quickly. Maybe I've lost my touch. Well, to be honest it was the Charlie lady who did the most damage!"

"What do you mean, Charlie did it?"

"Well it was her that hit me on the head with the rock." He rubbed his head.

Joseph laughed. "By the Gods, Hakim, you were felled by a girl! You are mihakkah, you've had it old man. Oh my, wait till I tell the troop." He started to giggle and Hakim glowered at him.

"Shut up, don't you dare tell, you old goat. I've got some stories I could tell about you."

66

Jacqui and Mohammad were waiting for Andy and Charlie in the next bar. Jacqui looked up concerned as she saw Charlie's pure white face and her eyes blazing like black coals.

"Hey, Chas, you look terrible. Are you still feeling the effects of yesterday?"

"No, no I'm fine. But I've got to speak to you." She pulled Jacqui to one side. "Jac, I'm so angry I can hardly speak." Her voice wavered.

Jacqui put out a hand to touch her arm but Charlie flinched and drew away. "Hey, babe, what is it. Spit it out," Jac said.

"Did you or did you not dig up the bits of paper we buried on the Isis Island?"

"What? What?" Jacqui jumped up, her voice close to a shout. "No. I certainly did not, how could you think I would? Good God, Charlie, don't you know me better than that?"

"Well, I thought I did, but the paper has gone, disappeared, vanished. Once I realised how important it is I got cold feet about leaving it there so Andy took me back to find it. The stone's been moved and the paper has gone."

"Well, I most certainly didn't take it. Bloody hell! What made you think it was me?" Jacqui's face glowed red.

"Well, I picked up your phone by mistake and there was a message about you meeting someone and bringing something for money."

"That was a secret. Sam asked me to buy a gold pendant for his girlfriend. I'd told him of a gold shop in the souk that Mohammad had taken me to. They give a special discount to the tour guides but we have to keep it secret else the whole boat would want a discount. I said I would buy it for him if he gave me the money. It's a cartouche with his girlfriend's name engraved on it in hieroglyphics. I bought one for Mohammad too as a goodbye present."

She picked up her bag. "Here's the one I bought for Mohammad." Jac opened a black velvet box and showed her a gold pendant with hieroglyphics on one side, on the reverse a letter J and a letter M entwined. "I was going to pick it up for Sam last night but, of course, I didn't get there – too busy rescuing you."

Charlie blushed. "Oh, but that's beautiful, Jac. Oh dear, I've made a terrible mistake. Will you ever forgive me?" Charlie had tears in her eyes now.

She sat heavily in one of the chairs and put her head in her hands, the tension of the last few days poured out of her as she sobbed.

Jacqui put away the box and stepped over to her friend and took her in her arms. "There, there, sweetie, don't cry, you've been under so much pressure I'm not surprised you've lost it a little."

"A little!" Charlie looked up at her friend from behind the handkerchief. "How could I even have thought it was you. I've lost it big time. I'm so, so sorry, darling." She hugged Jacqui tight. Jacqui rubbed her back and gradually Charlie calmed down.

"So, if Jacqui didn't take it then who did?" asked Andy.

"One of those watchers maybe. Oh God, I've been so stupid I never should have left it there. I feel as though I have failed before I've even started."

Jacqui put her arm around her again. "This just goes to prove just how important these symbols are. I wonder if those guys have already got into the Sphinx."

"Probably, it's probably all over now." Charlie wiped her eyes. "Sorry to be such a wimp but I guess the tension of the last few days is just coming out now. I hate being beaten and I feel as though I have lost now – and the stakes are so high." She sighed.

Andy stood up. "Well it's definitely time to find Joseph and let him give us the lowdown on what this is all about."

"Let me tidy myself up first." Charlie slipped off to the ladies while the others mulled over the events and tried to make some sense of what had been happening. Charlie came back and dejectedly they trooped into the next bar where they had agreed to meet up with Joseph and Hakim.

"Ah, here they are." Joseph jumped up to greet them as they arrived next door. Hakim pulled up extra chairs and called a waiter. "What do you want to drink?"

Charlie came up to Hakim, with a rueful look. "I am so, so sorry, Hakim. I gather you were there to help me and I hit you! I was scared that I'd killed you. I'm delighted that you survived. I feel so awful, fancy attacking you like that. How do you feel now?"

"I am OK, no problems. Thank you." He gave her a full smile and they clasped hands.

Charlie hugged him. "Thank God for that."

Muffled by her hair he replied quietly, "Yes and thanks be to Allah, you are safe too. What a dreadful time."

Joseph pushed his friend in the arm. "He's, as you say, a tough nut to crack." They moved tables and chairs together and settled down.

Jacqui sat with her hands entwined with Mohammad. "I've brought Charlie up to date with who you are, Joseph, dear. I still feel bad that we thought you, Malik and Hakim were baddies and… "

"Yes," Charlie interrupted looking at Joseph. "I'm really sorry for all the trouble I've caused."

"My dear, we are just so happy that you are safe. By the way Hakim has been watching you since you arrived in Egypt. He was on the bank at Luxor – you saw a small stage act we put on for the other watchers, those turkeys working for the London crowd. They had begun to suspect us. To fool them we wanted to appear as enemies of each other – which is why we staged the fight in Luxor. I also acted out the helpless old man to put them off the scent as it were.

"Hakim tried to warn you about Garneesh in the Temple at Edfu but he came back too soon and he also came to your cabin one night. He was impressed by your fighting skills. Have you ever been in the army, Charlie, you surely do know how to pack a punch!" He laughed.

"Oh, God I'm so sorry, I thought he was trying to abduct me!"

Joseph leant over and took Charlie's hand. "By the way you look upset, have you been crying, dear one? Is it the effects of that awful man kidnapping you?"

"No, no. I've more or less recovered from that thank you Joseph. But no, I've done something incredibly stupid. I copied down a secret code, a chant, a sort of magical spell that I had in a dream… "

Joseph interrupted. "Yes, yes I know about your dream and code, Jacqui told me yesterday."

Charlie shared her fears about the missing code. "I should have destroyed it." She looked into Joseph's eyes, remorse and guilt all over her face.

Joseph stood up and pulled out an envelope from his back pocket and handed it to her. "Is this what you are missing?" he asked, smiling at her.

She took the envelope and with her hands shaking opened it. "Oh, thank God. Yes this is it. How did you get it?" She let out a huge sigh and collapsed back in her chair with relief.

"Master sleuth, your stalker, Hakim, was on the island checking on you and when he saw you going through your ritual he guessed it was something important. Anyway, you can thank him."

Charlie jumped up and pulled Hakim into her arms for a huge hug. "I've so much to thank you for, Hakim. God you've saved my life again!"

Hakim looked embarrassed and extricated himself from her clutches. "Oh, it's OK, Miss Charlie, happy to help you."

Joseph slurped his coffee. "Be careful, Miss Charlie, he's not had a woman for five years, don't get too close to him!" Hakim blushed again. "We were just talking about your experience with that Garneesh, donkey. How come you didn't give in to him and his interrogation; he's considered quite a master at it you know. How did you manage to stop him getting what he wanted?"

"Oh, that's easy," she laughed. "To be honest I was scared witless at the beginning then I just felt determined not to let the bastard win. I kept thinking of my nan, Miranda. She is so strong and just thinking of her helped. I also thought about my life as Khamet and the symbols that I have to find – I realised that if he was so desperate to get them from me, then they must be something very special. He actually did me a favour because by being so passionate about finding the symbols himself and taking such risks to get them from me he really cleared away all my doubts about their importance. It just strengthened my resolve to follow my vow to bring them back. And I promise you I didn't tell him anything."

Joseph put his hand on her arm. "Well done, young lady, well done. It's essential that you share this information with no-one. It's been kept a secret for hundreds if not thousands of years and it needs to be kept that way for a while longer. By the way may I suggest we burn that paper now." He pointed to the envelope sitting on the coffee table in front of Charlie.

"Good idea," Andy said. "Pass me the ashtray; I'll do it right now." He pulled a lighter from his pocket and taking the small fragments of paper he set them alight. They ordered more coffee while Andy burnt every scrap of paper.

"It's so frustrating to have had all those dreams or whatever they were. Nan calls them past life recalls, and yet I can't remember what the symbols look like." She sat up very straight pulling in her resolve. "You know I think the only way forward is for me to go to Cairo and visit the Sphinx and try the chant and see if the paw moves then I can get into that underground room and find them, where I left them as Khamet." Charlie turned towards Joseph and held his hand. "What do you think Joseph? Do you think you could pull some strings to get me close to the Sphinx?"

"Well, my dear. I think that will be quite difficult. The authorities are very sticky now about visitors going into the Pyramids at night, entering these sacred places without official attendants etc. But I will see what I can do, I'll call Ali. I shall be seriously in his debt now; I've just about used up all my favours with him! Anyway I think it's probably your best chance now. Leave it with me."

They sat for a few minutes drinking their coffees quietly with their own thoughts.

Charlie sighed. "At least I can share all this with you guys now." She looked around at them and smiled. "I owe you all big time. Especially Andy."

She turned to Joseph. "I've one more favour to ask from you, Joseph. We have a couple of days before we return to Luxor and Cairo and Andy would love to go to Abu Simbel. I believe we need a permit if we wish to drive there. Is there anything you can do?"

Jacqui turned to Mohammad. "Oooh, that's a good idea. Let's go as well, shall we? I would love to go with you. It's a very special place. Could we take your car?"

Mohammad smiled. "Well, for sure, but I am concerned about the permit, it's not easy to get one."

"Don't worry I can arrange it. You have to bring passports with you, that's all. I'll get a permit organised, I will, how you say, pull some strings," Joseph squeezed Charlie's hand.

"Watch out, Charlie. You're too old for her, Joseph," Andy laughed.

"Oh it's never too late to try," Joseph chuckled and twinkled at her.

Mohammad slipped off to fetch his car and Joseph made a call to organise the permit, then turned towards Andy. "By the way, Andy, all this is not New Age nonsense. There are many individuals on Earth at this time – specially chosen to come and help the world shift into a new age of consciousness."

"God, you sound like my grandmother now!" Charlie laughed.

"Well it's true. We are the Guardians of the Sacred Knowledge that includes the symbols. But it is not our job to bring it to those who need it. There are people here, people like you, Charlie, who need to wake up first. They then in turn will wake up the rest of us. These pioneers have missions to teach people that they are more powerful than they think. They are here to connect to their spiritual powers. Then when they have made that connection they can show and teach others – like making ripples. Many of these movers and shakers are already awake – you will know some by name for they will be in the forefront of our society as leaders, writers, innovators, spiritual leaders. Others will be working away quietly teaching the benefits of love rather than hate, living their lives as role models for others to copy."

He paused and sipped his coffee and then turned full on to Charlie. "Charlie, when you get these symbols out there to the world there will be many who will use them to activate their forgotten and hidden powers; you could call them magical powers as they will allow people to do things they would never have dreamt possible. This is the beginning of a very special time for mankind that has been prophesised for centuries. It is the New Dawn, the beginning of a great new spiritual age, a time of individuals accepting their personal power and reconnecting to spirit and will eventually replace the era we are now in – the era of materialism."

"Hey, yeah, my grandmother, Miranda, has often talked about this. She must be one of the pioneers you referred to. I never thought I would be one too." Charlie grinned at Joseph. "So is this New Dawn just about beginning?"

"Yes. About now, the shift started in 2012. For centuries there has been dominance by religions, the ruling aristocracy and then social leaders. This has knocked all belief in personal power out of people. In the old days and the Ancient Egyptian times, similarly for the Mayans, Aztecs and so on, it was the Priesthood who had the power and they certainly didn't want the ordinary man to have it too." Joseph shrugged and opened his hands.

"There is one particular group who are working to stop this happening, a Society, I started to tell Jacqui about them. They are a group of influential businessmen, members of the aristocracy who call themselves the Society of Ammonites. They are based in London, although they have members in most countries, and they are all set to prevent any power getting to the world. Same old story, the few desire to dominate the masses. Those men who attacked us at the farm were recruited by that crowd. Also Garneesh was employed by them. He *is* a doctor, by the way, but he's been locked into the Society since his university days. He had an affair with the daughter of a certain Lord, and they got him in their clutches by paying for all his university fees and supporting him in London. In return he had to work for them from time to time. As you now know, he's a nasty piece of work and not averse to seducing his clients, many of them rich women who fall for his charms. He has a practice in Knightsbridge in London and in Kuala Lumpur, Malaysia. Cosmetic surgery is lucrative and he supplements his income with seduction, blackmail and the odd job for the Society. Also, he's a master of the dark arts, trained by his grandmother in Malaysia. He'll do anything for money."

Charlie shuddered. "He's certainly a master of evil. What a shame, he could be such a great guy. I suppose in a way he really compromised himself when he got mixed up with the Society. He told me he came from an incredibly poor family and was bullied because of it. I suppose it left him vulnerable to being seduced by money."

"Yes, they paid him well, but he got side-tracked and greedy and he sought the power of the symbols for his own use."

"Well I'm now determined to follow this through. I will definitely go to Cairo and see if I can get inside the Sphinx. I really must get the symbols."

"It's essential that you do. They have been lost for far too long. They are really needed now, really needed." Joseph nodded gently to himself.

Andy had been sitting frowning as he listened to Joseph. He had a question of his own. "Joseph, Charlie, I was wondering, do you think that Al Qaeda are some part of this? They seem to me similar to the dark forces that Charlie's been telling me were around in Ancient Egypt."

Joseph turned to Andy and looked at him long and hard, thinking about the question. "I don't know. But I think you could be right. The dark priests in the past were fanatical and they also thought nothing of killing people for their cause. They were desperate to take over power and force the people to do things their way. So you are most probably right."

"Yes, yes, I can see the connection." Andy continued to frown and sat back deep in thought.

"One last thing, Joseph. You mentioned Garneesh being a black magician. Don't they use symbols too? Won't people wonder if the symbols are evil? Nan told me that the swastika was a powerful symbol for good used by Hindus and Buddhists, she saw it painted all over buildings in Tibet to keep them safe," Charlie asked.

"The symbols that you are seeking were hidden to save them being perverted. They work with the combined energies of the user and their positive intentions. They lose their power otherwise."

Andy stood up. "Time to get ready for our day trip now, Charlie, we can discuss all this on the way."

Charlie leant forward and took Joseph by the hand. "Thanks, Joseph, thanks so much for your wisdom, your help and your friends too. Please thank little Malik, he was so brave, fancy just jumping on that man's back like that, you have a tough family, Joseph." She stood up and gave each of the men a hug. "I'll keep in touch and let you know how we get on."

She got out a notebook from her bag. "Give me your numbers and email addresses. Do you have Facebook?"

"No, my dear, it's a bit beyond the old soldier." Joseph laughed.

Charlie smiled. "OK, I will text you."

"Take care, precious one. Don't forget to keep in touch. I shall be thinking of you."

One of the boat crew ran up holding an envelope for Joseph. "Aha, the permit, good. This will be a good trip, but please listen to me, you must all take care that road is not really at all secure."

Mohammad arrived back and picked up the permit. "I'll take care of them, Joseph, and we have the demon fighter Andy with us, we'll be fine."

They said their goodbyes and the four took themselves off to the quay and Mohammad's car – an old Mercedes that looked like it owed its owner nothing. Mohammad introduced them to the driver, Moktar. Mohammad got in the front and Andy climbed into the back with the girls.

Mohammad opened the envelope that Joseph had handed him. "I'm glad we've got Andy with us, I must say. This is the area where in the past the Brotherhood terrorised the locals and by attacking the tourist buses hoped to disrupt the tourist business here in Egypt."

"Is it dangerous then?" Jacqui asked.

"No, not really, since the uprising there hasn't been much activity in the area but the authorities cannot afford any bad publicity. Abu Simbel is one of our greatest attractions. I see the passes Joseph arranged for us say we are press! In case you are asked just say you are journalists for a travel magazine. When we stop keep your eyes open and don't wander too far from the car."

"OK, and thanks, Mohammad," they called from the back.

"Hey this is exciting. Did we bring any food for lunch?" asked Jacqui, "and more to the point have we anything to drink?"

"Well, your favourite tour guide hasn't let you down, how could I?" Mohammad laughed and pulled up his backpack. "I have in here a bottle of wine, an opener – of course, and the cook made us sandwiches and there are olives, pita and hummus. We'll stop for a picnic at Wadi El Nil." For this he got a round of applause.

They started off, soon leaving the town of Aswan and the fertile area around the Nile.

"Tell us about this place Abu Simbel, Mohammad," Andy asked. "I know it was moved bit by bit because of the threat of flooding at the time the Dam was built – I'm sure I read somewhere it cost eighty mill US, but who is this guy Ramses, his name crops up all over?"

Mohammad stepped into tour guide mode. "Well, Ramses the Second built this for his favourite wife Nefertari… "

Charlie yawned, her past twenty-four hours catching up with her and she and Jacqui snuggled down in the back; they both fell asleep on Andy's shoulders.

He tapped Mohammad on the shoulder. "It's OK, Mohammad. Carry on I'm interested in the history but I think the girls are done in."

"One pharaoh story too many," Charlie whispered and fell asleep.

67

"Jared Mustof?"

"Yes."

"The meeting will be at the Lansdowne Club, Mayfair. We have a room booked; check at reception. Be there at two p.m. sharp. Only you, none of your men." Lord Dennington's secretary put down the phone.

Jared left his desk and walked to the window and looked out over London. A grey day, the town was quiet. He hated Sundays – too quiet, no action. He looked at his watch, two hours to go.

He pulled out his Blackberry and hit a key. "Binwani, how many men can I get into action in the next twenty-four hours into Egypt, apart from the two new ones already assigned in Aswan?" He listened to the response.

"Just tell them it's an anti-capitalist job, sell them the idea that they're doing it for the cause. What Arms?"

There was a pause on the other end of the line.

"Good, right, we're going to wrap this up and I can't have any more bungling. I'm meeting the chief in two hours and I'll have my arse wiped all over the carpet as it is, so I need a good plan. How are you keeping tabs on the girl and that motley crew she's met up with?"

"Did you say phone? Christ! Would have thought that ex forces guy would have tumbled that one by now. Hey ho."

Another pause.

"The line is really rough, did you say Abu Dhabi?"

"Oh, oh, where the hell is that?"

"OK, see if this Brotherhood crowd can sort them out there then. Good, but put the backup plan into action anyway, can't take any chances now." He ended the call.

Good. Binwani would sort it, he has all the connections.

He took his jacket off the back of the chair and left the room.

Time for lunch then to face the music.

68

Moktar drove the old Mercedes into the parking lot near the temple site. Andy and the girls had slept through most of the three hundred kilometre journey, catching up on lost sleep, just stopping for a short break to eat at Wadi El Nil – not quite the romantic oasis they had hoped for. Mohammad had handled the two road blocks and with a transfer of small notes and after a lot of arm waving they had been allowed through.

Mohammad looked at his watch. "We have two hours till they close at five, just enough time to explore the site."

He led them to a monument to love, Egypt's equivalent of the Taj Mahal. He was in his element. "Did you know this is now a World Heritage site." Mohammad was in full flow and the others peered up at the huge statues of Ramses guarding the temple entrance.

Charlie turned to Jacqui. "Jac, I do hope I don't have another turn here. This place is so isolated and I still feel exhausted."

"Well, just tell them upstairs that you have no intention of doing anything and you just want to be a tourist for the day. Your nan was telling me that she speaks to her spirit guides every day and gives them instructions."

"Oh, sure, she does that, but I always thought she was a nutter, now it's me that's talking to disembodied beings. It must be in the genes!"

"I'm going to go back to the temple he built for his wife, that's so romantic. I'll see you in a mo." Jacqui wandered off.

Andy, Charlie and Mohammad entered the Great Temple and walked through the enormous hallway filled with pillars and rock carvings.

"Twice a year at sunrise the sun shines directly onto these statues of Ramses, Ra and Amun, once on the anniversary of the temple being built and once on his birthday." Mohammad continued with his guided tour.

Deeper into the complex a shadowy figure nodded to one of the many Arab tourists that were wending their way through the site. The two of them had a short conversation then left. They walked purposefully but without attracting notice and made their way to the entrance of the smaller temple nearby. Here four tall statues of Ramses and two of his queen stared out over Lake Nasser, way into the distance far above their heads.

The two men stood to the side of the temple and watched; their eyes searching the tourists as they sought out their target. Eventually they found her in a corner leaning against a pillar by the Holy of Holies where the goddess Hathor held the sacred energies.

Jacqui was oblivious of their interest. She held up her guidebook and read out loud the words written by Ramses about his favourite wife.

"For whose sake the very sun doeth shine." She looked up at the statue again, her eyes shining, overwhelmed by the idea of such remarkable love.

Two middle aged English women stood next to her; they too were impressed by the act of devotion. "How amazing to have a statue put up by the man you love, how romantic. Did you ever visit the Taj Mahal? That is the most extraordinary monument of love too. Oh, well, Jane, maybe one day, you never know, we might meet a man who cares enough."

"Most my old man ever gave me was a take-away Chinese on a Saturday night." The women laughed.

The watchers whispered to each other again.

The crowds were thinning now as it was getting close to closing time for the complex. The women moved away from Jacqui's side and wandered off.

She stood alone. Lost in her thoughts she continued to gaze at the face of the Hathor, the goddess of love and beauty. The men moved behind the nearest pillar. One by one they edged closer and closer.

69

Mohammad stopped his discourse and looked around. "Where's Jacqui?"

"She wanted to spend more time in Nefertari's temple. She was fascinated by the thought that a man would build something so magnificent for his wife. This might be a total change of heart by her about men." Charlie laughed. "I never thought the day would come, but who knows."

Andy frowned. "I'm not sure it's a good idea for us to split up."

"Oh, it's fine here," said Mohammad. "There's a lot of police and army presence to protect the tourists."

"OK, you're probably right." Andy looked at his watch. "Anyway, why don't we go and join her. We've only got half an hour left here." He ran his fingers through his short dark hair, not entirely convinced and his instincts were putting him onto high alert.

* * *

Jacqui stood stock still staring at the statue as she absorbed the realisation that love was a reality, a reality that she too was now experiencing. She felt her old beliefs crumbling and dissolving. She sensed that she could now dare to let go her entrenched belief, that love and sex were one, a belief that had destroyed every relationship she had experienced with men so far. She felt tears on her cheeks. Suddenly, she became aware of time. She looked down at her watch. Soon time to go. She felt an overwhelming desire to find Mohammad and share her new found feelings.

The men moved towards her, in the open now. They were within twenty yards and closing in. As she moved towards the entrance they walked faster to cut her off. They were within grabbing distance now. Suddenly she began to run. They too ran, gaining on her.

A dark figure stepped into the entrance of the temple. She let out a cry and hurled herself into Mohammad's arms, oblivious of the danger she had missed by a few seconds.

The men cursed and walked away.

Charlie and Andy stepped up beside Mohammad. Charlie smiled. "We thought we had lost you to the goddess there for a moment, Jacqui. We could see you in the distance – we called you but you seemed lost in another world."

"Well this time it wasn't another dimension just a rosy glow of the love that this king had for his queen. That's the sort of love I want," she squeezed Mohammad's hand.

He looked down at her and a huge smile spread across his face. He sighed and holding her hand tightly they slowly meandered their way through the temple and out to see the long shadows stretching down to the lake as the sun began to slip down and settle for the night.

Jacqui waved her guidebook at Mohammad. "They have a sound and light show here tonight."

"We don't have time now, Habibe. We must start to get back before it gets too dark, the road is not really that great, we'll be navigating around potholes and all sorts. I should be happier if we went to the light show at Luxor in the Temples of Karnak tomorrow night, that one is quite spectacular."

A man in the shadows glared at them and made a phone call.

70

Mohammad and Andy ushered the girls along, trying to get some urgency into their meanderings. Mohammad urged them on. "Come, come, there is no time, we must get on the road."

"Sorry, guys, I need the loo before we start back," Jacqui said.

"Me too." The girls headed towards the toilets.

"For heaven's sake be quick, girls." Andy seemed really hassled and Charlie threw him a look.

"What's up, Andy, where's Mr Cool gone?"

"Sorry, sweet pea, I just feel we need to be on our way."

Andy and Mohammad also decided to use the men's facilities and they went off in deep discussion.

The two men watched the party split up. They looked at each other. "Donkey's ass, we had the wrong one. Quick."

The girls made their way across the car park. The men headed towards them. They were getting in touching distance. They were right behind them in front of the toilet block.

"Hey," a shout from a policeman brought them to a standstill. He walked over, swore and pushed them away. Unaware, the girls went inside. The men ran to their jeep and drove off fast into the evening light.

A few minutes later Andy gathered his small group together and urged them towards the car park and Mohammad's parked car. They found Moktar sleeping with the front seat pushed right back.

Mohammad roused him and sat in the front beside him. Andy and the girls took the back seats again. He leant across and put on the radio and picked up a station playing sultry Arabic music. The girls dozed in the back. Jacqui closed her eyes and smiled.

She sighed and turned to see Charlie sleeping snuggled up to Andy. The events of the last few days had taken all her energy.

Jacqui smiled again. Then she too slipped into dreams.

71

The countryside away from the river was desolate and there were few farms and little habitation. The road was virtually free of traffic; just a few local farmers in old pick-ups, bullock carts or leading donkeys. As they left the town even this traffic disappeared. It got darker and they could see little from the car.

Andy leaned forward and nudged Mohammad gently. He whispered, "I don't want to frighten the girls but I think we're being followed. There are a set of lights that have been more or less the same distance behind us for some time now."

"Yes, I was wondering about that too."

"Tell the driver to pull over for a minute." Andy peeled himself from Charlie's arms, got out and opened the passenger door. "Mohammad, I think I would feel happier riding shotgun. You get in the back with the girls. Be prepared to duck if I shout."

They swopped places quietly. The girls stirred but fell back to sleep as the car continued. They motored on for another half kilometre when suddenly a number of lights appeared ahead.

Mohammad's voice from the back woke the girls. "Looks like another road block, damnation, what sort of time is this to stop a car."

He shifted in his seat and Andy leaned over the seat. "Have you all the papers, Mohammad?"

"Sure, sure, it will be no problem." He pulled them onto his lap.

Andy shook the girls awake. "We should be all right but just be on guard."

They sat up, rubbed their faces and looked around at the scene; their car headlights shone on a line of oil drums blocking the road. Set back behind the barrier two dark jeeps were parked by the side of the road.

The driver drew up to the oil drum barrier that blocked the road and wound down the window on his side.

Andy whispered to Mohammad, "Tell Moktar to keep the engine running. Under no circumstances turn it off and keep the handbrake off. Be ready if I tell you to react. I don't know for sure but this doesn't feel good to me."

Mohammad passed on the message in a hiss of Arabic.

Two soldiers fully armed and carrying rifles sauntered up, leant over and spewed Arabic at the driver through the open window. He nodded his head. One of the men called to another two soldiers who had been waiting at the barrier.

"What do they want?" Andy whispered to Mohammad.

"They are asking him if we have a permit. But I don't like the feel of this, Andy. They don't seem quite right."

With that the first soldier jerked open the car door and pulled Moktar out, hoisting him out bodily and threw him to the ground. He lay there cowering and covering his face with his arm. The two of them then started to shout and rant at him. He shook his head vehemently as though denying some charge they were putting to him. Again the men shouted and swore at him. Again he shook his head. Then suddenly, without warning the second soldier pulled out a pistol and shot him in the chest.

The sound of the shot reverberated through the car. Charlie and Jacqui started screaming.

Andy shouted, "Everyone duck, down, down, down."

In an instant he scrambled over the gear lever and dropped into the driver's seat and pushed the car into reverse. He leant out and pulled shut the door. At that same time another set of headlights illuminated the scene as the car that had been following them pulled up with a screech of tyres and brakes. Three men leapt from this car and ducked behind it. Gun shots started to fill the desert air.

Mohammad shouted and pointed at the men behind the car. "Alhamdullela, thank God. Joseph and Hakim are here."

Andy changed to second gear and drove forward with his foot on the accelerator, the engine screaming in the low gear as they hurled towards the soldiers and the barrier. His unexpected approach caught them by surprise and he knocked two of them with the front of the car as he careered through oil drums and bodies. He then braked and swerved and turned around for another battering ram approach. Through the windscreen he saw one of the original soldiers fall, hit by a stream of bullets. Two others jumped down from the jeeps shooting at the second car and their attackers. One of the men hit by Andy's onslaught crawled away in the sand holding his leg that looked broken; the other limped off to the parked jeeps.

"Three to go," shouted Andy, "keep your heads down, right down."

He then drove fast towards the men crouching behind the oil drums, more shots were fired and just as he hit the drums a piercing scream came from behind Joseph's car.

Charlie screamed and lifted her head to see. "Oh, God, I think that's Joseph."

Mohammad and Jacqui pulled her back down. "Get down, get down," they shouted.

"But, I think Joseph's been hurt," she cried.

At that point the car slewed and the women fell on top of each other in the back.

In the gloom they saw one of the jeeps start up. It hurtled around the barricade, wheels spinning and sending out a stream of gravel and sand and head straight towards their car. They could see the grim face of the driver, gripping the steering wheel with a fierce determination. The two passengers were leaning out of the windows pointing their pistols towards them.

Andy immediately put his foot down and drove towards them, spinning the wheel at the last moment before collision, taking a U turn and driving back down the road they had travelled. The jeep swerved to avoid the impact then righted itself and gave chase.

Andy screamed, "Keep down, keep down."

Mohammad and the girls cowered in the back with their hands over their heads.

The car bounced and lurched over the potholes and bullets flew past. Crack, the side mirror took a direct hit and glass shattered and flew out as they sped on. Ahead the road sloped up as they mounted an embankment leading to a bridge over a dry river bed.

"Hold on," screamed Andy. He had his foot on the floor, pushing the old car to its limits. The jeep was twenty meters behind and the men spewed bullets at them out of the windows, their aim hindered by the bucking and bumping of the country road.

Crack. This time the rear window took a full blast. The bullet flew past Andy's head. "Bloody hell, close one," he muttered. Then he shouted, "HOLD ON TIGHT," and slewed the car down the embankment.

The driver of the following jeep took longer to react and was committed to the bridge. It drove over and the driver had to negotiate a three point turn to come back. Andy had jumped out of the car as soon as it stopped and from behind the bonnet he took up a shooting position. As the jeep returned over the bridge he had a good purchase on his pistol and aimed from a firm base. He shot out the tyres of the jeep, then pumped bullets into the windows. The jeep careered off the road and fell onto its side. After a few moments of quiet there was a huge explosion and the petrol tank caught fire.

Andy, running doubled over, approached the burning jeep. From the back of the car the girls heard two shots and they clung to each other in horror. Andy then ran back to the car, jumped in and quickly turned it around and flew back along the road to the barricade. He turned his head slightly to the back of the car. "Sorry, girls, but that was necessary. The odds were against us."

Within minutes they were back at the barricade. The car skidded sideways as Andy pulled on the handbrake and pumped the brakes. He jumped out, ducked and ran towards the other car. Halfway he paused and turned and shot at the one remaining attacker; he caught the man in the arm and his pistol went flying.

The second jeep that had been parked up suddenly appeared from the gloom of the night and two men jumped out but instead of joining the fire fight they bent down and picked up the injured soldiers. They ignored the bodies of those shot and drove off at great speed into the night. A hush came over the scene. The only sound the heavy breathing as everyone gathered themselves.

Andy ran firstly to check on Moktar. He felt his pulse in his neck and shook his head. Then quickly ran around the second car.

They shouted for Mohammad, "Quick, quick, Joseph's down."

Hakim knelt beside his friend giving rudimentary first aid. Joseph had been hit in his side, blood seeping out at an alarming rate. Malik with tears pouring down his face brought the car's first aid kit to his side.

Hakim pushed it away. "Nothing any good in there." He pulled off his own shirt and folded it into a pad which he held over the wound.

Charlie ran up. "Oh, Joseph, darling Joseph. You're hurt. Oh, Andy, what can we do?" She turned to Andy distraught and panicking.

Joseph smiled at her. His voice hoarse and rasping but still strong. "Calm down, pretty one. I shall be OK. It takes more than a bullet to put an old soldier down."

Mohammad was already on the phone, dialling 123 for an ambulance and 122 for the police. "We have to report this," he said. "This time we cannot cover up. I hope we get some sort of response; we are still half an hour from Aswan here. Let's pray Allah is merciful."

Joseph's voice was a little quieter now. "Tell the police they were terrorists. Don't tell them about anything else. Just say we were attacked as we made our way back from Abu Simbel. Least said the better to those donkeys." He slumped back down, the effort of speaking draining his energy.

Andy walked over to the body of the first victim of the shoot out. He bent over and looked through his pockets. He pulled out an ID card. "You don't look like a soldier to me, my lad," he said as he peered at the card. "Mohammad, what do you make of this?"

Mohammad walked over and took the document. "Well, he's Libyan for a start. That's about enough to get the authorities nervous."

Andy pulled out the man's mobile phone. "I think we'll take this one. There could be some interesting messages on this." He handed it to Mohammad. "See what you can pick up."

Mohammad listened to the last messages on the phone. Suddenly he lifted his hand to hush everyone. "By Allah, there's a call here about Charlie from someone called Binwani." He listened intently then replayed it again focused and intent on the message. "They planned to kill us. Allah be praised we stopped them. Allah be praised you were

242

here, Andy." He looked at Andy as though he had been struck. "This is really serious. This is so bad." He shook his head. "I don't believe this."

After a brief silence while they took in the news they all started speaking at once, their voices shrill from the shock of the attack and the realisation of what they were up against. The men did their best to help staunch Joseph's wound.

Sirens sounded in the distance. Hakim held up his hand. "Shush, shush, here they come. Leave the talking to me and Mohammad. You know nothing, you are shocked and you are innocent travel writers; just stick to that story."

Andy slipped the phone into his pocket.

The first vehicle on the scene was a bright orange Volkswagen ambulance.

"Thanks be to Allah," muttered Hakim. "This is good; one of their better vehicles."

When the back doors opened there was an impressive array of equipment from oxygen to emergency blood. The two man crew quickly began to cut through Joseph's shirt. This set off a series of oaths – strong Arabic oaths that cut through the air and brought a smile to all. "Hmar, you donkey, how much do you think I paid for this?" He scowled up at the young paramedic.

"Hey, you boy, have you passed your driving test?" He then laughed his great guffaw that brought out even greater smiles. Gently they lifted him to the stretcher and carried him to the ambulance. "Orange, why did they paint this wagon orange? I'm going to hell in a tangerine." His voice wavered.

They passed him an oxygen mask to assist his courageous heart as it pumped away and his blood seeped.

"Bye, Charlie, my sweet child," he called from the back of the ambulance. She jumped up and knelt beside him. Jacqui joined her.

Charlie took his hand. "Be strong, Joseph. We have to hear your tales of daring do, your wartime exploits, so much to still learn of you and from you."

"There's plenty of time for that, my dear. You are well looked after by your soldier. I hate to say this but he's more use to you than this old, one-eyed goat. He is a good man, a brave man. Listen to him, he will keep you safe. Now you have to leave." His voice muffled by the mask.

The attendants ushered them out. They stood at the bottom of the steps, Hakim, Andy, Mohammad, Jacqui and Malik, all exhausted, all deflated. Malik, Charlie and Jacqui with tears coursing down their faces. Mohammad chewed his lip. Hakim held his arms crossed over his heart silently praying and Andy looked grim.

Joseph with no more than a hoarse whisper had more to say. "Charlie, don't forget the New Dawn, you are the key to the New Dawn. Those symbols are the keys to a better life for all. Get yourself to the Sphinx immediately. Malik, if I die you get my pistol, Hakim if I die I will haunt you... "

Just as the doors of the ambulance were about to close Hakim turned to Andy and Mohammad. "I want to go with Joseph; I need to protect him in case those donkeys are after him. They may know he's a guardian. You two can look after Charlie, I must be there with Joseph. Malik stay with the others."

He jumped into the ambulance and after a few terse moments of debate with the attendants they closed the doors and the ambulance swept them away.

Charlie cried into Andy's shoulder. "Oh God, I hope he will be all right. I love that man. I feel like I've known him all my life."

Jacqui put her arm around her friend. "Well, if he was around in your past life in Egypt I expect you are soulmates. Your nan says we often have the same bunch of people around each lifetime. That's why we feel we know someone when we meet. I think Mohammad and I are soulmates too don't we?" She looked at Mohammad who smiled and nodded.

Charlie put her arm around Jacqui and gave her a big hug. "Well, I know that you and I were definitely together before. Thank heavens you have been with me through all these ghastly experiences." She turned to Andy. "Thank you, for driving like a pervert – never thought I would say that but, your mad driving saved the day."

He smiled. "Not sure those guys who got shot will think the same. I wonder if their mates have taken them to a hospital – if they are who I think they are they may well just put a bullet in them."

Mohammad turned to Andy. "Who do you think they were? Local thieves?"

"No. The way they dispatched the driver so cold bloodedly like that, I reckon they are the Brotherhood."

Mohammad nodded. "I agree. Islamic Brotherhood bastards. No feelings. He broke into a string of curses."

Andy stood quietly for a moment. Then he looked hard at Mohammad. "Hell, we have to get out of here right now. The police will be here any minute and how are we going to explain this carnage? Let's go. Come on, girls. Get in the car. Quickly now."

He went to the back of the car and attempted to shut the boot that had flown up in the collision. After three attempts he looked at Mohammad. "Bloody thing."

Mohammad stepped up. "Don't be gentle with it, Andy. Look, like this. He lifted it to its maximum height and brought it down with a huge crash. It closed. "See, we treat our cars and our women rough over here."

He then opened the driver's door got in and turned the key. It started straight away.

Andy got in the back with Charlie and Jacqui sat next to Mohammad.

Malik ran over and leant into the car to shake their hands. "I take Joseph's car. I go to hospital now. Please, take care. Mr Andy, you look after Miss Charlie, she is very special. It is very important that you keep her safe."

He looked at Charlie, he frowned; his face took a serious set as his young brown fists clasped around her smooth, white hands. He looked into her deep brown eyes. "Joseph tell me you are very, very special."

"Bless you, dear Malik. You take care too."

Andy shouted across them. "Go now, Malik, quick we have to get away before the police arrive."

He ran back to the car that had suffered a few bullet hits but otherwise was unharmed.

Charlie called out of the window after him. "By the way, Malik. What made you follow us – I thought we'd said goodbye to you before?"

He turned. "Joseph. He felt it here," he touched his heart. "He thought you were in danger."

Charlie smiled. "Dear Joseph, my guardian angel."

Mohammad started the car and with a spin of wheels spraying grit and sand they turned towards Aswan.

Andy looked back and saw Malik's car safely behind them. He looked down at his hands. They were shaking. He took four deep breaths and dropped his shoulders. "God, that was a tight one."

Charlie looked rueful. "I'm a liability! But you were tremendous. Bless you." She took his hand and held it tight. The shaking stopped.

Jacqui put her hand on Mohammad's arm. She leant towards him and whispered, "You were tremendous too. I love you."

"Thank you, Habibe. I did nothing. But your words are like nectar to me, my dear. May Allah be praised that I found you. No one has touched my heart before. I am so lucky." He grabbed her hand and squeezed. Smiling, he let go and placed his hands firmly on the wheel as he focused on the dark road ahead.

In the back Charlie looked up at Andy. "Why do you look so grim, Ands?"

Andy was grinding his teeth and glaring out of the window. "I wish I'd got those bastards who got away. Wish I'd finished them off for good and all."

"Hey, babe, no need to be so violent. They're out of action, surely that's all that matters?"

"I'd be happier if they were dead." Andy looked fierce and stared out into the darkness. "They're nothing but scum," he muttered.

Charlie shivered. "Andy, babe, please, calm down. Come back."

He sighed and tore his eyes away from the murk and looked down at her. "Sorry, babe, I just get a bit fired up sometimes, you're right, it's over."

But after a few moments Charlie was sleeping on his shoulder and his eyes were again drawn to the dark and gloomy night, his eyes narrowed, his frown returned and his lips turned down. He looked down at his hands. They were shaking again. He felt a familiar tightness in his chest. He stared hard out into the darkness of the desert.

72

Andy organised room service the next morning. Charlie was sat curled up in a comfy chair sipping her orange juice. "I feel as though I have lived through a nightmare. I feel shaky inside, cold right through and it's not just the air con." She shivered. "I woke a couple of times in the night and I felt that I was going through it all again. I could hear the noise of the car crashing, the bullets and worst of all," she wiped tears from her face, "worst of all was seeing poor Joseph going off in that ambulance."

"I'll call Hakim. I'll find out how the old soldier's doing."

His call was answered immediately and he chatted with Hakim for a few minutes. He put the phone down and came over and took Charlie in his arms.

"It's not good, sweetie pie. He's in intensive care. They are not sure if he'll survive this one. Apparently he's been hit a few times in the past. They are going to operate this morning. Malik and Hakim are with him and his family are there too. There's not much we can do though, I'm afraid. Hakim will call us if there's any change."

Charlie sighed and shed a few more tears. "How did you cope with this sort of thing for all those years? Didn't it affect you, Andy? God I'm finding this difficult."

Andy took her hands. "You take on an armour suiting after your first mate gets injured or killed and something inside starts to shut down. But you never really get over it."

248

"I guess it's just as well, you could become an automaton without feelings. But don't you get angry and frustrated?"

Andy stood up. "Yes." He looked down at his hands which were still trembling a little. "Yes, I do get angry." He shrugged his shoulders. "But let's talk about you now. What do you want to do next, where do you want to take this?"

Charlie clasped her arms around herself. "To be honest I feel a bit sick. I feel dreadful that Joseph has been hurt because of me. When I woke in the night I could see his face and I had time to think. Such a brave man and I feel the cause of all this bother. But what I did decide is that to give up now would be letting him down. So, although it's a long shot, I need to go to the Sphinx and see if I can get this chamber to open up. God knows how it would work and what I would do if does open. But, I'll worry about it when it happens."

"OK, if that's what you want to do. I know this is your call, your choice, but I personally think you should get back to England and forget this whole affair. It feels totally whacky to me and it seems that you have been in danger ever since you started messing with the occult."

Charlie glared at him. "I am not messing with the occult. I had a dream. I didn't ask for this to happen." She jumped up and started striding round the room. "It's not been my desire to be hounded by a pervert, kidnapped and tortured then chased over the desert by terrorists. Funnily enough, that wasn't my idea of a holiday." She shouted, "So get off my back. Either you are with me or against me."

She stormed into the bathroom and her angry voice echoed against the tiles. "I could do with some support here not mockery or cynicism." Anything else she said got lost in the sound of the shower.

"OK, OK. So we'll go directly to Cairo. Jacqui and Mohammad will be here soon and we can find out if she wants to go with us. I doubt that he'll be able to get away, he's got his job to do."

Andy got his laptop out of his travel bag and plugged it into the hotel system. He started trawling for plane times and a hotel to stay in Cairo.

Charlie came out of the bathroom wrapped in a towel and rubbing her hair dry with another. "Sorry, Andy. This isn't your fault, God you were the one that saved our lives yesterday. I know I'm a bit edgy about this and I might seem unreasonable but I feel very nervous and I do want to get this sorted. The sooner I get these symbols, the quicker I can get them out to the world and then maybe I won't have these ghastly people trying to kill me." She flopped onto the bed. "It's an awful strain having people trying to kill you, you know."

"Well, I certainly know how that feels," he said. "I can do the physical protection angle but I'm totally out of my depth with this spooky stuff."

He sat on the bed next to her and gave her a cuddle. She leant into his arms. "I feel safe when your arms are around me," she said.

The room phone rang. Andy picked up. "Good," he said, "we'll be down in a moment." He turned to Charlie. "Jac and Mohammad are downstairs."

Charlie jumped up and pulled some clothes out of her overnight bag. She put on a pair of lightweight jean cut offs and a white short sleeved blouse. She slipped into a pair of pumps and was ready to go.

Andy looked down at her and grimaced. "I'm sorry to keep on about the danger but it's real, sweet pea. You are going to be exposed in Cairo. That Binwani character will be chasing up on his men and I don't think for one moment they will pull back now. Not at all. In fact they will be all the more determined." His eyes grew dark. "And they will want revenge too."

73

"Mustof?"

"Yes."

"It's Binwani here. I have some bad news to pass you. The situation did not work as we desired."

"What do you mean? That you f**ked up?"

"Not me personally, you understand. The men sent to take out the Charlie Masters woman, well they got beaten by the soldier. Also the police turned up on the scene. But there is good news. They brought down Sayyid, Joseph Sayyid."

"But he was hardly a threat, you idiot, I heard he was ancient. A toothless old man." Jared's left eye began to twitch, a sure sign that the big man was upset.

"Bloody hell, Binwani, this is bad news. Lord D thinks this job is as good as done. He'll go out of his box when I tell him this news. This one is really personal to him. The girl getting those symbols or whatever they are really rattles his cage. I don't get it. She's not exactly wonder woman – she seems a frail little bitch. But he seems to think she's a major threat, to what I don't know. But it's his thing. He'll go mental." He continued with a string of profanities and stomped up and down his office. He stopped by the window and stared out at London.

Sensibly Binwani was silent on the other end of the line.

"Listen, keep a watch; deploy more men if you have to. His Lordship is throwing money at this. We don't know what she'll do now and we *need* to know. Come back to me when you find out their next plans. Follow her every move."

"OK but I've only got four men I can deploy now. The cell I used doesn't want to know. They say the man is too dangerous."

"I don't care how you do it but you sort this out right now!" he shouted, spittle everywhere. Eye twitch on overdrive.

"Now, Binwani, listen carefully. I will whisper in your shell-like what I will do to you personally if you fail again..." It took at least a minute to get his message across.

Binwani's stomach churned as he listened. Click.

74

The departure area of Aswan's Dawar airport was busy, noisy and hot despite a newly installed air conditioning system. The air was filled with the sound of crying of babies, a hubbub of farewells, flight announcements and a constant buzz from conversations in the cafes and bars.

He watched them wave to the tall Egyptian and disappear into security, then made his call. "They're on the 15.40 arriving 17.05."

"No, just the women and the Englishman." He clicked his phone closed and left the airport and joined the afternoon traffic.

75

It was late afternoon by the time they arrived in Cairo. The city was covered in a pall of pale grey-pink polluted haze and the traffic was dreadful as ever; noisy, impatient and chaotic. Andy had booked rooms at the Sofitel Le Sphinx Hotel in Alexandria Road with adjoining rooms and balconies with views of the Pyramids and Giza plateau site. The events of the previous days had left them exhausted and emotionally drained so they planned an early dinner and night in the hotel. Only Charlie had a spark of life. She repeated the chant continuously in her head like a mantra and every few minutes felt a quick thrill rush through her as she thought of the possibilities of the next day. Her head was full of thoughts about what might occur. The entrance to the Pyramid and Sphinx was closed by the time they arrived so they made plans for an early start the next day.

They sat in the bar having a drink before dinner.

"I hope you haven't got your hopes up too high, sweet pea," said Andy.

Jacqui nodded. "That's right; we don't want you cast down with disappointment if it doesn't work."

"Oh, I'll be OK, don't worry about me. I always bounce back. After what happened at the farm and on the desert road a bit of a let-down now won't deter me." Charlie sipped her wine and picked at the bowl of peanuts on the table. Andy and Jacqui looked at each other. They were not so sure.

"I wonder how Joseph is getting on. Has anyone heard from Hakim, since he had the operation?" Jacqui asked.

Neither of them had.

Andy looked thoughtful. "I've been wondering how on earth you are going to be able to do your chanting thing surrounded by tourists. That site is very popular and apparently, according to Mohammad, it's busy all day. Even when it opens at eight he said there will definitely be a number of people around. It doesn't seem the sort of place that you could perform a ritual or even use a chant without being heard or seen. And anyway what are you going to do if the paw does move and you can get inside. The authorities are bound to try and stop you. I just don't see how this is going to pan out. Sorry to be a damper, Babe, but it just doesn't seem practical to me."

"I must admit now we're getting close to it I have been wondering the same thing." Charlie fingered the paper napkin that had come with her drink.

Jacqui said, "It's a pity you can't get in there at night when there's no one around. Your nan told me that she'd stayed the night in the Pyramid once years ago. They bunged a handful of pounds to the local policeman and he let them in. They slept on the floor of the King's Chamber – can you imagine how spooky that would be."

"But I don't know any policemen to bung," Charlie said.

Just then Andy's phone rang. He stood up and as he answered the call he left the room.

Charlie said, "He always does that. Whenever he gets a call, wherever we are, he gets up and takes it outside."

"That's just polite isn't it? I can't bear those people who shout into their phones so that we can all hear their business, it's just so rude."

"Well, it makes me think he's got even more secrets," Charlie said.

Andy walked back into the bar shutting his phone. He looked serious and sat down. He took a large gulp of his drink and turned towards Charlie.

"That was Hakim. Joseph is hanging on and they are hopeful he will get better by tomorrow, seems he has developed some sort of a fever, maybe picked up an infection. I sent greetings and best wishes to him from all of us and Hakim says he's still upbeat and cheerful. And," he paused and pulled a face, "there is some, what you would consider, good news, although I'm not happy about it. Before we went to Abu Simbel Joseph asked his friend, Ali, the police chief here in Cairo, to help you get close to the Sphinx. He's just come back to them and agreed. He's given us the telephone number of a local officer who can help us, but we will have to go at night, after the last Son et Lumiere session and when the tourists have left the site and the grounds. Apparently it's quite quiet around about here at night, there's not much going on in the evenings apart from the light show so we should be able to do this without being disturbed."

"Oh, that's brilliant, well done, Joseph, again." Charlie was all smiles.

Andy frowned. "As I said, I'm not keen on the idea at all – I know how these 'undercover'," he flicked his fingers to emphasise the quotes, "situations can go wrong. I also think we are still being watched. We will be sitting ducks creeping around by torchlight alone on the site in the middle of the night."

"Oh, but Andy, this is a perfect solution. I feel immensely relieved as I won't have to do this in full view of the public and if anything does occur we can recover the symbols without being seen. You will just have to be extra vigilant and play your minder role for me. I like the idea of you being my bodyguard," she grinned. She was really getting hyped up now. "Oh, this is so exciting, don't you think so Jac?" She turned to her friend for confirmation.

Jacqui grinned back. "You know me I'm always up for fun and games, sounds a great scheme to me and, as you say, Andy, we trust you to watch out for us."

"You girls are one hell of a responsibility. I would rather be guarding the President of the US than you right now." But he did relax and smile.

"I presume this police officer who is going to let us in will hang around while we are there, I can get him to keep watch too." She put her arm around Andy. "Sorry, Andy, I know you are worried for me."

"Well, yes, these are dangerous men that we are up against. Anyway, let me ring this guy. Are you OK for tonight if he can do it? The sooner the better as far as I'm concerned."

Jackie and Charlie nodded. "Yes please. Let's do it," Charlie said.

Andy stood up and went outside to make the call.

Charlie turned to Jacqui. "He's really quite cross about this, I've never seen him so rattled. I suppose I've caused a lot of trouble to a lot of people, but you know when you just have to do something you won't let anything stop you. Well, that's how I feel about this."

"You're like a woman with a mission. In a way I suppose you really are. Let's have another drink, that'll help soothe the nerves." She called over the waiter. "By the way you haven't mentioned Nan lately. Have you been in touch?" she asked.

"No, I didn't want to tell her about the farm drama and have her worrying about me. Then the attack on the road. She'd be out of her mind. But the odd thing is she hasn't been in touch with me either. Let me call her now."

She rang Miranda and sat and listened to the ring tone until the message system kicked in. "That's odd, there's no answer." Charlie looked at Jacqui. "I do hope she's OK. That's the second time I've rung and not got an answer."

76

Jared Mustof was angry. Actually he was furious. His eye was twitching beyond control now. He had some explaining to do. He stormed up and down his office, shouting at the walls, kicking the furniture. He picked up the phone several times before he gritted his teeth and actually made the call.

"Tracked a call from that McNab guy, the boyfriend. Bloody SAS or whatever – caused mayhem at the roadblock. The cell we used are furious, said we told them they were a soft target. I've got some sweet talking to do there and some serious backsheesh to hand out. Anyway our man on the spot found out they have been in touch with the police and it seems they are going to the Sphinx tonight. I've only got four men on the ground there now. My lot are going down like flies." He paused and listened. He closed his eyes in an attempt to keep the twitch under control. He screwed up his face as he listened to the cut glass aristocratic tongue lashing. Lord D also gave him a message for the operatives.

"Yes, your lordship. Will do. Yes, I have already told them… Yes, yes I will tell them again… Yes, I'll let you know when it's done. Cheers, your lordship. 'Night."

He slammed the phone on the desk and made a gesture into the night air and swore. "Patronising bastard, one day… one day… "

77

Andy woke Charlie and Jacqui at one forty five and following his recommendations they wore black trousers and T-shirts and both brought a fleece for the night time chill. The girls brought cameras, torches and water and Andy had a back pack holding what he called his bodyguard kit. They didn't like to ask what that was, but after the last two occasions when there had been action they had a pretty good guess. They walked through the sleeping hotel, crossed the sumptuous reception area into the gardens and arrived on the road outside the hotel with a few minutes to spare.

The moon was up and full. Cool silver light illuminated the hotel complex and gardens.

At twenty past a man arrived dressed in Diesel jeans, white shirt and smart leather jacket and he introduced himself as Sergeant Mustapha. He looked the girls up and down and smiled appreciatively. They made their introductions. He held Charlie's hand just a little too long for Andy's comfort.

"How's this going to work, Mustapha, how do we get in?"

He held up a bunch of keys. "I have taken the emergency keys from the station. We keep spares in case of fire or terrorist attack".

He pulled his eyes away from Charlie and directed his question at Andy. "Which part of the site do you wish to see?"

"The Sphinx," Andy answered.

"Aha, Abu el-Hol, The Father of Terror, that's what we Egyptians call it. Built by King Khafre. My father was guide for Department of Culture at the Pyramids for many, many years. I know area very well. Two brothers also work there today. I work in police. Good job, good pension."

"While we are there can you stand watch for us, please, Mustapha? The girls are a little bit scared that there may be a terrorist attack, they're a bit nervous." Charlie shot Andy a look and frowned.

But Mustapha didn't seem to think the request at all unusual; maybe he was used to nervous women. "I, myself, cannot enter. I will not know you if are in any trouble. You must be on your own. Me not responsible. But I stand outside and guard gate. No-one come at this time. All Egyptians sleeping or… " he winked at Andy and grinned, "having good time."

He gestured towards his car parked at the side of the road and the girls got into the back, Andy in the front. "It short drive." With crashing and grinding of gears he shot off down the road.

The fact that it was in the middle of the night didn't seem to faze Mustapha. He was full of life and, in Andy's view, far too jolly. He kept glancing in the mirror to get another glance at Charlie. She leant towards Andy and whispered in his ear, "Don't worry, sweetie, it's my blonde hair. I've been getting this attention the entire trip. I've had my fill of dark skinned men."

In minutes they drew up by the silent gates of the complex.

"Bags of atmosphere here," murmured Jacqui. And it was. They could make out the dim shapes of ancient buildings and, as they entered, they could see what looked like a graveyard off to the side. "Oh, my God, is that a cemetery?" Jacqui asked.

"Yes, Habibe, that is the Eastern Cemetery for the bodies of the workers who built the Great Cheops pyramid. Twenty thousand men build these pyramids. Over there the village where they lived," he widened his eyes and swept his hand around pointing out the village and the cemetery, "and died!"

"Why you want to see Sphinx in middle of night?" He directed his question at Andy again.

"We are writing a travel article for a magazine and want some special effect photographs. Egypt by night," he added lamely.

"You see the light show yet?" This police officer obviously doubled as tour guide.

"No, maybe tomorrow. So thank you, Mustapha. Where shall we meet up with you when we have finished?" He was now keen to get rid of him and beside him Charlie was hopping from foot to foot in her impatience to get going.

"Outside gate, I wait. You go through there," he said, pointing at the murky outline of a temple. He stood and watched them as they walked off, shaking his head he gave Charlie's backside one more appreciative glance and turned and left the complex.

"Thank God he's gone. He gives me the creeps," said Charlie. "The guidebook says you get the best view of the Sphinx by going through the Valley Temple, which must be this building here."

They walked through the pillars of the temple.

"Wow," she stopped short as she came through the other side of the temple and got her first full view of the object of her dream. The Sphinx with its body of a lion and face of a pharaoh, the ancient king Khafra, was illuminated by the soft light of the moon. She shivered and felt familiar whooshes run through her body.

"Here at last. Oh, I feel so nervous now," she said.

"Well, you go ahead and do your thing," said Andy, "and I'll go stand over there and keep watch."

"I'll come with you," said Jacqui following Andy. "I'm not supposed to hear this chant either."

They slipped away into the shadows leaving Charlie standing in front of the huge stone figure. She looked at the paw and sighed. It was at least fifty feet long.

How was that going to move?

She thought back to her dream and recalled that just a portion of the paw moved to disclose the steps down to the chamber below. She pulled herself together, no point in getting the heebie jeebies or doubts at this stage. She reminded herself that she had nothing to lose and everything to gain.

"This isn't about you," she said to herself. So, holding her chin up high she spoke out the chant clearly and succinctly.

"O poh ker ray men

O poh ker ray men

Ban di poh key

Ban di poh key

Bah lah so ray

Bah lah so ray"

She paused. No response. No shifting of paw, no movement at all. She closed her eyes. Maybe she didn't say it loud enough, in the dream she had used a huge voice. So she repeated the words using her deepest and strongest voice.

Nothing. No whooshy feelings, no past life recall or trance, nothing at all.

As she repeated the magical words for the third time she felt a slight tingling in her hands and thought she could hear a far distant throb of drums, but they were indistinct and soon passed. Again, no reaction from the huge statue. It continued to look impassively into the far distance.

She could feel her face burning. Her stomach was churning and head thumping, she felt sick. After all this to get nothing was a disaster.

Andy and Jacqui appeared at her side.

"Did you say the words, Chas?" Jacqui asked.

In a very small voice she answered, "Yes." Then burst into tears and sobbed onto her friend's shoulder.

Jacqui wrapped her arms around her. "There, there, it's OK. Obviously, it's not meant to happen."

Andy threw his eyes to the sky.

"Not meant to happen," he mimicked. "Come on let's go. I was against this from the get go. We've just exposed you to more danger here. The sooner we get back home the better." He walked ahead briskly. "We can talk about this back at the hotel. I have to pay off Mustapha, let's get out of here. I've just about had enough of all this woohoo nonsense; putting our lives at risk for a lot of non-existent symbols."

"God, sometimes I really hate him," whispered Charlie. "I don't think he ever believed this was going to work."

"Well, who knows, his lack of belief may have stopped it happening," said Jacqui. "Maybe you should come back on your own."

"No way, no way, absolutely not," Charlie shook herself free from Jacqui's arms. "That's it now. I've given it my best shot; I've suffered kidnap, as well as nearly being killed a couple of times. That is most definitely it. Now with Andy's sarcasm and cynical attitude I've had enough. I want to go home now."

She squared up her shoulders, wiped her eyes and her face took on a steely determined look. "I shall get back to living my life as it was before. I was beginning to believe in the spiritual way, the power of the symbols and all that. But now I've had it. Had it up to here," she glared fiercely at Jacqui and drew a hand under her chin. "Now where's Andy gone?"

"He went back to the gate. He was mad."

The moon went behind a cloud at that point and Charlie clutched Jacqui's arm as they stood alone in the darkness. "Get your torch out, Jacqui, it's so dark, I can't see a thing." The girls fumbled in their bags searching for their torches.

The peace of the quiet night was suddenly disturbed by a screech of tyres and a series of shots. Next an outburst of loud Egyptian profanities. Then a scream cut through the night. More shots.

"Oh, my God, what the hell was that?" Jacqui clutched Charlie in fear.

78

Andy had just arrived at the gate when the car roared around the corner and braked into a skid fifty yards in front of the entrance.

Mustapha had been leaning against the boundary wall smoking and he leapt to one side ducking down as he pulled out his Glock. Four men threw themselves from the car as it screeched across the tarmac. They fired at Mustapha and Andy as he came running up on the inside of the locked gate. Mustapha let out a torrent of Arabic profanities and fired back at the men as he moved to take cover.

Andy threw himself to the ground and grappled with his bag. He drew out a pistol with night sights and rolled into position and aimed through the bars at the gate. He immediately brought down one man and wounded another in the arm. The man let out a primal scream and ran back off into the night clutching his arm, blood spurting.

Mustapha shouted out to Andy. "Take cover." He threw the keys over the wall where they landed a few feet from where Andy lay.

The remaining two men were within feet of the gate. They ran forward shooting randomly into the night unable to see their opponents. They realised that they were obvious targets for the shooter at the gate and threw themselves by the wall on the opposite side to Mustapha. They crouched behind the small version of the Sphinx that guarded the site entrance and waited.

Andy screamed into the night. "Charlie, stay where you are. Don't speak and turn off your torches."

Thirty yards away the girls huddled behind a souvenir kiosk and switched off their torches. They held onto each other tightly.

Andy couldn't open the gate without becoming exposed. With their attackers still for a moment he started to crawl back behind the wall dragging his kit bag after him. Once there he got up and, bent double, ran further down the wall beyond the gunmen's position.

Mustapha peered out from the statue and let off a number of shots in the general direction of the men.

Andy again dug deep in his bag and pulled out a second pistol that he shoved into his waistband.

The night was filled with gunfire as Mustapha and the two men exchanged more shots.

Andy quietly stood up and looked up at the six foot wall, just visible in the gloom. He turned and walked ten yards and then ran full on at the wall and threw himself up, his feet gripping the rough stones and propelling him higher up as his hands grabbed a hold on the top of the wall. For a moment he hung there breathing deeply as he gathered his strength to pull himself up to the top. With muscles screaming and heart pounding he managed to pull himself onto the top of wall. The two men continued to crouch behind the second Sphinx and bullets ricocheted around them hitting the Sphinx, the wall and the gate portal.

Andy ducked as a stray bullet from Mustapha's pistol winged past his ear. He grinned.

Stupid bastard amateur cop.

He pulled out his two pistols and leapt down the six foot drop and fired as he landed. He caught them completely unprepared and both men went down in the stream of bullets. The men twitched then lay still, their blood pooling around their bodies on the pavement.

Silence.

Mustapha stood up and came toward Andy. Embraced him.

"Good shooting, partner. We gave those dogs a good beating, yes man. Thanks be to Allah."

Andy smiled. "Yes, and thanks to Mr Glock."

He opened the gate and ran back towards the girls.

"Where are you, Charlie?" he shouted as he peered for them in the darkness.

"Oh, Andy we're here," called Jacqui. They stepped out and Andy took them into his arms. Mustapha stepped up and joined in.

"It's OK, mate, they are fine." Andy peeled off the amorous arms of the policeman. "They are just fine thank you," he said more firmly and pulled him off the girls.

Mustapha was full of smiles. "I make sure the ladies are OK," he laughed.

The girls also laughed. The tension broken. They made their way back to the car. Mustapha waited till they were outside and locked the gate.

"I will call the station. I will disguise my voice and tell them I am a man walking my dog and heard shots. Must not say I am here. Let us get away, quickly now."

They all jumped into Mustapha's car.

"Thank you, Mustapha." Andy pulled out a bundle of notes and selected a few to hand to him.

"Those men were not from here. They look like terrorists, Al Qaeda scum!" he muttered.

Andy shrugged. He looked down at his hands. Still shaking a little. His adrenalin levels coming back down now.

Outside the hotel they thanked Mustapha and hurried into the building in silence. As they got to their floor, Andy's phone rang. He gestured Jacqui and Charlie to go on into their room. He stayed in the corridor to take the call.

He looked grave as he listened. "I am so sorry," he said. "I am so very, very sorry. Yes, of course I'll tell her." He closed his phone. With a deep sigh he followed the girls into the bedroom.

Charlie was sitting on the sofa, head down her disappointment tangible. Andy walked over and sat down on his haunches in front of her and took her hands. "Petal, I have some bad news for you. I am so sorry. That was Hakim. Joseph died of his wounds half an hour ago."

Her scream rent the air. She flew across the room and hurled herself onto her bed in floods of tears. Andy turned to Jacqui and shrugged his shoulders and sighed.

They knew there was nothing that they could say. Her grief was raw and her whole body shook with the sobs. "Oh, no, oh, no," was all she could say for some five minutes. Jacqui sat and soothed her hair. Andy went to the mini bar and poured whiskey for the girls and a brandy for himself.

Eventually, her heaving subsided and she sat up. Her face was wet and small tears continued to trickle down her cheeks. She looked so dejected it sent arrows into their hearts.

"It was my fault," she said. "None of this would have happened if I hadn't had this flight of fancy. Joseph would not have died if it wasn't for me. Can we go home? That's definitely it now. I want to get as far away from Egypt as I can."

79

Jared drove his car up the long gravel drive and parked outside in the large parking and turning area in front of the Queen Anne mansion. He looked around at the sloping lawns, the laid out flower beds, the swathes of colour in the herbaceous borders. A path led down to the river frontage. The house and grounds were magnificent. He turned to the girl in the passenger seat.

"This, my dear, is old money," he muttered. "Old money off the back of us worker ants and the bloody slave trade. And it's only his weekend cottage, lucky bugger."

The blonde giggled. "Oh my God, a cottage!"

Jared sighed. "No not really a cottage. Oh, forget it, stay here, don't leave the car I'll be a short while." He climbed out of the car as she tuned into Heart radio and settled back to listen.

A housekeeper met him at the door and led him through to the back garden where Lord Dennington sat at a garden table with a group of men. They all wore the establishment-at-ease uniform; button down T-shirts, loafers and chinos. He looked relaxed as he sprawled in his chair, calm and in total control.

"Come and join us, Jared. His host waved a welcoming hand to an empty seat beside him. He poured him a Pimms from the jug in front of him.

"This is the first day this year the weather's been good enough for us to enjoy the garden." He sounded almost jolly.

Jared frowned. *Why so pleasant today?*

"So let's decide where we go from here with Little Miss Charlie. Tell me exactly what happened at the farm, on the Abu Simbel road and at the Sphinx."

Jared took a sip and tried to relax. He wasn't fooled by the attractive scene and the cosy set up. Despite the smiles he could feel the menace. One wrong step, one mistake and he knew he'd be gone. He knew about menace, he knew about knife edge, he knew about fear, he spent his life putting others in this very spot.

He could feel the heat on his back as he recounted the best rendition of the events in Egypt that he could. He declared Garneesh as a traitor, self serving and disloyal to the cause. He trashed his name without a backward glance. He wrote off Binwani's men as dolts, amateurs, fumbling idiots.

"And the Sphinx, did she manage to find any of the symbols?" Lord D asked.

"No, nothing happened at all."

"Did they try to dig underneath it?"

"No. No they didn't dig. They did nothing. She was obviously upset."

"Our plan was to take her out at the site, what happened?" His steely look cut straight through even Mustof's tough exterior.

He swallowed. "Well, this is how it went down. I have never entirely trusted Binwani and his band of bloody terrorists. They are guns for hire and I'm never sure of the intelligence I get back from them. So I sent a man of me own over and bugged our friends' rooms and 'ad him keep watch. Binwani's blokes arrived but again totally bungled the attack. They are complete morons three out of the four of them were eliminated by the Scottish soldier boy. They 'ad a local copper helping them. My man reported that they all went back to the hotel and flew out the next day. From the bug in their room it would seem they had given up on the idea of getting the symbols. She wanted to go home and the boy soldier thought the whole thing a farce. We also picked up from his phone that the old Egyptian is dead. He was a key player in the whole affair. I think it's all going to die a death, me Lord."

"So you are confident that we have nothing to fear now, Jared, my son?" Lord D patted Jared on his knee. "Well that good news for me and good news for you."

He lit a cigar and blew the smoke overhead. He didn't offer one to Jared.

"You came close to the edge on this assignment, you know that don't you?" He looked hard at Jared. No smile. No warmth.

Jared nodded.

"Put one small team to watch that Jamieson guy, I don't trust him, by the way he's a naval man, SBS. And keep tabs on the granny's phone. That's all. You may go now. Marcus, pay him off and show him out."

Jared cleared his throat. "About the granny. I thought you wanted her taken out."

"No just tap her phone. I don't need unnecessary drama and the police all over the place. If they haven't got the symbols there's no need they are all as pathetic and useless as the rest of the common herd." He waved his cigar to indicate the masses. "Have you done something else stupid, you moron?"

"No. We had plans but not executed them. Only 'er phone."

"Well, that's very lucky for you then isn't it?" He looked down at Jared with a false smile.

Jared turned and walked away clenching his fists and gritting his teeth. He arrived back at the car and threw the package of money onto the back seat.

The blonde looked up at him. "Oh, honey you're hot, look you're sweating. You feel OK?"

"Shut up, you bitch. Let's get the hell out of here." He spun the wheel and sped out of the grounds.

80

Charlie curled her legs up on the sofa in Nan Miranda's cottage. She felt better than she had for days. It was good to be in familiar and comfortable surroundings again. Tabitha, black and fat walked in, made a circuit of the kitchen and jumped up and snuggled up to her.

"So what's next?" Miranda put a large mug of hot chocolate and a plate of freshly baked ginger biscuits on the side table.

"Well, I'm not sure. I go back to work tomorrow. I've been a wreck this last week. All I've done is cry a deluge of tears. I think I'm all cried out now and feel a bit stronger. When I first got back I had the most dreadful dreams – of the farm and that man, of the poor driver getting shot and of course, dear Joseph. I didn't know guilt could make you feel so dreadful. I have a constant ache inside and from time to time I get a sharp stabbing pain in my solar plexus, as though being pierced by a dagger. I'm now going through the 'if onlys'."

Miranda sat at the wooden kitchen table and sipped her own hot chocolate and munched a biscuit as she listened to her grandaughter's anguish. "Well, guilt and regret both hurt. Then you can add a layer of self hate and sprinkle it with self doubt and then a lashing of self pity!"

"You're right. I don't want to get onto the pity pot. All of this was my own making so I just need to pull myself together and get over it. I shall be fine once I get back into my work. A couple of my accounts are up for a new campaign so I'll have plenty to do for the next few months."

"How's Andy?" Miranda asked.

"Well he's back in UK but I've moved out from his place."

"What do you mean? You've finished with him? I thought you were a bit warmer to him after the dramas of Egypt."

"Well I was warming to him for sure, especially after he rescued me at the farm and he was very brave in the desert. But it's the way he speaks to me Nan, and his attitude."

Miranda frowned.

"As far as I'm concerned it's over." Charlie tossed her hair back, almost defiantly.

"Why?"

"Several reasons really. Although Garneesh was an absolute bastard, I absolutely loved the way he treated me when we were on the boat. He was sweet and attentive, something Andy never is."

"Yes, but that was just an act. You are comparing an evil phoney to a real man; a man with a few problems and maybe the odd dark secret for sure, but at least Andy is real."

"Yes, yes, I know but it's more than that. When I couldn't get the opening spell, or whatever it was to work I felt so stupid. I felt let down, I felt guilty about Joseph and I felt really low. It seemed that everything I had gone through was for nothing. And Andy just blew off at me. He was impatient and irritable all the time we were in Cairo. He just doesn't seem to have it in him to feel for me, to see what I want and need. He's so caught up with his own issues that he's... he's actually quite a selfish bastard." She stared defiantly at Miranda. Her face flushed red and her eyes blazing.

"Putting his life in danger to rescue and protect you hardly seems the actions of a selfish man, my dear."

"God I knew you would stand up for him, Nan."

Charlie stood up and walked to the window. "I know he was brave and I really appreciated all he did for me. But life is also about the day to day issues and the way he is with me in the ordinary times. Hopefully, there won't too many times when he has to play the White Knight or Action Man and rescue me as a damsel in distress. I want him to play out the Mr Nice Guy who is gentle and understanding and allows me to get close to him. And I don't honestly think he can do that."

She looked around at Miranda. She had tears in her eyes.

"Bless you, darling. Come here."

Miranda wrapped her arms around Charlie and gave her a long loving hug. She stroked her hair. "There, there. These are sad days." She too had tears in her eyes. She let her granddaughter go and they both wiped their eyes.

Miranda took their mugs over to the sink. "Do you think the danger is over now, Nan?"

"The worst of it should be, my dear. They know you haven't got the symbols and therefore you are not a threat. I am sure they have been keeping watch and once they realise you've given up they will slide off into the slime where they came from. But take care, my darling, you cannot be too careful."

"Yes, I will, Nan, dear." She walked up behind Miranda as she stood at the sink and wrapped her arms around her. "Thank you for being here for me. You always have been, bless you. Although, I don't want to go any further with this situation and I've abandoned the search for the symbols, what I have understood is that there is much more to this spiritual woohoo than I ever realised. When I was in that farm I felt such a strong presence of being protected and when I had those visions my fingers really did tingle from the energy. And the whooshes of energy or whatever it is that I had all through that trip were very real. I'm sorry to have dissed you over it in the past."

Miranda turned from the sink and held her hands. "Well, you were shut down, and for good reason. You probably won't remember this but when you were a little girl you were able to see and speak to angels. You would point them out to me and tell me their names and share your conversations with me. We spent a lot of time together angel spotting!"

"Oh, really, Nan, I don't remember that at all. Although, I do have memories of spending time with you and laughing a lot."

"Well, you lost your memory at the time of the car crash. That also left you with guilt, that you were in some way responsible for the accident," Miranda said.

"Yes, I get a sinking feeling in my stomach whenever I think of my parents and sometimes it feels as though my heart is being squeezed."

"Well, of course, I don't know exactly what happened that day, but I do know that you never mentioned angels again after the accident."

"Oh, Nan, how frustrating this must have been for you, watching me as I fumbled about in the dark!" Charlie said.

Miranda gave her a big hug and walked with her to the door. "That's fine, darling, I knew you'd wake up one day. Now, drive carefully and keep your car doors locked at all times. Your cards are still showing you need to take care. And don't forget to eat, you're looking far too thin."

"Well, that's one good thing to come out of it!" She smiled and got into her Audi TT. "The past catches up with us all the time really, doesn't it? I wonder if we ever escape it. Anyway, I must dash; see you, Nan, thanks for everything as always. Love you."

She put her foot down and drove off waving her arm out of the window.

Miranda shook her head, walked back into the kitchen and sat for a while at the table with her thoughts. Then she stood up, picked up her phone and called Andy. He didn't answer so she left a message. "Andy, can you come down to Brockenhurst and see me urgently?"

81

"I'm sorry to bother you, my dear," said Miranda giving Andy a hug and leading him into the kitchen. "What can I get you to drink?"

"A beer would be great thanks, Nan. I'll help myself." He went to the fridge and took a can of Speckled Hen from the supply she kept in just for him.

He sat spread legged on the sofa, both his physical and energy presence filling the small kitchen. Miranda was making a lemon meringue pie at the kitchen table. As she grated the lemons she looked over at him. "As you know, Charlie was here yesterday and I gather she has decided to split up with you."

"Yes, I just can't seem to be the person she wants me to be. She complains that I have too much armour on and am insensitive to her. Miranda, I'm not much good with feelings and this analysis of what people feel. I really try but I just don't get it, I don't understand it and I am out of my depth. But one thing I do know. I love her. I realised that at the farm. When I saw what that bastard was trying to do to her I have never felt anything like it in my life. I could have killed ten men with my bare hands I was so mad."

"What are you going to do now?" Miranda continued with her baking.

"Not sure really. In fact no idea. I feel gutted at the moment. The flat feels completely empty without her. You know, it's only now that I realise how much she really means to me. I thought I'd wait a bit and see if she would see me sometime when she's got over the trauma of that trip. S**t, I feel absolutely s**t. Sorry, Miranda, sorry." He put his head in his hands.

"You're not doing badly for someone who isn't in touch with his feelings, young man." Miranda smiled. "Best to back off for a while. She's still very upset about it all. By the way, does she know about the black ops?"

"Yes. I had to come clean as I had a bag of my ops gear with me and I also had to show my hand a couple of times over there."

"Probably better to be honest. Still don't compromise yourself. Your work is too important to do that." Miranda was beating eggs so had to shout over the noise of the whisk. She paused to look at Andy. "Just take care, it's dangerous work."

"Yes, it's caused me some of my worst nightmares and greatest moments." He paused. "I know you are aware that I have some issues. When I was in the SBS I had to make a choice one night that left a buddy dead. I've had nightmares about it ever since. I actually feel a bit of worthless scum if I'm honest."

He looked out of the window and paused for a moment. "I had some counselling for it. I know all the psycho babble. But nothing seems to help. However, and here's the good news." He turned to Miranda with a trace of a smile. "I've definitely been sleeping better since all the drama in Egypt."

"Good."

"But I'm... I'm a bit of a loss what to do about Charlie. What do you think, Nan? Do you think we might be able to sort out our relationship?"

"Yes, I think you might. You've both been battling your inner demons and guilt is a tough one to work through. You could probably help each other if you were a little more honest and opened up a bit more." She waved the whisk at him to emphasise her point. "Give Charlie time you never know she might give you another chance yet."

She turned back to her cake and began to dollop the mixture into the cake case and added the meringue to the top. A few deft swirls with a fork for effect and the pie was ready for the oven. She pushed it to one side for a moment and with her arms on the table she stared hard at Andy.

"Now. What I have to say may sound like I've seen one too many Bond films. The reason I've asked you down is that I am seriously concerned that my phone has been tapped. In fact both of them, the landline and my mobile. Having heard the full story from Charlie I am convinced that the Society was listening into the conversations and messages between Charlie and me when she was in Egypt; probably before and since as well. I thought I heard a clicking sound one day so I stopped contacting her.

She pushed her mobile towards him. "I've gone off the phone altogether. They seemed to be too well informed about what she was doing and where she was. After all, how did they find out that she was going to Egypt in the first place?"

"OK, Miss Marple, I'll get the lines checked out for you. I don't need your phone to do that though." He gave her back her mobile.

"And another thing, I'm worried that my girl is still in danger. What are you going to do about that?" She heaved herself off her chair and carried the pie to the oven. Slamming the oven door she turned to Andy again.

He smiled at her. He was very fond of this eccentric old lady. "Yes I agree. I don't like this situation at all and although it's gone quiet now I think we must remain cautious. There is a possibility that I could put a tail onto her – for a time at least. I will have to pull a few strings as we daren't try and explain this story to the army or the police, let alone my hairy backed crowd."

"Good, thank you very much, young man. That will allow me to sleep at night. Now, on to more pleasant matters. It's Charlie's birthday next month. I thought to have a small tea party in the Georgian Room at Harrods. This could be a chance for you to make a good impression on Charlie again. Can you make it?"

"Love to come, Nan, thank you. But how do you think she will feel about me being there?"

"Leave that to me. It will be afternoon tea, three o'clock on the 4th March, don't forget. I'm going to ask Jacqui and see if her new man, Mohammad, will be able to come. I would like to meet him and give him a look over. I'm interested to meet the man who has tamed our man-eater. Charlie said she saw a copy of the Koran in her bag the other day. Maybe she'll be wearing a hajib next." Miranda chuckled. "What a turn around. I am so pleased for her, poor girl, she's been short of love in her life."

"Yeh, he seems a good guy."

"So glad you can come. It'll be fun. I don't get out much these days, life's a bit quiet down here."

Andy raised his eyebrows as Miranda went to check on her pie. "That's just great, Nan, it will be fun." He entered the date in his i-Phone.

"Now do you want to wait for a piece of this pie?"

"Love to."

"Good. Help yourself to another beer"

82

"Hi, Nan," Jacqui bounced through the door of the cottage. She was her usual outrageous self in the shortest black velvet skirt, opaque black tights and a purple sweater and high heeled black boots laced up the front that would have looked at home in the Folies Bergère. She had her dark hair piled high and huge gold hoops in her ears.

"So how's my second granddaughter doing?" Miranda enveloped her in her arms then held her at arm's length to check her over. "Charlie told me you met someone in Egypt and you certainly look like a woman in love, you look radiant; romance obviously suits you."

"Oh, Nan, I feel amazing and he's gorgeous, so kind, so considerate and I think he actually has fallen for me too."

"Good, come and tell me all about him. I was half expecting you to be wearing a hajib." She laughed as she looked Jacqui up and down. "Come, my sweet, I made a pie this morning and it's sitting waiting for you. I want to hear all your gossip."

She bustled Jacqui into the kitchen and set about serving coffee and pie while Jacqui chattered on about Mohammad.

Half an hour later, she had brought Miranda up to speed with her romance and had eaten two large slices of pie with cream; she leant back on the sofa with Tabitha on her lap.

"Gosh, I'm full; I do wish you didn't cook so well, Nan, I put on two pounds every time I visit you." She patted her trim flat stomach. "So that's all my good news. I do have a problem though; I don't think

Mohammad's parents approve of me. Whenever I wanted to talk about them he changed the subject and I asked to meet them when we were in Aswan. He said that it wouldn't be a good idea but didn't say why. I think they may disapprove of me not being a Muslim."

Miranda sat at the table and watched Jacqui stroking Tabitha, deflated now as she looked reality in the face. Her heart went out to her, poor girl; she'd had such a terrible start in life yet still managed to keep such a sunny personality.

Miranda got up and sat next to her on the sofa. "My darling, they are probably unsure and nervous at the thought of their son getting involved with someone of another culture. I have a feeling you will face some opposition from the family. But it's early days yet, I wouldn't worry about it for a while. Have some fun and enjoy being with someone who cares about you. When are you seeing him next?"

Jacqui looked up and smiled. "Thanks, Nan, you're right, one day at a time. That's always been my motto. He's supposed to be coming over in a couple of weeks."

"Good, well bring him along to meet me won't you? Maybe he can join us at Harrods for Charlie's birthday. Will he be staying with you at Mudeford?" Jacqui lived in an old coastguard's cottage by the Christchurch estuary.

"Yes I'm taking another week's holiday – hey, I need a holiday to get over the last one!" She laughed. "The other thing I wanted to talk to you about is Charlie. She started back at work a week ago and she's gone ballistic. She's working fourteen hour days. You know she's devastated about the symbols and she feels she's let Joseph down. And what's more she's split up with Andy."

"Yes, and she told me about Andy. I've asked him to her birthday party too, I hope that she might change her mind about him. As for her using work to heal her wounds, well, there's nothing you or anyone else can do just now. This is something that Charlie must work through herself. Through all the danger and so on she certainly found something about herself. At last she doesn't think that I am talking hocus pocus anymore." Miranda laughed her deep chortle. "Now would you like a glass of wine or do you have to drive home? You can stay the night if you wish. Charlie's bed's made up."

"Oh, go on then, Nan." Jacqui unlaced her boots and made herself comfortable on the sofa.

"Good, let me tell you about some of my own adventures in Egypt."

Miranda threw a large log on the fire, brought over two glasses and cold bottle of Sancerre and the story telling began.

83

The taxi drew up outside the front entrance of Harrods. Charlie pulled out her purse to pay the fifteen pound registered on the clock.

Damn.

She realised that she was nearly out of cash. She paid the taxi driver and entered the store. Her phone rang, it was Jacqui.

"Hi, Babe, where are you, we're all here waiting for Birthday Girl."

"I've just arrived but I've no money, I'll have to go down to the basement there's a bank down there. See you in about ten minutes max."

She dashed into the store. It was, as ever, heaving with tourists. She slipped through the crowds enveloped in the fragrance of the Perfumery department and made her way to the down escalator for the lower ground floor. As she stepped onto the escalator her heart missed a beat. She had forgotten about the sumptuous Egyptian theme that the Fayed brothers, the previous owners of the store, had commissioned for this escalator. The walls were covered in sculptures, reliefs and rich paintings of Ancient Egyptian gods and scenes as seen in the tombs and temples. She felt a familiar shiver shimmy down her back as the escalator took her down to the lower ground floor.

She turned to find the bank and as she did came face to face with a glorious statue that sent shivers through her and sent her senses reeling. Oh, my God. She looked into the golden face of the Sphinx. Her head began to spin, her legs started to tremble and she felt her entire body and senses slipping into meltdown. She grabbed the escalator rail to steady herself. She focused hard on the statue and stepped closer, hardly able to breathe. She could hear nothing but a thrumming in her ears and her eyes were locked to the golden face. The scene swam before her and she felt faint and she slid to the floor. She sensed herself floating as her consciousness slipped. She saw a clear gold symbol appear and a great force of light energy surged through her.

A voice resonated clearly.

"To you who was known as Khamet, High Priest of all Egypt. Now is the TIME. Behold the Symbol of Healing – the first of the lost symbols of the universe. It is the key for the individual to access the universal energies of love – the key to healing. Go forth – use it and share it with the world. So be it."

The vision faded and the vision of the symbol dissolved. But she had seen it and seen it clearly. She would never forget its shape, form and the energy that it unlocked. She became aware of sounds and movement around her.

"Are you all right dear?" A kindly silver haired man bent down to assist her.

"Oh, yes, so sorry, no I'm fine, thank you." She stood up and smiled, oh, yes she did feel fine, very fine indeed. She brushed down her skirt. Her head felt swimmy but the energies still coursed through her. She felt she could fly. She was uplifted, transformed and alive, truly alive again. WOW. All thoughts of banks and money were wiped from her mind and she dashed around to the up escalator.

She had to phone Miranda, she couldn't wait to share her news.

Miranda jumped as she heard her phone calling from the depths of her voluptuous bag. "Goodness, I'd forgotten I had it with me, how embarrassing." She fumbled to turn it to silent and clutched it to her ear.

"Hi, Nan, I've got one of the symbols, I've got the one for healing. I'll be with you just now. Oh, I'm so excited."

"Fantastic. Quick come up and join us." Miranda turned to the others with a huge grin. "She's got a symbol."

As ever Miranda forgot to turn off her phone and Charlie laughed at the squeals of joy from the other end. She was literally bouncing now and dodged around the other passengers, pushing her way through the crowd to the next level. It seemed to take forever to get to the fourth floor. She arrived breathless and excited at the stunning room, lit with glistening chandeliers, filled with tables covered with white starched clothes laid for high tea of delicate cakes, scones and minute sandwiches served on tiered silver platters. How glorious, how magical it looked. She saw Andy standing at the far end of the room waving her over. Her knees were shaking and she felt a thrill of excitement and anticipation flash through her as she walked across the thick carpet, weaving her way through the iconic and busy restaurant towards her table.

Miranda, Andy and Jacqui stood up as she arrived at their table. After she had hugged, kissed and received their Happy Birthday blessings she sat and beamed at them all.

"So what do you think about my amazing news?" she said.

Andy and Jacqui nodded. "Brilliant. Tell us all about it. Give, give, give," Jacqui bounced on her seat.

"I've actually got one of the symbols. I can't believe it but I've got it."

She looked at each of them and paused giving them a chance to assimilate in her extraordinary news.

Miranda smiled, reached over and took her hand and said, "It's about time too."

Jacqui asked, "How did you get it then, Chas, how did it come, in a dream?"

"No, no, not a dream. Just now, I used the Egyptian escalator to go to the bank and I came face to face with the Sphinx. I had all the whooshes and tingles that I've had in the past but no drums, I am happy to say no drums. I went into a sort of trance and then I saw it. AND I can remember it. Give me a pen quick – I must draw it in case I forget it again."

Andy passed her a pen from his jacket and Jacqui found a small notebook in her handbag. She looked up at him as he handed over the pen. He smiled at her and touched her hand. She paused and then whispered, "I wasn't expecting to see you here." He shrugged and smiled again. She stared for a moment then looked down to the notebook.

She drew the symbol and passed it around. "It has to be drawn three times from right to left, that's how it was presented to me. It unlocks the power to channel healing energies. Isn't it clever?"

Andy pursed his lips. "It is if it works."

Charlie flashed him a hard look. "Oh, here we go again… "

Miranda interrupted her. She flapped her hand at him. "Oh, Andy, of course it will work. Don't be such an old sceptic."

Jacqui also chirped in. "Yes of course it works I saw it in my dream on that island near Aswan."

Miranda stretched out her arm. "Well you can practise on my elbow it's so stiff. I fell on the ice in the winter. Try it on me."

The waiter interrupted to take their order. Miranda asked for four afternoon teas and four flutes of champagne.

"What tea, Madam? We have a selection you can choose from, Chamomile, Roibos, Moroccan Mint, Blackcurrant, Earl Grey… "

Impatiently they interrupted him with a request for Moroccan Mint for all of them.

Charlie looked around, "Where's Mohammad, Jacqui, I thought he was coming over to join you?"

"Oh, Chas, don't ask. It's been awful, we have had the most dreadful argument. It's all about his parents. I think our relationship is all but over. But let's not talk about it now – I don't want to spoil your afternoon." She put on a brave face. "Come on then, show us how this healing works."

"Hey, I don't really know, but I'll give it a try."

She drew the symbol in the air three times and placed her hand onto Miranda's elbow. "I can feel a pulse in the middle of my hand," she said. "Nan, can you feel anything?"

"My elbow is really getting very, very hot already," said Miranda.

"I believe I can use it hands on or off," said Charlie, all smiles now.

"Can it do any harm?" Jacqui asked.

"No," said Miranda, "it's just pure love. Clever isn't it. My elbow really is feeling better."

The waiter brought their tea, delicate sandwiches, cakes and scones beautifully presented, but they were too excited with the healing and they simply took the champagne and toasted Charlie's birthday.

"I'm getting a tingling sensation in my arm now," said Miranda.

"Are you sure, Nan, you're not humouring me are you?"

"Not at all, you know you always get a straight answer from me," she threw her a reproving look. After a few more minutes they took a break to eat their tea and Miranda confirmed that her elbow was much, much easier than before and insisted on a hug to seal the healing.

"Hey, you must try these macaroons they are great." Jacqui passed the plate round the table.

"Your appetite is amazing, and you never put on weight. It's not fair," said Charlie.

"Ah well, I think everything I eat gets burned up by my dynamic and effervescent personality which is another way of saying I have ADHD!" she laughed and took another scone and cream. "Let me test my theory out some more." They all laughed.

Charlie's relief at finally finding her Holy Grail created a sense of euphoria and they were all affected.

"Hey, Chas, heal my knee, I twisted it this morning running down the stairs at Bond Street; these damn heels gave way." She glared at her six inch high heels.

They moved round so that Charlie could sit with her hand on Jacqui's knee. "Hey, you're right, Nan, it gets hot. Wow, it feels funny too, a sort of pulsing. Your turn next, Andy."

"I'm OK, I don't need healing; I'll leave that to you ladies."

Miranda put a hand on his knee and leant close to Andy. She whispered, "It's good for sorting out personal demons, Andy. You should try it sometime."

"Maybe, one day, not now, but thanks, Nan." He smiled at the old lady and turned back to the table. "Hey, guys, anyone like another glass of champagne? We should celebrate this moment."

They all decided to have another glass and raised a toast to Charlie the Healer.

"Cheers, Charlie," Andy raised his glass. "I am so sorry that I was such a disbeliever! I can see by the way your first patients have responded that you certainly have the gift."

Charlie blushed. "Well, to be honest, I think it's more to do with the symbol and the energy it calls in rather than anything I'm doing. But I must say it feels as though a great weight has lifted from my shoulders. It makes everything that happened in Egypt seem right now."

Andy took her hand. "I'm sorry, darling; truly sorry for being a sceptic."

"It's OK. I was more than sceptical too!" She smiled up at him. Blushed then turned in embarrassment to Miranda.

"So, Nan, how does this work?" asked Charlie as she took her hand from Jacqui's knee and sipped her champagne.

"Well, my dear, it's all about energy. You are channelling in a high vibration energy to uplift a low vibration energy – the damaged knee will be a lower frequency than the incoming energy and as it flows through it clears any blocks and knots of energy that the body is holding. It works on emotions, you know, old stuff, baggage and issues – fear, anger, depression; it sort of raises spirits."

"What are you going to do now?" Jacqui asked.

"I don't know. It seems anyone who uses the symbol can do this. So I need to share it. Anyway, that's what the voice I heard told me to do."

"How?" Andy asked.

There was a pause while she considered this. "I could make a website – you could help me with that couldn't you, Jac?"

"Sure I will, babe."

"I guess Twitter and Facebook would work too."

"Good idea," said Miranda.

Charlie turned to her frowning. "You didn't seem very surprised that I've got a symbol at last?"

"Well, no. I knew that you would get there eventually. You used the code at the Sphinx in Egypt and that unlocked the seal. It didn't move the paw but it unlocked your own memory. Those symbols were not really lost, they were held in your cellular memory from the time you used them when you were Khamet. The magic seal and chant were the lock and key to your memory."

"Wow, so there are more?"

"Many more. But you may need a trigger to jolt your memory into remembering them. The Sphinx downstairs was the trigger for this first one."

"So do you think I need to find more Sphinxes?" Charlie asked. She was getting excited again now and she pulled her hair back and twirled it in her hand. "I need to find the others now, or I should say, I need to remember them, right, Nan?"

"Yes, that's right, sweet child."

"But where will I find another Sphinx outside of Egypt? Oh, please don't say we have to go back to Cairo again." She looked scared.

"No, I don't think you have to go there again. But the Sphinx downstairs is also a clue that will lead you to the next one."

"The British Museum," answered Andy. "The Egyptian room at the museum is famous. You may find a Sphinx there to trigger your memory for the next symbol. It's definitely worth a try."

"Let's go now," said Charlie, wiping her hands and getting her bag ready to leave. "I feel I am on a quest now, a woman with a mission."

"OK, you go and I'll pay the bill. I don't feel up to chasing around museums. You won't need me if you go with Jacqui and Andy. I'll meet you up at your apartment, Andy," Miranda said. "Keep me informed. I shall want to know what's happening."

"I still have a set of your keys, Andy." Charlie delved in deep into her Gucci bag and passed them over to Miranda. "And here is the door code." She passed her a piece of paper with the security code.

Andy had been Googling on his Blackberry and looked up. "We must get going. The Museum closes at five thirty and it'll take us about half an hour to get there. It's four now. Quickly now." He stood up.

"My car's parked in the Harrods' car park. Oh, by the way, Miranda, I had your phone checked. You were right. It's definitely being bugged, so you need to replace it." He stopped and stood stock still. The look on Miranda's face scared him. She looked at him wide eyed.

"Oh, God, Andy." She looked down at her mobile phone. "Charlie called me from the escalator about the symbol. What shall we do?"

"Hell. Well, there's not a lot we can do. We just mustn't use our mobiles any more, none of us. My phone is clear so I'll call the apartment phone if I want to talk to you, Miranda. OK? When you get there don't let anyone in unless you know for sure who they are. We must all be on our toes now. Those bastards may be mobilising."

She sighed. His tension was catching. Jacqui and Charlie had heard their exchange. They looked at each other with startled eyes. Charlie experienced the frisson of fear that she'd so often felt in Egypt.

Andy pulled the girls away. "Come, we'll talk on the way to the car. There's nothing to be gained in making a drama. We'll deal with things as they come up."

They blew kisses at Miranda and rushed out of the door towards the escalator. She called a waiter for the bill and cautiously slipped the drawing of the symbol into her bag.

84

"We're in place and we're following the two women and the man. The old woman is still in the restaurant. Have you got someone who can tail her?"

Jared grinned. The more activity the bigger the bill for Lord D, and assassinations paid far more than surveillance. Now there was serious work to be done – his kind of work and on his patch. He was in control now. At last things were falling into his hands. "Yeah, yeah, don't you worry your little head over 'er, I'll sort it. Just you stick like glue to the others. When you get an idea where they're making for, give us a buzz."

Brilliant, bloody brilliant. Alleluia.

He made a call. He took the smile from his face and spoke slowly and used his deepest voice. "Lord Dennington, I am sorry to say she's found one of them symbols."

He listened.

"No 'ere in London." He listened to the stream of instructions. "Yeah, onto it." He paused. "Let you know. Bye."

The silence of his office just broken by the faint refrain of Leonard Cohen's song 'Alleluia, alleluia' whispering through his fleshy lips as he stared out of the window watching the traffic and planning. Planning the end game.

85

The journey to the British Museum in Great Russell Street took over half an hour. Andy found a parking slot nearby in Russell Square not far from the main entrance. Even this early in the year the huge front forecourt was filled with tourists and school groups. They threaded their way through the crowd to the steps leading to the Museum's impressive Victorian main entrance. Once inside they were taken aback by the enormous glass domed atrium, a more recent addition and in the centre a huge inner building that contained more rooms and the library. But today there was no time for sightseeing; they ran over to the information desk and were given a guide map that showed the main Egyptian rooms were on the ground floor to the left of the entrance.

They stepped into the entrance of a complex of interlinking rooms filled with antiquities from Egypt's cultural past. Charlie looked around and saw hundreds of statues and carvings of pharaohs and deities lining the walls. "We are looking for a Sphinx. There's so much, where do we start!"

Andy held up his phone. "I've already Googled but there seems to be only a pair of female Sphinxes – they should be down the end of this room."

"OK, let's go there then," Charlie said.

Andy led the way down the room.

At the end they found two large glass cases that held similar figures of a female Sphinx with braided hair and large breasts. Charlie stood staring at them. "Oh dear, I can't feel a thing."

She continued to stare hoping that she might get a reaction.

Nothing.

"The only thing I feel is jealousy for those boobs."

"Well, maybe there's something else here that will trigger your memory," said Jacqui still optimistic. "Come on, let's go through this room again."

Charlie stopped in front of each statue in the hopes of getting a reaction. She passed the famous Rosetta Stone that helped historians to translate the hieroglyphic writing found on all the temple and tomb walls.

Nothing.

She looked into the eyes of the great cat god, Sekmet.

Nothing.

She stood head to head with the pharaoh, Ramses 11.

"There's your friend, Jac," she nodded towards the king who built Abu Simbel. But for her, not a single shimmer, shiver or tingle. Nothing at all.

"None of these are doing it for me. How many more rooms here to walk through, Andy?"

"I don't know, just a few I think."

He led the way through several adjoining rooms with walls covered by tablets and friezes. Still no reaction from Charlie.

Andy looked at his watch. "We don't have much more time before it closes. I must say, Chas, I do hope you find something soon. I'm really concerned about the phone tapping. If the Society knows you've found a symbol they will be looking for you and you are in danger. You need to get it out on Facebook or something then there won't be any point in killing you. You need to act fast."

"Oh, Andy, it sounds so chilling when you say that."

"Well, it's the truth. I think we should cut our losses and get you to the apartment and then you can get working on it."

Jacqui was reading the guide. "There is another set of rooms upstairs in that centre area, where mummies and sarcophagi are on show."

"Oh, yes let's go there. Just for a few minutes, Andy. They won't kill me here with all these people around now will they?" She gave him her full charm smile and put her arms around him.

"OK, but be quick. Come on let's go."

They ran out of the room and into the circular corridor back to the front of the atrium and found the staircase that would take them up to room sixty-two and the mummies.

* * *

"George, can you still see them?"

"Yes, yes they're going upstairs now. It's easy to follow them without being seen, this place is teeming."

"Good keep close, but watch out for the soldier boy, he's savvy."

86

Charlie tried to calm herself down. After the excitement of her discovery in Harrods she had been on a high but Andy had brought her well and truly down to earth with his doom and gloom warnings. She felt desperation creeping in. She was against the clock; they had only half an hour at best in the museum. She could feel the menace that she had experienced in Egypt. She could sense the danger. Several times she felt the presence of someone behind her, the feeling of being watched; but when she swung round to see who it might be she was faced with a wall of total strangers. No one stood out as different or dangerous. She felt scared of them all.

She shared her fears with the others. Andy too could sense someone watching them.

"I can actually feel the hairs on the back of my neck quivering," said Jacqui, rubbing her neck as though to settle them.

When they entered the first room of mummies a shiver ran down Charlie's spine. Was that a sign or was it the closeness of the death in the cabinets.

"These dead bodies give me the shivers," she said.

There were cases and cases of brightly painted coffins, sarcophagi covered with hieroglyphics; messages to guide the soul on its onward journey and a pair of boldly painted eyes to keep away the bad spirits of the underworld. In some cases, bodies that were two, even three thousand years old lay wrapped in their embalming linens, again painted and decorated in sumptuous colours and gold.

How could these be a trigger?

Jacqui had wandered off into another room and Andy was hovering behind her, chivvying her along.

"I won't sense anything if you hassle me," she snapped. "Give me some space, please."

He shrugged and stepped back. "Well hurry up."

The rooms up here were quiet as closing time approached. Suddenly there was a loud clacking of running feet along marble floors. Jacqui appeared flustered and excited. "Quick, quick Chas, I think I may have found something."

They ran after her to the next room. "Here, over here," she called them to a glass case with another highly decorated sarcophagus. "Look." She pointed to the description. But even before she started to read it Charlie could feel the familiar woozy feelings, the throbbing in her ears. As the entire scene in front of her first swirled then faded she slipped to the floor. She heard the now familiar voice.

"*To you who was known as Khamet, High Priest of all Egypt. Before you see the Protection Symbol – the second of the lost symbols of the universe. It is the key for the individual to access the power to protect their energy with strength from the negative forces of your world. Go forth – use it and share it with all. So be it.*"

A huge golden symbol of light appeared before her. A triangle within which sat a line drawing of an eye similar to the Eye of Horus that decorated the coffins.

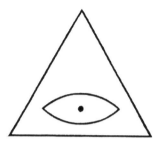

As quickly as she had slipped away she came back into full consciousness again. Andy and Jacqui were leaning over her with a concerned look on their faces.

"It's OK," she muttered, her voice hoarse and faint. "I'm fine and I have another symbol."

"Good, good, but we must go back to the apartment."

Andy lifted her to her feet and she stood shaking a little in front of the cabinet signage. This was the body of a High Priest Hornedjitef, who lived in Karnak and served the God Amun, the Sun God in the Ptolemaic era.

"It's me," she whispered. "That's my body. That's Khamet. Oh, my God." She was really shaking now. "How amazing."

The girls wanted to read the whole narrative but Andy was getting very agitated. "We must get out of here," he insisted. He took her arm and almost carried her out of the room towards the stairs. "Are you OK to walk?"

"Sure." She sounded a little drunk and her legs were slightly wobbly but with help from the others she managed to get down the stairs.

Andy looked around them checking the thinning crowd. He sensed but couldn't see a source of danger. They walked as fast as Charlie could manage, across the huge open floor space and out of the building. She took a couple of deep breaths and started to regain her strength. She managed the walk back to the car unaided, dropped into the front seat and closed her eyes.

Andy started the car and began to weave through the heavy traffic. "Right. Back to the apartment," he said.

Jacqui dived into her bag. "It's Mohammad." She pulled out her phone. "He's wishing you happy birthday, Chas." Her eyes filled with tears. "He sent a picture of us at Abu Simbel. He says we are the modern version of two of the Great Egyptian Lovers. Oh, how romantic."

"Who were the others then?" Andy asked.

Charlie opened her eyes. "Nefertari and Ramses and Anthony and Cleopatra are the only ones I know." She sat bolt upright. "Oh my God! Cleopatra. Wait a minute, wait a minute," she said urgency making her voice shrill. "That's it. We have to go to Cleopatra's Needle on the Embankment. I am absolutely sure there are two Sphinx figures on either side of the column, and they are just like the one in Giza. I'm sorry, Andy, I know you want to get back but we should go there. Will it take us far out of our way going to the Embankment?"

"Well. No, not really. OK, OK, we'll go."

Andy wasn't listening to her any more. He was staring in his rear view mirror.

"I'm sure we're being followed," he said. "We've some unwanted interest from that silver Mercedes behind us. It's been with us since Russell Square. Hold on. I'll try to lose them."

Immediately he spun the wheel and drove down a small side street. They careered down the narrow road and then he quickly took a turn to the left, dodging an oncoming car and wove his way through around parked cars. The Mercedes was still right behind them.

87

George was driving. He turned to Ashley, sitting beside him and Paul in the back. "Bugger, 'e's spotted us. He won't go home with us on his tail. I've got another idea. Give Les a call and see if they've still got the old bird in their sights."

George had his own way of relieving stress. He dipped into the box of gum he kept in the car between the front seats. He stuffed four pieces into his mouth and chewed vigorously.

Ashley made the call. "Les says they're in St Katherine Docks. The old lady went into Heron block. Don't know which number but should be easy to find that out from Security."

"OK, we'll get moving and join him there. They're heading in that direction."

"They must all be meeting up there. I'll go along Holborn, should be clear at this time of day. Tell Les we'll meet him there and we'll nail them as they arrive into the garage, won't be too many spectators down there, that garage is like a grave in the daytime; most of the owners live overseas. I got myself a Roller from down there once." He grinned.

Ashley passed on the message.

"OK, Les is sending Stig to get the flat number."

George's voice came smothered in white gum. "He's probably got an underground parking bay. Get the boys to find out about that too."

Ashley hesitated before passing this request on. "How'll they do that? Security won't tell him. How's he going to find that out?"

George pushed the gum into his cheek; he grinned and spoke each word deliberately and slowly. "Tell him to ask the old lady."

Ashley, looked at him hard. "You sure?" He scratched his head vigorously.

"Yeah, I'm sure."

In the back Paul giggled.

Ashley started to say something then swallowed his words. "If you say so." He rubbed his hands over his stubbly head once more. "You're in charge, but I don't like it."

George smirked. "When you've called him then give the boss a call, tell him what we're doing." He braked hard as an elderly woman pulling a shopping basket stepped out in front of him on the crossing.

"God help us. Silly old mare. I 'ate old age. You can shoot me when I start to lose it, bruvver."

"You'll be lucky to get there, someone will probably do you in before then, you evil bastard." Ashley shook his head and picked up his phone.

Once the old lady had crossed over George revved up the car and sped down the road and took the next turn left into High Holborn.

88

Miranda dropped her bags on the sofa and looked around the apartment. Not to her taste, far too Zen. No ornaments, just a couple of boldly coloured oils of boats, probably on the Solent. The sofas were cream and the wide glass windows overlooking the dock were dressed with simple cream dress curtains on stainless steel rods. She shrugged. Looked like any number of others in any city estate agent's window, not what she would have chosen but attractive in its own way; an A1 location for the city and a fun place to stay.

She walked into the small galley kitchen, shining and good as new. Not too many Sunday roasts or cakes cooked here. She put the kettle on and searched the cupboards for coffee.

As the water heated she wandered back into the lounge and looked out of the window at the dock below. There were a number of small yachts and motor boats moored in the basin. Opposite she could see the back of the Dickens Inn, a popular pub for tourists. She could also see the Tower of London over the trees and Tower Bridge.

She thought about her granddaughter. She could see why she enjoyed staying up here with Andy. She sighed.

How will her life unfold? Charlie will most likely be moving off in a different direction now. Maybe she could include her new spiritual knowledge with her current job, but I doubt it. Would the powers of symbols really impact the world? Maybe, maybe not. Maybe they would for those who wanted to discover their own powers and were ready to explore the possibility of magic.

She stopped her musings and stared hard at the two men leaning on the guard rail around the dock. The one in the denim jacket had most definitely been pointing at this apartment. He now nudged the second man who flicked his half smoked cigarette into the water and they walked towards the back entrance of the block. They arrived at the security gate at the same time as a middle aged woman, one of the residents; they gave her a reassuring smile and walked in with her. Miranda heard the gate click shut. Her intuition and personal radar sent a shiver of warning through her. She went to use her mobile then remembered Andy's warning that it was bugged. So she walked into the hallway where she found the landline phone in its socket. She dialled Charlie's mobile number. She was directed to voicemail.

89

"See, I told you there was nothing to worry about," Charlie said. The Mercedes hadn't been seen for some minutes. "You've become paranoid, Andy."

She laughed. She was on a high now. She had found symbols at last – what a relief. She felt vindicated and all the trauma of Egypt faded into a sense of purpose and excitement. She could also feel real again. All those bizarre and unworldly experiences were a reality, a strange one, but a reality.

"Still, I don't feel we should hang about long. Here's Cleopatra's Needle."

Andy pulled his BMW over to the side of the road. "I'll give you just two minutes. We – or at least you – are in danger while you've got those signs or whatever they are. Miranda's phone was definitely bugged and we were definitely followed, so hurry up."

Charlie looked over to her right at the stone obelisk built by Cleopatra in honour of her lover Mark Antony. It had been gifted some two hundred years ago to Britain by the ruler of Egypt to commemorate the success of the Battle of the Nile by Lord Nelson. She closed her eyes for a moment and as she opened them took in the two Sphinx figures in bronze at the base of the pillar. Again her eyes closed and she felt a gentle throbbing of energy coursing through her. Her inner vision filled with white light and the now familiar voice.

"Dear one, known as Khamet. We present to you the great Manifestation Symbol. We bring it forth from your memory and previous lifetimes into your current consciousness."

A clear gold symbol blazed through the white light in her mind. She could see the shape easily as it hovered in front of her. Its form seemed familiar. She had a sense of knowing. The throbbing increased through her entire body and she felt herself shaking as it came fully into her awareness.

"This symbol when held with a pure intention will create and attract all you need. Visualize your dream, your goal, your need and, given that its time is right, that it is for your highest good, so YOUR DREAM WILL COME TRUE."

The voice and the vision dispersed. The connection was ended and she felt herself coming back fully into the present, back to earth.

Her eyes opened. Andy held her hand. "You OK?" he asked.

"Yes, yes," she whispered.

"Right, here we go." He joined the traffic and they made their way down the Embankment towards the City.

Suddenly, Charlie sat up. "Oh, my God. I've heard those words before."

She put her hands around her head, willing her memory to work. "I've got it, I've got it," she cried. "I remember now. When I first met Joseph by the boat, he said those words to me in Egypt, in Luxor; when

I bought the bandana and the cross. When he gave me the silver ring, he said it would help me make my dreams come true. The voice said the same words. Oh this is amazing." She looked down at the ring that she still wore.

She screamed. "There it is, it's the symbol, look." She turned to Jacqui and showed her the ring. "See that symbol inside it's the same as the one I've just been shown. Oh, my God. Wow. I can't wait to tell Nan. I'll buzz her now. She should be at your place by now, shouldn't she Andy?"

"Yes, most likely sitting drinking a cup of tea or smudging my apartment to get rid of my demons, she has a theory I'm affected by what she calls negative energies!"

Jacqui laughed. "She spent two days clearing my place last year. She said I had an elf in the garden and an old fisherman haunting the cottage. I must say that it did feel lighter after she'd finished but the smell of incense hung around for days."

"Oh, I've had a missed call from your place, Andy," Charlie said. She hit recall. The phone rang and rang. "She's not answering."

"She may have popped over to Waitrose for a few bits," said Jacqui.

"We'll be there in about ten minutes. Try again in a minute," said Andy.

Charlie looked at her ring and gave it a kiss. "To think I had this with me all the time. How amazing. Dear old Joseph."

There was a lump in her throat and she stared out at the river thinking back to their time on the Nile. "That all seems like a dream now."

"Nightmare you mean," Jacqui said.

It was getting darker. They were slowed to a crawl by the rush hour traffic that added office commuters to the stream of vans, buses and taxis that continuously flowed into and out of the City to the East End and on to Essex.

Charlie tried calling Miranda again. No answer. She shivered and looked at Jacqui. "I wish Nan would answer. I am getting bad vibes. I've called her mobile and the landline and she's not answering either. I'm getting worried now."

"Me too," said Jacqui. "Still she's a game old bird; she's been getting herself out of trouble for years now. I'm sure she can look after herself."

"Check to see if she left you a message," Andy said.

Charlie dialled her message service. She lifted her hand to hush the others. "Oh, my God." She turned pale as the colour drained from her face. "Nan says that there were two suspicious looking men at the back by the dock. She saw them entering the gate when another resident came in. She sounds really anxious. I've never heard fear in her voice before. Hurry we must get to her. Oh I couldn't bear anything to happen to Nan!"

90

It took Les ten seconds to slide his patent door opener along the lock of number twenty-four.

"Gotcha," he whispered as he heard the slight click as the mechanism responded. He gestured to Stig to shush.

Miranda was looking out of the window checking the back of the block for anyone else suspicious. She started to wonder if she had imagined that the men were a threat. They could have just been friends of a resident. She guessed that these flats were full of businessmen, foreigners having a pied-à-terre and other transients. Not much chance of a strong community spirit here. Not like her village.

She started from her thoughts as she heard a sound at the front door.

Oh, heavens I should have put on the chain.

She started to make her way out of the sitting room.

"Who is it?" she shouted.

The door slammed back and the two men hurled themselves forward. Les grabbed Miranda in an embrace, a hurtful and forceful embrace.

"Get your hands of me, you beast," she shouted at his face. "Get off."

Stig shut the door and he and Les forced Miranda back into the sitting room and pushed her down onto the sofa.

"How dare you!" she said. "How dare you." She smoothed down her kaftan and straightened her turban.

"What do you want?" she asked.

"Simple, we just need the number of the garage space downstairs. Give us that and we'll leave you in peace. Get difficult and we'll have to resort to tricks that old ladies shouldn't be part of. Save yourself the suffering. Give us the number."

Stig braced his tall and muscular frame as he stood close, looking down on her. His hands on his hips made him look even larger and more oppressive, the archetypal bully.

"I most certainly shall not, you come in here barging your way through the door and then expect me to co-operate with you. Forget it."

The phone rang. She put out a hand to pick it up but Stig reached out his own, large, covered in tattoos and prevented her from picking it up. "No phones, Granny, no phones."

Les sat down on the chair opposite. "Look here, Gran, we don't want to harm you. Just help us out here. We need the parking slot number."

"No." Miranda clenched her fists and her lips. "No."

Les leant into her face. "Now, listen carefully, *if* you don't co-operate it will go badly for your granddaughter."

Stig grinned, a humourless grimace. "Yeah, we'll get her when she arrives. We'll get her right here."

"You are evil, positively evil."

Miranda felt herself filling with anger. Rage pulsed through her. She tried to keep it under control. "IF you promise not to touch or harm Charlie I'll give it to you, but only if you promise."

The landline rang again. "Ignore it," said Stig.

"Yeah, sure we promise, don't we Stig?" The men both nodded. Their faces bland.

"OK, it's number one hundred and two. It's down three levels of parking. It's the bottom level. You have to take the stairs; the lift doesn't go that far."

"Good. Well done, Grandma."

Les took out his phone. "Ready, George? It's one hundred and two. Good luck, mate. See yer!"

He looked around the apartment grinning. "Nice gaff. Worth a bob or two." He looked more relaxed now.

His phone signalled an incoming call. George listened intently, frowning. "OK. Will do. Come on Stig. Time to move." The men left the room.

Miranda leaned over to pick up the phone.

"Oh, no you don't, Grandma." Stig had slipped back into the room. He picked the phone up and pocketed it. "Have you got a mobile?"

"Don't be ridiculous what would I be doing with one of those things?"

He bent over and picked up her handbag and threw the contents onto the sofa. Her phone fell to the floor. The paper with the symbol slipped out too.

Miranda held her breath as the man dived on the phone.

"Oh, wouldn't have one of these ridiculous things," he mimicked her as he took it and put it in his other pocket.

She moved her foot and placed it on top of the paper.

"I don't trust you, Granny. I think you're a bit smarter than the average."

He looked around the apartment for a minute, then spotted the navy curtain tie backs. He walked over and ripped two of them from the wall.

"Be careful," Miranda called. "You'll damage the plaster."

She shuffled her feet to push the paper under the sofa.

"Will you shut up?" Stig snarled at her now. "You are f**king trying my patience. What are you doing? Sit still."

"Nothing. You make me nervous with your shouting."

"Put your hands together. Nice prayers now," he said.

She obeyed. "I shall pray for your soul, young man. I'll pray that you see the light and step out of the darkness," she smiled.

Les shouted from outside the flat. "Hurry up, Stig, we've got to go. They'll be here in a minute."

"Just stopping this old witch from setting off the alarm," he called back. "There that'll slow you down." He'd tied both hands together and her ankles. "You are going nowhere." He gave her a false smile.

"OK, OK, you nasty young man. Your karmic card is marked – this will come back to bite you for sure. Get out now."

"Yes, I'm going to sort out your precious granddaughter." He left the room and slammed the door. She heard the door intercom buzzer go in the hallway. She let out a huge sigh. A tear slid down her cheek.

91

"How are we going to get through the security gate?" asked Paul.

They had parked their car in visitors parking and were standing outside the main entrance.

George smiled. "Leave this to Uncle George. We're not taking the car down. No point. Now we know the number we'll just have to get through the doors into the block and go down the stairs to the downstairs security gate. Leave this to me, I've been here before."

Les answered the intercom from Andy's flat. "Hi, guys, welcome, welcome." He could see their faces peering into the miniature screen and he pressed the entry key and the main entrance door opened.

The three men walked into the foyer and towards the stairs to the parking. At the security door to the basement parking Les took out a small electronic device and after a few beeps and buzzes the door opened.

"Abra-bloody-ca-Dabra, see! Ready for action, got your piece Ashley? I'll try the blade, quieter. Ready my boy?"

He turned to Paul and clapped him on the back. He stared up close into his face. His eyes dead, his grin a macabre distortion of a smile. "First blood, my boy, your first blood."

92

"There's still no answer from Nan. Those men must have got into the apartment, I am seriously worried now," Charlie said.

Jacqui clutched at Charlie's sleeve. "Do those symbols of yours work at a distance?"

"I don't know why?"

"I was just thinking you could use the protection symbol to keep her safe."

"Great idea." Charlie drew the symbol in the air three times. "Protect Nan, please." She sighed. "We'll just have to trust it works."

They were drawing close to Tower Hill and only a few minutes from the apartment. Andy frowned as he weighed up the possibilities and probabilities of their situation. "Right. We need to make a plan here. I am going to take charge now and I want you two girls to do just as I say. It's the only way that we can sort this mess out."

"Andy, do you think this is serious?" Jacqui asked.

"Well, yes. There are a number of likelihoods and some maybes." He spelled them out emphasising each point with a finger.

"Firstly, probable; there are a number of men employed by the Society waiting for us ahead at the dock. Secondly, probable; they are planning to kill Charlie, maybe all of us.

"Thirdly, this one's a possible; Miranda has been either killed, heaven forbid, taken or attacked in my apartment. At the moment I am working out why they might have done that.

"Fourthly, and this is wishful thinking, Miranda made a mistake and the men are no threat and she's popped out shopping as Jacqui suggested. Whatever, we must plan for the worst situation."

He looked at Charlie, his frown turning into a full scowl. "We must secure Miranda and get you onto a computer fast so that you can broadcast your spooky stuff. Once you have done there can be no reason to kill you and then we can breathe easily again."

He banged his hand on the steering wheel. "What on earth can they want that Miranda knows?"

"Maybe it's something they think she knows?" Charlie said.

"But what? If they were following us, which I am sure they were, they would know that she isn't with us."

They had reached the crossroads with Tower Bridge and waiting at traffic lights. Andy was pale, the stress affecting him. "Right, we need to park the car and get up to the apartment pronto. Whatever else is going on we must check on Miranda first."

Charlie put her hands on her heart. "Oh, please, Andy, I would die if anything happened to Nan."

They turned into Thomas More Street and Andy drove slowly towards the parking barrier.

"How do we get from the car to the apartment?" Jacqui asked. "Aren't we a little exposed as we enter the building?"

"It's fine, my parking slot is down two floors then there's a staircase that only goes to the ground floor. It's designed to be secure and stop non-residents getting to the apartments from the parking levels," Andy said.

The barrier lifted and they drove underneath down into the underground parking. To the left was the secure parking for the residents of their block and to the right public parking. Andy opened the secure gate with his pass key and they drove slowly into the first car park level. The place was empty. Just a few cars parked and some left long-term, covered with dust covers, owned by overseas owners who only came to London from time to time.

Suddenly, Andy thumped the wheel. "God, I am stupid, where's my brain? They are probably trying to get my parking bay number, so then they can catch us as we arrive in the car."

"What can we do?" Jacqui asked.

"Get ready. I'm going to leave the car here. We can't drive out because we can only get out via the bottom floor. We'll go by foot and use the security gate key to get out and then we make for the stairs up to the ground floor. We'll go in through the front doors."

"Do you think they'll still be in the apartment waiting for us there?"

Just then Charlie's phone rang. "It's Nan, it's Nan," she shouted. "Nan, are you OK?" She put the phone on loudspeaker.

"I was attacked by a couple of thugs. They wanted the parking number and they tied me up. I managed to get undone and found the bedroom phone."

"Oh, hell. Are you OK?"

"Yes, yes, sweet child, of course I am."

Andy asked, "Have they left the flat?"

"Yes, yes. Some time ago. About five minutes at least. They were meeting up with some of their mates. Beastly men. Evil. Charlie, do take care they are out to get you, my sweetness."

"OK, Nan, we are all fine here," Andy interrupted. "We're coming up now."

"By the way, darling boy, I made up the number for the parking slot."

"What number did you give them then, Nan?"

"One hundred and two."

"Well done, Nan. Thanks. " Andy smiled and passed the phone back to Charlie. He shook his head. "Great, my number is ninety-nine. We would have walked straight into them. Still she thought she was doing well, bless her."

Charlie took the phone and put it away. "Well, the symbol worked!"

Jacqui gave her a quick hug. "Thank God for that."

They entered the block through the glass front doors into the carpeted foyer.

"Lift or stairs?" Charlie asked Andy.

"Lift, the stairs are hardly used, we're more vulnerable there."

They got out on the first floor. Andy's apartment was straight ahead of them. He unlocked the door and they stepped inside.

They ran through to the lounge where Miranda was sitting looking completely composed. Apart from the odd spiral of grey hair hanging from her turban, there were no other side effects at all from her drama.

"Welcome, my dears. What an adventure. What dreadful men. Thank God you are all right, my darling." She stood up and gave Charlie a hug. Despite her bravado she could feel Nan trembling a little.

"Shall I make some tea?" Miranda asked.

"Sorry, Nan, we've no time we have to get going on the website and Facebook. We have to make the symbols public." Charlie grabbed Andy's laptop and ran to the table; quick Jacqui, come and help me."

Andy went straight to the window and pulled back the curtains to check the area around the dock. The street lights were creating pools of light along the walkway and several of the boats moored up in the basin were lit. The lights were full on in the Dickens Inn and they cast tongues of light across the water. There were the usual passers-by taking a short cut through to the supermarket off Thomas More Street. "Seems quiet enough." He turned to join the girls.

At that moment the sitting room door flew open and two men hurled themselves into the room. They were holding pistols and waving them around; they looked serious, very serious. They also looked nervous and unpredictable.

"Get down on the floor, all of you right now," they shouted.

"Oh God, not again," muttered Miranda.

Andy shouted, "Do as they say." He dropped down and lay next to the sofa.

Charlie and Jacqui helped Miranda down. "God, my knees are not made for this," she said as she got to her knees then gently went down to the floor.

"Give us your phones," Stig screamed pushing his gun into Andy's back.

"I thought you two had left," said Miranda, her voice muffled by the khoum rug.

"Not so smart hey, Grandma," Stig leered down at her. "We've been in your bedroom cupboard, waiting for these lovely people to arrive. Our mates have got the garage covered. Do you think we are stupid or what?"

"My phone is in my bag," said Jacqui.

"Mine too," said Charlie.

The men shook out their bags and grabbed the phones. They took all the phones and the landline handsets and laid them on the floor. Les went into the kitchen and returned with a meat tenderiser and set about destroying them. The apartment was filled with the harsh sound of the phones cracking and plastic splitting. One by one they were shattered.

Suddenly, Miranda turned onto her side and started to wheeze. "Oh my God, I can't breathe," she stated to choke. The girls sat up to help her.

"Get yerselves down," Stig snarled.

"But she's choking," Charlie screamed.

"Water, water," Miranda cried. "Let me up, I must have water."

Stig and Les paused as they looked across the room at each other and down to the old lady thrashing about gasping for air.

Andy saw his moment and brought his feet up and pushed hard on the coffee table sending it flying across the floor. He heaved himself back against the sofa and used it to propel himself up and at Stig. He knocked the gun from his hand and whacked him in the face.

Les tried to aim his gun at Andy but Stig was in the way. Andy grabbed Stig and pulled his right arm behind his back. Andy's arm was around Stig's throat and he was twisting it hard to the left.

"Drop the gun or I'll kill your mate," he shouted at Les.

"Charlie, Jacqui, get to the window – it's open already, get on the balcony."

The girls slipped quickly through the open window and waited for Andy.

Once the girls were out of the way he shifted his hold and threw Stig bodily at Les. There was a crack and a scream as Stig caught his leg on the coffee table. He fell to the floor sobbing and yelling. "You bastard, you've broken me leg, you bastard."

Les had been thrown off balance and Andy threw a vicious kick at his left leg. It caught him directly on the shin and he followed up with a swift uppercut to his chin. The big man toppled over onto the sofa and lay there panting.

Andy helped Miranda to her feet. "Are you OK, Nan?"

"Of course I am, dear boy, of course. Just a touch of the Sarah Bernhardt's for distraction."

"Well played, Nan, now we must all get away from here, the others will be coming up soon. They'll be in the garage but it won't take them long to realise that we've slipped past them."

"Of course, my dear, of course. What's that?"

There was a thumping on the front door. "I put the chain on just now but they'll be trying to beat the door down. Come, Miranda. Quickly now."

He took her by the arm and pulled her towards the window.

"Heavens, must I?" she protested but she pulled back to pick up her handbag and then followed him out through the window.

On the balcony they could hear groaning from the two men on the floor and crashing as the men outside beat the front door. Andy locked the glass door behind them. The balcony was well lit by the nearby street light and long shadows slicked along the ground beneath.

"Sorry, ladies, we have to jump. Take off your heels, Jac. Charlie, Jac, Nan come. After me. I'll catch you. Girls help Nan over the railings." He leapt over the balcony to the grass below.

The girls helped Miranda to straddle the balcony then she said a swift prayer and hurled herself over, knocking Andy to the ground as he attempted to catch her. She quickly struggled to her feet and Andy jumped up, a wry smile. "Well done, Nan."

Charlie looked at Jac as they heard the front door of the apartment splintering. Jac followed then Charlie. Andy caught them both as they landed and led the way out of the garden. He used his pass key to open the back gate and then led the way running along the dockside.

"What we need now is a boat," Andy shouted back to the girls.

"I'll use the manifestation symbol." Charlie drew her latest symbol in the air and closed her eyes and quickly visualised a boat. "We need a boat now," she declared.

93

Andy ran on head. When he reached the turn at the corner of the dock he called back to the women. "Hurry up. We have to get out of this dock."

The girls were being slowed down by Miranda who was struggling to keep up; she was breathing heavily now.

Andy shouted. "Hey, this will do." He pointed to a motor boat moored at the quay. "This is the club captain's boat. He's a mate of mine."

He ran down the steps at the quayside to the boat level and ran up to a forty foot white cruiser. He unhitched the mooring guys as the women arrived, Jacqui and Charlie almost carrying Miranda.

"Get on board, fast, they are just behind us." He leapt up the stairs to the cockpit in the bows and opened a box that held flares, life jackets and a spare set of keys.

"Sorry, John," he muttered, "needs must."

The engine started at his first attempt and he pushed the boat into reverse. As they started to move away from the quayside they could see four men running along the footpath towards them.

"Nan, Charlie, Jac, get down just in case they start shooting."

The boat reversed fast into the dock basin and Andy swung the wheel around to face the second basin and the way out to the river.

"Please, God, let the lock be open," he said. "Charlie, we need your manifestation and protection symbols now. If the lock is closed we won't be able to get out into the river, it all depends on the state of the tide – the lock is only open about three and a half hours each day when the tide is right."

He looked over his shoulder at the men on the quay. They were standing on the quayside arguing between them.

"OK, girls you can come up now. Keep an eye on those bastards will you. I think they'll be following us, they just have to find a boat."

They turned into the second basin and towards the exit. The lock gate was closed.

"Damn, damn," muttered Andy. "Girls, what are those guys doing now?"

Charlie ran back to the stern of the boat to check and came back to the cockpit breathless and agitated. "They seem to have got onboard one of the boats that we passed. But I think there was someone on that boat. God, do you think they will take them hostage or something?"

"Wouldn't be surprised," replied Andy.

A yacht slowly chugged on her engine and crossed their bows. As it got close to the gate the winch operator came out of the harbour master's office and moved towards the sluice mechanism. The yacht's crew, a middle aged couple, started a conversation with the man, obviously they were regulars. Andy could feel his heartbeat speeding up as they got into a deep conversation.

"Shut up, you old fools," Andy muttered. "Get on with it. What's happening now, Charlie?"

"Jac's gone back to check," she replied.

Jacqui came running back. "Quick, Andy, they've got one of the boats and are coming through."

The lock keeper finally finished his conversation and pulled a lever and the sluice gate slowly opened.

"Thank God." Andy's shoulders relaxed. He brought the boat up close to the yacht and slid into the lock.

Would the other boat get there before the lock was closed?

"They're waving to the winchman – he's waved them in," Jacqui shouted.

"Damn, damn, damn." Andy stared at Charlie. "I don't know what to do now. I can't start shooting them here in broad daylight. We are sitting ducks. S**t, s**t, s**t."

Charlie looked at Andy's white face. His hands gripped the steering wheel. His eyes dark.

She put her hand on his shoulder then turned to the others. She pulled herself up tall. "OK, guys. It's time to get serious with these symbols and let them vent their full power for us."

She faced the stern of the boat and stared at the boat behind. The front windows unlit, menacing, like two Darth Vader eyes staring them down. She glared back. She pulled her shoulders back, braced herself and with both hands drew the protection symbol, once, twice three times. In a commanding voice demanded, "Protect us."

The night air was still but as she spoke an energy spiral swirled out from her hands and seemed to envelope their boat. The shimmering light of a force field surrounded them.

Miranda and Jacqui looked at her, their eyes large. "Wow that feels so strong, Chas. Like the Force is with us."

Miranda looked at her granddaughter and smiled. "Wonderful, darling. Well done you. That will work. You've created a protective shield of energy. Great."

Unaware, Andy continued to stare ahead as if in a trance. Then he shook himself. "You girls go down below, there's a small cabin, keep out of sight. When we get into open water they are more likely to try something but at least we can manoeuvre there. I feel like a sitting duck here. I just hope the number of witnesses will stop them doing anything serious here."

Charlie turned towards him. "It's OK, Andy. I will stay here. Jacqui, Nan, please go down. I will stay up here with Andy now."

They looked at her. She had a new air of strength and confidence about her.

Miranda nodded. "Of course, darling, come on Jacqueline." She turned to Andy and Charlie. "By the way I'm not doing the kamikaze act from the balcony again, my ribs are still sore where I landed on Andy. Sorry, boy, you'll be bruised for weeks. And my ankles have blown up like balloons."

Miranda hobbled towards the gangway to go below decks. She turned to Andy and Charlie. "By the way I have every faith in the two of you and the symbols."

"Nan, you are always so positive," said Charlie.

"Just now I feel like I'm in a video game. I wonder if life will ever come back to normal," Miranda said.

"This lock seems to be taking forever to fill. It's so cold. Why don't you see if there are any spare jackets down there?"

Miranda and Jacqui disappeared below and Charlie could hear them rooting around in the cabin cupboards.

She put her arm around Andy. "Don't look so grim, sweetie. I'm sure we will be all right, we've survived everything they've thrown at us so far."

"Yeh, but these guys are serious gangsters. The only reason we are safe so far is there are too many witnesses."

"And I've used the protection symbol. I know you're not sure of them but I do believe that the symbols work."

"Well, you'll be able to find out soon. I don't know what's going to happen when we get out of the dock. We can't even call the police;

we don't have a phone between us." He looked back at the other boat, but there was no sign of life.

"I can't bear this," Jacqui called up from below. "We're too exposed here. When are we going to move?"

"Just a couple of minutes, the dock's nearly full."

"I'd rather be up there, anything could happen and we are trapped down here. Can we come up?"

"OK, I don't think they'll do anything here and they have no escape route themselves, but be careful."

Miranda decided to stay below but Jacqui climbed up and joined them in the cockpit. She brought up a couple of thick fleeces and a waterproof jacket.

"My heart is beating so hard I think it will burst out," Jacqui said, her face pale in the dim light of the dockside lamps. Charlie grasped her hand.

"Me too. It's ghastly just sitting here waiting knowing those dreadful men are just behind us. It's amazing that Nan can even function after her experience with them."

"She's tough," Jacqui said.

"And so is her granddaughter," Andy said grimly and nodded at Charlie who was standing glaring back at the boat behind.

Andy followed her gaze. They could make out just one man in the cockpit. There was no sign of the others.

"Should be soon now." He looked down at the water line. The sluice gate started to open. The yacht in front moved forward.

"Thank God." Andy steadied himself as he opened the throttle and the boat surged forward.

Within seconds they were in the open water of the Thames and he revved up the engine and sped away downstream away from Tower Bridge.

The girls stood beside him as the boat travelled down the river alongside Wapping on the left and Butlers Wharf on the right. Both sides of the river developed now with high end restaurants and apartments created from old warehouses that had once stored spices, sugar and tea.

The river was dark, lit only by the occasional reflection of lights from the buildings and streets on the river banks.

The other cruiser stayed a short distance behind them; a constant menace lurking in the dark.

"This stretch of the river is actively patrolled by the police so I think they'll make their move once we are round this next bend." Andy kept one eye on the river ahead and one on the mirror in front of him where he could just see the boat behind in the gloom.

He shook his head. "Girls I am so sorry, but this is rather stacked against us. We can't call the police, I don't have even a pistol and they are probably armed."

He weighed up the best option. Stay on board and take his chances on the water where he had experience or try to make a dash down one of the exit points along the banks. He squinted out at the sides of the river with piers, inlets and ladders.

He made his decision.

"Charlie, will you look into that box, the one with the life jackets? See if there are any flares in there." He shared his plan.

The river bent around to left. In the near distance they could see the lights and hear the voices of drinkers from the Prospect of Whitby pub overhanging the river. They passed a couple of barges and a dredger that was anchored close to the bank but it was evening and winter so there were few boats using the river. The water looked dark and strong currents caused eddies and flurries of water pouring from holes that were once waterway entrances to the warehouses and docks of the old City of London.

Andy looked behind him; still no move from the boat that shadowed them. It followed along some fifty feet behind them. As they left the Prospect the only sound was the chugging of the motors of the two cruisers and the slurping of the water.

"I feel like a mouse about to be pounced on by a cat." Jacqui couldn't take her eyes of the boat behind. "I wonder what they are planning, why haven't they attacked us yet?"

"Probably waiting for a quieter stretch of the river," said Andy.

They continued over the Rotherhithe Tunnel and the river started to bend to the right. Still no sound from the boat behind.

"It feels eerie out here – it's so dark, just as well there's a moon out tonight, it would be even worse without any light," said Jacqui.

Miranda came up to join them on deck. "What's happening?"

Andy answered between his teeth. "Nothing yet. They are still behind us. Bastards. What's their game? Why don't they do something? Keep your eyes peeled. If anything starts, Miranda, you must go below decks."

"Aye, aye, Captain." Miranda saluted and they laughed. A break of tension.

"Andy, do you have a plan of where to go?" Charlie whispered.

"I don't. My idea was to get the hell out of the dock. Didn't think they would be able to get a boat. Now quite honestly I don't know what to do. Just hope I'm a better sailor than they are."

"When I used the symbol it seemed to put a sort of protective shield around the boat. Maybe they just can't break through it."

"Well, you may be right. I've no other idea why they haven't had a go at us yet, unless they've called for reinforcements."

A tug with a trail of barges chugged towards them creating a wake that set the boat rocking for a few minutes. They were now well and truly in old dockland with Rotherhithe on the right bank and Millwall Docks on the left.

"I can feel my heart thumping and my mouth is dry. Soldiers must feel like this before a battle." Jacqui licked her lips and hugged herself.

"They do. This is the worst part. In action you have no time to think or get scared. This is when your imagination can really terrify you," Andy said.

"Well, mine's achieved that all right, I'm freezing inside me and every shadow out there looks like a monster. I hate the dark," Jacqui said quietly.

"We'll be coming up to The Isle of Dogs and Greenwich soon. I can remember being taken to the Cutty Sark on a school trip once," said Charlie.

"Round this bend, past O2 and we'll be coming up to the Thames Barrier."

Andy peered back again at the boat behind. The sound of the steady throb of the engines was a constant reminder of the danger behind them. "That noise is getting on my nerves," he said.

He cast another look behind to see if anything moved on the deck of the cruiser. All he could see was the dark form of one of the men at the helm. Still no sight of the others and still no sign of any move from them.

As they were passing the O2 Stadium on their right hand side they became suddenly aware of a boat speeding towards them out of the gloom. It was a rib, an inflatable and it was approaching them fast, very fast.

94

The sound of the rib filled the night and they froze as it bore down on them through the gloom, creating waves across the river.

Andy peered hard to check whether it was the river police or port authorities. He could see no markings and no navigation lights. His intuition set off alarm bells that spurred him into action.

"Action stations, action stations," Andy shouted. "Miranda, below, please." She picked up her kaftan skirts and dived down the steps into the safety of below decks. The girls crouched in their allotted places waiting for orders.

The cruiser behind burst into speed and started to draw beside them.

Andy put on full throttle and the boat leapt forward. The girls struggled to keep their balance. They staggered and grabbed the hand rails then dropped down as Andy had planned. They both picked up three flares and lighters that they had placed ready.

Andy began a zig zag course, creating waves that hit the small inflatable sending it bobbing. Bullets started to wing across their bows, fly over their heads and ping into the body of the boat. Andy could make out three men in the rib, one steering and two shooting at them. He threw a quick look over his shoulder and now he could make out three men on the cruiser. Two were taking aim at them with pistols.

95

Andy knew he had to act quickly.

"I will shout 'now', then you fire, OK girls?" His face set firm, he looked confident now – he was in his element.

He cast a quick glance around and saw no other craft within range. He began to weave the boat from side to side of the river. The moon caught the choppy water and cast pools of silver across the surface.

The rib was faster than the cruiser and easily caught up with him but the helmsman was finding it difficult to keep it steady enough for the shooters to aim straight. Despite Andy's manoeuvres, bullets were still hitting the boat. He would have to do something clever soon, otherwise one of the bullets would definitely be finding its target.

Just as the rib was drawing very close on his right hand side he swung the wheel round fast and changed the boat's course; he had completed a full u-turn before the other boats could react. He was on a collision course for the rib.

"Aim and fire," he shouted. "Fire now. Right now."

The girls lit their first distress flare and aimed the launch canisters at the rib. The flares faltered at first then ignited and the bright red light shot forward like a firework rocket directly into the men on the boat. The men were blinded by the intense light and they fell onto the floor of the rib believing they were under serious gunfire. The helmsman swung his wheel and the boat tipped dangerously as they swung off into a huge arc to avoid the cruiser as it headed straight towards them. One of the men fell over the shallow sides of the rib into the Thames.

By now Andy had the larger boat in his sights and he too created a full arc of the river this time to the left bringing him up behind the other boat.

"Get down, girls, get down," he shouted. Bullets started to wing around his head as one of the marksmen took aim from the rear of the boat in front. Andy swung their boat round once more and aimed at the side of the cruiser, away from the flying bullets.

"Fire, fire." Again they pointed their distress rockets. This time Charlie's failed to light. Jacqui's rocket went straight into the cockpit of the cruiser and the scream from the man taking the direct hit ricocheted around the river. Charlie grabbed her third flare and aimed it at the other two who had run forward to take the wheel from their injured partner. Her flare hit the wheel itself and the men fell back onto the deck. Jacqui's flare hit the engine and started a fire which soon set off a small explosion.

"Well done, well done," shouted Andy.

He turned the wheel and started to race back down the river leaving the burning cruiser in his wake. The rib without a man at the wheel was careering off towards the Thames Barrier. There was a thunderous explosion as it hit one of the huge silver gates and burst into flames.

The girls were shaking now and they clutched each other as they huddled by the side of the boat.

"Oh my God. Oh my God. That was terrifying. Well done, Jac."

Jac wiped blood from her friend's face with her hand. "You're bleeding, Chas, have you been hit?"

"No, maybe cut by some of the glass when they hit the windscreen."

"Are you OK, girls?" Andy shouted.

"Charlie's been cut by glass but otherwise we're OK. I'll go and check on Nan."

"No need, she's just fine." Miranda's turbaned head appeared at the top of the stairwell. "Is it safe to come out now?" she asked.

"Sure," said Andy. "We're going back home now. We've still got work to do, haven't we girls?"

"Hell, yes we've got to get onto the computer." Charlie looked down at her hands. "Hope I can type, my hands won't stop shaking."

They were up to Wapping when they heard the thrup thrup of a helicopter rotor. They looked up to see the ominous form of a large black helicopter circling overhead.

"That's probably the police," said Charlie. "We must have woken up the whole of London."

Andy looked hard at the helicopter. "That is not a police helicopter."

96

Jared stared hard at the man opposite him. Jared was an angry man, he was very angry. His mouth was working but there were no words, no sound of any kind. His fat fists clutched his mobile in one hand and a pen in the other; he was in danger of breaking them both.

Binwani, the man opposite, sat forward on the edge of his chair as though poised for flight. Probably a good option. He wore a leather jacket and scarf tied around his neck, fashionable tight jeans. He was a handsome man but right now his good looks were marred by the fear that gripped from his bowels up. This was the first time he had been summoned to the office. All his connections so far had been by phone. As he watched the fat man splutter and seethe he most definitely would have preferred to have kept it that way.

Gradually Jared regained control of his vocal chords. He swore in Arabic for a full two minutes, describing the man's mother, father, children, what he would do to them, where they would go where they died and so on, and on. At each oath Binwani twitched, tensed and winced. After the onslaught there was silence.

Jared leant forward. "Eight men lost or injured in Egypt. Two injured and eight lost in London. And some of those were my own men. You are a total waste of space. If I didn't need your contacts I would kill you with my own hands right here, right now." He thumped the desk so hard the windows rattled.

He leant over even further, as far as his belly would allow. He started quietly. "Listen to me, you son of an ass, I want you out of my sight right now. Get out and I will call you when I have decided what to do with you. GET OUT," he screamed, "GET OUT OF MY SIGHT YOU JACKASS, YOU IDIOT," he continued to scream in Arabic as Binwani hurtled out of the room slamming the door behind him.

Jared reached into the drawer of his desk and brought out a bottle of Johnnie Walker Blue Label and a crystal glass. He poured himself a triple measure and threw it back in one gulp.

He was waiting for report-backs from his own men.

God help them if they also fail.

He looked out into the pitch black of the night. No reports from them so far.

He sighed, rapped his manicured nails on the leather desk top and thought for a few moments. He picked up his phone and made a call. "Hi, Mog, how are you doing?"

"Good, we need to talk, are you free?" He paused to listen.

"Good man, we can meet today, this afternoon. My office. Two thirty."

"Great, see you then."

The big man stood up, smoothed down his suit. Walked around the room once, back in control, then picked up his phone and made a call. "Can I speak to His Lordship please, Tracey."

97

The helicopter flew low over their boat. They craned their necks looking up. Black or white; good or bad; friend or enemy? They held their breath. It swooped down over them. No-one moved, they stopped breathing and stared as it dropped so low they could see the face of the pilot. It hovered for a minute then swooped off down the river towards Woolwich. Just as they dropped their shoulders and started breathing again two large ribs appeared from the direction of Tower Bridge. The boats were dark and all on board were dressed in black, like dark riders racing through the night. But they ignored them and sped past down the river.

"I think they might be sorting out our friends down there," said Andy. "But we don't want to hang around to be asked difficult questions. Let's get out of here."

He gunned the engine and they moved swiftly towards home. The lock was closed and no sign of a lock keeper when they finally drew up to the dock.

"We'll moor here at the pier till morning then I'll sort things out with John." Andy and Charlie secured the cruiser and they left the boat.

"Thank you, John, thank you, John," said Charlie and Jacqui and they patted the boat as they left. "And thank you again, Andy, for an incredible ride and escape!" Jacqui and Charlie hugged Andy and put their arms around Miranda helping her along as they walked slowly back to the apartment.

"Do you think those men will have left the apartment by now?" asked Charlie.

"Yes, I'm sure one of their mates would have rescued them. If not we'll call the police, although I would much rather not try and explain all of this palaver. I am hoping that the authorities will think that those two boats caused the damage to each other. There will be signs of bullets and fire-fight on both boats. My job will be explaining to John why he's got bullet holes in his cruiser!" Andy turned down his mouth and shrugged his shoulders. "That won't be easy. I'll have to offer to pay for the damage."

They wearily made their way up to the apartment which was empty as Andy thought, and the girls spent a few minutes putting the furniture back in place while Miranda set to in the kitchen.

"Here we are," she called with a flourish as she brought in two large plates of sandwiches. "The best I could do from your store cupboard, Andy. Typical man there's only wine in your fridge!"

"Thanks, Nan, I suggest we eat this as we get started. You go and get some sleep." Charlie put her arms round Miranda. "You must be totally exhausted, darling Nan."

"Oh I've loved the adventure, my life's been very dull lately; it was just what I needed." Miranda plonked herself on the sofa and started on a sandwich, but her hands were shaking. "However, I think I will retire to the country after this. If you want to see me you'll have to come down to me. I feel quite shaken up – not sure if it was my flying off the balcony, my dash along the dock or being flung around in a boat all the while being shot at. Either way, I'm definitely too old for this." She tucked an escaping lock of grey hair back into her turban.

"Me too," said Charlie. "My stomach is still in my mouth and my heart is beating too fast. My hands are also shaking, Jacqui, how come you still seem so calm?"

"It's an illusion. I am totally wrecked inside. I guess there's a narrow line between excitement, fear and outright dread! Right now I'm dropping out of dread into fear."

Charlie took Jacqui's hands in hers. "Thanks for being such a great friend, Jac, you are so supportive bless you. This has definitely been a good test of our friendship."

"You can say that again! I've lost my best shoes. I went out this afternoon for a posh tea at Harrods and now look at me!"

"Right we must get started." Charlie looked around for the laptop. "Didn't we leave your laptop on the table? I'd just started working on it when those men came in. It's not here now." Charlie looked around hoping that it would appear.

"Oh, no, they must have taken it. Perhaps they thought you'd recorded the symbols on it already."

"My laptop is in the office. Oh, God, what are we going to do now?" Charlie slumped into the chair and dropped her head onto the table in despair. "I can't bear this, it's one thing after another."

"Hey, come on sweetheart." Andy stroked her back. "You've been brilliant so far. We'll find a way." He sounded reassuring but he looked grim. He didn't tell the girls but he was still sure that the danger was not yet over. "Do you have your office keys? I could go there and get it now." He looked at his watch.

"No," Charlie looked up and wiped her face.

"It's four thirty. What time is the first person likely to arrive? Do you have cleaners in the morning?" Andy asked.

"No, they come in the evening. Jo gets in at about seven-thirty and opens up. OK, I'll go and get it then."

"Miranda, you get off to bed now." He disappeared into the hall.

Miranda kissed the girls and followed him out of the room.

Charlie stood up and stretched. "Although I feel exhausted physically, my mind is racing; I don't think I can sleep."

Andy came in carrying a spare duvet and pillows. "Hope you don't mind sleeping on the sofa, Jac. I've given the spare room to Miranda."

"Don't worry, I don't think I can sleep yet either." Jac pulled out a notebook from her bag. "Maybe we should sit and plan out exactly what we are going to do. We can type it up went we get your laptop."

"Yes, doing something would help. Might settle my nerves," said Charlie.

The door opened and Miranda came back in. "I can't settle to sleep, can I join in?"

"Of course, Nan."

"I'll do the website, I know what I'm doing with that," said Jacqui. "You do the Facebook and Twitter accounts."

"I think we should put the symbols and how to use them on the website then I can direct anyone interested there through the Facebook entries."

"Why don't you tell your story, what happened in Egypt, and put that on the web too?" Miranda suggested. "That will make it all much more real and believable. Don't forget there are many more sceptics than believers out there, so the more facts you can include the more likely it will be accepted."

"Good idea, Nan." Charlie sat with a pen in her mouth, thinking. "I'll explain how I've changed too. After all it's all happened in just a few weeks really and yet I feel I'm very different now. I feel more relaxed, more energised, more fulfilled and more than that I feel more confident."

Andy was attempting to repair one of his chairs damaged in the fight. He grinned. "Good. Maybe you won't go beetroot whenever anyone confronts you or gives you too much attention. And it would be great to see you stop being a doormat for all those tricky bastards in your company."

Jacqui looked up. "Too true. Give a bit more focus on your needs, sweetie pie. You could be a little less of a pleaser and do what you want not just what everyone else wants."

"Well one thing is for sure. I will be very wary of cosmetic surgeons especially if they come from Malaysia." She grimaced and shuddered. "I'm still amazed I was so duped."

"We all were, sweetie. It wasn't just you."

Miranda said, "A good lesson to learn, to see beyond the good looks and surface charisma. Sounds to me he was like a Champagne Charlie! I think you will be fine now. You certainly were working too hard. It doesn't make for a balanced and happy life. Now I sense you will be a woman with a mission but the mission will in itself bring happiness. Helping others find their potential – what could be better than that. Once you have explained the power they can tap into when they use the symbols it will open their minds to the possibility of even more personal power. You'll be like a spiritual life coach."

"Thanks, Nan, I do feel older and wiser!"

"Yes," said Andy, "stick with boring old white wine and a boring, not quite so good looking Englishman. I may not be so good with words but I can tie a mean reef knot and am pretty handy with a bowie knife." He pulled a frightening face at her.

They all laughed.

Jacqui turned back to her notebook. "So back to this website. What do you want to call the site, Charlie Masters? Ancient Symbols?"

"Oh, I don't know, what will appeal do you think? What do you think, Nan?" Charlie scratched her head and looked at Miranda.

"How about charlie-masters.com? I suspect you will have more sacred information to share in the future.

"Got it!" shouted Jacqui, "Great we're off!"

For the next two hours the girls got their heads together and designed the website and decided how to present the symbols and how they worked to the world. Miranda helped them put the words together in a way that could be understood and accepted.

Andy eventually gave up on the chair. "I'm going to your office now and wait for Jo to arrive."

"Can you scan these, Andy?" Charlie handed him three sheets of paper. "I've drawn the symbols." She yawned. "I am totally bushed now."

"OK and I'll buy us some phones. Later I'll search out John; I've some difficult explaining to do." As he reached the door he turned. "And please be careful. Although we sorted out those guys last night, I don't think you should open the door to anyone you don't know. I'm not sure we've seen the last of them."

98

The girls were now alone together for the first time since their return from Egypt.

"We've done as much as we can before we get the computer. Jac, tell me what's going on with you and Mohammad? Why hasn't he come over?"

"Oh, Charlie, it's horrible. His parents have become so difficult about our relationship. To start with they were fine. I think Mohammad's had a load of girlfriends from the cruise ships, one night stands and quickies. So I think they got used to that but once they saw that we were serious and that he loved me then they turned against me. You know out there parents have big dreams about the wife their son will marry and those dreams never include a woman like me, certainly not a non-Muslim. They have been putting immense pressure on him to give me up and to marry a local girl. They have even found one that they think is suitable."

"Oh, sweetheart, that's dreadful, you poor thing. What are you going to do?"

"Well, Mohammad has such respect for his folks, you know they love their families in his culture, they give them a very high priority. He wants to please his parents so he has agreed that we will have a cooling off period. We won't see each other for three months and if we are still serious then we will take it from there. But I know that they won't give in easily. I think the relationship is doomed, quite honestly." She was crying now; heaving sobs and her mascara trickled black rivers down her face.

"Oh, bless you, sweetie." Charlie handed her a bundle of tissues and wrapped her arms around her.

"You know this is the first time I have ever truly experienced love, Charlie," she said in between sobs. "It's wonderful and I just don't want it to end. I can't bear the thought of him with another woman." She snuffled into Charlie's shoulder.

After a minute her sobs subsided and she pushed Charlie away. She pulled back her shoulders. "Look, don't worry about me. You've got much more important things to sort. I'll be all right, you know me, the proverbial bouncing ball. The work we've got to do here is more important."

She wiped her face, pushed back her hair and even tried a smile. "I promise you I'll be fine; let's take a nap while we wait for Andy." The girls snuggled down on the sofas and were asleep in minutes.

99

It was six o'clock and dark outside.

Charlie stretched and yawned. Andy had come back with her laptop and another that he had borrowed for Jacqui. Since nine o'clock that morning she had been working hard with hardly a break. Jacqui stood up and declared, "I'm bushed. I cannot type another thing; my fingers are going into cramp. I need a drink now please."

"And you shall have one, my sweet child." Miranda walked in with a bottle of chilled Pinot Grigio. "Your favourite, I believe." She also laid out three small bowls of olives, pistachios and crisps. You must stop now, girls. How have you done?"

They moved over and sat on the sofa helping themselves to nibbles and wine.

"I've set up accounts for Twitter and Facebook and spent the day sending out preliminary messages, saying what I have experienced and that very soon there will be a website where they can find the symbols. Andy scanned my drawings of them and Jacqui has got them now. I have also started writing my story for the website."

Jacqui stretched again. "I am on my way to making the most incredible website. It's full of spooky, Miranda, you will love it. It was fun working with something other than F and B products, much more inspiring. I'll show you what I've done when I've recovered. I reckon one more day and it will be done and then we can go live."

Andy poured himself a glass and sat opposite them. "I've grovelled in front of John and offered to pay him for the damage. I told him we were caught in the crossfire of some incident on the river. I hope that doesn't go against me on judgement day, Miranda! Fortunately, it's been on the news today so he believed me. They did kidnap the skipper of that cruiser but fortunately just tied him up and kept him below decks and he's OK.

"The media are speculating that the incident was a gang fight; talking about drug cartels and such like. Anyway, it's made me into a bit of a local hero at the yacht club and the boys all wanted to buy me a drink and hear my story!

"Oh, by the way, I also called on all our neighbours to apologise about the noise last night and the crashing and banging in the hall today as the new door was fixed. Most of them are away, thank goodness," Andy said.

Miranda flomped onto a dining chair and sipped her wine. "And I have been busy making crab ravioli and salad. AND I think you need some comfort food to boost you up so I've made an apple crumble with custard. So here's to us!"

They laughed and raised their glasses. "To us."

Just then the doorbell went accompanied by heavy knocking on the door. They all looked at each other.

Andy stood up and said, "Put down our glasses and just be ready for anything."

He walked to his drinks cupboard and took out a brown paper bag then made his way to the front door. He put on the chain and cautiously opened the door a short way and peered out.

"Police, can I come in?"

Andy opened the door a little further and a man flapped a card in his face. He peered at it, nodded and let him into the hall.

"OK, you can come in but you don't look much like any copper I've seen before," Andy said.

The man followed him into the sitting room. With his tan, handsome face, unkempt long blonde hair, he certainly looked more like an aging beach boy than a policeman. As he entered the room the girls stared at him then stared at each other, disbelief on their faces. They looked back at him in amazement.

"Oh, my god, it's Sam. Sam from Texas. What on earth are you doing here?" screamed Jacqui.

"Sure is. Sorry to intrude, ladies." Sam grinned and shook their hands. Andy and Sam clapped each other on the back. Charlie looked startled by this and stared hard at Andy.

"This is my Nan, Miranda, meet Sam from Texas, he was on our tour in Egypt." She motioned him to take a seat. Miranda fetched a glass and another bottle. "Drink, Sam?"

"Sure thing, good idea, thank you, Ma'am."

"So, what ARE you doing here, Sam? And Andy, do you know each other? And how?" Charlie asked.

"Well, I have some explaining to do to you two ladies. Firstly, I'm sorry to have deceived you. I left Texas when I was two and since then I've lived in New York and more recently Virginia so my Texan act was just that, an act. I am actually a senior operative with the CIA and I work undercover alongside your MI6 and sometimes MI5 too. He looked at Andy. We are in fact colleagues and both assigned to anti-terrorist, covert operations. My task is to find the men who fund and support terrorist operations. Andy is more of a hands-on man as you have recently discovered."

"So you know each other?" Charlie asked.

"Yes, we do, but not well. We've met a few times on training ops, by the way, Sam, I don't generally announce what I do, just for the record," replied Andy.

"OK, sorry, I sort of thought your nearest and dearest would know."

Andy shrugged and nodded for him to continue.

"Charlie, Jacqui, you may not have noticed but I didn't join the cruise on day one. I came on board after a contact of ours in Egypt by the name of Joseph Sayidd called me."

"Oh, that's our Joseph," said Charlie.

"That's right. He is ex-army but still works with the security forces from time to time. He has a lot of knowledge about the region and the terrorist organisations that use Syria, Libya and Egypt for training purposes. Andy was there on his project as you know, that was to take out one of those training cells. Anyway, Joseph had identified a doctor called Garneesh Vellupillai who worked for a sort of New World Order sect here in London, calling themselves The Ammonites. This crowd fund terrorist activities to destabilise any government or sector of society that it feels is getting too powerful, especially socialist and left wing groups." He paused to sip his wine. "We had been following the good doctor's movements for a while. We came across him when he was used by this organisation a couple of years ago acting as a courier between terrorists groups. Garneesh was therefore on our radar. When we got the tip off from Joseph I decided to take a trip up the Nile. Something I've always wanted to do as I actually do have a personal interest in Ancient Egypt."

"You were certainly very knowledgeable," said Jacqui.

"Well, thank you, Ma'am, I know a little. There's much to learn. So, I was there keeping an eye on this Garneesh character. Not a very successful one, I might add, as I was in Abu Simbel, as you know

Jacqui, when Charlie was kidnapped. I didn't realise that Garneesh had taken you off the bus until it was too late, but anyway, Joseph said he was onto the situation and had sent his man Hakim to shadow you. So my apologies, Charlie and to you too, Andy. Just as well you turned up on the scene yourself." Sam took a few more sips. He sat back, his relaxed demeanour and startling revelations holding the women in his spell.

"I still can't take this in," said Charlie. "I even thought at one time that you were one of the baddies."

"Well, I was in disguise, if you can call this haircut and my accent a disguise," he laughed and self-consciously smoothed his hair. I haven't had time to sort it; things are moving a bit too fast just now."

"By the way, Sam, did you know that Joseph has been killed?"

"Yes, sadly I did hear that; by terrorists on the Abu Simbel road."

Andy leant forward. "Those helicopters and ribs last night looked suspiciously like black ops. Were they anything to do with you?"

"Sure thing. We picked up that you were in some bother and as it happened we only had to do a cleanup op, you sorted it very well, congratulations."

"How did you know that?"

"Your bug." Sam looked really embarrassed now. He looked around at the girls, "all the operatives have a chip in their neck."

"You have got to be joking!" Jacqui glared at Sam.

"It's not as bad as it seems. It's for their benefit. They are used as locators and can help us to recover operatives who go missing in action or kidnapped."

"Did you know about that Andy?" Charlie looked hard at Andy.

"Yes, of course." He nodded rubbing his neck.

Sam turned back to Andy. "What you may not be aware of is that we also decided to put a camera in your flat and bug your phones to see if your cover was blown in any way. We did that the night you spent drinking with Guthrie. He did a good job of diverting you so we could bug your place. Just as well we did because we picked up the attack here at the apartment. We were the ones that took those goons away."

"Oh, I thought that their own people had taken them."

"No, we did."

Miranda waved the wine bottle at him. "Yes, I would love another glass, thank you, Miranda or can I call you Nan?"

"Nan will do fine, young man."

"Thank you."

"Did you take Andy's laptop by any chance?"

"Yes we did. We needed to check if it had been infiltrated with spyware."

"Had it?" Charlie asked.

"No, we will return it tomorrow; sorry Charlie, but we have to be careful. Now, I have to tell you the real reason why I am here."

100

"As you know I have been trailing this Garneesh character, but he is just a small operator as far as the organisation who hires him goes. This is an organisation that I dearly wish to bust wide open. I want the men who are the organisers, the links between London and the terrorists – like the Brotherhood they used in Aswan. My main goal is to take out the guy at the top, the guy with the funds, for without funds the cells cannot sustain themselves. They cannot live on ideology alone. If we take out the money supply the cell dies."

He stopped to take breath and sip his wine. The women were hanging on his every word.

"The operational cells are everywhere, as you know they have infiltrated into Afghanistan and Pakistan. More recently they have moved into the North African Maghreb region, which is now full of their training camps. But, as I was saying we need to find a way to get to the middle and men at the top. They stay in the shadows; they cover their tracks and hide with scrambled phones, false identities and pseudo business operations. They can be anywhere in the world and most are not to be found in the centre of operations, they prefer to run the organisations from a safe distance. They also hire cells for their own use.

"All we know about the man at the top of the organisation is the same one who is the leader of the society that is behind the problems you have encountered, Charlie. He is powerful and elusive. We have identified his side-kick who does his dirty work; it's a gangster by the name of Jared Mustof. He is also well heeled. He was brought up in Bermondsey, London, and has criminal connections throughout the world. He uses a man called Binwani as his link to Al Qaeda and other extremist Islamic terrorist groups. In your river conflict you have already disposed of his UK gang leader, Les; Leszek Zolinski. Congratulations."

He took a breath and sip of wine.

"Once I have Mustof I have a link and a chance of getting the top man and then I have closure on a case that has taken me years to crack." He looked grim. "I have a task force here with me and we are getting intelligence together – with the odd bit of help from our British friends here." He waved a hand at Andy. "Although I have to say they seem to be blocking us more than helping us, as usual." He grimaced.

"Well, there's a bit of history between the CIA and MI5 and MI6, Sam. There's been a long time rivalry between our country's special forces too," replied Andy.

"Yes. You could say that," said Sam. "There seems to be more competition than co-operation since the debacle in Kenya. Anyway I am confident that we will nail these bastards soon."

He stood up and stretched and looked out of the window for a few moments while they all mused on his words.

He turned to look at Charlie. "Enough of my woes. How about you? Am I right in thinking that you have found some important hidden knowledge that this Society are interested in?"

He came and sat next to Charlie as she brought him up to date with her experiences of the dreams and the symbols.

"Wow. How amazing! That is one hell of a story, Charlie. My sister's into Reiki and all that energy stuff. She also believes in past lives, so I know a little about these things."

Andy interrupted. "Actually this isn't just a case of interest – they want to kill her to stop her from making them public. Until she does she is in danger, there have already made several attempts on her life, that scene on the river was the latest."

Sam went quiet. "So how close are you to getting these symbols out to the world then, Charlie?"

"Very close. We have a few more hours work to do on the website and then we'll be ready to go."

Sam sat and thought for a few minutes. "Well, your life is the most important thing here, hey Andy?"

Andy nodded. "Of course."

"I don't know about how much of an impact a few symbols will have on the world, sorry no disrespect, Charlie." He touched her knee and smiled at her. "But I think I may have a way for you to get this stuff out quickly – at least you would then be safe."

"Well that would be brilliant." Charlie smiled and turned to Miranda. "That would put your mind at rest, Nan."

"It most certainly would, sweetheart. What's your idea then, Sam?" asked Miranda.

"Well, my cousin is the Director of CNN in Europe and he's based here in London. I am sure I could get him to give you a live slot, especially if I tell him your life's in danger."

"Wow, that would be tremendous," said Charlie. Her eyes were shining now.

"So if someone would pour me another drink I will try and get him on the phone tonight and see what we can arrange." Jacqui immediately rushed up with the bottle and filled Sam's glass.

Sam took a hefty sip and stood up. "His number is on my personal phone in the car. I won't be long. I'll see what we can sort out."

As Sam left the apartment filled with a hubbub of noise as they all started to speak at once.

"I can't believe our luck. That's a brilliant breakthrough," said Jacqui. "Wow fancy you being on telly, Charlie."

"Well, we'll have to see if he can arrange it first, Jac, before we get too excited," said Andy.

"Oh, don't be a killjoy, Andy. Do I suspect you don't like him very much?" Charlie said.

"Well, he's a cocky bastard and the yanks have been bloody arrogant and push their weight around in my field of work. They can't bear to play second fiddle and don't care whose toes they tread on to achieve their goals. They are not averse at stealing the glory of group ops either."

"Well, whatever," said Charlie. "If he can get me on TV that would be a great achievement and I will love him for it." She sparkled at Andy. "Not as much as you though, sweetie." She laughed and cosied up to him on the sofa. "It seems all our troubles are over, at last and I can fulfil my promise to Joseph."

101

Jared picked up the phone, hoping he wasn't in for another roasting from Lord D. The last one had blistered his ear.

He could hardly hear the soft, muffled voice. He certainly didn't recognise it. He strained hard to catch the mumbled words and asked for the man on the other end to repeat his message; he needed to be really sure of what he was hearing.

When the call ended Jared smiled. The smile grew and grew and turned into a full belly laugh as he rose from his seat and pumped the air.

"Gotcha, gotcha!" he thumped the desk then reached for his mobile.

"Mog, listen good. This is what you have to do."

102

Once the excitement of Sam's announcement had died down Andy got up and put the brown paper bag and its contents back in his drinks cupboard. He then started to hunt through the apartment for the bugs.

"I don't like being spied upon by anyone, whosever side they are on," he said. The others sat quietly and watched.

After he had disposed of all the bugs and cameras he sat down with the others to wait.

Sam had been gone over fifteen minutes.

"Where the hell is he?" asked Jacqui.

"Maybe his cousin isn't answering his phone," said Charlie.

"Does anyone know where the CNN studios are in London?" asked Andy.

There was a rap on the door.

"I'll go," said Andy.

Sam came in beaming. "Hi, Guys. Good news. Just been onto my cousin, Jaques Parcell, apparently he's the vice president European operations not the director. Anyway he's going to play ball. I told him how urgent it is and he has come up with a suggestion. He can't do a live recording as the studio is set for news reports only at this time of the day, but he can get a small film crew together in a couple of hours to interview Charlie. I told him about the attack on the river and he wants to bring that into play. CNN is primarily a news channel and he would need to have a news story as cover in order to interview you and get to show your symbols? How do you feel about that, Charlie?"

"Well, I guess that's OK, what do you think, Andy?"

"As long as I'm kept out of any filming and we don't mention names, then I can't see any problem."

"He knows a small industrial estate down by the river that will be quiet at this time of the night. He feels it would give just the right atmosphere for the shoot." Sam passed Andy an envelope with a scribbled address. "Can you read it; sorry it's a bit of a scrawl."

"That's OK we'll use SATNAV to get us there."

"OK, then I'll see you there at twenty-two hundred hours sharp. That gives you four hours. Let's wrap this up now." Sam stood up to leave.

"By the way I just need your phone numbers in case I need to get in touch and Jaques will want that for his reference. I believe you lost all your phones yesterday, we watched those characters having fun bashing them to bits."

They gave him email addresses and phone numbers; they said their farewells and Sam left and the rest of them sat and looked at each other.

"Right," said Jacqui. "This is right up my street. I am now your PR agent! Charlie, why don't you print out the symbols nice and clear so that they'll be picked up well on the cameras and let's start practising what you're going to say. You've got to get a clear and concise message out there."

"Oh God, now I feel nervous," said Charlie.

"You'll be fine. I'll coach you sweetie. Slip out of your dress – it looks the worse for wear. I'll give it a press."

103

It was cold and wet. Charlie looked out of the car window into the darkness of the industrial estate. Dim lights cast shadows on shadows; dark buildings with faceless windows; warehouses with no windows at all standing square and formidable, huge locked doors and gates, ugly metal fences; this place was full of menace. She felt dark and heavy vibes pouring from every building across the large tarmac car park. They were parked just inside the main security gate which had been left open for their arrival. They were on one of the abandoned wharves that had been converted into industrial buildings in recent years and they could see the dark murk of the river just twenty yards away to the right.

She shivered. Her stomach was turning over and over. She had a lump in her throat and her heart was thumping. She held Andy's hand to prevent her own from shaking.

"Don't worry, sweetheart, I am right here. You'll be fine."

"What a scary place, certainly plenty of atsmosphere!" she said.

A car arrived; headlights flashed across the buildings and it came to a stop on the other side of the car park.

"That must be Sam or his cousin."

Silence returned.

The car door opened, the driver stepped out and slammed the car door; the sound echoed around the estate. Charlie relaxed as Sam walked across to join them and they stepped out to meet him.

He was full of smiles. "How you doin'?" He kissed Charlie.

"Terrified!" she said. "But excited as well. This is such a great opportunity thanks so much, Sam."

"Cool, no problem," he said. "Jaques should be here any minute."

With that a large black truck swung into the lot.

Charlie's stomach churned again. Her throat so dry she couldn't speak. She thought of Joseph and Miranda. "OK," she whispered. She took a couple of deep breaths and drew back her shoulders.

Three men got out of the truck and Sam took Charlie's hand and led her to meet them. Andy followed.

The sound of a falling bin on the left. They all turned quickly, jumpy, nerves taut. A cat scurried across the yard.

"Is this the film crew, Sam?" asked Charlie.

Suddenly, the air was filled with the shock waves of a gunshot. The vibrations bounced around the yard, the sound ricocheting off the factory walls.

The man who had been standing at the front of the group collapsed, tumbling to the ground. A flood of blood flowed across the wet tarmac.

At first Andy and Charlie stood frozen with the sudden violence. Then Andy recovered and ran over to him. He knelt on the ground beside him and bent over checking his pulse and listening for his breath. The man's breathing was heavy and laboured. His lips moved and Andy knelt close. The man whispered his name. Andy moved his head closer.

The man struggled to breathe but Andy managed to catch the few words that were all Jared Mustof would ever mutter again. "Screw the bastard for me. Check the safe." His head sank and his eyes closed. Andy stood up and swung round.

"Hey, Sam, what the f**k is going on. This is Jared Mustof." His face went white as realisation hit.

He threw himself towards Charlie but before he could reach her the night was pierced with the sound of a second shot. He gasped as right in front of him Charlie fell forward face down on the tarmac. Her cry of shock and anguish spun around the darkness, chilling the air. Immediately Andy dropped to her side.

"No, Charlie, no," he screamed in outrage and disbelief. "Oh, no, Charlie, please don't die." His voice thick with emotion and shock.

He put his arms around her and rocked back and forth, covering her with his body, too late to protect her.

The back of the truck flew open and a dozen black clad figures jumped down. The lot was filled with the sound of running footsteps as men in black rushed through the yard.

Sam ran over and looking down at them, swore. "F**k, this was never meant to happen, f**k." He turned to his men and screamed at them, calling them into action. "Find the bastard, find him fast, now."

The wharf became a turmoil of shouts, slamming car doors, whistles and yells as the troops entered the buildings searching for the sniper and probing the ground near Charlie and Jared, looking for clues and spent bullets.

Out of sight, a dark figure abseiled down the back of the furthest warehouse. He slipped off into the night, his job done.

From his vantage spot up on the roof, Mog made a dash for the fire escape; two of Sam's men were on the second floor level and they caught up with him and dragged him down to the ground and cuffed him. They half carried half pulled him down the staircase and brought him and his rifle to Sam.

They turned to see who had snatched their prize from under their noses. Sam walked up to the Russian and glared into his face. "Who are you working for?" One of his men handed Sam the gun. He looked it over. "It's a Heckler and Koch PSG1."

"Only one shot fired from this, boss."

Sam nodded. "I know. The one that shot Charlie. But the bullet that got Jared didn't come from that gun. Different pitch, different sound. Sounded suspiciously like a L96 to me. Get out there and find the other shooter. Make it quick." Four of the team spun off to continue the search in the buildings surrounding the car park.

He nodded towards the Russian. "Take him away, he's one of Jared's men."

"Sorry, my friend. I had to get my men here just in case they were tailing Charlie."

Andy didn't respond but kept his head down as he continued to clutch the still form of Charlie in his arms.

Sam kicked the ground, his face grim and tight. "But who's the arsehole who dropped Jared? Who was he working for?" He looked around as though the answer lay in the gloom of their surroundings.

"My God, I wanted that man – he's my key to the son of a bitch at the top, the mastermind of this set up. I've been working on this for years."

One of Sam's men came running up. He had a bullet casing in his hand. "You're right, boss, this has come from a L115A3."

Sam turned to Andy, his face a mask of anger and hatred. "Bloody SAS gun. You did that didn't you? You bastard, I needed that man. Years I've been hunting him. Tonight I was so close… You bastard."

Andy ignored him. He continued to bend over Charlie. He picked up her prone body in his arms and carried her back to his car and laid her gently on the back seat.

He turned to Sam. "You mean evil murdering bastard. You were giving them Charlie on a plate. You just wanted to draw out Jared. You didn't give a damn about Charlie. You are right, my man took out Jared. My mistake was we didn't spot the Russian before he took out Charlie. Interrogate him to your heart's content, I'm sure he's got plenty of leads for you. Now get out of my way."

Sam glared at him but moved out of the way.

104

Andy drove the car around the corner, stopped and picked up his phone. His voice cold, stripped of emotion. "Thanks, Guthers, good job done."

"Beat the Yank at his own game, enjoyed that," Guthrie answered.

"Get to Jared's place pronto. Quick as you like. Don't want the Yank stealing a march on us there."

Andy listened to his reply. He paused for a few moments. "No, she was shot by Jared's man, Mog, after you left."

Guthrie swore.

The line went silent.

105

The rain fell hard and fast and created puddles on the concrete farmyard. Animals hadn't been kept on this farm for over ten years. The locals knew there were strange and mysterious goings on at the secluded Black Dyke Farm. The regulars at the Three Kings had speculated and gossiped for years about the odd and sinister goings on at the farm. Old Peggy and Reg had kept themselves to themselves and there were mysterious late night visitors even in their day. They did say they were holding poker nights for a group of friends from their old village of Deadworth, but that didn't stop the gossip. The boys were slightly disappointed when no bodies were found buried there, a group of them had crept up there one Sunday after the old couple died to have a good look around, but nothing apart from a lot of old defunct machinery.

Now they had plenty to gossip about; black painted vehicles, helicopters and barbed wire and Keep Out signs just fuelled their suspicions that it was now a camp for training SAS and Black operations. Which is exactly what it was. The MOD had acquired the farm and the buildings for their covert operations.

Tonight a group of men were gathered in the converted milking shed to hear their latest instructions. Tim Guthrie looked over his team of ten men standing in front of him poised for action as he went through the op plan one more time. They wore black combat trousers and jackets; each had a balaclava in their back pocket and around their waist ammunition belt, grenades and stun guns.

"Everyone understood?" he asked.

They all nodded; they were eager to get into action. Revenge and action. He led them out to the two Range Rovers that would take them into the City.

They drove through the dark wet streets to their destination, an office block in Blackfriars and drew up outside the ten storey building. The men left the car quietly and entered the main entrance. Guthrie showed his pass to the security guard. He was expecting them.

"Eighth floor, use the two lifts, turn left as you come out of the lift. The name on the office door is Mustof Trading, Import Exports. Good luck, the owner is a total son of a bitch, never had a single good word from him, fat pig."

The office block was silent apart from the sound of the two lifts as the men followed his directions. They regrouped outside the office and Guthrie signalled the man carrying the enforcer battering ram to step forward. He nodded to him to break in the door. With three swift blows the wooden door crashed inwards.

"Get down, get down, this is a raid." The men ran in as Guthrie shouted.

But as expected the office was empty. On the far side of the outer office was a door marked Jared Mustof, CEO. They crashed through that door then the entire team were deployed into their allotted roles as they comprehensively searched the filing cabinets and desks. Two of the men carrying a kit bag stepped up to the safe in the corner of the room and proceeded to set explosives to blast the safe door open. When they were ready they retreated to the outer office while the fuses were lit; the explosion shook the windows and rattled the furniture and the safe door fell off its hinges.

Guthrie started to search the bundle of envelopes and papers inside. He soon found what he was looking for. The envelope containing a memory stick. Every conversation between Jared Mustof and Lord D had been meticulously recorded and saved. Addresses, identities and all he knew about the Society boss were there. Jared's vengeance, his final retribution. Guthrie grinned.

Guthrie called his men together. "Job done here. Now we go for the big fish. Let's really piss off our Yankee friends. We're off to Kent. Follow me."

They left the office in chaos but the owner didn't care, his spirit hovered overhead, gloating – this will be sweet revenge – teach the toff to patronise him, sweet revenge indeed.

106

Andy crashed through the door and fell into the apartment. Miranda and Jacqui ran from the bedroom to meet him. He laid down Charlie's body on the sofa.

"Oh my God," screamed Jacqui and she and Miranda rushed over. "Is she dead?"

"No. She was shot but the bullet deflected. It hit the pendant she was wearing. The bullet has bruised her. Sam double crossed us. He had tipped off Jared and he brought his own special forces men in."

"Are you all right, darling?"

Charlie was shaking, literally shaking as her grandmother swept her up in her arms. Her teeth were chattering but she managed a little smile. "I'm OK, Nan. Your pendant protected me! Can you believe it?"

"Heavens, child, it must have been terrifying. You are so brave. What happened? What about the film crew, how did you get shot?" So many questions.

Andy explained how they had been ambushed by Jared and his Russian sniper Mog had tried to kill Charlie. That Sam had set them up and must have tipped off Jared about where he was taking Charlie.

"But, Andy, who shot Jared?" asked Jacqui.

"Well," Andy smiled. "Although I had no proof, I felt that Sam was being just a bit too helpful getting Charlie on TV at such short notice. One of you said that it's too good to be true and, in my opinion, if you think that then it *is* too good to be true!"

Miranda nodded. "You are right there, young man."

"Anyway, I decided to get my mate Guthrie involved as a precautionary measure and had him bring some of our special ops guys along to make the site secure. Unfortunately, they missed Mog who must have slipped in at the last minute."

Miranda continued to fuss over Charlie and insisted on bathing the bruise that was coming up livid and blue on her chest. She applied a hot poultice and drew the healing symbol placing her hands gently on her chest.

"We'll use my kind of medicine for now and get you to a doctor tomorrow to check it out. Thank God, the skin's not broken and the pendant took the full blast of the bullet."

"How lucky is that?" exclaimed Jacqui.

"Not lucky, it was doing its job, bless it," smiled Miranda. "Rest now, my girl, no more escapades, no more flirting with death. Tomorrow Jacqui can finish the website, let's hope that you have no more enemies from this lifetime or any other. Hopefully we can have some peace now."

Charlie lay back on the sofa. She looked pale but was recovering fast. She managed a big smile for Miranda. "Don't worry, Nan. I'm fine and it seems they have caught the top men. Andy just got a message from Guthrie, didn't you darling?"

"Yeh, Guthrie's men raided the country pad of the head of the society. Turns out he's Lord Dennington, owner of the media empire. They've taken him into custody. This is going to cause one hell of a stir. They've got evidence too, thanks to Jared's revenge. Seems he hated the Lord's guts and had recorded all their conversations."

"Andy saved my life again. Didn't you, my darling?" She put her arms around his neck and smothered him with kisses.

"But it was incredibly scary."

"I should never have let you go. I must admit I had my doubts about that Sam," said Miranda.

"I guess the old adage is true; what doesn't kill you makes you stronger. Anyway, did they get everyone?"

"No, there was no sign of the middle east connection, Binwani. He seems elusive and there's no record of him at Jared's place or Lord D's, but he was a hired hand and has no motive to harm Charlie. We can go after him another time."

"What will happen to Sam?" asked Jacqui.

Andy smiled. "Well he's finished. Guthrie and I will be putting in our reports and I don't think we'll be seeing him in international operations again. He may well get court-martialed too, unless the authorities do a cover up; it won't be the first time if they do. The really great thing is," he rubbed his hands and grinned, "we got one over on him and his troop. Guthrie and his men are over the moon."

"Well, I suppose that's a good result for you. Anyway we must take the website live, and then I can breathe again," said Charlie.

Jacqui pulled a face. "Oh, of course. Look you rest up. I've been working on it while you were out getting killed. There's not much more to do, I've cut some corners and we can go live just now."

She went to the laptop on the dining table and set the system quickly into action and activated the website.

Charlie started to calm down and once her shaking had stopped she sent out an announcement on Facebook and Twitter that the symbols were there for anyone to use.

"I'm ready for a drink now," cried Jacqui, "Andy, we need to celebrate. What've you got?"

"Leave it to me," Miranda bustled off into the kitchen and returned with a tray and four glasses and a cold bottle of Lanson.

"Great idea," said Andy.

"Brilliant, bring it on, Nan," said Jacqui.

"Thank God you didn't buy Cristal, I'll never drink that again," said Charlie. She raised her glass. "A toast." They lifted up their glasses. "To the good guys!"

They chorused, "To the good guys."

"And to Charlie and Andy," said Jacqui.

At that moment their celebration was interrupted by the door bell. They stood stock still and looked at each other. "Oh, no, what now?" cried Charlie flopping back onto the sofa. "I don't want to see anyone or speak to anyone for at least twenty-four hours, I've had it."

Jacqui called out after Andy as he went to the door. "Shoot them or send them away, Andy."

He opened the door then popped his head around the door. "I heard that, but I think you might change your mind, Jac," he laughed.

He stepped back and let the visitor into the sitting room. A good looking Arab in black jeans, pink shirt and loafers stepped into the room.

"Is there a glass for me?" he asked.

Jacqui exploded from her seat. "Oh my God. Mohammad. How wonderful," and hurled herself into his arms. She wrapped her legs around his waist and he spun her around and around, their joy filling the apartment.

"What happened, how did you get away? What about your parents. How long are you staying, since when did you start drinking?" She pulled him down to sit on the sofa with her and threw her legs over his, locking him down.

374

She suddenly jumped up. "Oh, I'm sorry, Nan, this is Mohammad." He stood up and went over to Miranda and bowed and took her hand. She clasped him to her and gave him one of her huge hugs.

"How wonderful, I am so glad you could make it. This will cheer up Jacqueline; she's been quite cast down since she's been back."

He looked over to Jacqui and smiled. "Me too. I've felt quite dreadful since you left."

"Come and sit down here and tell us what's happened."

"Yes, of course. I'm sorry to come unannounced but I thought it would be a good surprise. Andy gave me his number when we were at Abu Simbel so I was able to text him. He was in the plot." He threw a glance at Andy.

Andy chuckled. "Yes I got your text this morning."

"I had hoped to meet up with you at Harrods for your birthday, Charlie, but I had a lot of things to sort out and I needed to get a visa."

"Well, when I tell you everything that's happened in the last twenty-four hours I think you'll be delighted with yourself for not coming earlier," Jacqui said. "By the way," she said grinning at everyone in the room. "I manifested this."

"What do you mean?" asked Charlie.

"Well when you discovered the manifesting symbol at Cleopatra's Needle I thought let me try it and I did and, as you can see, it most definitely worked." She bowed to them and they stood up and applauded her.

"Brilliant, Jac. Well done." Charlie gave her a hug.

Jacqui turned back to Mohammad. "Now, my love, do you really want a drink?"

"Well, I do have the occasional glass of wine or a beer when I'm away from home." He turned to the others. "I worked in London for four years and you can't live in England without going to the pub."

Andy handed him a glass of champagne. "Cheers. So come on let's have the lowdown."

"I'd been feeling so unhappy, since Jacqui left Egypt. One morning I woke up and realised that this is **my** life and I've only got one and I want it to be as good as it can be." He looked down at his hands. He clenched them and looked up. "So I went to my parents and explained how I felt. They didn't exactly give me their blessings but I guess they will come round eventually. Anyway, I left my job and applied for a visa to work here. My godfather works at the Egyptian Embassy here so he pulled a few strings and here I am. I have a job working on the cruise ships out of Southampton. I thought that way I could at least see you in between trips, my dear." He looked at Jacqui and took her hands in his. Her face was wet with tears.

"Oh, that's wonderful, just wonderful," she cried.

"You see, I love you." He paused and took a deep breath. "I just wondered, but you don't have to say yes, but I just wondered, if, by any chance... would you let me live with you?"

They all held their breath.

Jacqui sighed and wiping away the tears from her cheeks she smiled at him and whispered, "I love you too and I would love you to live with me."

They all cheered.

"Thanks be to Allah!" Mohammad jumped up and picked up Jacqui and twirled her around.

"Careful," she cried, "mind my champagne." Everyone laughed.

Andy's phone rang. He took the call out in the hall and Charlie made a face. "Still mister secret squirrel," she said to Jacqui.

He came back in after a few minutes with his pocketbook in his hand. He looked grim. "Miranda, Charlie, I've got something to tell you which is actually quite shocking."

107

"That call was from Guthrie. After they took down Dennington they did a thorough search of both his homes and office and they made an interesting discovery. He had a large file on you, sweet pea."

"Oh, really," said Charlie.

"Your name came to his attention just after you were born. Not sure how, there is just a short paragraph cut from a newspaper about your birth – 4th October 1980 Charlotte Jane born to local artist, Annabelle and horse breeder, Jonnie Masters. Lord Dennington had written in the margin." Andy checked his notebook, "*This is the one, ref. Valdosa's prophecy.* Guthrie hasn't found any further reference to a Valdosa in the papers he's sifted so far so we don't know what that is but I guess it's something to do with the symbols. Anyway, the disturbing part is that there is a note in a diary November 5th 1983. Took out A & J M but CM survived. And there is a document that gives full instructions on how to cut the brakes of a Triumph TR7 in such a way as they would go undetected by a cursory glance." He shut his book and looked up at Charlie.

Charlie stared back at him. "I don't believe it. Do you mean for all those years I thought… " She sat still and cold. She stared at the wall.

Tears started to flow down her face and as Miranda went to sit by her she stood up and rushed from the room. "Leave me," she cried.

They could hear her crying in her bedroom. Miranda and Jacqui held each other's hands as they waited.

Five minutes later she returned. She curled up on the sofa next to Miranda who hugged her close. "OK, darling?"

"I'm fine, Nan, really fine." She let out a huge sigh. "It's a huge relief to find out that I didn't cause the accident but ghastly to think they were murdered."

Miranda turned to Mohammad. "Sorry, Mohammad, this is all a bit of a turn up for us and really shocking but you need to know what's been going on. Jacqui you'd better tell him about our dramas."

They spent the next hour bringing Mohammad up to date with the events of the last few days. Charlie fully recovered her composure after an hour and became involved in the recaps and replays. She then drew and explained the use of the symbols. As she drew the healing symbol she paused and stared at it tapping her fingers on the table.

"You know this symbol feels really familiar. I've been trying to remember where and when I've seen it. It's a bit like the Cancer and Aids awareness symbols but upside down."

Miranda nodded. "If you turn it on its side it also looks a bit like the fish symbol the early Christians used."

Charlie frowned. "But there's something else niggling away at the back of my mind. I know, I know." She jumped up and scrummaged in her bag and pulled out the bandana she had bought from Joseph. Here it is. I thought so. Look." She showed them the small pattern on the black material. "This is the symbol. Look, Nan."

"So it is, my dear one. So it is."

"So that means I had it with me all along, just like the manifestation symbol – see, Mohammad, that's on the ring that Joseph gave me." She showed him the ring. "That is used to turn our intentions and visualisations into reality." Charlie looked thoughtful.

"You know it's amazing that I had those two symbols on me all the time. I wonder if I had the other one, the one for protection."

Miranda suddenly jumped up. "Oh, my goodness, you may have. Look on the back of the pendant I gave you, there is a symbol on that, I never knew what it was for, just knew the pendant was meant to work like a protective charm."

Charlie screamed and dug out the pendant from under her sweater. "Oh, God, here it is on the back. The scarab on the front and the symbol on the back." She showed the others.

"Fantastic. Protective symbols work by strengthening the wearer's energy field. If your energy field is strong you can withstand the negative thoughts and energies of others. It also seems to keep you physically protected too. It calls in assistance from the spirit world, a bit like calling in angels when you need help," Miranda said.

"I wish I'd known before," Charlie said.

"Well, my dear, you had to find them for yourself. That's part of your journey. Your persistence, your courage and your determination were tested. Since you broke the spell at the Sphinx you will remember more of them as time goes by."

"Great, I'm certainly up for anything that comes now," said Charlie.

"Now, I've got something to share with you. I haven't told you everything. I've actually known that something like this was all in store for you since you were very young. Like Joseph I am a Guardian. But, we were sworn to secrecy and couldn't tell you anything."

Charlie jumped up. "Nan, a Guardian, how amazing. But how could you have kept that from me?"

"This had to be your own journey. It's not been easy. I would have loved to warn you about it – the part of it that I knew. I didn't know the symbols by the way. You have done brilliantly, my sweet child.

And, as I said, I was only shown a very small part of the picture but you will see it all in time."

"Well the ones I've used… "

"And me too," interrupted Jacqui smiling at Mohammad.

"Well, they have worked, they really have."

"Of course they do. Anyway, in celebration, I have something for you." Miranda leant down and dug into her handbag. "I've got a special present for you; something to celebrate the amazing events that you have experienced." She handed her a small black velvet box.

Inside the box was a pendant of the healing symbol with an amethyst.

"How beautiful, it's absolutely lovely." She passed the silver pendant around to show everyone.

"However did you organise this, Nan?"

"You left the piece of paper with the drawing of the symbol on the table when you rushed off to the British Museum and I snaffled it. I thought it would be a good idea to have this made for you. Andy organised it for me with a local jeweller when he went out for the laptop. They made it up in a couple of hours and have made a fine job of it too." She beamed at her granddaughter. "You deserve this."

Mohammad looked at Charlie. "I'm amazed to think that all this came about because of a Nile cruise – my Nile cruise. I feel honoured to have been part of this." Jacqui hugged him.

"Everyone was involved one way or another," said Charlie.

"That is as a result of the spiritual connection. There will be many times when just the right person comes along with a solution or assistance just when you need them. It works like magic – in fact it is magic," said Miranda.

"Well, all I can say is that I couldn't have got there on my own."

"By the way, Nan, there's something I've been meaning to ask you but we keep being interrupted by drama. Did you know Joseph?"

"Yes I did. I met him in Cairo years ago. We were both guardians but more than that he was a dear friend. So I too am grieving for the dear man. He was a bit of a rascal in his youth and there was many a night where I had to bat him off." She laughed. "Oh, yes I knew Joseph, a remarkable man and a great loss. So sad." She shook her head.

Charlie touched her hand. "Let's have another toast; to all my friends who helped me on this journey and a special one to dear Joseph."

They raised their glasses.

"Just don't ask me to come on holiday with you again, my sweetness, I have had all the excitement I can handle for a long time," Jacqui said laughing. "Mind you, I did find my man," she squeezed Mohammad's hand.

"What are you planning next, Charlie?" Miranda asked.

"Well, Andy and I are going to give our relationship a new kick start. After all the drama of the last few months we decided we need a break together. We are thinking of flying to Bali for a real holiday to get over the last one." She smiled at Andy. "We thought we would go somewhere quiet and peaceful. We are planning a two week break in the sun."

"Wonderful idea," said Miranda. "It's a very spiritual place; you will probably get a lot more of the symbols while you are there."

At that moment there was a bleep from the laptop. They looked across where it sat on the table top.

A message appeared on the screen: GO TO INDIA. J.

The End

Epilogue

Unfortunately, Andy had to delay their trip to India but this gave Charlie the chance to try out her symbols further. She went to a psychic fair and met a man with the latest digital camera. She was delighted to find that he could record conclusively the energy stream that the symbols created – just what she needed to convince Andy's sceptism.

She uploaded these and further insights on the symbols to her website www.charlie-masters.com.

Author's note

Although all the characters in this book are fictional the story is based on my own experiences as a spiritual healer.

I started my working life as a bank clerk then moved onto roles as computer programmer, trainer and saleswoman and travelled throughout the world selling and teaching the use of computers. This was at a time when computers were just beginning to be used in businesses.

However, my working life took an abrupt change of direction when twenty years ago, while living in Malaysia, I had a very mystical experience – very similar to that which affected Charlie. One afternoon while I was resting in my bedroom after a morning instructing expats on the use of PCs I heard a voice that prompted me, in a rather demanding fashion, to start healing. I was told to contact a lady called Sal who would explain further my new role. To say I was excited by this very first experience of spiritual connection is an understatement, I was exhilarated and overwhelmed. I spoke to Sal and she told me that she had been expecting me! This was when I started to feel the whooshes that Charlie experienced through her Egyptian adventure!

Since then I have continued to experience thrilling and mystical experiences. Two were particularly significant to the ideas behind this book. One was a vision I had of a spirit guide who gave me a symbol that triggers the flow of universal energies of love and healing. This was the first of over thirty such symbols.

The second experience that prompted this storyline was a vision/dream of myself as a priest in Egypt hiding away the symbols under the Sphinx just as Charlie did as Khamet. The spells in the book for opening and closing the energies of the Sphinx are the actual words I heard in that past life recall.

I have gone on to share the symbols with people around the world through my books, workshops, jewellery design and a set of oracle symbol cards. I have appeared on television and radio and am a frequent guest speaker at seminars and conferences.

You can use the symbols yourself. Be prepared to be amazed! I am constantly astounded at the results that my readers and students achieve. Good luck and enjoy!

www.annejones.org

Further Information on the symbols and Anne Jones:

"Heal and be Healed" – discover the secrets of ancient symbols by Anne Jones, available from www.smashwords.com as a download or www.annejones.org for printed version.

Ancient Symbol Oracle Cards. – using ancient symbols for guidance and connecting to universal energies for healing and empowerment. www.annejones.org

Books published by Piatkus/Little Brown Books
Heal Yourself.
Healing Negative Energies

The Ripple Effect
Open Your Heart
The Soul Connection
The Power of You

Connect to Anne and her work.

Facebook: AnneJonesHealer
YouTube: AnneJonesHealer
Twitter: AnneJonesHealer
Blog: www.annejonesblog.org
Website: www.annejones.org

The Keys are real...

Some of the symbols have been made into beautiful silver jewellery, which can be worn to bring their energy whenever you need it.

To discover the power of the keys for healing yourself and others you can read how to use them in this pocket book or use the symbol oracle cards to help you decide which ancient key you need to use...

All of these items are available from the shop on Anne Jones website www.annejones.org

Also available from Anne are a series of comprehensive online healing workshops, including Symbol Healing for the Heart and Soul which demonstrates the use for all of the ancient symbols. This and other workshops are available from Anne's community website, www.the-powerofyou.com